ice on the bay

Books by Dale E. Lehman

Howard County Mysteries

The Fibonacci Murders
True Death
Ice on the Bay
A Day for Bones

Bernard and Melody Capers

Weasel Words

Science Fiction

Space Operatic
The Belt
Penitence

Short Story Collections

The Realm of Tiny Giants
Found by the Road
Manifest Secrets

ice on the bay
a howard county mystery

Dale E. Lehman with
Kathleen Lehman

RED TALES

Chase, Maryland

Ice on the Bay
Dale E. Lehman and Kathleen Lehman

Copyright © 2018,2019 by Dale E. Lehman and Kathleen Lehman

All rights reserved. Except as permitted under U.S. Copyright Act of 1976, no part of this publication may be reproduced, distributed, or transmitted in any form or by any means, or stored in a database or retrieval system, without the prior written permission of the publisher.

This is a work of fiction. All the characters, organizations, and events portrayed in this book are either products of the author's imagination or are used fictitiously.

Cover design by Proi
https://99designs.com/profiles/proi

Book design by Kathleen Lehman
Text set in 11-pt. Calluna
Chapter headings set in 30-pt. Almaq Rough.

First published by Serpent Cliff, an imprint of One Voice Press, LLC, 2018
Published by Red Tales, 2019
Essex, Maryland
United States of America
https://www.DaleELehman.com

Trade paperback: 978-1-940135-67-0
ebook: 978-1-940135-68-7

*For our daughter Andrea, a.k.a. "Super Tech."
Where would the animals be without you?*

Assorted Disclaimers

Howard County, Maryland is real, as was the extreme winter described herein. Some setting elements have been changed to suit the story, while others are complete fabrications. Kathleen did her best to ensure accuracy in all Catholic content. Nevertheless, she cautions that some story elements may stray from the Catechism. Dale accepts the blame for all other errors, but gently reminds you that this is, after all, a work of fiction.

Were it not for the cold, how would the heat of Thy words prevail, O Expounder of the worlds?

—Bahá'u'lláh, *The Fire Tablet*

1

"I'm freezing, Harold."

His attention on the old house before them, Harold didn't answer his wife's complaint. Pale golden light leaked through gaps in the blinds covering the first-floor windows while the second floor slumbered in darkness. Built sixty or seventy years past, the house was a home no more, but a veterinary clinic. A brilliant white floodlight splashed across the front of the pale blue structure. Harold's eyes didn't register the color in the glare; he only knew it because he'd been here two days earlier, casing the place in daylight.

"Harold!" She whispered it fiercely and tugged on his sleeve.

He absently wrapped his arm around her shoulders, but his attention remained fixed on the house. Situated in an otherwise deserted block on a sparsely-populated road, it hid among the winter-bare trees, a loner or an outcast. A perfect target. Better still, the security light's glare washed out the burglars' white coats, white hoods, and white pants as cleanly as the house. They might have been one with the walls. At least, that's what they'd been told. Harold felt terribly exposed here and stole a glance back at the road. Not that passersby were likely at this hour anyway. Even so, he planned to enter through a back window, where the trees would swallow any sounds they made.

He started forward, arm still around her, but she didn't move. "What?" he asked sharply.

"Lights are on inside."

"Just security lights."

She leaned into him and shook her head. Her hair, long and thick, lightly stroked his arm.

"You backing out on me, Hannah?" Harold felt her tension in her touch. He knew her that well. After all, they'd been together for six years, ever since Howard Community College, where he had been a pitcher on the school's baseball team and she an aspiring actress in the theater program. A mutual friend had introduced them, and Harold had fallen hard. Hannah's radiant smile, golden hair, and shapely body instantly attracted, and the eagerness with which she attached herself to a star athlete amply fed his ego. Hannah's prettiness and Harold's rugged good looks, together with the uncanny alliteration of their names, seemed to cast a spell about them that other students were loath to attempt to penetrate, preferring instead to regard them with a respect bordering on awe. Yet they'd ended up neither on the stage nor on the diamond, but here in the chill night.

Hannah shook her head a bit too emphatically. "Of course not." A good actress, she faked determination well. But she couldn't fool him. She wanted out of this, out of the cold, out of the danger, out of the whole business. Only loyalty kept her here. He admired her for that. Little had gone right for him since college. Hannah alone had stuck by him. Why? He'd never fathomed that mystery. Oh, he knew that once she had needed his protection, but those days were long gone, and here she was, still with him, defying the urge to run, standing firm by his side when she could have been sleeping warm and secure in a better man's bed.

"Come on." He tugged at her, and this time she moved.

"At least it'll be warm in there," she muttered.

They crept through the darkness along the left side of the house and came to the rear. A waning moon illuminated the landscape, its light dimmed now and again as ragged patches of cloud raced by. The date was December twenty-fourth, Christmas Eve; the time two-twenty in the morning; the temperature forty-one degrees with a stiff breeze that chilled them all the more. Somewhere inside the house lay their objective: a supply of morphine and ketamine, cash literally in liquid form.

They paused to check the four darkened windows that flanked the back door, two on each side. Here, too, a security light pretended to deter thieves while contrarily revealing to them every detail of their intended target. The light from within, washed out by the exterior glare, shone faint but steady.

Hannah took two pairs of latex gloves from her pocket and handed one pair to Harold. They pulled them on, careful not to rip them, then Harold eased up the short flight of wooden steps leading to the door, his footfalls quieter than a rabbit's. He gently rotated the knob. Of course it was locked, but it never hurt to check. No sense smashing things if the owner had invited them in. Leaning to the left, he felt around the nearest window, examined it in detail, and gingerly tried to push up the lower sash. Again, no luck. Again, none expected.

Hannah tiptoed up the steps while he worked and stood close behind him. "Hammer," she whispered, pulling the tool from her coat pocket and handing it to him like a nurse handing a scalpel to a surgeon.

He took the hammer and with a swift stroke smashed the pane, then cleaned the jagged shards from the sash with the head. Falling splinters chattered as they struck the floor inside. Once satisfied the opening was clean, he helped Hannah through the window. She moved so quietly she might have vanished, but in his mind Harold could see her go to the door, disarm the alarm with the code they had been given, and unlock the deadbolt. The door whispered open.

He slipped inside and eased the door shut, then took her face in his hands and kissed her on the forehead. She beamed, a dog basking in her master's approval.

The very next instant, the job went horribly wrong.

*

Social affairs had never been Detective Lieutenant Rick Peller's forte, although his late wife Sandra had possessed a knack for spur-of-the-moment entertaining. She could conjure what appeared to be perfectly planned, if simple, dinners with a wave of her hand. Whatever her secret to success, her husband had definitely not absorbed it. Since her death four and a half years before, he often felt her whispering at his side, but she had never offered advice on hosting a party.

So it was fortunate, he thought, that when he decided to light up the winter darkness with a small gathering of friends on the evening of Saturday, January fourteenth, Detective Sergeant Corina Montufar offered to help. She took charge of planning, shopping, and cooking, and dragged Detective Sergeant Eric Dumas into the fray against his will. Under Montufar's management, the evening materialized as if by Sandra's magic. Peller secretly thought that maybe it had been.

In addition to the three of them, he had invited Montufar's brother Eduardo; Eduardo's wife Sylvia; Peller's next-door neighbor Jerry Souter; Tomio "Tom" Kaneko, the mathematician who had helped the detectives with a major case the previous spring; and Kaneko's wife Sarah. He had also invited Montufar's younger sister Ella, but she declined, having already made other plans. "I think she's got a new boyfriend," Montufar had confided to Peller. "Lately her wardrobe's gotten fancier."

Peller had no need to suggest that Dumas and Montufar each invite a friend. Although they had concealed it fairly well, he'd noticed the looks passing between them, the occasional meeting of hands, how frequently they met outside of work. Peller didn't think anyone else in the department had caught on, but he knew the pair better than most. Nor did their increasing closeness surprise him, although he did wonder how long the pretense would last. Or was it pretense? Maybe Montufar and Dumas themselves didn't fully understand their relationship.

But tonight Peller wasn't dwelling on that. He wanted to simply relax, enjoy some time with his friends, and carry on an intelligent, insightful conversation about something trivial. The evening didn't disappoint him. As the group worked their way through a tossed salad, a zippy chili, and a heaping basket of corn muffins, they launched into an intelligent, insightful conversation about the weather.

"What I don't get," Jerry Souter said, emphasizing his point with a wave of his spoon, "is how it can be so dang cold. Global warming? Ha!

Coldest winter I remember. Snow as early as Thanksgiving, bay freezing over. That's global warming?"

A round of nods and affirmative murmurs emanated from the group. At ninety-three years of age, Souter's memory was the longest at the table, and his imposing ebony figure spoke vividly of his days in World War II. Jerry, Peller thought, would always be on the Italian Alps.

"It does seem counterintuitive," Dumas agreed. "But I'm sure Corina is perfectly comfortable." He winked at her.

"I hate it." Montufar didn't need to remind anyone that she'd been born in Guatemala. "And so do you, Eduardo, so don't start."

Her brother closed his mouth hurriedly, then faked a crestfallen look and turned to Sylvia for help.

Sylvia rolled her eyes.

"Global warming," Kaneko informed them in a classroom voice, "refers to the increasing average temperature of the whole planet, not to circumstances in any one location. Consider an illustration. Suppose you put your left hand in a bucket of almost frozen water with a temperature of thirty-two degrees. Then you put your right hand in a bucket of water with a temperature of one hundred twenty degrees, nearly hot enough to scald." His eyes fairly sparkled as he paused for effect. "On average, the heat you experience is a little above room temperature."

Everyone laughed.

Peller considered his chili and iced tea. "Good illustration, Professor. But that doesn't change the fact that one can't buy a decent winter coat here in the Piedmont."

Surprised, Sarah Kaneko set down the muffin she'd been lifting to her mouth. "I can."

"Yes, but you're not used to New York winters. I'm from upstate. To me, the typical Howard County winter could be autumn. The fall after we were married, Sandra bought me a heavy parka. I only had it two seasons. I got rid of it after one winter down here. It never got cold enough to wear it."

"She was one wonderful lady," Souter proclaimed, his voice rich and vibrant.

Montufar and Dumas nodded. The other guests looked anywhere but at Peller.

Raising a spoonful of steaming chili in salute, Souter added, "This is a meal worthy of her." He leaned towards Peller and added, "You didn't cook it, did you?"

"Hey, now," Peller laughed. "I'm not that bad of a cook."

"Probably not. Guys in our position learn quick or starve." He looked around the table, his intense eyes commanding the attention of the others. "It's part of life, folks. I seen more death than any of you. Lots more. Every one of them a person worth remembering."

Dumas pushed back from the table and set his napkin by his now-empty bowl. "I don't mind remembering Sandra." So quietly the others had to strain to hear, he added "It's the living that bug me."

"How so, son?"

Dumas looked around in surprise but said nothing. Peller wondered if his colleague had inadvertently voiced some buried regret.

"Must be running from his past," Montufar deadpanned. "All those women back home want him so desperately."

Dumas tried to smile, but the attempt made him look ill.

Eduardo put a hand to his mouth as if to whisper, which he didn't. "Then you'd better marry him, little sister, before they catch up with him."

Everyone laughed, and several guests spoke at once. Peller felt a tap on his shoulder and turned to his neighbor. "When this circus is over," Souter said in a low voice, "I gotta talk to you."

*

At around nine-fifteen the party began to wind down, and by nine-thirty Corina and Sylvia had disappeared into the kitchen with the empty plates and dishes. Dumas and the Montufar clan waved goodbye as the clock was striking ten. A shivering Sylvia pulled on her coat as she walked out the door into a biting wind. Only Souter remained, resting comfortably on the old blue sofa, gazing at the family photos on the wall opposite him: photos of Peller and Sandra and their son Jason spanning some three decades.

Peller sank into an easy chair to Souter's left and yawned. "I'm too old for this wild life."

Souter waved off his comment. "Folks are as young as they think they are."

"For some of us, it's been a long year. But I expect you're ready to lead another charge into battle."

"If duty calls."

Souter's voice was sober—strained, in fact. That wasn't like Jerry at all. Peller sat forward, studied the old man's lined face and the firm set of his jaw, followed his dark gaze to the photos on the wall. "Is it calling now?"

Souter pointed at the gallery. "You got a fine family, there."

Peller nodded.

"And you know what it's like to lose someone."

"What's wrong, Jerry?"

Souter shifted and met Peller's gaze. "Nothing's wrong with me, son. Question is, what would you do if your boy up and vanished without a trace? You don't know if he's dead or alive, killed or kidnapped or just run away from home. What would you do to know?"

"Whatever it takes, of course. Why?"

"Friend of mine, a lady who goes to my church, is in that boat. Her grandson vanished."

"When?"

Souter leaned back and contemplated the ceiling.

"Jerry?"

"Two years ago, Rick. Two years."

Peller knew the feel of days stretching into weeks and months and years, of emptiness descending into numbness. "I assume she reported it at the time."

"Sure. Your guys looked into it but came up empty."

"When did you find out about it?"

"Just last week. I had a cold and didn't go to church. Some of the folks thought I must've died in my sleep. Don't know why they'd think that, but this lady volunteered to check up on me. I invited her in for coffee and we got to talking. I had no idea."

Peller waited for the inevitable.

Souter looked sheepish, no mean feat for him. "I told her my neighbor was the best detective on the force."

Peller couldn't help but smile. "Yeah, I figured as much."

"I know you guys got rules, but could you check up on it? Maybe see if something got missed?"

"I suppose, but don't expect too much. I'm sure the investigators knew what they were doing."

Looking relieved, Souter nodded his thanks.

"How much did she tell you about it?"

"The kid's name is Jayvon. Jayvon Fletcher. He was living with his grandma Wanda and worked at an animal hospital. Christmas Eve he was pulling third shift, keeping an eye on the critters. He never came home. Your guys found a broken window and blood on the floor nearby. The back door was open, unlocked from inside. More blood on the back steps. Nothin' else."

"Sounds like a break-in," Peller said.

"That's what the cops told Wanda. They think Jayvon's dead."

Barring evidence to the contrary, Peller would have thought the same thing. "And she doesn't want to hear that, of course."

"No, but not knowing is worse. She's hired and fired a couple PI's and offered rewards and I don't know what else." Souter shrugged. "She just wants to know."

"All right," Peller told him. "I'll look over the reports and see what I can see. But like I said, don't expect too much."

"I appreciate it, Rick."

Peller yawned and stretched. "But," he said lightly, "I'll remember this next time I assemble the guest list for a party."

2

Monday morning the temperature struggled upward to twenty and faltered. In a North Laurel neighborhood of large trees and small townhomes, Eric Dumas gingerly brought his car to a halt atop an ice-patched pavement, just behind three squad cars and an ambulance. Flashing red lights painted the snow-dusted scene with menace, giving an infernal tint to the knot of curious neighbors gathered across the street. It was ten-thirty A.M. but somehow most of the gathering, including police and paramedics, looked half asleep. Maybe it was the cold.

Dumas climbed out of the car, shoved his gloved hands into his coat pockets, and approached the nearest rank of houses, where yellow crime scene tape had already been strung. A tall evergreen shook free its burden of snow as he passed by. Behind the townhouses, a steel tower strung with high-voltage power lines played roost to a group of turkey vultures.

The townhomes alternated styles from left to right: one brick, one sided in pale wood, another brick, another sided. The front door of the leftmost unit stood open. Dumas could see the forensics team working inside. He ducked the tape and carefully moved into their midst, passing through a small foyer floored in dingy green tile. A flight of stairs on the right, carpeted in a muddy brown fabric, led up to the second floor. The living room, identically floored, featured a huge flat-screen TV on the wall to the left. A battered tan sofa and matching chairs lounged before it, accompanied by two cheap wooden tables and a similar coffee table. Used paper plates dotted with pizza sauce and bits of crust and cheese littered the coffee table, alongside a half-empty bottle of vodka and a white serving bowl full of redskin peanuts. Some battered cardboard boxes were stacked along the back wall, tops folded shut.

"Hey, Detective," one of the team said. "Want some pizza?"

Dumas wasn't in the mood for gallows humor. "No, thanks."

The dead man on the sofa looked peaceful, except for the bullet holes through his head and chest. Dumas' first impression was that the kill had been remarkably clean: the only blood in evidence was that staining the victim's clothing and wicking into the upholstery in a hellish halo. No blood on the floor, none on the walls.

The deceased looked like anybody having dinner in front of a TV. Dumas noted that he was Asian, of average height and build, wearing jeans and a plain black t-shirt. Wool socks. No shoes. Nothing in the room appeared out of place. It was as though the man had been shot while he slept. Or maybe, Dumas thought, eyeing the bottle, while passed out. At any rate, this was neither an accident nor a heat-of-the-moment attack. The shooter had meant to kill, and kill he had, with cold efficiency.

The air had the warm, sharp smell of fresh cigarette smoke, but none of the team would be puffing on tobacco at the crime scene. Dumas looked toward the back of the house, where a wisp of smoke swirled in the draft near a sliding glass door. Following it, he found a cluttered kitchen and small dining area to the right. Dirty dishes filled the sink, and the tiny counter overflowed with small appliances and spent food containers. At a wooden table covered with more dirty dishes, mail, and other papers, a rail-thin woman in a dark-green robe sat smoking, gazing at nothing, possibly not even aware of the activity in the next room.

"Ma'am?" Dumas asked quietly.

"Denise," she said in a whiskey voice, not looking up. She took a long drag on her cancer stick. "Denise Newville. I suppose you already met Michio Tamai." She waved toward the living room. "Some people called him Mike."

"Your husband?" Dumas pulled out a chair and sat opposite her. She appeared to be in her mid-thirties, with a tangle of sandy brown hair and eyes that had seen too much.

"Nah."

"You lived together, though."

"If you can call it living. He gave me food and a roof over my head. One guess what I gave him." She paused to take another even longer drag on her cigarette and slowly blow out the smoke. Dumas turned his head slightly and held his breath until the cloud passed. "This complicates things," Newville added, "but I'm not sad about it. Sleazeball deserved it."

Dumas gave her an inquiring look.

With a nod she stood up, put her bare left foot on her chair, and pulled back her robe to expose most of her thigh. A livid purple bruise spread from her knee up her leg until it vanished beneath the fabric. "I could show you more, but you'd arrest me for flashing a cop." She covered up and sat.

Dumas wondered how she could be so flippant about it. "When did he do that?"

"Last night. He'd been out drinking, somehow managed to find his way home, and wanted me to fix him a big meal. At one in the morning." She dragged a hand through her hair and gave Dumas a crooked smile. "I wasn't inclined. So, you know."

"How long had this been going on?"

Denise took another puff. "A year or so."

"Why didn't you leave?"

"Nowhere to go."

"Did you kill him?"

She looked up, shocked, then laughed harshly. "If I had, I'd have someplace to go. But no, sorry, it wasn't me."

"Do you know who it was?"

"Could've been almost anybody he knew. He had a knack for making enemies out of friends." Finishing her cigarette, she crushed it out in an overflowing ash tray and fished another one out of a pack lying before her.

While she lit up, Dumas asked, "For instance?"

"Michio used to do odd jobs with a guy named Silas. Skinny creep who knew how to get into locked buildings. They'd *acquire* merchandise from warehouses and sell it. Made pretty good money, I guess. That was before I knew him. Silas moved on to other things, but they liked to brag about it over drinks. Until Michio had a bit too much one night and let slip that he'd cheated Silas on the profits. Laughed about it right in his face. That ended that friendship. Broken noses, missing teeth, and no more bragging over drinks."

"He was like that with everybody?" Dumas asked.

"You want to see my leg again?"

"Point taken. You think Silas killed him?

She blew out smoke, careful this time not to aim it at Dumas, and watched it drift away. "Not really. He hasn't been around for a good while. Then again, who knows?"

"I gather you didn't see it happen, then."

"Nope."

"Were you home?"

Denise gave him a disappointed look. "Do I look like I've been out, Mr. Detective?"

Dumas wondered if she was trying to get him to smile. He didn't. "You must have heard the gunshot, then," he said intentionally misstating the count.

"Gunshots," she corrected. "Two of them. I know because I counted the holes before calling 911. No, I didn't hear them. I wasn't feeling very relaxed after he beat me up last night, so I took a little something to knock myself out. He was dead by the time it wore off and I woke up."

Dumas believed her. She would have had good reason to kill Tamai, but her lack of pretense felt real to him. Far more likely was a scenario in which one of Tamai's accomplices either had a score to settle or had simply grown tired of him. "What time was that?"

"About a quarter to ten."

Dumas rose. "We'll need a list of Michio's contacts and background on his relationships with them, but we can do that later today. You'll be around?" He handed his business card to her.

"Where else would I go?" Denise read the card. "Unless you're in the market." She might have been joking, but her world-weary words ended in a cough instead of a come-on.

"Sorry," he replied.

With a cool smile she waved him on. He returned to the living room where a tall young woman was standing watch as a pair of middle-aged men bagged up the body. Dumas thought that crime scene investigator Geri Franklin looked barely old enough to be out of high school, but he knew her bland expression masked an intense focus. "Anything noteworthy?" he asked.

She didn't lift her gaze. "Only how clean the room is. He probably was shot where he lies. We'll go over the couch in detail as soon as the body's out of the way."

"All right. Give me a call if anything startling turns up."

"It won't," she replied, eyes still fixed on the proceedings.

Dumas couldn't help smile in spite of the circumstances. He crossed to the back of the room to inspect the stacked boxes. "What's in these?" He glanced back at Newville, still seated in the kitchen, still smoking like a chimney.

"Old books," she said.

Dumas donned a pair of latex gloves and opened one of the boxes. The books weren't old, but mint science fiction paperbacks stripped of their covers. He noticed multiple copies of several titles. "Yours or his?" he asked.

She blew out a puff of smoke and coughed. "His. I think he got them from dumpsters at the mall. Sometimes he could unload a box or two."

Unsold books reported to the publisher as destroyed, Dumas knew. Dumpster divers collected them and sold them to friends or at flea markets.

He closed up the box and left. He returned to his car, paying no attention to the neighbors still hanging around. There seemed to be a few more of them, waiting expectantly. For what? A glimpse of the shrouded body on its way to the morgue?

It's too early in the year for a murder, he thought. *It's definitely too cold to be out chasing a murderer.*

Behind the house, several of the vultures took wing and flapped lazily into the blue.

*

"The nursing home just called. Papá's not well."

Corina Montufar, digging through a pile of papers on her desk, jammed the receiver between her shoulder and ear. "What's wrong?"

Her sister Ella's timorous voice sounded distant. "They think he has pneumonia. They're transferring him to the hospital."

"You need me to go over there?" Finding the document she wanted, the fire marshal's report on a recent arson, she leaned back. They had moved their father, Felipe Montufar, to a nursing home three years earlier as Alzheimer's overtook him. Since then he'd been in generally good health but frequently unable to recognize his children or his surroundings. Montufar had been to the nursing home the prior weekend for a painful two hours during which he seemed to think she was one of his cousins. He had reminisced at great length about their youth in Amatitlán, Guatemala, of family Christmases and hot summer days swimming in the crystalline waters of Lago de Amatitlán. She wondered if he even knew anymore the fate of his beloved lake, which had long since been despoiled by industrial waste and raw sewage. She wondered if in any part of his mind he still remembered he had a son and two daughters, or if time itself any longer held meaning for him.

"Maybe," Ella said, then quickly added, "No, it's okay. I'll be fine."

Montufar gazed blankly at the report. The text appeared as meaningless blots before her eyes. "I can if you want."

"I can't ask you to leave work, Corina."

"He's my father, too. I'll be there if—"

"Don't keep offering," Ella snapped.

Montufar laid the report down. She'd never heard that tone of voice from her little sister before. Ella was more likely to cower than come out swinging. What had suddenly caused her to grow a backbone? "Are you okay?"

"I'm a big girl. I'll be fine." When Montufar didn't answer, she added, "I can do this. I have to." But before she finished the sentence, the determination slipped from her voice and she sounded like her timid self again.

"Okay. Let me know what they find. I'll stop by this evening."

After she hung up, Montufar turned and looked out the window across the room. It was another cold day. Even from a distance, she thought she could feel the chill seeping in.

Not only had the weather turned strange, life itself had followed its lead. She couldn't imagine her little sister taking charge of a situation. Ella had always been fainthearted, hiding behind her siblings at the first sign of trouble. But maybe recent trials had toughened her. Their mother had died, their father's mind had slipped away, and last year Eduardo had had a close brush with death. Was Ella finally learning to stand on her own feet? That life goes on despite sorrows?

Enough of that, though. She had work to do. Drawing a long breath, she picked up the report again and read about someone else's tragedy. The Dibble family's home had burned to the ground, taking all their worldly possessions with it, but fortunately no lives had been lost. Husband and father Vincent, wife and mother Candace, and their two children Peter and Andrew had been out to dinner when the fire erupted. Montufar felt sorry for the victims, but she knew they would bounce back, rebuild, be stronger for the experience. Life would go on.

She already knew the fire marshal had ruled the incident arson, but she hadn't yet read the report in detail. She did so now. Evidence indicated the presence in unusual locations of combustible liquids containing ethyl alcohol: near the living room window where the fire appeared to have started, along nearby baseboards, and on the floor alongside some of the furniture. Additionally, glass fragments recovered from the scene suggested breakage of a number of different bottles containing alcoholic beverages. Since nobody had been home to throw a wild party, the fire marshal concluded that the alcohol had been intentionally used as an accelerant.

None of this particularly surprised Montufar. What brought her up short was a comment at the bottom of the report: *Aspects of this case bear strong resemblance to three cases investigated in April of last year.* The case numbers followed. Turning to her computer, Montufar looked them up. Detective Lieutenant Bill Trengove had handled them. In those cases, too, ethyl alcohol had been used as an accelerant, poured beneath curtains and on furniture in the living room. Bottles had been smashed, leaving chunks and shards nearby.

But an arrest had been made. The suspect, one Carl Bradley, had been charged with three counts of second degree arson, tried, convicted, and sentenced to the maximum: twenty years for each fire, sentences to run concurrently. As Bradley was nowhere near parole, he obviously hadn't committed the more recent crime.

So was this a coincidence? A copycat? Or could Bradley have been wrongly convicted? As Montufar reviewed the information, the latter possibility grew farfetched. Trengove had somehow thought to check for fingerprints on the mailboxes, which in two of the three cases were mounted near the street rather than on the houses and thus not destroyed in the fires. Bradley's prints had no business being on either mailbox yet had been lifted from both of them. Bradley had of course protested his innocence but had been unable to present any credible alibi. Moreover, he had a moderately violent record to begin with, so his attorney didn't dare put him on the witness stand. Counsel for the defense had struggled valiantly to cast doubt on the prosecution's evidence, but the jury had deliberated for less than fifteen minutes before returning a guilty verdict.

Still, something didn't sit right with Montufar. She called Trengove's extension.

"Detective Lieutenant Bill Trengove," his gruff voice answered.

"Bill, I've—"

"I'm out today. Leave a message."

Montufar hung up as the beep sounded and sent him an email instead.

*

While Montufar was talking with her sister, Peller reviewed the strange case of Jayvon Fletcher, veterinary technician and missing person presumed dead. The photo his grandmother had provided showed a promising young man: tall, strong, and clean-shaven, with even features and a smile that seemed to say nothing could possibly be wrong with the world. He stood at the entrance to an apartment building, shaded by an oak tree of impressive girth. One meandering branch hung low over the door and Fletcher's head. The number on the building matched his address, so that must have been where he had lived with his grandmother Wanda.

He set the photo aside and took another from the file. This one depicted a pale blue house that looked to be over half a century old: the South Howard Veterinary Clinic, Fletcher's place of employment and the last place he was seen alive. Ever seen, Peller corrected himself. Two years ago a pair of colleagues, a veterinarian and a fellow tech, had updated him on the status of the patients and boarders left in his keep on the night of December twenty-fourth, then bade him Merry Christmas. Jayvon had seemed his usual cheerful self.

Peller shuffled through other crime-scene photos showing the back of the clinic. The broken window to the left of the rear door. Shards of broken glass on the ground below. The bulk of the smashed window on the floor inside. A few drops of blood scattered on the floor nearby. More blood streaked across the wooden steps as though an injured person had been dragged down them.

Something odd caught Peller's eye. The smears weren't as strong as he would have expected. It might have been the light, but he wondered if someone had tried to clean it up, leaving only what had stained the wood.

Lab analysis compared with Fletcher's medical records indicated that the smear was his blood, as were the drops found inside. But how had it been spilled? All fingerprints lifted from the scene had been eliminated as belonging to the clinic staff. That in itself didn't rule out the presence of anyone else, though. Detective Sergeant Andy Newton, who had investigated the case, had considered several scenarios.

First, Fletcher might have broken the window himself, either intentionally or accidentally, cut himself badly, and wandered off in search of medical help. Bleeding profusely, he never made it. Not likely, Newton had thought, and Peller agreed. No blood had been found on the broken glass itself, and too little dotted the floor. Moreover, the window had clearly been broken from the outside. Fletcher hadn't smoked, so it seemed unlikely he would have gone outside. But suppose he had? Could he have locked himself out and broken the window to get back in? Sure, but the same problem arose. He couldn't have seriously injured himself in the process without leaving blood on the glass and significantly more on the floor than had actually been present.

Suppose a would-be thief, assuming the clinic to be empty on a holiday night, broke in. Hearing the window shatter, Fletcher might have confronted the intruder and lost in a struggle. Sergeant Newton didn't like that alternative, either. Nothing had been stolen. If the incident had begun as robbery, the thief must have panicked and fled, taking Fletcher—alive or dead—with him. But again, why so little blood?

Newton's final hypothesis involved an intrusion of a different sort: Fletcher may have had an enemy who choose to attack while the tech was alone in a secluded location. A calculated killing could have left time to clean up any resulting mess, accounting for the lack of blood inside. While not flawless, that scenario seemed most likely, aside from one tiny problem: Fletcher appeared to have had no enemies. His life sparkled as clean as his photograph. He'd never been in trouble, never been involved with drugs, was liked by friends and family, and was a stellar employee. In his quest for an enemy, Newton questioned everyone connected with Fletcher and struck out across the board.

Peller put everything back in the file and stretched his legs. He hated to disappoint Souter's church friend, but he didn't see how he could make any more of it than Andy Newton had.

Yet the blood smears on the steps puzzled him. The more he considered it, the more he was sure someone had tried to clean up. That pointed to Newton's third hypothesis. But why wouldn't the killer have taken precautions against leaving blood on such a hard-to-clean surface in the first place?

Shaking his head, he returned the file to its drawer.

3

Hannah had never felt particularly courageous. Harold surely was the brave one, the strong one, not her. In high school and college, the only time she ever felt in control was on stage, where she could be anyone. Otherwise, she stood alone in a threatening world. She could never please her parents, no matter how hard she tried. Her older brother thought she was a flake and never wasted an opportunity to remind her. Academic subjects so baffled her that most of her teachers considered her hopeless. As she matured, girls envious of her growing beauty spread rumors that she was sleeping around—she wasn't—and certain boys, hoping the rumors were true, relentlessly pursued her. Too often she had grappled with clutching hands and fierce mouths, escaping only to be cornered another day. If anyone in authority ever noticed her distress, they hadn't intervened or even inquired. Tormented by fear, desperate for escape, her teenage years dragged on in exhausting, endless days.

And then she'd met Harold, her knight in shining armor who treated her as a woman rather than a useless appendage or a piece of meat. The pack hounding her quickly learned that she had a strong protector. The girls, now motivated by a fresh and unexpected jealousy, wished they could be her. Even Hannah's parents seemed to cut her some slack when Harold was around. Her brother still thought she was a flake, but he was, after all, her brother. Harold shielded her, worshiped her, and brought her to the self-respect she had long lacked. Even when their dreams sublimated into nothing and they descended into petty crime, he kept her from losing heart.

And yet, in the most desperate moments of their shared lives, Harold had not rescued Hannah. She had rescued him. She didn't understand how this unlooked-for courage and resolve had been born, but she didn't question it. She was glad she could give back to him. He deserved it.

And here, now, was another such moment. His head cradled in his hands, Harold sat on the austere beige couch in the tiny living room of their small apartment in Savage, muttering, "Bad move. Terrible move. Why the hell did we do it?"

"You know why." She stood at the window looking out over the frozen grass and parking lot. Cold seeped in around the edges of its sagging old frame. This winter was the coldest she'd ever known, but somehow she liked it. That was as odd as her courage. Marylanders didn't generally like the cold. She herself had hated it once, but that was before.

"We should have paid him off," Harold said.

"With what? We'll never have that kind of money. Besides, he couldn't be trusted. He'd just hit us up again. And again. It was the only way."

Harold looked up, his face twisted with misery. "He was my friend. He helped us."

"He stabbed us in the back."

"I know. I just…I'm afraid, Hannah. We can't keep doing things like this. Sooner or later, we'll get caught."

Hannah went to his side, sat, put her arms around him. "So long as we're true to each other, nobody can touch us."

He looked into her eyes, those blue eyes that had bewitched him. She knew because he'd told her time and again over the years. His own eyes were hazel and usually intense, but now they seemed incapable of grasping the nature of anything they saw. He sat lost in a familiar world, searching for something he could not find.

"What?" she asked.

"Why do you bother with me?"

"What does that mean?"

"Look at yourself. You could have any man you want. You know you could. Why me?"

"Because you're mine."

"That's no answer."

She embraced him more tightly. "It is so."

He pondered that for some moments. "Do you love me?"

She wished he'd shut up before he wandered into territory he couldn't safely traverse. "Sure."

"As much as before?"

So much for wishes. But she had never lied to him, and she wouldn't now. "No."

Strangely, he didn't look hurt. "Then how?"

"Come here." She took his hand and rose. He followed her to the window. Still holding his hand, she breathed gently on the pane. It fogged up, and in the frigid air currents the moisture transmuted into delicate traces of frost. "That's my heart."

Harold regarded the frost as though content to become lost in its tiny crystalline maze.

"Nobody is going to hurt you. Nobody is going to take you away from me. Nobody."

He nodded.

"You're okay with that?"

He nodded again, and as she felt his hand relax she knew that winter had seeped into his heart, too.

"Let's forget about it. Let's forget about him. All there is, is us."

Harold slipped his arm around Hannah's waist, pulling her body tight against his. She imagined their joined forms etched in frost on the window. The image pleased her. She vowed that it would always be this way.

"You know," he said, "I don't think I even remember his name."

*

Shortly after noon, Dumas received a call from Denise Newville, ready to talk details. He pulled on his coat and drove back to the townhouse she had shared with the late Michio Tamai. The cloudless day hadn't warmed noticeably, and the light felt unusually feeble, as though the sun itself had retreated to some warmer clime. He got out of his car and studied his surroundings before approaching her place.

The neighborhood sat quiet under the winter sky. The gawkers had moved on to work or withdrawn into the warmth of their homes. The electric tower behind the townhouses no longer played host to the turkey vultures. Where, he wondered, would they go on a day like this?

Dumas started for the front door but had taken only a few steps before a car door slammed behind him and someone called, "Sergeant Dumas! Could I have a word with you?" He turned to find a short young fellow bundled in an electric blue coat, matching ski cap, and thick black gloves hurrying up the sidewalk. The man's narrow face looked pale. Dumas wondered if he was really that fair-complexioned or whether it was a trick of the light. A tag of dark brown hair thrust haphazardly from under the left side of his cap.

"Jack Collins," he said breathlessly, coming to a halt and extending a hand.

Dumas accepted the handshake. "What can I do for you, Mr. Collins?"

"I'm a reporter with the *Columbia Flier*."

Dumas put up a hand to stop him. "I'm sorry, but I can't talk about this case right now. You can call Public Information for whatever details are available."

"Actually, I'd like to do an article on how cases are processed."

What? Dumas thought, but just looked at him.

Collins shivered and shuffled his feet. "How evidence is gathered, how you put it together to solve a case, stuff like that." He nodded toward Tamai's front door. "This would make for a dramatic backdrop."

"You want to exploit a man's death to sell papers."

"No, no, I just—"

Stone-faced, Dumas shook his head. "It's too cold to argue. If you'll excuse me." He turned away.

"I could drop by Northern District Headquarters at your convenience, Sergeant."

Dumas looked back. The reporter waited like a dog begging for a handout. "How do you know my name?"

The reporter shuffled his feet again, either out of embarrassment or to keep warm. "I'm sort of a friend of the Montufar family."

"You don't say."

"Ella's friend mostly."

Recognition dawned. "Wait, I remember you. You're the fellow who asked Corina about Eduardo's accident at that press conference last year."

Collins nodded.

"What, you're hoping to score points with Ella?"

"So—" He made a vague motion with his hands. "No, it's just my job."

Dumas choked back a laugh. "All right, Mr. Collins, maybe I can talk later today. Call first, though, huh?"

"I will!"

The detective started for the door again.

"Thank you, sir!" Collins called.

Of all the dumb things. Dumas knocked on the door. So quick she must have been watching his approach, Denise Newville admitted him. The place looked no different than it had earlier in the day, except that the couch, now covered with a worn earthtone afghan, no longer cradled Tamai's spent body. "How are you holding up?" Dumas asked her.

"Passable." Newville motioned vaguely around. "Kitchen again, or out here? The table's still a mess. I don't think I'm going to clean it up. Ever."

Dumas motioned to the chairs near the sofa, and they sat. "I thought you had nowhere to go."

"Not really, but I have a cousin who might take me in for a while. She lives in Virginia." She had traded in her robe for jeans and a sky blue turtleneck covered by a plaid flannel shirt buttoned only halfway up. While she talked, she fished in the shirt's breast pocket but came up empty. "Left my cigarettes upstairs."

Dumas could have done without the secondhand smoke but said, "Go ahead, I'll wait."

"Nah, that's okay. I've already doubled my usual daily habit. One death a day is enough." She forced a smile.

Dumas understood the deflection. On the outside, people often pushed aside tragedy, as though mere denial might undo it. On the inside, it pushed back. "About Michio's friends."

"Yeah, so I told you about Silas. His last name is Hudnall. But like I said, he hasn't been around for a long time. Ken Farmer was another guy. His first name's Kennedy. Never heard of anyone with that first name, have you?"

Dumas shook his head.

"Ken's a real smart guy, played chess online, always had some scheme cooking. He was Michio's ideas man, until he figured out that he wasn't getting a fair cut."

"What kind of jobs did he do?"

"He didn't do them, he just planned them. A lot of it was just petty theft. They did a good business in cell phones for a few months. Another time it was bicycles. I think they were working out some kind of online scam when they had their falling out."

"Do you know where Ken lives?"

Newville smiled demurely and rose. She sashayed into the kitchen and returned a moment later clutching an address book to her chest with both hands. She sat and looked into Dumas' eyes. "If I give you this, how grateful will you be?"

Dumas needed her cooperation, but he had little patience for games today.

She batted her eyes theatrically.

"Ma'am—"

"Oh well, can't blame a girl for trying." She set the book on her lap and opened it. "Here's another guy I remember. Henry Carver. He and Michio robbed prostitutes in Baltimore County a few times."

"Armed robbery?"

She nodded. "Michio had a gun. I'm sure he took it along. I don't know about the other guy."

"Any run-ins with the cops over that?"

"There wouldn't have been, would there? Not likely a hooker would go to the police."

"Maybe, maybe not. What kind of gun did he have?"

"The kind you shoot people with. I don't know anything about guns other than that." Newville turned pages in the address book and ran her finger down the entries. "They did a few other jobs together, too, but Michio stopped working with him. Said Henry was getting edgy and making mistakes. Oh, here's a real gem. Wolf."

"Wolf?"

"Wolf Spensely. Tall, skinny black guy. Strong. You wouldn't guess from looking at him how strong he is. He makes heavy electronics disappear from delivery trucks without breaking a sweat. He's not above bashing in a head or two if needed. Michio needed his skills sometimes, but he was afraid of him, too. He was about the only guy Michio didn't cheat. At least as far as I know. But now that I think about it, nobody would be more likely to pop a friend than Wolf."

After pondering the book for a few more moments, Newville closed it and offered it to Dumas. "All the contact info Michio had is in here. You can have it. No charge."

Dumas took it. "Thank you."

"Are you always so dead serious?"

"Probably."

"I make you nervous, don't I? You must be married."

"Actually, no."

"Spoken for?"

"I did have a few more questions."

She leaned back and laughed. "I hope you're more relaxed around her."

Dumas couldn't help but smile at that. "She thinks I'm funnier than Robin Williams. But I do have a few more questions."

"Fire away."

"What was Michio up to in the last couple of weeks?"

Folding her hands together, Newville studied her fingers. "I don't know for sure. I usually tried to ignore his business. But somehow I knew he was headed for trouble." Before Dumas could ask, she added, "I don't know how I knew. He wasn't upset or troubled or anything. Just the opposite, really. He was always confident, but lately he'd been downright smug. I didn't ask and he didn't say why. But I didn't like it. Something was happening, something big, and with him that could mean big trouble."

When she looked up, he noticed for the first time that her eyes were red; she'd been crying recently. "Does that make any sense?"

Dumas decided it might be best to cut the interview short. Tamai's death must have affected her more than she let on. "It makes a lot of sense. And I think that will do for now." He rose and she followed him to the door. "If you do go to Virginia, let me know your address and phone number down there. I may have more questions, and I'll want to let you know what we find."

With a nod, Newville touched his hand, carefully, only for a moment. "Thank you, Sergeant."

"Of course." As he traversed the walk back to his car, he felt her eyes on him, but when he looked back the door was closed and the windows were empty.

∗

The bloodstains on the steps increasingly bothered Peller, to the point that shortly after noon he shoved aside his pile of paperwork and walked over to Andy Newton's desk. Newton was busy filling in forms of his own and didn't raise his eyes when Peller pulled up a chair. "Not bored, are you, sir?" he asked blandly.

"Not yet."

"Be with you in a moment."

Peller waited patiently, musing over Newton's appearance as he did so. The man reminded him of a character from Washington Irving or Nathaniel Hawthorne, with a befuddled-scarecrow look that concealed a formidable skill at drawing information from those he questioned. People always felt a need to offer extra detail when talking to him, just to be sure he understood.

"You remember the Jayvon Fletcher case, I'm sure," Peller said once Newton looked up.

"I wish I could forget it. Why?"

"How about I buy you lunch and we can talk it over."

Newton grinned. "For lunch, you can have the whole case."

"Name the place."

"You like Thai?"

Peller grimaced.

Eager to be off, Newton rose. "Italian, then. That place in Golden Triangle."

"Stella Notte. Deal."

Peller drove the surprisingly congested mile to the restaurant, a nice sit-down place at the east end of the Golden Triangle shopping center's parking lot. The hostess led them to his favorite of the two distinctly-decorated dining rooms: the Terraza Room, an airy sunroom. Hanging spider plants and ivies basked in the afternoon light. Peller was delighted to find that not many diners were present despite the hour, and their table was a restful spot in which to think.

They didn't talk shop until the waitress had returned with iced tea for both of them. Newton ordered lasagna without even looking at the menu. Peller hesitated between several choices, finally settling on chicken parmigiana.

"So what's got you interested in Jayvon?" Newton asked.

Peller unfolded his napkin into his lap. "Turns out Fletcher's grandmother goes to the same church as my next-door neighbor. He twisted my arm into checking up on it. Not that I think I can contribute anything."

Newton picked up his fork and twirled it absently. "I wouldn't mind another set of eyes, to be honest. That case still bugs me. I don't think we'll ever resolve it."

"Barring a miracle," Peller agreed. "What did you make of the bloodstains on the back steps?"

"You got me. They don't fit, do they? Inside, broken glass under the window and a tiny bit of blood on the floor. Then those nasty smears outside. You read the report?" He looked up.

Peller nodded affirmation.

Newton put the fork down and drummed his fingers on the table, his eyes focused not on the present but on his visits to the crime scene. "My best guess wasn't a great one, but it's the only scenario that makes any sense to me."

The waitress glided up and placed salads on the table. "Your food will be up shortly. Anything else I can get you?"

"We're fine, thanks," Peller told her with a smile. After she left, he asked Newton, "Could somebody have cleaned up the mess?"

"I think they must have. But that's kind of strange."

Peller agreed, and wondered whether Newton's thinking on the subject matched his own. "How so?"

"The perp removes the body without taking precautions to keep blood off the back steps, then thoroughly cleans the wood and the floor inside. But he leaves the broken glass?" He took a drink of tea. "If you're going to clean up after a premeditated attack, wouldn't you limit the mess in the first place and make a better job of dealing with the rest? And if it wasn't premeditated, wouldn't you have left the mess and bolted?"

"People do strange things when they're scared," Peller observed. "You remember Morgan Parsons last year? Committed a robbery, killed a man who tried to stop him, absconded with the body, and ditched it in a pond?"

"Point," Newton agreed. "Besides, Fletcher had no enemies. I couldn't find a single reason why anyone short of Charles Manson would kill him. Maybe it was unpremeditated after all."

"So a break-in."

"Which turns into a manslaughter, after which the assailant removes the body without stopping to think. I can almost go along with that. But they *do* stop to clean the blood from the floor and steps?"

The waitress, approaching with their entrees, gave the detectives a curious look. As she slid the dishes onto the table, Newton smiled sheepishly. "Sorry. We work in a rough business."

She returned the smile. "I grew up in Baltimore city," she said. "Be careful, the plate's hot. Anything else I can get you?"

"We're good."

As she retreated, Newton continued. "The worst thing is, it almost doesn't matter what happened. We have no link to the perp. Either way, Fletcher's gone without a trace."

"Well." Peller cut into his meal. "Time for lunch. Thanks, Andy."

"My pleasure. Let me know if you do pull a rabbit out of the hat."

"That's Eric's pastime," Peller said with a grin.

Newton laughed, then casually asked, "How are you holding up these days?"

"I keep myself occupied."

"Glad to hear it. We haven't talked much since...you know."

Peller knew. Everyone tiptoed around the subject of his late wife and the revelation last spring that her death hadn't been entirely accidental.

"I've made peace with that. Besides, Sandra wouldn't want me wasting the rest of my life in grief."

Newton worked on his lasagna in silence for a few minutes. "That's good," he finally said. "And, uh, I don't know if you'd be interested, but my wife has a friend who might like to meet you."

"So long as she doesn't want me to solve another one of your cases," Peller quipped without thinking. But then he realized what Newton meant and put his fork down.

"From that look," Newton said drily, "I guess you're not ready for that yet."

"No, Andy. I don't think I ever will be."

"Come on, you've got a lot of good years ahead of you. You might not want to spend them alone."

"I'm not alone."

Newton turned his perpetually surprised eyes on Peller, then shook his head and resumed eating. "Okay, sir. But if you change your mind, let me know. She's a nice lady."

*

When Montufar walked through the doors of Howard County General Hospital, she felt as though all the world was passing away before her eyes. She hated hospitals. With each step she took, her revulsion grew. The cool antiseptic-tinted air, the art carefully composed to suggest serenity, the lab-coated doctors whisking by, reminded her over and over of her mother's passing. Outwardly she didn't show it, but her insides quivered in anticipation of the moment when the place of healing would unmask itself as truly a place of death.

By her side holding her hand, Eric Dumas felt her tension and gently squeezed. The moment he'd learned about her father's illness, he volunteered to accompany her. She hoped his presence might provide warmth and strength enough to fend off the icy hand of fear clawing at her neck. But could even Dumas save her from her demons?

They found Felipe Montufar asleep in his third-floor room. Corina took a step back. Dumas' hand steadied her. Seventeen years her mother's elder, her father had always been "old" to her friends, but only now did she see him that way. Her father's face, a parchment mask stretched over bone, was turned toward the door as though he had anticipated her arrival. IV lines snaked into his left arm; more lines ran oxygen from the wall behind into his failing lungs.

He's only seventy-one, Corina thought. *Why does he look ready for the grave?*

Ella had pulled her chair close to their father. Her hands were clenched tightly on the edge of his bed, and her hair spilled haphazardly over her shoulders, as though she hadn't had the energy or desire to put it in order. She looked up when Corina and Dumas stepped through the doorway, and her face, bare of cosmetics, was ghastly pale.

Corina felt as though she were standing on a precipice over an unfathomable abyss. She knew her younger sister was given to emotion and exaggeration, but the starkness of her face was genuine. Ella was certain that the end was near. "How is he?" Corina asked.

Ella shook her head.

Fear turned to anger. "Hasn't anyone said *anything*?" Dumas put an arm around her shoulder and drew her close.

"Oh. Yeah. A doctor looked in on him about two hours ago. It's a lower respiratory infection."

"Pneumonia?"

Ella stroked her father's gray hair. "Not yet. But it will be."

At the sound of his daughter's voices Felipe's eyes opened halfway. "Ah," he said weakly. He tried to reach, but his hand barely rose from the bed.

Ella took his right hand while Corina hurried to the opposite side of the bed and enclosed his left in hers. "Hola, papá," Corina said. "¿Cómo estás?"

"Cansado." His voice was a dry whisper, but his eyes sharpened as he looked at her, hinting at his past strength. "Ingles por favor. Es más importante para vernos en los Estados Unidos."

Corina patted his hand. "I know, papá. I speak English all the time now."

He nodded and closed his eyes again, drifting away, although Corina couldn't tell if he slept normally or was simply lost to the drugs they were giving him. Moments passed. No one spoke. Ella and Corina held their father's hands. The voices of the nurses as they went about their rounds and the quiet blips of monitors swelled in the silence. Felipe breathed slowly. Corina half-expected that soft sound to stop, but it continued. She found herself wishing they were indeed in Guatemala, as her father had thought, preparing for the journey north. *So long ago*, she thought. *Almost nineteen years. How could so much time vanish?* Then her father had been the family's strength. Whatever life brought, he could safely guide them through it. She wanted those days back, wanted to live them again and again.

"He just needs rest. He's sick, that's all," she told the room, as though doing so might restore order to her universe. Not that she could even convince herself. How could mere words make the world right?

"It's worse than that, Corina. The doctor didn't exactly say pneumonia, but it could go that way. You know what happens to old people with pneumonia." Ella wiped away a tear on her sleeve and turned to face her sister. She released their father's hand and stretched her fingers as though forcing them to relax. "We should be talking about funeral arrangements."

The words struck Corina with almost physical force. Dumas must have felt her tense, because he drew her closer. She could only manage a single, faint word. "What?"

Ella's mouth quivered. "He's so weak. Besides, his mind..." She motioned vaguely as though that might explain all.

Corina's fingers contracted into fists. Fear and anger rose in her throat, choking her. A chorus of furious voices clamored in her head: *Who let this happen? What were they doing at that nursing home? Weren't they paying attention? How could you do this to us, papá? You have to stay, you have to take care of us! Damn it Ella, how dare you give up! How can you speak what I can't bring myself to think? You're still afraid of the dark!*

Dumas gave her shoulders a comforting squeeze. She met his eyes and found his gaze steady, his presence solid and reassuring. Something in those eyes and the set of his mouth triggered a memory.

On the day of her grandfather's funeral, surrounded by grieving aunts and uncles and cousins, she recalled her grandmother Alessandra sitting straight and calm, eyes closed, her silver rosary threaded through her fingers. Corina thought she should be clenching them, clinging desperately to them in her grief. But no.

"*Abuela,*" she had whispered, and her grandmother had opened her eyes and smiled at her.

"Yes, *niña?*"

"Why aren't you crying like everyone else?"

Her grandmother smiled again. "You are sad because your *abuelo* is gone."

"Yes."

"But, you see, he is not." Grandmother lifted the rosary to show her. "We have prayed for each other all our lives. I still pray for him, and he for me. And now his prayers are so much stronger than they were when he was alive."

"I don't understand," the memory-Corina said.

"No, not yet. But one day you will find the one who will pray for you, and you will pray for him. And your prayers for each other will be strong. So strong they will hold you up always. Even when the world shakes under you."

The moment passed, and she was again by her father's bedside. *I understand now,* abuela, she told her grandmother's soul. *I do understand.*

Dumas studied her face. "You all right?"

Had it been memory, or had her grandmother, far in the past, spoken to her of this moment, or had she visited her in this moment to remind her of that day? It didn't matter. God had not forsaken her. Eric was His gift. Eric loved her and would support her no matter what.

"Yes," she told him. "I'll be fine." Turning to Ella, she drew an unsteady breath. "Is it that serious?"

Ella shook her head. "Maybe not. I hope not. But look at him, Corina. It's going to happen, probably sooner than any of us want. We should be ready."

Montufar stroked her father's hand and said nothing. Dumas' grip on her shoulders was strong and gentle. Quietly, he said, "I'm sure he'll recover, Corina, but Ella has a point. It's best to be prepared."

"Eduardo's going to talk to Father Owen," Ella said.

Corina nodded absently. *Prepare for the worst. Hope for the best.* She watched her father sleeping and felt a great weariness herself. She reached out to Felipe and gingerly touched his hand.

She must have looked ready to fall apart again, because Ella came to her side and wrapped her hands around both sister's and father's. "It's okay, Corina. You've been strong for me so many times over so many years. I don't know how I would have lasted without you. Maybe it's my turn to be strong for you."

Montufar felt tears forming, and for some time her mind drifted, hollow save for a profound sense of loss. And then the irony of Ella's words struck her and she couldn't help but laugh. She wrapped an arm around Ella to pull her close. "That is just so wrong!"

In a moment, Ella was laughing, too, leaving Dumas to puzzle over them.

Felipe woke at their laughter. After a moment of confusion, he found his daughters and focused on them. He smiled a weak but joyful smile. "¡Ah, mi hermanas bonitas! Te amo. Te amo." Then closed his eyes and lapsed into sleep once more.

The women's laughter faltered. Dumas watched sadness creep back into their eyes. "What is it? What did he say?"

Ella drew a ragged breath. "He said he loves us." She glanced at Corina, then looked up at the ceiling.

"And something else, obviously."

Corina closed her eyes, settled her forehead against Ella's, and explained, "He thinks we're his sisters."

4

Jack Collins, young reporter and apparently Ella Montufar's latest catch, got pulled onto an assignment Monday afternoon. He called Dumas Tuesday morning to profusely apologize for going AWOL and begged for a second chance. Against his better judgement, Dumas took pity on him and invited him to come by.

Collins arrived with lightning speed and was now shrugging out of his electric blue coat. Combing his fingers through his mop of brown hair, he seated himself next to Dumas' desk. "I really, really appreciate this, Sergeant. You have no idea what it means to me."

"I can guess," Dumas said dryly. "So how do we start?"

"I'd like to see your work firsthand. Since I missed the initial stages of the investigation, it would help if you walked me through what's already happened."

"You'll take notes?"

"I'll make recordings, if that's okay. It's a lot easier."

"I don't mind," Dumas said, not quite sure that was the truth, "but we need some ground rules."

"Of course. Just let me know what they are."

Dumas picked up a pen and studied it as though the rules might be written on its casing. "First, you don't release anything—and I do mean anything—without my approval. We routinely withhold certain information from the public to avoid compromising ongoing investigations."

"Understood."

"Second, at a crime scene you stay back and follow all instructions I or any other officer gives you. We have to be very careful about recording and recovering evidence. One wrong step can compromise our ability to bring a criminal to justice."

"Of course."

"I'll make up the rest once I find out how much of a distraction your presence will be."

"Oh, I wouldn't—" Collins started to protest, but when Dumas grinned at him, he backpedaled. "You were joking."

Dumas dropped the pen and opened a file folder that had been waiting on his desk. "Not entirely, but that's the third rule. You don't have to be afraid of me. I'm an easygoing guy most of the time."

Collins shed some of his nervousness and almost smiled in return. He pulled a tape recorder from one of the deep pockets in his coat, switched it on, and set it gently on the desk.

Dumas eyed the device with distaste. "Okay, let's get started on the backstory. The lady of the house, Denise Newville, called 911 at about nine forty-five and reported that the man she was living with had been shot to death..."

He related the essentials as quickly as possible, gave Collins a cursory look at Tamai's address book, and pulled up a map on his computer. "I plan to interview a number of Tamai's contacts, starting with Wolf Spensely. Denise Newville fingered him."

"She thinks he did it?"

"She didn't say so, but maybe. Or, she might want me to focus on him."

"Why?"

Dumas wondered whether his curiosity was genuine or just a way to extract information. "Maybe she's deflecting me to protect the killer. Maybe she is the killer. I doubt it, but she could be. Or maybe she has it in for Spensely, or deep down actually does think he's the killer." Dumas picked up the phone and dialed a number. "Whatever the reason, he's as good a starting point as any."

Collins looked eager to start, but Dumas didn't want to go it alone. Newville had painted Spensely as potentially dangerous. So he called for backup, hoping his friend Officer Kevin Graham would be available. He was. Graham joined Dumas and Collins in the parking lot, and they set course for Spensley's, an address bordering a farm some eight miles west of where Michio Tamai drew his last breath.

They arrived to find not a house but a trailer set well back from the road. By then, a featureless, gray sheet had been pulled over the sky and wind picked at the bare branches of the trees surrounding the trailer. As trailers went, it was on the small side, old, and tired. Its dirt-streaked white sides bore a barely-visible mark that might once have been a dashing blue stripe. A faded logo clung to its forward end. The door stood about in the middle, overspread by a spavined awning that sagged to the left. Rusting lawnmowers and power tools, decaying wooden pallets, discarded cans faded beyond identification, and other detritus littered the sea of dead weeds and tall dormant grasses poking up through the thin layer of snow. Trees and bushes and brambles grew where they had sprouted at Mother Nature's direction. She was apparently partial to thorns. One ferocious clump of vine had rambled up the forward end of the trailer, where it hung patiently down from the roof as though waiting to snatch up and devour an unwary trespasser.

"Home sweet home," Dumas remarked as he and Graham picked their way up the rimed gravel drive with Jack Collins on their heels. They had parked at the lower end of the drive to avoid warning Spensely that he had guests. A battered black Honda Civic rested at the top beside the trailer. Dumas wondered if it ran any better than the abandoned lawnmowers.

"Wolf is obviously neither a gardener nor a mechanic," Graham commented.

"Astute observation. You really should transfer to CID. You're cut out for this."

Graham, a powerful six-foot three immigrant from Jamaica, shook his head. He and Dumas had long worked together, at first by happenstance but increasingly at Dumas' request. "I like patrol work. Keeps you on your toes."

"And this doesn't?"

"You CID guys don't know how good you have it."

"I've been shot at a few times, you know."

"I've been hit."

"Really?" Dumas couldn't keep the surprise from his voice; he hadn't heard about that before.

Graham nodded. "In the left leg, eleven years ago, by a woman with a .38."

"How did that happen?"

"A domestic. She caught her husband messing around and wanted to make sure he stopped. She was a lousy shot. Closed her eyes before she fired." He slapped his left thigh. "It wasn't bad, just winged me. She turned out to be a sweet lady, though. She apologized a million times and took care of me until the ambulance got there. She even sent me flowers next day."

Dumas stared at him, incredulous. "Sweet lady. Only you could say something like that."

Graham shrugged. "She wasn't aiming at me, mon."

"She wasn't aiming at all." They arrived at the door and Dumas knocked. "I'm serious about you transferring. We're a great team. Besides, it'd be a lot easier than having to request your presence all the time." He glanced back at Collins and saw that their conversation was being recorded. He made a note to make sure he watched what he said. He hadn't counted on his every word being captured.

Graham gazed at the recorder for a moment, too, but turned back to the door, unconcerned. Momentarily, the door opened.

To Dumas, Wolf Spensely looked like a half-starved basketball player. Jeans and a t-shirt hung on his lanky frame; an unbuttoned khaki flannel draped limply over them. His bronzed face was darker than Corina's but not as dark as Graham's. "Mornin', folks," he said easily in a Virginia accent muffled by the gum he chewed. Dumas wondered if cops made a habit of showing up on his doorstep.

"Mr. Wolf Spensely?" Dumas asked, and the other nodded. He showed Spensely his badge. "Detective Sergeant Dumas, Howard County Police. This is Officer Graham. Could we have a word?"

"Sure, c'mon in." He held the door open for them, his eyes lingering over Collins and his whirring tape recorder. "You boys want a drink?"

"Kind of early, isn't it?" Graham asked.

Spensely flashed a disconcerting smile. His mouth somehow looked crooked even when closed, its left side angling upward where it shouldn't. Smiling exaggerated the effect. "Never too early. 'Course, you're on duty."

The door opened directly on a cramped living room where a white couch grayed by use competed with some wooden chairs and a paperback-crammed rank of bookcases. Dumas was surprised at the wealth of reading material. He went to the shelves and surveyed the titles, which included a healthy collection of Civil War history and spy fiction. All of the spines looked well-worn, and many of the covers were missing, reminding him of the boxes at Tamai's place. *Probably where he got them*, Dumas mused. "You must spend your days reading."

"Some. Those are all secondhand. I didn't wear them out by my lonesome. Help yourselves to a seat." He stationed himself in one of the wooden chairs, where his ramrod-straight posture still caused him to tower over his guests. "What's with the tape recorder?"

Although Spensely didn't seem ill at ease, Dumas didn't want him turning belligerent, so he signaled Collins to turn it off. "Mr. Collins is a reporter. He's doing a documentary on police work. He's here to report on me, not on you. Do you know why I'm here, Mr. Spensely?"

As Dumas spoke, he took in the artwork on the wall opposite the bookcases. A series of four original paintings by an artist of almost modest talent depicted bay-area landscapes in glaring, straight-from-the-tube acrylics. In their midst, a very different painting had been given pride of place: a shapely blonde woman tightly clad in black leather, half turned towards the viewer. Her legs were planted so far apart that the model—if there had been one—must have fractured something. As a final touch, her outstretched hand brandished a coiled whip. Dumas wondered if Spensely was the artist. He couldn't read the signatures from where he sat.

"Can't be a social visit," Spensely replied.

"An acquaintance of yours was found dead yesterday morning. Michio Tamai." Dumas noted that Spensely's eyes widened a touch. "What do you know about that?"

"Mike," Spensely said thoughtfully. "Well I'll be damned."

"You worked with him," Graham said. "Word is, he was scared of you."

"I ain't admitting to working with him, but yeah, he was a bit edgy around me. Some folks are." He seemed to find that amusing. "I guess I do have a bit of a temper."

"Word is," Graham continued, "a long list of people might have wanted him dead, and you're somewhere near the top of it."

"Nah, he never did me wrong."

"He did everyone else wrong," Dumas said. "Why not you?"

"Like your partner said, he was scared of me."

"When did you see him last?"

"Probably…" Spensely looked at the ceiling, eyes narrowed in concentration. "Two weeks ago? I stopped by for a social visit. It was a Saturday afternoon. We talked, had a few drinks, nothing much."

"Talked business," Graham interjected.

"Nope."

"What did you talk about, then?" Dumas asked.

"Just guy stuff. Football. Women. You know."

"Just a couple of mates hangin' out," Graham mused, sounding thoroughly unconvinced. "Seems alcohol usually loosened Mike's tongue. Was that your plan? Get him to talk, find out if he'd cheated you like he'd cheated everyone else? And if so, take him out?"

Spensely laughed. "What's this, good cop bad cop? Won't work on me, guys. I guess you know my record, but I got tired of that life. I got nothin' to hide these days. I'm a painter now." He motioned to the artwork. "It's not much of a living, but I enjoy it."

Dumas could tell it wasn't much of a living. "Then why did you stay in touch with Tamai? He couldn't have been a good influence on a reformed ex-con."

"Oh, well." Spensely smiled slyly. "I kinda have a thing for his woman."

"You were sleeping with her." Graham injected a healthy dose of disgust into the statement.

Spensely's smile grew even more crooked, perhaps in an attempt to rattle Graham. "I would've if I could've, but Mike's possessive. I made do with enjoying her socially."

"Did you ever tell her how you felt about her?" Dumas asked.

He shook his head. "I don't think the feeling was mutual."

Thank God for small favors, Dumas thought. The last thing Denise Newville needed was another crook in her life. Although, Spensely had just admitted to a motive for killing Tamai. "Tell me where you were on the night of January fifteenth."

Spensely looked up at the ceiling as though his activities calendar might be pasted there. "He was killed Sunday night, huh? I didn't go nowhere Sunday. I was here all day and all night and slept in late Monday with a hangover."

"Drinking on your own?" Graham asked.

"Only after the girl left." Spensely grinned his crooked grin again. Dumas wished he'd stop that.

It didn't seem to rattle Graham, though. "Name, address, and phone number."

"You're not her type."

"Not if she's been with you. But if she's your alibi, let's have it."

Spensely shrugged. "Didn't catch her name. If I see her again, I'll sure get that info for you. I'm telling the truth, guys. I didn't leave this trailer that night."

Sure, Dumas thought. *Everybody always tells the truth about not being the killer.* "Do you own any guns, Mr. Spensely?"

"Yep, I got some in the back. All licensed and legal. I'll show 'em to you if you want."

"Not going to insist on a warrant?"

"Ends up the same either way, right?"

"Pretty much," Dumas acknowledged. "Let's have a look, then."

Spensely rose from his chair and motioned them to follow. He led them through a tiny, untidy kitchen down a short hall where they passed a bathroom to the right and a bedroom opposite. At the end of the trailer a room probably intended as a second bedroom opened before them. This room, however, was crowded with battered cardboard boxes, some overflowing with books, others with painting supplies. A folded easel and several stacks of canvases of varying size huddled in the back corner beside an antique oak gun cabinet.

The cabinet was the only piece of furniture in the entire trailer that looked at all cared for. Its polished wood glowed warmly, and through the spotless glass that reflected Dumas' figure he could see a pair of rifles, a side-by-side shotgun, and four handguns.

Spensley fished a set of keys out of his pocket and unlocked the cabinet. "My granddad made this," he said. "Inspect away, but be careful." He opened the door and stood aside. Dumas removed each weapon and read off its serial number while Graham recorded it along with model information. The inventory included a Browning semi-automatic .22 rifle with a walnut stock, a black Bushmaster Predator, and a beautifully detailed Winchester 101 twelve-gauge. The handguns were all Smith & Wessons: a nine millimeter, a .38, a .40, and a .44 Magnum.

When they were done and the guns all returned to their resting places, Spensely relocked the cabinet and pocketed the keys. "Anything else?"

"Do you keep any other weapons?" Dumas asked.

"Nope. If you don't trust me, feel free to look around."

Dumas glanced at Graham, who replied with a tiny shake of his head. "That won't be necessary right now," Dumas said. He didn't relish the idea of digging through Spensely's garbage dump, especially when it was unlikely they'd find anything of interest. At least he couldn't say the guy hadn't cooperated.

*

When Peller stopped by Captain Whitney Morris' office mid-morning, he found her with elbows planted firmly on her desk, piercing her monitor with a murderous glare. Outside her office window a gray sky hung drearily, punctuated by a few tiny snowflakes eddying in an errant wind. "Is Tuesday being Monday?" he asked cheerfully.

Morris glanced up, expression unsoftened, then returned to the monitor. "Budget cuts. Apparently, somebody thinks we're a bunch of spendthrifts."

Peller pulled a chair close to her desk, sat, and grinned. As usual, her desktop was clear except for a pad of paper, a pen, and a photo of her husband with their three children. "You really shouldn't have bought us those Lamborghinis."

She pushed back from the desk. "You're in a good mood today."

"I got a letter from my brother David yesterday. He and his wife want to visit this summer. I haven't seen him in over four years."

"That's wonderful." Morris nearly cracked a smile. "If you stopped by to cheer me up, it's almost working."

"That, and I wanted to let you know I'm taking a semi-official jaunt to the South Howard Veterinary Clinic. I have an appointment to meet with the owner, Dr. Barbara Meadows."

"I vaguely remember that name. What's going on?"

"A young vet tech named Jayvon Fletcher disappeared from her clinic a couple of years ago. Andy worked the case, but Fletcher never turned up."

"Right. You've found a new angle?"

"Not really. My neighbor Jerry—you've heard me talk about him—knows Fletcher's mom."

Morris rolled her eyes. "Say no more."

"Andy's okay with me digging around. I just want to be able to say I looked when I tell Jerry I came up empty."

"Can't hurt to look." Morris tapped the top of her monitor. "Just get it done before I have to make these cuts. After that, I'll have to confiscate your Lamborghini."

Peller rose and gave her a quick salute. "You got it, boss."

The drive through the on-again, off-again flurries took less time than he would have expected. The snow might have scared some people off the roads. When he arrived, he parked and stood beside his car for a moment, taking in the clinic and its surroundings. Barricaded on all sides by trees, it felt like a quiet old house except for the parking lot half full of cars and the hysterical barking of a nervous Chihuahua.

Once inside, he found the house completely transformed to suit its medical purpose. The waiting room, furnished with pale blue cushioned benches, occupied much of the front. A huge bulletin board covered in photos of smiling clients with their pets hung on one wall. Two receptionists staffed telephones and computers at a long counter separating the waiting area from shelves filled with files, flea treatments, and prescription foods. A corridor to the left of the desk led into the recesses of the building. Peller could see the numbered doors of exam rooms. Behind the center of the counter another door led, probably, to the surgery and kennels.

Barbara Meadows, DVM, stethoscope draped over her lab coat, greeted Peller within a minute of his arrival. His immediate impression was that of a sturdy country girl somehow misplaced in this suburban setting. The brown ringlets that draped over her shoulders and her frank brown eyes reminded him of the young women with whom he had attended high school in upper New York half a lifetime ago.

The doctor extended a friendly hand. "Welcome, Lieutenant. I hope you didn't have any trouble finding us?"

"None at all." From the strength of her grip, Peller suspected Dr. Meadows spent her days bench-pressing mastiffs. "I appreciate you seeing me on such short notice."

"My pleasure. Come on back to my office and we can talk."

She led him down the corridor past the exam rooms and around a corner. The contents of her modest-sized office were almost monastic in simplicity: a desk, chairs for herself and two guests, and a gray metal filing cabinet. Her desktop held a computer and a neat stack of file folders. Behind the desk, more photos of animals congregated. She noticed Peller studying them and said, "Those guys were all mine. I've had six dogs and twelve cats. So far."

"That's quite a family."

"All rescues. All amazing creatures, each in their own way." She looked over her shoulder at them. "Maybe I'm weird, but I think the most important experience for a veterinarian is losing a pet."

"I suppose it helps you empathize with your patients' owners."

She returned her attention to him. "Exactly. And it makes you consider the mystery of life and death. But I could have done without losing somebody like Jayvon. His poor grandmother. Did you ever find out what happened to him?"

"Unfortunately not," Peller said. "I'm taking another look at his disappearance, but it's not likely anything will come of it."

"This is what you call a cold case, I suppose?"

"Stone cold. Still. What do you remember about Jayvon?"

"He was a wonderful tech and a wonderful person. He had a way with both the animals and the people, which is no small thing. You have no idea how some people act."

Peller raised his eyebrows. Cops knew all about that.

She got it. "Well, maybe you do. But Jayvon, he had boundless patience. Everyone liked him. I suspect a couple of the young ladies on my staff were smitten." She smiled at the desk, maybe remembering a longing gaze or snippet of giggle-filled conversation.

"Was he involved with any of them?"

"Not that I know of. He may have had a girlfriend, but not anyone on staff, I don't believe."

"What do you think happened that night?"

"Robbery."

She'd said it with such conviction that he wondered if they'd overlooked something obvious. "Why?"

"A window broken from the outside? Jayvon would have heard the noise and investigated. If they were armed, it wouldn't have ended well for him. Nobody ever told me, but I've always assumed the blood was his." She sighed. "It's a bad world out there."

"Was anything stolen?" The reports said no, but it never hurt to double-check. Maybe something had turned up missing later and hadn't been reported.

"No, but that just tells me the thief didn't do his homework."

"Because?"

Dr. Meadows crossed her arms on her desk and leaned forward as though to share a confidence. "What do you steal from a veterinary clinic, Lieutenant? Drugs. Controlled substances. Morphine and ketamine—it's an anesthetic—are popular targets. The regulations concerning storage of controlled substances require us to keep them locked up in metal cabinets secured to the premises. Nobody is going to steal those drugs from my clinic. Or any other clinic that knows its business."

Peller considered the implications. It happened all the time: an unprepared thief interrupted by someone he didn't expect to find in the building. He recalled an incident a few years back—in Ohio, he thought—

where a thief trying to steal opioids from a veterinary clinic tried to shimmy through the ventilation system and got stuck until police rescued him in the morning and hauled him off to jail. But what if the thief knew the drugs would be under lock and key? He'd need a way to get at them, and a simple way existed. He knew Meadows wouldn't like it, but he had to ask.

"Could Jayvon have been the thief's accomplice?"

"No," she said firmly. "Absolutely not."

"No offense," Peller said calmly. "But I have to consider all the alternatives." When she started to protest, he went on, "A smart thief wouldn't break in without a plan for getting to the drugs and without knowing who was here. Granted, there are a lot of dumb thieves out there, but if this guy was smart, Jayvon could be involved. It would explain a few odd things about the incident. Maybe the thief planned to kill Jayvon all along so he didn't have to share the profits, or maybe they had an argument while the robbery was in progress."

Meadows' jaw was set defiantly. Peller decided not to press the point. "What about other staff members. Did anyone have any other thoughts?"

She shook her head. "Not really. Everyone was very upset by the break-in and especially by Jayvon's disappearance. At the time, I think we expected the police to find him, but when that didn't happen...." She looked out the window. "We replaced the treads on the back steps. People didn't want to walk over the bloodstains. I lost a couple of good employees who couldn't face working here at all anymore."

The mixture of anger and sorrow on her face was plain. Before she could lose herself completely in past tragedy, Peller rose and ended the interview. "Thank you for your time, Doctor. I'll let you get back to your work."

She smiled, relieved. "You're quite welcome. Do let me know if you manage to find anything."

"Of course."

She rose and led him out of the office. Just before they reached the waiting room, she turned, her eyes intense. "Jayvon was a good man,

Lieutenant. I can't believe he went bad. If he did, how can any of us ever be trusted?"

Peller didn't have an answer, but he didn't need one for himself. He knew from experience that some people's goodness could be very fragile, while that of others could be a fortress.

*

Detective Lieutenant Bill Trengove stood a hair under six feet tall with a round, harsh face that reflected his personality. Montufar had never been sure whether irritation was his default position or an emotional form of crime scene tape. Either way, he looked plenty miffed as he read over the arson report she brought him Tuesday morning.

"Copycat." He slapped the papers down on his desk. "Has to be."

"That was my first thought," she admitted.

"Bradley's in jail."

"I know, but—"

"Damn it, Corina, it was him. Even his lawyer admitted it."

"In court?" she asked, stunned.

Disappointment mixed with disgust in his eyes. "Of course not. I ran into him a week later at the bar in Bare Bones. Bradley had been sentenced and locked up and there weren't going to be any appeals, so he talked about it. A little."

"What did he say?"

"Just that he knew Bradley had done the arsons. The rat had been scared, evasive, couldn't keep his story straight, stuff like that."

"What was the lawyer's name?"

"Matthew Cantor." Trengove leaned back and locked his hands behind his head. "You're not going to interview him, are you?"

"I might. Tell me about the fingerprints."

He gave her a tight-lipped smile. "They looked like a bunch of little swirled lines."

Okay, that was funny. But not to disappoint him, Montufar just shook her head and replied, deadpan, "I mean, why did you check the mailbox for them? I wouldn't have thought of that."

"One of the homeowners, Karla York, received a stupid note in her mailbox a week before the fire. Unfortunately, she didn't keep it. She and her husband thought it was a prank. They'd had occasional trouble with neighborhood kids. She said it was written in pencil on notebook paper and pretty vague, something like what a shame it would be if your couch blew up."

Montufar thought the note cast light on the matter. Sometimes arson had a specific motive—revenge, destruction of evidence from another crime—while some arsonists simply enjoyed watching buildings go up in smoke. She knew from the reports that no particular motive had surfaced. Bradley hadn't known any of his victims, nor had the victims been connected in any clear way, which might have suggested the latter. But the threat didn't fit with arson for thrills.

"No indications Bradley had an accomplice?"

Trengove shook his head. "Fingerprints notwithstanding, he never admitted to being involved himself, much less working with someone. It's possible he worked on contract, but no evidence turned up. Nothing in his apartment or in his email indicated such. The few contacts he had were just run-of-the-mill lowlifes."

Montufar tapped her fingers on Trengove's desk. She didn't like it, but with nothing to go on, she'd have to proceed for the moment as though the cases were unconnected.

Trengove watched her tapping fingers. "I know. That note doesn't make any sense to me, either. Then again, Bradley wasn't the sharpest crayon in the box. He might have thought he was being funny."

"I guess." Montufar rose. "Some joke, huh? Thanks, Bill."

Still not convinced, Montufar returned to her desk for her purse and coat and set out to learn what she could from the victims. The Dibble family, who had come home from dinner Saturday evening to find their house engulfed in flames and firefighters hard at work trying to contain the blaze, had been fortunate enough to receive offers of shelter from several friends and family members. They'd temporarily moved in with Mrs. Dibble's brother about a mile southeast of Dayton, not far from where their own home had once stood.

That situated them in a pricey area where huge houses, surrounded by attendant spas and pools, clustered in densely-wooded lots. Montufar felt distinctly out of place as she crept up the drive. Although she wasn't knowledgeable about real estate values, she figured this place had to be worth over a million dollars. All angles and strongly-pitched roofs, one end of the place was fashioned of dark stone, while a matching chimney scaled the opposite end of the house. Tall narrow windows stretched toward the leafy canopy. Montufar half-expected them to be stained glass, but they were ordinary panes. The rest of the house was covered in cedar siding.

Montufar parked and approached the front door, which was flanked by a pair of two-story square columns. A flagpole stood at stern attention to the left of the house, the Stars and Stripes fluttering at its head. Neatly-squared hedges in stepped lines barricaded the first floor windows. Pristine snow blanketed the land, although the drive was scraped clean, and it was clear that at least one animal with a lack of proper military discipline had scampered across the yard. She rang the bell and looked up at the decorative fanlight above. She could imagine a uniformed butler on the other side of the door, or perhaps a maid in a starched apron and cap, but when the door opened, a slim black teenage girl wearing blue jeans and a white sweater smiled at her. Her hair had been streaked in blues and greens that Montufar thought looked surprisingly elegant. "Hello?" the girl said brightly.

"Hi, I'm Detective Sergeant Montufar." She displayed her shield. "I'm looking for Vincent or Candace Dibble. I'm here to talk to them about the fire."

"Oh, sure, come on in. They're in the kitchen going over insurance paperwork."

The girl led Montufar through an overwhelmingly white foyer, where the walls bled into blond parquetry. Abstract paintings in delicate hues hung on the walls, lighted from above. They might have been hanging in a museum.

"What's your name?" the detective asked.

"Ruth," she said, making a bit of a face.

"You don't like it?"

"My family's big on Biblical names. They all sound old-fashioned to me."

"I think it's a pretty name."

"Yeah?"

"Yeah."

It was clear that someone had attempted to soften the austerity of the decor. A number of large potted plants occupied the room, but despite the gardener's intent, an invisible force appeared to have drawn them up into parade ranks. Montufar wasn't sure that they were real. Their leaves had a glossy look that suggested plastic. Ruth turned left and led Montufar through a room the size of her entire first apartment, scattered with mint-condition furniture. The lines were all clean, the colors all light. From there, they turned again toward the back of the house and passed through a dining room equally as large and immaculate. The centerpiece here was a masterpiece of the cabinetmaker's art—a golden oak table, laid out for twelve in china and silver. Double china cabinets, buffets, and sideboards edged the room, interspersed with what might have been more fake foliage. The table would have been beautiful, Montufar thought, if not for the conference-room effect. She wondered if the owners had a maid to keep everything spotless and in its place.

A right turn brought them into the kitchen.

The kitchen stretched easily across half the back of the house, filled with a seemingly endless expanse of golden oak cabinetry, coolly lit by skylights and a picture window that overlooked the undulating land and woods behind the house. A wood-topped island big enough for half a dozen chefs dominated the center. Montufar counted two stoves, four ovens, and an array of polished chrome appliances, some of which she couldn't even name. *Do they really need all this?* she wondered.

Beside the picture window, Vincent and Candace Dibble stared at a pair of laptop computers competing for space on an oval table otherwise covered in file folders and papers. This table wasn't as big as the dining room table, but Montufar noticed it could seat six without effort. Intent upon their insurance work, the Dibbles didn't look up. They didn't even seem to belong together, Montufar thought: he was a short, slightly overweight, balding white man; she a lanky black woman. Like his niece Ruth, he was dressed in jeans and a white sweater. Mrs. Dibble was elegant in a long amethyst skirt patterned with flowers and a lavender long-sleeved top. The stones in the cross that hung about her neck on a gold chain matched the color of her skirt.

"Uncle Vincent," Ruth said. Mr. Dibble looked up, expressionless. "There's a police lady here."

Vincent maintained his blank stare, but Candace stood and extended her hand. "Of course, welcome." Montufar shook hands and introduced herself. "Please, have a seat," Candace continued. "We were just going over insurance paperwork. It's a nightmare."

"Have a seat, Officer," Dibble said belatedly.

"Thank you," Montufar said, sitting opposite them. "I imagine it must be horrid."

"Vincent took today off from work so we could get this started," Candace explained. She looked at him, concern showing in every feature of her elegant face. "But I told him he should get back to the office tomorrow. He's the type that needs to stay busy, and I can handle most of this myself."

"Do you work outside the home?"

"Yes, I teach economics at Howard Community College, but they're letting me take the week off. Everyone's been very supportive."

"That's good to hear. I have some information for you and need to ask a few questions, if that's okay."

"Absolutely."

"This will be a shock, I'm afraid. The fire marshal has ruled the case an arson."

Vincent looked shaken but said nothing.

"Arson!" Candace gasped. "Who would do that to us?" She looked helplessly to her husband, who shook his head and scowled down at the papers in front of him.

"I was hoping you might have an idea," Montufar said.

"No, none at all," Candace replied. "It makes no sense. We're an honest, hardworking Christian family. We don't have any enemies. Do we, honey?"

"Uh-uh," Vincent muttered without looking up.

"It could be a random act," Montufar said. "Some arsonists get their kicks by setting fires. That's all the motive they need. It's also possible…" She wasn't comfortable making this suggestion, not knowing how the couple would take it, but they needed to consider it. "It could have been a racist act."

Candace stared openmouthed. It took her a moment to form a reply. "I'm sure it wasn't. We've never had any trouble like that. Mixed couples don't have the stigma they used to. Do they?"

"Not generally, but there are still plenty of racists out there, some of them violent."

"I know, but…" She looked to Vincent for support.

"Not likely," he agreed, still refusing to look at either his wife or the detective.

Montufar wondered what was up with him. Did he know something he was afraid to admit? "Okay. Let's set that aside for now. Did you happen to receive any unusual or threatening notes lately?"

"Nothing like that," Candace said.

"You're sure? It may not have been obviously connected."

"I sort through the mail every day. I'd know if anything like that had been delivered."

Vincent maintained his distance. Either he was the silent partner in the marriage, or he was intentionally keeping his mouth shut. Montufar decided to address him directly. "Where do you work, Mr. Dibble?"

That got him to look at her. "Filson Control Industries. I'm director of marketing."

"Never heard of them."

"You probably wouldn't have. We specialize in industrial controls. Computerized sensors and monitors, that kind of thing."

"Has business been good?"

"What's that got to do with anything?"

"I'm grasping at straws," Montufar admitted. "Looking for any reason at all that somebody might have wanted to harm you. Maybe you've had to let employees go recently, either for performance or for economic reasons?"

"No." He looked down again.

"You can't think of any reason why anybody would want to do this."

Almost imperceptibly, Vincent shook his head.

"How about you, Mrs. Dibble?"

"I can't think of a thing that's happened at work that could be related to this. Anyway, all I do is teach economics. It's not a subject people get worked up over." She smiled weakly.

Montufar could tell she wouldn't get anything from either of them. Candace could barely process the idea of arson, and Vincent wasn't ready to volunteer anything. "In that case, we're probably looking at a random act. I'll let you get on with your paperwork. Thank you for your time." She stood.

Vincent relaxed now that the grilling was over. Candace stood with her. "I'll see you out," she said, and led Montufar back through the dining room, living room, and foyer. At the front door, she put her hand on the knob but didn't open it right away. "Vincent's taken this really hard," she said in a confidential tone. "I hate to see him like this."

"Understandable," Montufar told her. "You've lost everything."

"Not everything. The family is safe, thank God, and we have our faith. Things can be replaced."

"You must be a strong family." She looked back the way they had come, still wondering what was going in inside the man's head. "You think he's more disturbed than he normally would be?"

"Normally? I don't know. This is hardly normal." Candace cast her eyes back toward the kitchen, too. "I think we might need some counseling."

Montufar thought the observation significant, but she said nothing. Instead, she touched Candace's arm to comfort her. "You'll be fine. Thank you again."

Outside, she wondered how fine they would be. She couldn't be sure, but she had the distinct feeling that Vincent Dibble knew a lot more than he was admitting.

5

"Bored to tears yet?" Dumas asked.

"Not at all," Collins said, puffing in his struggle to keep up with Dumas and Graham. Ahead of them stretched a long, sloping driveway leading to a nondescript ranch home perched atop a hill. "I'm finding this quite interesting."

Dumas doubted that, but he had to admire Collins' pluck.

A plow blade had neatly cut the snow along the edges of the well-cleared driveway, but no sign of the removed mass remained. Dumas wondered whether it had been hauled away or illegally dumped in the street for the county plows to handle.

"Some background," Dumas said, and Collins readied his tape recorder. "Kennedy Farmer lives up there. Denise Newville called him Tamai's ideas man. She said they had a falling out when Farmer discovered Tamai had cheated him."

"And that makes him a suspect," Collins said.

"A person of interest. It's possible he killed Tamai, but we don't know enough to call him a suspect. Nor to clear him, for that matter."

They reached the top of the hill and approached the door. "We're expected," Graham said, motioning toward the picture window to the right of the door. The left edge of the drawn curtain, pushed aside by an invisible hand, fell back into place.

Before Dumas could ring the bell, the door flew open. The petite, freckled redhead in the doorway set a trembling hand to her mouth. "Oh God," she squeaked. "Oh God."

Did we hit the jackpot already? Dumas wondered. He hadn't even said hello yet. What could have rattled her other than Graham' uniform?

"It's not Dad, is it?"

That made even less sense. "I'm sorry?"

"My dad. He's a state trooper. He—"

Dumas quickly put up a hand to stop her. "We're here to talk to Kennedy Farmer."

The redhead leaned against the door and took a deep breath. "Thank God. I thought something awful had happened."

Dumas and Graham waited while she collected herself. Her fright over, she didn't seem to know what to do next.

Graham peered into the house. "Is Mr. Farmer home, ma'am?"

She straightened and smoothed the waist of her full-length floral dress. Its clingy blues and greens shimmered. "Yes, I'm sorry. Please come in." She led them into the living room, a cheery place that competed with her for attention. She pointed to a pair of Louis XV-style chairs. "Have a seat. I'll get him."

Without sitting, Dumas surveyed the French art prints and Rococo mirrors. Beneath them, a blue and gold sofa and matching loveseat completed the seating arrangements. He couldn't think of anyplace he'd seen this kind of furniture except in museums and old movies. He wondered if it was all custom work. None of it seemed cheap, except for a pair of some-assembly-required end tables that glared against their opulent setting. Were they leftovers from less affluent days?

Neither Graham nor Collins sat, either. Dumas knew Graham preferred to be on his feet as much as possible. He figured Collins was merely following their lead. Collins did, though, turn off the tape recorder without prompting and stuffed it into his deep coat pocket.

Graham waved at their surroundings. "He's done pretty well for himself," he remarked quietly. "Much better than our friend Wolf."

"Obviously," Dumas agreed. "I wonder if his lady friend knows about his line of work."

"If she does, she's kept it from daddy."

"I feel like I'm in a museum," Collins said. "There's a Boucher, and a Watteau. Isn't that a Fragonard?" He pointed to a print of a lady on a swing. The detectives looked curiously at him. He shrugged. "My great-aunt's a curator. Went to school in Europe and everything. She tried to get me interested in art once."

"But you weren't?" Dumas asked.

"I was. The journalism bug just bit me harder."

They heard the woman talking in the recesses of the house, and a man answered. Presently, he put in an appearance and took in his trio of visitors with a quick shift of his eyes. "Is something wrong?" His bland voice answered his own question. Nothing possibly could be.

"We're investigating a homicide," Dumas said. "A friend of yours, Michio Tamai, was killed early Monday morning."

Farmer's blue eyes widened behind his wire-rimmed glasses, and he dropped into the loveseat. "My God. How?"

Dumas ignored the question. "When was the last time you saw Michio?"

"I don't know. It's been awhile. We had a falling-out."

"Over what?" Dumas took a seat on the sofa. With a glance at each other, Graham and Collins followed suit.

"Business."

Graham leaned forward. "Oh yeah? What kind of business?"

Farmer eyed Graham's uniform but revealed no emotion. "Our business."

"Mike didn't do honest business," Graham told him.

"That's why we had a falling-out."

"I hear," Dumas said, "that he cheated you out of some earnings."

Leaning back, Farmer regarded Dumas as though working out a complex problem. "Is this relevant?"

"It's a murder investigation, sir. Anything could be relevant. Michio was in the habit of cheating his partners. You were one of his victims. Do the math."

From his look of concentration, Farmer did just that and decided slightly more openness would be prudent. "Yes, he cheated me. But I didn't' kill him. I haven't gone near him since I discovered his true colors."

"How did you get mixed up with him in the first place?"

"A mutual acquaintance introduced us. I guess that was, what, seven years ago. I was down on my luck. I was told Mike needed some ideas for his business and I was just the man for the job. I was dumb enough to jump on board." Farmer stood and shoved his hands into the pockets of his well-tailored trousers. He walked to the picture window, pulled open the curtains, and stared at the snow. "A bit over a year ago, I guess. That's when I found out he hadn't paid me what I was owed. We got into an argument. He slugged me in the gut. I returned the favor and we had a bit of a scuffle. We both got banged up, and afterwards I never went back. Lesson learned."

Dumas wondered if Farmer could really have held his own against Tamai, but decided a bit of post-scuffle bravado was natural enough. His lady friend might be listening in the wings. "What kind of work do you do now?"

"Same as then. I design websites."

"Back *then* you were stealing cell phones," Graham said. "Among other things."

Farmer looked over his shoulder at Graham, his face bland, before returning his attention to the snow. "Fifth amendment."

"We're not after you," Dumas said in a reassuring tone. "We're looking for a killer."

"Then you're in the wrong house."

"Whose house should we visit?"

Farmer turned and met Dumas' eyes. His round face remained impassive, but his voice was tinged with irritation. "How should I know? Mike was a fun guy to be around most of the time. He liked to party and had a lot of friends. But if he treated them the way he treated me, he must have had a long list of enemies, too. I didn't kill him, but to be frank, I'm glad he's dead." He turned back to the window.

"Then I'm sure you can tell me what you were doing the night of January fifteenth."

"I was here watching a movie with Rachael."

"Your wife?" Graham asked.

"Don't try to be funny. You're no good at it."

Graham blinked in astonishment. It had been a natural enough question, hadn't it?

"You think we find murder funny?" Dumas snapped. "Answer the question."

Farmer didn't bother looking at them this time. "Yes, Rachael is my wife. You want our marriage certificate for evidence?"

Dumas rolled his eyes, but Graham decided it was worth pressing the inadvertent attack. "Maybe we should talk to Rachael. A good husband like you wouldn't keep secrets from his wife. She must know about your past."

Farmer turned a reddened face on Graham. "Leave her out of this. She had nothing to do with..." He pressed his lips tight and turned away again. "Just leave her alone."

"With what?" Graham asked.

"Anything. Everything. Nothing."

"Uh-huh."

When Farmer didn't protest further, Dumas asked, "Did Rachael ever meet Tamai?"

"No."

"Did she help you with any of the, ah, work you did for Tamai?"

Still looking out the window, Farmer shoved his hands in his pockets. "I don't know anything about Mike's death, okay? I haven't spoken to him in over a year. I can't tell you anything more."

Dumas and Graham looked at each other. Graham nodded sagely.

Dumas rose. "All right, Mr. Farmer. I'm leaving my card here on the table. If you do think of anything that might help, please give me a call."

Farmer didn't acknowledge him. Dumas led Graham and Collins out into the cold and down the long driveway to his car. "What do you think?" he asked Graham.

"He's one angry dude. He could have done it."

"But his bride will give him an alibi."

"Sure. She's in on it."

"She's in on something, all right, and he's determined to protect her." Dumas looked back at the house. Farmer was still at the window, staring out, neither at them nor the winter landscape. Something else, something invisible, seemed to hold his attention.

※

On the drive back to Northern District Headquarters, Peller mulled over what little he'd learned so far. Dr. Meadows was probably right: the incident had likely been a botched robbery attempt, but he wasn't so sure about Jayvon Fletcher's innocence. All accounts painted the young man in glowing colors, which in Peller's experience usually signaled dark secrets. That left him in a quandary, though: what if he had to tell Jayvon's grandmother that her grandson wasn't merely dead, but a dead criminal? He didn't relish that. Could Fletcher really be one of those rare pure souls? Or had Peller committed the sin of identifying with a potential suspect?

Great. Now I'm questioning my own objectivity.

He needed some unbiased input. He tapped a control on the steering wheel to activate his cell phone and called Dumas. "You busy?" he asked when the other answered.

"Just interviewing a horde of people who swear they didn't do it while trying to entertain a reporter. Why?"

"Let's meet somewhere for lunch. I need to borrow your brain."

"What, not Corina's?"

"I'm in the market for wild speculation."

Dumas laughed. "I'm your man, so long as you don't mind our conversation being recorded."

"How's that?"

"By Mr. Collins, my reporter friend. He keeps meticulous records."

Peller wasn't sure he liked the idea, but decided not to object. "Where are you?"

"Almost to HQ. I have to drop Kevin off. You?"

"Northbound on I-95, a mile south of 32." He eased his car into the right lane. "Let's meet in Clarksville. There are a few fast-food places there."

"Works for me."

They agreed on a burger joint and hung up. Peller arrived ten minutes later. With lunch hour in full swing, the drive-through line snaked almost completely around the building. Peller circled the lot twice before finding a parking place. Car safely stowed, he got out and leaned against its tail to wait. Sunlight streaming down from the blue warmed the air almost up to freezing. Peller enjoyed the balmy weather, although he might have been alone in that. He amused himself by watching Marylanders, some sufficiently insulated for an arctic expedition, scurrying between the warmth of their cars and the warmth of the restaurant.

Dumas soon pulled into the parking lot and was lucky enough to find a just-vacated parking space. He introduced Peller to Collins, and the trio entered the packed establishment.

"Does everybody live on burgers and fries?" Dumas asked rhetorically.

"That and chicken nuggets," Peller rejoined.

When they reached the head of the line, they placed their orders with a young woman whose hair was beginning to escape her cap and whose eyes simply begged for escape. Peller could sympathize. As they waited for their sandwiches, Peller picked up utensils and filled several ketchup cups. When the food arrived they made their way to a just-vacated corner table at the back of the restaurant. It hadn't been cleaned yet, but Dumas grabbed a couple of extra napkins and wiped off the spilled salt and drink rings.

"So what's the story?" Dumas asked as he unboxed his sandwich. He took a massive bite.

Collins turned on his tape recorder and set it on the table.

As he arranged his food, Peller related what he knew so far about the incident at the South Howard Veterinary Clinic and the disappearance of Jayvon Fletcher. Collins' tape recorder quietly whirred as it stored the information. The reporter, acutely interested, didn't interrupt Peller's narrative.

When the tale was told out, Dumas took a long pull on his drink, his face pensive. "I don't like it," he finally said.

Peller waited, but his colleague didn't continue. Even Collins grew impatient as his recorder registered dead air. "Don't like what?" Peller finally prompted.

"You've got elements of panic and calm, of stupidity and smarts." He picked up his remaining three French fries and held them up as though pressing them into service as props for one of his magic tricks. "Two outsiders, I think. And Fletcher makes three."

Peller studied the fries. They were ordinary sticks of potato. One had a singe mark on its side. They didn't disappear or sing or dance or anything else remotely entertaining. Dumas' three-man hypothesis, though, caught his interest. He started with the item he had independently considered: "Why Fletcher?"

"Stands to reason." Dumas placed the fries on the table between them one at a time as he spoke. "The brains. The muscle." Now it was the burned fry's turn. "The inside man."

"A broken window to mask Fletcher's involvement," Peller mused.

"Yep. But then an argument, and Fletcher gets clonked on the head. The other two have to clean up the mess and remove the body." He gathered up the fries and set them aside. "Could've been an argument over money.

Maybe Fletcher decided his cut wasn't sufficient and refused to produce the goods until he had better terms."

"I'm supposed to be helping his grandmother find him, not leveling accusations against him."

Dumas raised a surprised eyebrow but didn't otherwise chastise the boss.

Peller sighed. "I know, I know. And much as I hate to admit it, your scenario seems reasonable."

Dumas twirled the straw in his drink. The hideous squeak made Collins cringe, although his tape recorder didn't seem affected. Peller wondered how it would play back. "Without more evidence," Dumas told him, "it's just speculation. I'm afraid you'll have to ask his mother some pointed questions."

"Now you're being sadistic."

"The only other option is to tell her you don't have anything."

"Unfortunately." Peller swirled a French fry in ketchup. "At the time, she only talked about what a good boy he was. I doubt she'll have much new to say."

"It's been a few years. She's had plenty of time to reflect. Something might have occurred to her."

They fell silent. Collins frowned at his tape recorder. "Do you have any evidence to back this up? Most of it sounds like guesswork."

"It is," Dumas admitted. "But it's based on the available evidence. Police spend their lives hip-deep in stuff like this. Once you've seen it a couple hundred times, you recognize the patterns. Gut instinct often tells us where to look for additional evidence."

"And evidence," Peller added with a grin, "keeps gut instinct from running amok."

Collins' cell phone wailed like a muffled banshee. With a look of irritation, he turned off his recorder and fished the device from his pocket.

He tapped the screen a few times. "She's got to be kidding. I'll have to work all night!"

"Must be your editor," Dumas observed.

"She wants to run my first installment tomorrow!"

"Well," Peller said lightly, "you knew the job was dangerous when you took it, Fred," He wasn't unsympathetic, but he'd lived long enough to know that everyone had days like that. Besides, could a local reporter's worst day compare to a cop's? He doubted it.

Dumas and Collins turned quizzical looks on him.

"A line from an old Saturday morning cartoon," he said. "*Super Chicken.*"

"I don't think I want to know," Dumas told him.

"It was on with *George of the Jungle.*"

"George I know. That was Brendan Fraser."

Peller waved him off. "You're too young."

Dumas shrugged and asked Collins, "Do you have enough material to get started?"

"Yeah. But I sure could have used a bit more warning. I guess I'd better get back to the office. Can you drop me off at the station, Sergeant?"

Dumas nodded. "Whenever you're ready."

"In a few minutes. I'd better step outside and call in. No rush."

Collins exited, took up a position on the lee side of the building, and placed his call. Dumas had wolfed down his lunch, but Peller was lingering. He noticed Dumas eyeing him speculatively and looked up. "Something on your mind?"

Dumas shifted uncomfortably. "You haven't said anything about Corina and I."

Peller stopped mid-bite. "Should I?" Dumas had a habit of circling around subjects he found uncomfortable. It could be well-nigh impossible to know where he was going sometimes.

"You've noticed things, I'm sure."

"A few," Peller admitted, his mouth full. "But I try not to pry into other people's lives." He hoped this wasn't a request for personal advice. He had never pretended to be any good at that.

Dumas slowly gathered up the empty food packages and piled them on his tray. "You know, there's nobody in my family that's what you might call a great example. Not my parents, anyway. You and Sandra, though, I always thought you were wonderful together. Great marriage, good kid. I always wondered how you did it."

Peller felt out of his depth, but he could guess in general terms what Dumas was driving at in his inimitable, roundabout way. "Spit it out, Eric."

"You've noticed Corina's crucifix."

Peller nodded. She had started wearing it the previous year, although he didn't know why or what it meant to her. He hadn't ever seen her wear it before then. "It's kind of hard to miss," he said gently.

"She was raised Catholic. Obviously. Guatemala and all. But lately she's gotten more and more religious."

"That's not necessarily a bad thing," Peller told him. "I'm sure what's happened in her family is having some effect on her. Her brother was in that awful accident and now her father's dying. Maybe she needs the comfort and support. I don't know a lot about Catholicism, but she's not a member of the lunatic fringe, at any rate."

"I know, I know. It's just that I'm not religious. Not in any orthodox sense, anyway. I do believe there's more to life than this." He knocked lightly on the table. "But I'm not sure I'm cut out for her path. Actually, I don't even know much about her path."

"Then how do you know you're not cut out for it?"

Dumas fiddled with the wrappers on the tray. "I guess organized religion feels like someone dictating to you what's what. It's like stuffing some part of reality into a little bottle and saying that's all there is, and don't you dare question it."

"You don't have much experience with organized religion, do you?"

Dumas shook his head. "I feel like I'm walking a road that doesn't have any end. I want it to have an end, but right now I can't see anything but the lines fading into the distance. I think Corina must have found the end. That's great for her. But where does that leave *us*?"

Peller understood. He and Sandra had both been raised Methodist, but they had approached God differently. Her faith was deep and intensely personal. Vital. His had been more of a backdrop to life, not so passionate or active as hers. He looked out the window and saw Collins gesticulating wildly, probably deep in argument with his editor. "What does she think about it?"

"We haven't talked about it. Not yet, anyway."

"Well. I'm sure she respects you enough not to pressure you." From Dumas' expression, that didn't help, so he tried to dredge up some useful advice or example from the recesses of his memory. When it came, he wasn't sure it was memory at all; it was Sandra's voice, asking him, *Remember Jack and Martha?* He did, quite clearly.

"I had a friend on the force long ago," Peller told Dumas, "an Episcopalian engaged to a Jewish girl. At their rehearsal dinner a discussion broke out about their religious differences and how awkward it would make life. Mostly just ribbing, but it embarrassed the both of them. The woman's rabbi was at the dinner, too, and he came to their rescue with this."

Peller pushed a napkin to the middle of the table and got out his pen. He drew a small circle near the top of the napkin. "Look here. This is God."

"Doesn't look like Him." Dumas smiled weakly.

Peller drew two smaller circles below and to either side, forming a triangle. He tapped one. "This is you." Then he tapped the other. "This is Corina. This is her spiritual path." He drew a line connecting the Corina-circle to the God-circle. "And this is yours." He drew another line connecting the Eric-circle to the God-circle. "Here's the important bit, according to the rabbi. The closer you each get to God—" He drew two new circles up their respective lines, closer to the God-circle. "—the closer you get to each other." He finished by connecting the two people-circles.

Dumas leaned forward to study the image. "That sounds too simple."

Peller sat back and put away his pen. "As it should be. Don't give yourself ulcers, Eric. Just talk to her about it. The two of you will be fine."

Picking up the napkin, Dumas folded it carefully and put it in his pocket. "Thanks, boss."

"Don't mention it." Peller glanced outside. Collins shoved his phone into his pocket, looked heavenward, and spread his hands in pained inquiry to the divine. *He's advancing up his line at a rapid clip*, Peller joked to himself. "I think your shadow is ready to go."

Dumas looked over his shoulder. "Poor fellow," he said lightly. "I don't know how he survives."

✳

Good lawyers, in Montufar's experience, fell into three categories: pricey, very pricey, and you-must-be-insane. Matthew Cantor, she surmised, belonged in the second. While his name wasn't on the door—the partnership was branded Brookes, Kirchner, Spiegel, and Ludlow—the firm's sixth floor office in a building flanking the Columbia Town Center smelled luxuriantly of leather and polished wood. Besides, the radiantly blonde receptionist was clad in a Chanel suit. If she could afford that, the lawyers must command enviable salaries.

Cantor certainly did. A man of average build and tight-lipped smiles, he dressed to impress. His crisp charcoal double-breasted suit and knit silk tie made Montufar wonder what his dry-cleaner's bill looked like. He took her hand firmly. "Ms. Montufar. I was a bit surprised to hear you wanted to talk about Carl Bradley. But on reflection, it stands to reason he might have been suspected in other crimes. Come on back to my office and we can talk."

He led her down a corridor illuminated by clamshell fixtures on the walls. As they passed an empty conference room, Montufar swept her eyes over the huge table, leather chairs, and fifty inch flat-screen TV hanging on the wall. When they reached Cantor's office, he motioned her to a seat. While he settled himself behind the desk, she studied her surroundings. Cherry and walnut dominated. The full bookcases were neatly organized, the chairs well-padded. The window looked out on the mall. Had he been a partner, she bet he would have had a view of Symphony Woods instead.

He leaned back in his chair, so relaxed this couldn't possibly be business. Even the most guilty client would have been reassured. "So what can I do for you?"

"Why do you say it stands to reason Bradley might be suspected in other crimes?"

"You obviously didn't know him. He's an angry guy with a serious violent streak. Personally, I never liked working with him. When he was in the room, I made sure we weren't alone."

"That bad?"

"He never attacked me, but he did once break a lamp and throw a paperweight across the room. It left a mark on the paneling over there." He pointed to the wall to his left.

"Not one of your best customers," Montufar agreed. "What provoked him?"

Cantor's gaze wandered along the bookcases. "He knew I wasn't buying his story. Details changed every time he turned around. I got sick of it and pressed him to be straight with me. To put it politely, he told me to go to hell and punctuated the remark with a few projectiles."

Montufar wondered why anybody would agree to defend someone like that. She could never be a defense attorney. Quite aside from ungrateful clients, she didn't know how anybody could represent someone they knew to be guilty. "How did you end up with the case?"

Cantor smiled his thin smile. She found it unsettling, as though he had read her thoughts and judged them inferior. "Sheer dumb luck. I owed a colleague a favor, and she called it in. Apparently Bradley was some relative of some friend of hers. Her friend had pleaded with her to take his case. She didn't have time—or said she didn't, anyway—and volunteered me. The relative promised to cover Bradley's fees, so I figured why not?" He shook his head. "By the time I got to know him for real, it was too late to back out."

Montufar thought he could have if he'd wanted to, but maybe it had been a matter of principle. "He claimed he acted alone. Do you think he was lying about that?"

Cantor spread his hands helplessly. "All I know is what he said, or what he didn't say."

"Which was?"

"As you said."

"What about the note?"

"The note was hearsay. It didn't exist to be entered into evidence."

"I'm not the jury," Montufar told him.

Cantor leaned forward and folded his hands on the desk. His eyes looked beyond Montufar. "According to Lieutenant Trengove's testimony, it read like a sick joke. Sure, I can see Bradley writing it. But honestly? It makes zero sense."

"What about his motive?"

"Again, zero sense."

"So you think he torched three houses because he needed anger management classes."

The attorney chuckled but choked off his laughter, maybe recognizing it for poor taste. "If he had a better reason, he never let on. But this is old news, Sergeant. Why are you really here?"

"There's been another arson, very similar to the ones Bradley did. It could be coincidence or a copycat, but I'd like to rule out any direct connection."

"I think you can. He's in jail." There was that smile again. Montufar began to wish he wasn't in such a good mood.

"But if he had an accomplice," she said, "that person is still at large."

"If he had an accomplice, Sergeant, we'll never know it. He took the fall for them. But I don't believe there was one."

Montufar gave him a questioning look.

"Like I said," Cantor explained, "Bradley had anger issues. I can't see him quietly taking the fall for anyone. He'd have been up for murder as well as arson."

"All right," Montufar said, rising. "I guess I've taken up enough of your time. Thank you for seeing me."

But Cantor didn't respond. He was frowning at his desk as though he'd discovered something unpleasant lying there.

"What it is?" Montufar asked.

"I can't see him taking the fall for anyone," Cantor repeated, but then he looked up. "Unless he was scared to death of them?"

That set Montufar to thinking. An unknown boss orchestrating the arsons, keeping the arsonists in line through fear. It could explain the similarities between the previous and current fires.

But unless Bradley talked, how could she prove it?

6

Harold looked up from his coffee when Hannah came down the hall, her dark green flannel nightgown swishing at her ankles. As she passed from darkness into the morning light of the dining room, her golden hair brightened like the sun emerging from behind a cloud. Draped in the heavy fabric her body was almost shapeless, but he didn't care. She was the most beautiful woman in the world. *No*, he thought, *she is the only woman in the world.* No other existed for him anymore.

He never thought of himself as deep, but that thought had depth. If Hannah alone was real to him, if he alone was real to her, then they moved through a world of illusion, its people and places and things lacking substance. He remembered a word he had learned years before in school: *maya*. Hindu, he thought. Harold and Hannah, god and goddess in a universe of *maya*.

The image pleased him.

Hannah sat at the table and pulled to herself the steaming mug he had prepared for her. She smiled at him and took a sip. "Who killed who last night?" She said that most every morning. It began as a joke early in their relationship and solidified into tradition. She used to say it with a laugh, then a smile, then without expression, simply from habit.

He passed her the open newspaper. "You should read this."

She read in silence. At the end of the table, their laptop computer sat open but idle. Harold pulled it to himself and worked the keyboard while she read.

"That's very interesting," she said, poring through it a second time. "Almost like a gift."

"Yeah." Hannah tapped the paper. "This gives me an idea."

He took a drink of coffee. "I knew it would." He turned the laptop so she could see the screen.

She read what was there and gave him a coy look. "You always did work fast."

"I'll do the recon," Harold offered. "You'd attract too much attention."

"Not if I wear this thing." She fluttered the lapels of her robe.

"Gets my attention."

"Only 'cause you know what's underneath." Hannah pushed the laptop back to him. "What's for breakfast?"

"Whatever you want."

She yawned and stretched her legs under the table. "Don't knock yourself out. Cold cereal would be fine."

He rose and went to the kitchen. "I'll break out the chocolate stuff."

*

Dumas arrived at his desk Wednesday morning to find a sheet of printer paper taped to his computer monitor. On it was emblazoned a huge gold star. Inside the star, large boldface letters proclaimed, "Eric Dumas, World Famuos Detective!!"

"So guys," he called without hesitation. "Who doesn't know how to spell 'famous'?"

Laughter erupted from the surrounding cubicles, and Bill Trengove's voice arose from the din. "Might not be so much ignorance as uncoordinated fingers. Not that I'd know."

"But you might know who does know, is that it?" Dumas pulled the paper off the machine. The sign didn't seem quite Trengove's style, but he might very well have been an accomplice. There were plenty of likely perpetrators about, and Dumas had always suspected that Trengove's gruff exterior hid a lively prankster. "What did I do to deserve this, anyway?"

"You made the papers!" Detective Theresa Swan said from somewhere close by. "Haven't you seen?"

"I never read before ten o'clock. Except in the line of duty."

Too late, Dumas realized he'd left an opening a mile wide. Trengove rushed in: "Or even then." The laughter rose up before Dumas could deliver a suitable retort. Defeated, he parked himself in his chair.

Swan, rattling a copy of the *Columbia Flier*, walked toward him. "According to the reporter here, you're a genius." She set the paper on his desk. "On page eleven."

"Oh come on." Dumas took the paper and opened it. Jack Collins' byline sprang out at him.

Swan, who was leaning over his shoulder, read aloud. "'Detective Sergeant Eric Dumas is tracking a killer, wielding razor-sharp wits honed over a decade of experience. He'll need them. With astonishing speed, he's built up an extensive list of persons of interest and is digging out the clues that will transform one or more of them into suspects.'"

The squad room cheered. Dumas swore he heard Trengove laugh. *He must have been in on it*, he thought. "I did all that, huh?"

"'But wait, there's more!'" Swan said with a grin. "Have fun reading about yourself." She waggled her fingers in a good-natured farewell and returned to her work.

Dumas leaned back and finished the article, amazed both at the detail Collins had assembled in such short time and more than a little embarrassed by the reporter's descriptions of his subject's prowess. Honestly, he'd done no more than interview a few people and already he was Superman? Would Collins turn him into God by the time the case was solved?

"Looks like we have a superstar on the team," Montufar said behind him, her voice oozing ennui.

He put down the paper and swiveled around. "He's just making me look good to win your sister's favor."

"Ella?" She sat on the edge of his desk and brushed off her dark blue knee-length skirt. She frequently perched there when conferring with him, a fact that only now struck Dumas. She never sat on anyone else's desk, only his, yet their budding romance had nothing to do with it. She'd been perching there for years, as though she'd always been more comfortable around him than the others. Whatever the cause, he enjoyed it. She looked particularly beautiful in that pose.

"Yeah," he told her. "He knows her. Remember that press conference last year? The reporter who asked about Eduardo's accident?"

"Oh, good Lord."

"Yep."

"Maybe that explains why Ella's been acting so weird lately."

"Oh?"

Montufar looked around to make sure they weren't being observed. Leaning forward and lowering her voice, she said, "You know how it is when a girl likes a guy." She winked at him.

He had to cough to cover a laugh that almost escaped into the wilds of the office. "My experience in that area is a bit limited, but I think so."

"But now, Sergeant, you should train those eyes on your work."

"That may be difficult. Too many..." He looked at the newspaper, then gave her a once-over. "Distractions."

Montufar hopped to her feet. "Keep that up and you'll never catch that killer. What will the papers say, then?" Before he could respond, she smiled and waved him off. "I've got a case of my own to wrangle."

"What sort of case?" Dumas asked, slipping back into professional mode.

"Arson. The guy who should have done it is already in jail."

Dumas leaned back in his chair and locked his hands behind his head. "Copycat?"

"That's what Bill says. He's probably right." She frowned at nothing.

"But you're not buying it. Why not?"

"The original case wasn't high profile. I don't think it would have attracted a copycat."

Dumas thought she sounded uncharacteristically doubtful. Usually Montufar soaked up as much data as possible before settling on a theory. Holes in the picture would bother her. But this felt like something else operating. "Got a hunch? You want another set of eyes on it?" he offered.

"Not yet. I need to check a few things first."

"Okay. You know where to find me if you need me."

She started to say something but thought better of it and just winked. Then she was off at her usual quick pace to wherever she needed to be.

Dumas drew a deep breath and turned back to his desk, although honestly he didn't know how he was going to get focused today.

*

It looked just like the photograph.

Few places, Peller reflected, ever looked exactly like their photographs. Somehow this one did. Standing before one of the hindmost buildings in the Gateway Village apartments, awash in the rush of traffic behind him on State Route 32, he could imagine Jayvon Fletcher posing for the photo, just there in the shade of that stately oak tree, that thick old branch meandering just above his head. Behind Jayvon, pale siding covered the wall, the chocolate beams and railings of the balcony rose up, and sunlight glinted from windows. The photo, which he'd left in the file, had been taken on a green summer day, but the intervening time seemed to collapse to nothingness. He could see Fletcher standing before him, could hear him laugh as the shutter clicked.

"You lost or sellin' somethin'?"

The woman's voice, once full and rich but now ragged with encroaching age, challenged him from somewhere above. Peller looked up and saw an elderly black woman leaning out of an open window on the second floor. She looked neither alarmed nor upset, but it must have taken some gumption to open the window on a morning like this, with the temperature twenty-five degrees and the sun unable to make its presence felt. She was the guardian of the place, he thought, the Grandmother who watches over all.

"Neither, ma'am," he called back. "I'm looking for Wanda Fletcher. Do you know if she's home?"

"What you want with her?"

"I'm a Howard County police detective. I'm here to talk to her about her grandson."

The woman gripped the windowsill and closed her eyes. For a moment she seemed to be losing her balance. "You Mr. Souter's friend?"

Peller tensed, afraid she might fall. "Yes, ma'am. My name's Rick Peller. Jerry's my neighbor."

"Come on up. Two-oh-three." She disappeared inside and closed the window.

Peller went in and mounted the stairs. When he came to her door she already had it cracked, but the chain was still hooked. He showed identification without waiting for her to ask. "Can't be too careful these days," she said, rattling the chain and letting him in.

"Quite right," he told her. She was only a hair over five feet tall and looked frail, but Peller suspected she wasn't a bit of it.

"Detective *and* lieutenant. That higher than just lieutenant?"

"The same, just in a different division."

"Can't lord it over the uniformed cops, then?" She smiled impishly. "Come over here."

She led him into a spacious living room furnished in dark woods and bright reds and oranges. He could almost feel the sunlight on his face. The sofa and easy chairs could have swallowed a football player whole. The room came to a point in the back, with the dining area to the right opening onto the balcony. A short hall to the left led to the bedrooms, while the kitchen was opposite the dining area. Peller found the arrangement refreshing. So many apartments were built on the same floor plan, but not this place. Photos of Jayvon as a child and a young man dotted the walls, along with those of others who bore a reasonable family resemblance. A painting of Jesus with a group of children hung over the sofa.

"How is it you and Jerry go to the same church?" Peller asked. "You're not exactly neighbors."

Mrs. Fletcher pointed to one of the easy chairs, then sank into the sofa next to a mound of yarn skeins in bright spring colors. "I've been to St. Luke's all my life. My husband wanted to move down here to be closer to his job, but we kept going to church up there."

"Is that a Catholic church?"

"A.M.E." She fished a crochet hook out of the pile of yarn and held it close to examine it. "Did you find anything about my Jayvon?" She looked up, and although her voice had remained strong, her eyes looked scared. She started working the yarn into a panel of zig-zig color on its way to becoming, Peller guessed, an afghan.

"I'm afraid not, at least not yet. I've reviewed the files, talked with the detective who investigated the case, and visited the animal hospital where it happened. Nothing much stands out at this point. I'd like to know more about him, and you're the logical place to start."

She kept her eyes on her work, lips pinched tight. Peller understood the emotions churning beneath the surface: relief that he bore no bad news, frustration that he bore no news at all.

"I hate to ask," he added. "I think I understand what you're going through."

She looked up sharply. "Have you lost a grandchild?"

"No," Peller replied gently.

"Then don't you say that!"

He didn't take offense. He understood better than she could imagine. "My wife was killed in a hit-and-run four and a half years ago. The case was only resolved last spring. I may not know what it's like to lose a grandchild, but I do know how it feels to lose a part of yourself, and what it's like to spend years not knowing why it happened."

Mrs. Fletcher studied his face, then looked down and resumed crocheting. Her voice turned quiet. "What do you want to know?"

Peller relaxed, grateful for her cooperation. "We can't find a reason for what happened. I don't mean the break-in. That was common enough. If Jayvon had confronted the burglars and been hurt, that would have made sense."

"But not him disappearing," Mrs. Fletcher interjected.

"Exactly. A guy who was involved in the crime—an inside man—he might disappear. But Jayvon doesn't seem to fit that pattern. He was a good worker, wasn't ever in trouble, everyone loved him. Almost a superhero. Even you say so."

"I'm his grandmother. Of course I say so."

Peller couldn't help but smile, and noted that Mrs. Fletcher nearly did, too, in spite of herself. "You see my problem, though."

"You don't believe he could be that good?"

"I don't disbelieve it, but neither do I meet too many saints in my line of work. Does his grandmother believe it? Really believe it?"

Looping yarn around the hook and working it in, she gave the question serious thought. "We're all sinners, Lieutenant. But my Jayvon, he's something special. Oh, he got up to things when he was a kid, like any boy will. But so did you." She fixed Peller with a motherly look. After he smiled and nodded, she continued, "He never was a troublemaker. Fact is, the last few years before he vanished, he got real serious about his spiritual life."

"Was he active in your church?"

"For a time." A puzzled look crossed her face and she frowned at the wall behind Peller. "He'd been in the youth group through high school, but after he graduated he started hanging out with a bunch of people from some strange eastern religion. He spent more and more time with them and less and less with the church. Five months before he disappeared, he stopped going altogether. I told him I didn't like it, but he was an adult, so what could I do?"

"Did his behavior change?"

Mrs. Fletcher shook her head. "Not that I noticed." Suddenly laughing, she leaned back and said, "I said they were strange, not terrorists."

Peller almost wished they had been. That would have given him a hook on which to hang events, and an out should Jayvon turn out to be an accomplice. "Did you meet any of them?"

"Jayvon had them over a few times."

"What do you remember about them?"

"There were about ten all told. A funny group. Some must've been Arabs. A couple were black, a couple white. The Arabs had names I never heard of before."

"What did they talk about?"

Mrs. Fletcher shook her head and looked disgusted. "I couldn't make head or tail of it. They were reading from some book. Lots of big words and flowery talk. Like the King James Bible, only it wasn't."

Peller had grown up with the Revised Standard, only a step away from King James. "I take it you're not a fan of the king."

"I like plain talk. I can't see Jesus being all 'thee' and 'thou.'"

"Did they have a name for their group?"

"If you can call it that. I never could remember it. Hang on." She stood and went into the kitchen, where she rummaged through a drawer. "Here it is," she said. She returned, handed him a pamphlet, and sat, hands on her knees. "Jayvon gave me that to read. Never did."

Peller took it and studied it. The sky blue front featured the white silhouette of a dove in flight, with the words "Men and Women" above it and "Two Wings of a Bird" below. He turned it over and found, stamped on the bottom, the name of the group, along with a Columbia address and a telephone number. "The Baháʼís of Howard County, Maryland," he read. "Am I saying it right?"

Mrs. Fletcher shrugged and took up her work. Peller figured she neither knew nor cared. He opened the pamphlet and skimmed it. "Well," he told her, "there's nothing subversive here, anyway. At least, not so long as you live in twenty-first century America. Can I keep this?"

"Be my guest. Doubt I'll read it."

"Did you hear anything from Jayvon or his new friends that bothered you?"

"Not about stuff like that." She nodded at the pamphlet. "Seemed they were good enough people, and Jayvon didn't really change. If anything, maybe he tried harder to be a good person. But like I said, we're all sinners."

Peller waited, but she didn't add anything further. "Meaning?"

She fixed him with a stern look. He could imagine her giving Jayvon that look when he got up to that boyish mischief she'd alluded to earlier. "Are you a Christian?"

"Methodist," he replied with a nod.

"Then you know we can't do it on our own. All sinners need Jesus. No good can come of leaving him."

Peller skimmed through the pamphlet again. True, it didn't mention Jesus, and the names it did mention were unfamiliar to him. But neither could he find anything that felt wrong. Possibly these Baháʼís were hiding something, but on the surface they seemed innocuous enough. He folded the pamphlet and tucked it into his pocket. "Anything else you think I should know?"

"Just that I don't for a minute believe Jayvon was any kind of inside man. If you'd known him, you wouldn't think so, either."

Peller wanted to tell her that he didn't think that at all. More than that, he wanted to dismiss the idea altogether. He was tempted to do so. After all, he had no hard evidence for it. Surely some other explanation would turn up. Instead, he sidestepped the question. "I'll talk to these folks and see what they're about." He tapped the pocket that held the pamphlet. "I'll let you know what I find. And if you do think of anything else, please let me know. He rose and handed her a business card.

She took it and set it aside without looking at it. "I will," she promised.

The first item on Montufar's checklist was a visit to Filson Control Industries, where Vincent Dibble was director of marketing. Not knowing what to expect, she called FCI's human resources department, and once police had been mentioned in conjunction with Dibble's name, her request skyrocketed to the top. Company president Clair Watkins insisted on handling the matter personally.

At nine thirty, Montufar parked alongside the company's headquarters in Elkridge. The rush of traffic on U.S. Route 1 echoed from the white brick building while national and state flags snapped in the cold wind above the entrance. She pushed through the glass doors, noting the vibrant green logo emblazoned upon it. *FCI loves the environment*, she thought.

A young man smiled up at her from a walnut reception desk. "Good morning."

She returned the smile. "I'm here to see Ms. Watkins."

"Oh yes, you're with the police department."

"That's right."

He inspected Montufar while trying hard to avoid the impression of checking her out, which she could tell was his real intent. "I expected a uniform."

"It's in the laundry."

The receptionist didn't seem sure whether she was joking. He half smiled and phoned Watkins to announce Montufar's arrival, then rose. "I'll show you to the conference room. This way, please."

She followed and settled herself in a mostly comfortable chair at the end of a modest table. At the far end of the room, an entire wall painted to serve as a whiteboard bore cryptic lists and block diagrams. Montufar tried to figure them out but had no clue what they meant. She assumed they had something to do with the company's products.

In less than two minutes Watkins arrived. She struck Montufar as a no-nonsense woman. With her cropped dark hair, her light gray business suit, and age-obscuring makeup, she could have been a model for "modern businesswoman, age forty to sixty". She swooped into the room, sat straight-backed in the chair facing Montufar, and spoke without emotion. "What can I do for you, Sergeant?"

"I'm investigating the fire that destroyed Vincent Dibble's home."

"Obviously." Watkins' lean face was set in an expression that could have been either determination or disgust. "I don't see what that has to do with our company."

"We're treating it as arson. I—"

"Which has even less to do with us."

"The motive for the crime could lie with something that happened on the job. For example—"

"It doesn't." Watkins rose. "I have a full schedule, Sergeant, so—"

"Why not?" *Turnabout's fair play*, Montufar thought, not about to let Watkins brush her off.

The executive glared but reluctantly reseated herself.

Not used to being cut off yourself, are you? "Did Mr. Dibble fire anyone recently?"

"No."

"Did he have cause to reprimand anyone?"

"No."

"Could anyone have thought he had in any way treated them unfairly?"

Watkins continued to glare. "I'm not a mind reader, but I'm not aware of any such incidents. Frankly, I'd be shocked if any such thing happened. Our company has high ethical standards. Our employees are a close-knit family."

Montufar felt like laughing. This woman definitely didn't radiate warm family vibes. "Even so, things can happen. Was Mr. Dibble a good employee?"

"If he wasn't, he wouldn't be working here."

"How long has he been with you?"

"Just over a year."

"He didn't work his way up through the ranks, then."

"Not here."

It was clear she would get very little from this woman. Montufar purposely phrased her next question as an almost-accusation. "Wouldn't you ordinarily promote someone from within the company?"

"Are you investigating a crime or working on an M.B.A.?" Watkins remarked churlishly.

"Investigating an arson, Ms. Watkins. Arson. People could have died. I'd appreciate your cooperation."

Watkins held Montufar's gaze while working out her answer. "Our executive searches are open to both internal and external applicants. Mr. Dibble was chosen because he was the strongest candidate."

"Who was passed over?"

"That's an appalling suggestion. Our employees—"

"Are as human as anyone else. I'm suggesting nothing. I'm asking questions."

"I don't believe I have to answer that."

Montufar could have pressed the matter, but she decided on a different tack, one that might throw Watkins even more off balance than being interrupted. "Do you know Mr. Dibble's wife and children?"

"I've met them."

"What's your impression of them?"

"I don't really know."

Montufar gave her adversary a cool smile. "I thought you were a close-knit family, Ms. Watkins. You must have some opinion of them."

If Watkins was miffed at having her line thrown back at her, she didn't show it. "They seem nice enough."

"Were you surprised when you first met Candace Dibble?"

That earned Montufar a pair of raised eyebrows. "Really, Sergeant," was all Watkins managed. When Montufar said nothing, she added, "I don't care one way or the other about skin color. And anyway, it's none of my business."

"An admirable point of view. What about the rest of your corporate family? Do they share that sentiment?"

Watkins stood. "I've had about enough of this."

"That's not an answer. A family's home was destroyed. Not just any family, a family you claim is like your own. If they'd been there, they could have been killed. Don't you care about that?"

The executive's back stiffened. "Of course I do. I offered Vincent assistance. He said they would be okay. But frankly, I find the insinuation that one of his colleagues did this to him disgusting. If you have any further questions, Sergeant, you can speak to our attorney. I have to go now. I believe you know the way out." Without waiting for an acknowledgement, Watkins exited, head held high.

Montufar pondered the conversation before leaving the room. Just possibly, Claire Watkins actually did care about her employees and imagined she was defending them. But probably the potential for negative publicity concerned her more. Was she genuinely convinced that the arson had nothing to do with anyone at Filson? Not necessarily, but it wouldn't be easy to draw out any suspicions she harbored.

Still, Watkins had unwittingly provided one curious fact: Dibble had joined FCI about the same time as last year's arsons. It seems an odd coincidence, but before she could pursue it, her phone dinged, alerting her to a text message from Ella.

Please let it be good news, she pleaded.

But no. The doctor had just been by on his rounds. Felipe Montufar had double pneumonia.

✳

When Peller returned to Northern District Headquarters, he found Dumas poring through a little black book, making notes from it. His colleague had shut out everything else; he didn't as much as grimace when Peller joked in passing, "Nice article."

Oh well. Peller settled at his own desk to pursue his own leads. Not knowing what to expect, he put in a call to the number on the back of the pamphlet Wanda Fletcher had given him. He connected with a recording.

"You've reached the Bahá'ís of Howard County," a cheerful soprano greeted. "We thank you for calling and invite you to leave a message. Someone will return your call as soon as possible. Thank you!"

Friendly, or sales tactic? After the beep, he said, "This is Detective Lieutenant Rick Peller with the Howard County Police Department. I'm investigating the disappearance of a young man named Jayvon Fletcher. Jayvon had contact with members of your group. I'd like to speak with someone who knew him. I'd appreciate it if you'd return my call as soon as possible." He left his office and cell phone numbers and signed off with a thank you. Turning to his computer, he searched for the group's web site and found them along with several other—congregations, he supposed—in the region. He also found a site run by the Bahá'ís of the United States, and an international site. It wasn't a storefront church, anyway. In fact, he found they had a global membership in the millions.

He rather wished Montufar were here; she'd probably already know all about this religion and could save him some work. As it was, he settled in to read what they said about themselves.

*

Dumas' attention remained riveted on the address book Denise Newville had given him. The thing was massive, with more names than Dumas thought one person had any business knowing. Some had been scratched out, and contact information for others had been changed two or three times. Male names dominated female by a healthy margin, although

Tamai apparently knew a respectable number of women. He tried not to jump to any conclusions about that.

Fighting to stay focused, Dumas considered that tedium could be typified by working through such a list, checking for criminal records, separating names into in-state and out-of-state lists, trying phone numbers to see which still worked, which were still connected to the same names.

Jack Collins stopped by around noon to see if any action was in the offing but didn't stay long. Dumas couldn't tell him much. Various forensic reports had come in but revealed little. Tamai had been killed with his own gun, a nine millimeter he'd purchased about two years ago. It had been found, wiped clean of prints, under the sofa where he was killed. The medical reports revealed nothing new: two shots, one to the head, one to the heart, the combination fatal. No other marks had been found on the body. Tamai had been so stinking drunk pior to death that he'd likely passed out before being shot. Other than a predictable level of liver damage, his organs suggested general good health.

Collins digested those details, but once he discovered how Dumas planned to spend the rest of his day, he decided not to stick around. He asked a few questions about the process and extracted a promise from Dumas to call him if anything happened, then left. Dumas wasn't sorry to see him go. This sort of work taxed him enough without a reporter breathing over his shoulder. Maybe Corina would drop by and offer help. He didn't think he'd mind her breathing over his shoulder.

Don't start down that path, he scolded himself. *If you do, you'll never get through this.*

As it was, he barely finished by the end of his shift, and his end product looked a lot like the input: a list of names, addresses, and phone numbers, albeit shorter. Only then did Montufar return to the office and perch on his desk, haggard.

"Did you get anywhere?" he asked.

She shook her head. "You?"

He waggled his hand in a so-so motion.

Before she could reply, Bill Trengove poked his head around the corner. "Victoria's?"

Dumas had no idea what he was talking about.

"I'm gathering the troops for food and drinks," Trengove explained. "Like I've been doing every few months for, I dunno, maybe the past nine years?"

"Sorry," Dumas replied. "Long day. I think I'll just go home tonight, but thanks."

Trengove turned his steely eyes on Montufar.

"I think I'll pass, too," she said.

"Fine. I'll check in next month." He nodded at Dumas. "And explain it to you again."

Once he was gone, Montufar stretched and asked quietly, "What's for dinner at your place?"

"Frozen pizza. Pepperoni."

"I'll share it with you if you promise to heat it up first." She made a brave attempt at a smile.

He returned it. "If I must."

7

From the first time she had seen it, Montufar had liked Dumas' apartment. Its minimalist furnishings, while comfortable, were as unpretentious as their owner. The smattering of wood-framed prints featuring forests and rocky streams transported the visitor to a world far from the chaos of civilization. She could almost hear the quiet splash of water and a whisper of breeze in the leaves, could almost smell damp earth and greenery. Without invitation, she leaned back on the sofa, closed her eyes, and lost herself in the imagined sensations.

Dumas went straight to the kitchen to turn on the oven, then returned and sat next to her. He must have sensed her tension, for he took her hands in his and began to gently massage her fingers. Nothing was wrong with her hands, but the sensation was soothing.

"You want to talk about it or forget about it?" he asked. He sounded as though the day's work had sunk its teeth into him and refused to let go. She recognized her own exhaustion in his.

Without opening her eyes, she asked, "Do you want to talk about it?"

"Not really."

"Me, either."

He put an arm about her shoulders, drew her close, and kissed her hair. "In that case—"

A sudden pounding at the door made Montufar jump. Beside her, Dumas sprang to his feet and snapped, "I'll throttle him."

Montufar was about to ask who when she realized the answer. It could only be Dumas' neighbor, Ozzie White. Ozzie meant well, but Montufar thought he should have realized by now that his goal of getting Dumas safely married off could more effectively be realized by allowing them some privacy. Still, she found Ozzie's meddling strangely touching, even a bit endearing. Sure, it drove Dumas to distraction, yet Ozzie's innocence had a delightful quaintness. Questionable methods and atrocious timing notwithstanding, his intentions were good.

Dumas opened the door. "Hi, Ozzie," he said wearily. "What's up?"

"Hey, Eric! I heard you and Corina come in but didn't get to the door in time."

"Age slowing you down?"

From her perch on the sofa, Montufar couldn't see, but there was a childish enthusiasm in Ozzie's voice. "I was preoccupied. I want you to meet Cameron Terrell. Cameron, this is Eric, my neighbor and friend and the best detective in the state."

"Hi," a timid female voice peeped. "Pleased to meet you."

"Hello," Dumas said. After an awkward silence, he glanced back at Montufar. She could see the resignation in his eyes. *Resistance is useless*, he seemed to be saying. "We were about to have dinner, but you may as well come in for a minute."

Montufar rose as the trio entered the living room. Ozzie frequently reminded her of the character of Louis Tully from *Ghostbusters*—short and geeky, with a mop of light hair always on the verge of disarray—but what he lacked in stature he made up for in sheer enthusiasm. By contrast, the woman holding his hand might have stepped off of the page of *Elle*. A radiant blue ankle-length dress emphasized her full inch of height over Ozzie's. A gold cross with a small red gem in its center nestled in the deep v-neck of the dress, set off by an elegant pair of gold-rimmed glasses that glowed against luxurious brunette hair. Montufar wondered how Ozzie had scored such a catch and whether her personality would prove equally dazzling.

"And this is Corina," Ozzie told Cameron. "She's another of our great detectives."

Cameron waved timidly. "Hi, Corina."

"It's a pleasure," Montufar said with an encouraging smile. "Please, have a seat."

Cameron looked around the apartment as wide-eyed as though she'd entered a monastery. The reaction surprised Montufar, but then maybe the woman had never seen a place so understated.

Ozzie gently set his hand on Cameron's shoulder and motioned to the sofa. They sat while Montufar resettled herself on one of the chairs and Dumas took another. "How long have you two known each other?" Dumas asked, then looked down at his shoes as though wishing he could retract the trite question.

"We just met today," Ozzie said. "Cameron got lost. I found her out in the hall."

Dumas looked up and managed a smile. "That's a boring place to get lost," he quipped.

Cameron shrugged in embarrassment and said as though it would explain all, "I'm new to the area."

"What were you looking for?"

"A friend from college. She said to look her up if I was in Maryland, and I was, so I tried."

"One number higher than your apartment," Ozzie supplied.

"There is no number higher than mine," Dumas told him. "Not on this floor."

"I know. Wrong building."

"Maybe the wrong complex," Cameron said. She scrunched her shoulders up and smiled like a little girl trying to win approval. "I get turned around so easily. Thank goodness Ozzie was here to save me." She leaned over and kissed him on the cheek.

The couple beamed at each other. Montufar exchanged a skeptical glance with Dumas. Cameron's story sounded weird, all right, but some people did have lousy senses of direction. Corina had once had a friend who would get lost in a shopping mall. On the other hand, Ozzie would rush wide-eyed into a scam if a beautiful woman were involved. Montufar hadn't met his previous girlfriends, but Dumas had mentioned in passing how readily Ozzie plunged into obsession. And how hard he hit the ground when, inevitably, he tumbled back out of it.

"I've never met anyone so kind," Cameron said, and Ozzie beamed at her.

"Sounds like you hit it off right away." Dumas' voice held no trace of enthusiasm.

"Like magic," Ozzie said, then told Cameron, "Say, you should have Eric show you some of his magic tricks. He's real good!"

The change of subject nearly gave Montufar whiplash. Cameron gaped at Dumas in delight, her eyes begging him to pull a rabbit out of somebody's ear. "Um..." Dumas smiled weakly, but no rabbits appeared from anywhere.

Coming to his rescue, Montufar asked, "Do you live nearby, Cameron?"

"Sort of. I'm new to the area. Oh, I said that already! So I'm staying at the Courtyard off 175 until I find a place of my own." She looked significantly at Ozzie. Ozzie flashed a smile and opened his mouth to speak, but snapped it shut again. Probably he thought it imprudent to extend the invitation with Dumas and Montufar watching. Instead, he gave her a subtle wink.

Montufar thought of throwing a glass of ice water over him, or slapping him in the face but doubted that either cure for hysteria would snap Ozzie out of his trance. Naively, he'd already taken the plunge; in his imagination he was probably planning their honeymoon at some idyllic retreat. Whatever Cameron wanted from him, she'd get it, and there wasn't a thing anyone could do to stop her. Not without seriously offending Ozzie, at least.

A timer chimed in the kitchen, and Dumas rose. "Sorry, have to tend to dinner."

"So do we." Ozzie stood and helped Cameron to her feet. "We're going to that new steakhouse that opened down the road. I don't suppose..." He let the invitation hang there.

"That's very kind of you," Montufar told him, "but we already have plans."

He grinned and backed toward the door. "No problem. Maybe another time?"

Absolutely, Montufar thought. *Nonstop double-dating, so we can keep an eye on her.* "Why not?"

Ozzie and his lady friend said hasty goodbyes and wasted no time departing. Just before Montufar closed the door behind them, Ozzie called out, "Later, Eric!" and Dumas replied, "Later, Ozzie."

Montufar joined Dumas in the kitchen, where she found him unwrapping the pizza. She put her arms around his waist and pulled him against her. "Where does he find women like that? And how does he get them to pay attention to him?"

Dumas shrugged. "Mystery to me. Sheer animal magnetism, I guess."

"You think they'll last more than three days?"

"Not likely. She's either a crook or an airhead."

"Hmm."

"Oven," he said, and she backed up while he opened the oven door. A wave of heat engulfed them. He slid the pizza onto the rack where it began to sizzle as he closed the door. He turned around, face stony. "I'm not kidding. He's going to get burned again. As much as I grumble about Ozzie, he's a nice guy. I hate watching this happen over and over. He never learns."

"I didn't realize you cared that much about him," she teased.

"I can't help it. He's like an annoying little brother." He put his arm around her waist and guided her back to the sofa. Settled in again, she snuggled up to him, closed her eyes, and tried to clear her mind. She'd never found that easy. All manner of thoughts intruded without invitation: details of cases she was working, what she needed from the store, family woes, joys and sorrows long past. To all those were now added her feelings for Dumas and what might become of this relationship blossoming in the snow like an alpine flower. Here, in the dead of a strangely cold winter, she knew what she wanted—she wanted to be home, and she wanted a future with Eric Dumas. If only he wanted the same thing, the cold would be powerless to touch her.

She longed to tell him so but couldn't. Unanswered questions barred her way. What was Eric looking for? Home, family, faith? He'd had so little of any of that. His family, twisted and broken; his home an isle adrift; his faith, what? *Lost*, she thought in better moments; *discarded* might be a better word, although who had thrown it out was a question she couldn't resolve. His father? His mother? His Uncle Ethan? Maybe Eric himself didn't know. In her mind she often envisioned him sealed off in a protective bubble of his own making. Incapable of touching the outside world or being touched by it, sorrow could no longer reach him.

If she spoke, what would happen to that defense?

"Penny for your thoughts?"

"They aren't worth that much," she murmured.

She felt both his arms go around her and his voice, close to her ear, asked softly, "Is it your father?"

No, she thought, but answered, "Partly."

"What's the word?"

"Pneumonia."

"Not good."

"Not at his age, no."

"He's in good hands. They'll pull him through."

Montufar straightened. "I hope so. All we can do is pray and wait."

Dumas chucked her chin. "And stay positive. Speaking of that and of magic tricks, I've got a new one to show you. Come here, we have to sit at the table for this." Taking her hands, he pulled her to her feet and led her to the dinette. "You sit there. I have to be on the other side." Sitting across from her, he fished for something in his pocket, then dumped a pair of small paper wads on the table. "Now watch close." He began to count out loud, matching hand motions to numbers:

"One." He covered one paper with his right hand, palm down.

"Two." He covered the other with his left.

"Three." He turned his right hand palm up, leaving the paper on the table.

"Four." He turned up his other hand.

"Five." He scooped up the right paper into his right fist.

"Six." He tucked the paper into his left fist.

"Seven." He scooped up the left paper into his left fist.

"Eight." He extended both fists, fingers up.

"Nine.' He turned both fists over, fingers down.

"Ten." He opened both hands, and both papers fell out on the right!

Wide eyed, Montufar said, "How did you do that?"

He grinned. "Magic, of course!"

"Do it again!"

He repeated the trick for her three times before declaring, "That's enough for now. Any more and you'd figure it out."

"I promise I won't!" she laughed. "That would spoil it."

The oven timer chimed. Dumas rose. "For my next trick, I'll make a pizza appear out of thin air."

It was the best frozen pizza she'd ever had.

*

Hours later, after dinner and a movie and popcorn and a lot of talk about a lot of things not remotely approaching work, Montufar went home. Alone, Dumas sat at the table wondering why he'd failed yet again. He reached into his pocket and took out not the paper wads but a small velvet-covered box which he carefully placed before him. He didn't open it immediately, just glared at it as though it had betrayed him.

His plan had worked so well in rehearsal. Once through to introduce the trick; once again when she pounced curiously on it; the third time the gift box appeared on cue. With a flourish he presented it to his absent intended, who opened it to find within an elegant gold ring adorned with a single, brilliant diamond. He asked her to be his wife, and—

Except that he hadn't. Nothing appeared from his hand but paper wads.

Dumas had set up his proposal four times now, each time using a different magic effect, and each time had been unable to carry it through. He had no idea why.

Also on the table now, retrieved from the drawer in which he had stashed it, lay the napkin upon which Peller had diagrammed his explanation of how a relationship might accommodate differing religions. Somehow, he felt, this was the key to his predicament. Montufar was Catholic, with two thousand years' religious wealth behind her. He was some nondescript, generic sojourner looking for answers. Part of him imagined that maybe she could help him find them. Another part insisted that was stupid. A third part wished the first two would stop arguing.

Rick had told him to talk to Corina about it. *But how can I? It's not even that we're different religions. It's that she's something and I'm nothing. She's brilliant and I'm just me. She has a family and I have nothing. She has faith, and all I have are questions. What right do I have to impose my chaos on her order?*

He took in the details of Peller's drawing without thought. Simple, elegant, logical, it seemed to challenge his experience of the world as a messy, confusing, often hostile place. *Why did you make it this way?* he silently asked the God-circle at the top of the triangle.

The circle didn't answer.

Naturally. He hadn't expected it to. But as he considered his own question, the answer became plain. *You want us to work it out ourselves, don't you? Thanks a lot.*

Dumas didn't see how that put him any closer to resolution, though. He still had a ring, a woman he loved, and for about a hundred rotten reasons insufficient nerve to take the next step. On the plus side, there would be plenty more opportunities. He only needed one.

And enough determination to make it work.

Which possibly meant he needed a miracle.

*

Unaware of Dumas' dilemma, Peller was afflicted by its mirror image. The evening had begun simply enough, when he accepted Trengove's invitation to the bi-tri-whatever-monthly outing at Victoria's in Columbia. Although Peller, raised Methodist, didn't drink, he usually joined these parties for food and small talk. Spouses and significant others always joined in. Sandra, too, once upon a time. Even now, Peller still felt her presence at his side. When he'd told Andy Newton that he wasn't alone, he'd meant it quite literally.

Newton obviously hadn't understood. While Peller was sipping his root beer and listening to Captain Whitney Morris' husband Dr. Daniel Morris wax rhapsodic about the Baltimore Ravens' last Superbowl win—they hadn't made it this year—Newton slipped into the chair at Peller's left. Charity Newton, Andy's wife, stood behind him, her elegant hands resting gently on her husband's shoulders. Peller looked up at her. Charity was a petite woman with a toothy grin. In spite of the cold outside, she wore a little black dress with open-toe heels. *Brave woman*, Peller thought. *Of course. She married Andy.*

Peller nodded to the Newtons before realizing that someone else had settled into the chair to his right. Turning, he found a woman about his own age with a narrow face, pale skin, and a mass of dark hair expertly wound on top of her head. The deep red dress she wore seemed too elegant for the occasion. She smiled warmly but didn't introduce herself.

Charity moved a hand from her husband's shoulder to Peller's, gently, as though afraid of startling him. "Rick, this is a good friend of mine, Joan Churchill."

The woman offered her hand. "I'm pleased to meet you, Rick."

Peller accepted the handshake and found her touch as light as a breeze.

"She was free tonight, so I invited her along."

"Why not?" Peller said. "Nice to meet you, ma'am."

Newton laughed. "You're not on the job, Rick! We're all on a first-name basis here."

Peller forced an apologetic smile. "Old habits die hard. Sorry. Joan."

Churchill shrugged it off. "I hear you're one of the top people in your department."

"I don't know about that. We have a lot of talent on the team. I'm just one of the players. Whitney's the real gem, the brains behind the whole operation." Morris twisted her mouth and shook her head. Peller grinned at her. "I don't know how she puts up with us."

"I have to," Morris told him, voice dead serious although he knew she wasn't. "Somebody has to pay for Daniel's malpractice insurance."

"Hey now," Dr. Morris said, feigning shock.

Churchill laughed and leaned toward Peller as if to share a confidence. A subtle fragrance of gardenia clung to her. "Sounds like a great place to work."

"If you don't mind being hip-deep in crime." Peller suddenly realized what was up. He gave Newton a look of rebuke.

Far from denying the setup, Newton said to Charity, "Look, there's Theresa. Didn't you want to talk to her?"

"Ah, good," Charity replied. "Will you all excuse us?" Without waiting for an answer, they beat a hasty retreat across the room to where Detective Theresa Swan was hanging on her boyfriend's arm, laughing hysterically about something.

"Looks like you've been abandoned," Morris told Churchill.

"That's okay, I'm a big girl. At least they introduced me first." She smiled hopefully at Peller.

Peller found his mood darkening. He resented being pushed into this and had no desire to play along. He felt like stalking out and cloistering himself in his house for the next month. But a voice that only he could hear said with a hint of humor, *Be nice. It's not her fault.*

He never could deny Sandra. He composed himself as best he could. "So you're Charity's friend. Let me guess. You're coworkers."

Churchill looked both surprised and delighted. "Why yes, how did you know?"

"Well. Not to be indelicate, but she's enough your junior that you didn't go to school together. That and, as already stated, you're Charity's friend, not Andy's." Her eyes widened further, so he quickly added, "Not that he doesn't like you. I'm sure he does. I mean he knows you because of your relationship with his wife. So you're probably not neighbors. Coworker is a reasonable guess."

She actually applauded. "You're real name isn't Sherlock, is it?"

Peller wasn't sure whether to be amused or embarrassed. "No, it really is Rick. Well, Richard if you want to be technical, but my mother's the only one who ever calls me that, and when she does it usually isn't a good sign."

"And when was the last time she did?" Captain Morris asked, fixing him with a maternal stare.

"Fifth amendment."

A merry ruckus broke out at the bar where Trengove was holding forth on some subject, and one of the younger Detectives called, "Captain! We need you to resolve this for us!"

With a sigh, Morris downed her drink and made her way toward the bar. She hadn't gone three steps before her husband rose, too. "Duty calls," he said dryly. "She may look tough, but she has no chance against Bill's razor-sharp rejoinders." He shuffled off, leaving Peller alone with Churchill.

An awkward moment passed while Churchill fiddled with a napkin. "I'm sorry about this. You aren't in the market, are you?"

He didn't know how to respond. Anything he said might come out wrong.

"It's okay. Andy thought if we met something good might come of it. To be honest, I didn't really want to come tonight."

Peller met her eyes. Her voice had been serene, but that had been a mask. Beneath it, tension brewed. He felt an upwelling of sympathy. He wasn't the victim at the table. She was. "Why did you?"

"I wanted to see if you really were Superman." She looked away, smiling in embarrassment. "You've done Andy proud, I'll say that much."

"Uh, hmm, thank you. I think." Peller couldn't withhold a matching smile. "Andy doesn't impress people as being particularly creative, but you've got to watch him. He's devious. That face of his." Peller did a fair imitation of Newton's perpetual look of astonishment. "He's integrated it well into his toolkit."

Now they were both laughing, and Peller had to remind himself that people were watching, perhaps taking notes, even planning further romantic ambushes on his behalf.

"He told me about your wife," Churchill said, suddenly serious. "I'm so sorry."

Peller nodded. "And you? You don't strike me as the spinster type."

"No. I've been married and divorced twice." The napkin slipped from her fingers and vanished beneath the table. She absently folded her now empty hands in her lap, then looked at them as though wondering what they were doing there. "I had the bad luck to fall for two men who couldn't keep their pants zipped up."

"Now it's my turn to say I'm sorry."

"I've been on my own for five years. Andy said—well, I probably shouldn't tell you, actually. You'll think it's presumptuous and get mad at him."

"Don't worry. I can't stay mad at Andy for more than forty-eight hours at a time."

"He said that if by chance we hit it off, he'd guarantee you wouldn't treat me that way." She looked up, her lips smiling but her eyes moist. "So I thought, what the hell. Can't hurt to try."

"I guess not." Peller took another of the folded napkins from the table and handed it to her. She took it and dabbed at her eyes. "It's hard to explain, but I don't think I could remarry. Sandra would always be there. It would be awkward. You know?"

She thought about it. "I think so." Setting the napkin on the table, she leaned back and crossed her legs. He didn't want to think too hard about it, but she did have nice legs. "And I wouldn't mind being your friend, even if nothing else. Sherlock." She winked at him.

Oh God, he thought. *A nickname.* But he smiled back anyway.

*

Shortly before nine that evening, Peller walked through his own front door and went straight to the kitchen. He drew a glass of water and leaned heavily against the counter as he slowly drank. A large red "3" blinked urgently on his telephone, informing him of vital messages from organizations coveting his money. He thumped his empty glass down and jabbed the "play" button. A happy female voice informed him that he was pre-qualified for a loan.

He hit the delete button.

A serious male voice informed him that leaky toilet valves cost consumers thousands of—

He hit the delete button more forcefully. His finger remained on it as the last message began, another happy female voice saying—

Delete.

Odds were it wasn't important. If it was, they'd call back later.

He went upstairs to his bedroom and deposited his keys and cell phone on the dresser. Sitting on the edge of the bed, he took off his shoes, and only then realized that the controls on his cell were flashing, alerting him to more useless messages. *We're slaves to our technology*, he grumbled as he snatched up the phone and checked. One voice mail. Activating the app, he put it on speaker.

A happy female voice said—

He just about deleted that, too.

"Lieutenant Peller? My name is Vicki Manshadi. I'm with the Bahá'ís of Howard County, returning your call. I just wanted to let you know that

I'm working on finding out who talked with Jayvon Fletcher. I'll call back as soon as I have some information for you."

She gave a phone number where she could be reached and said goodbye.

Peller put the phone back on the dresser and gazed at it thoughtfully, thankful for something to occupy his mind other than Joan Churchill. Although he had no reason for suspicion so far, he wondered if Fletcher could have been led astray by his newfound friends. If his character had truly been so impeccable, it was far easier to believe he'd been subverted by religion than money. His grandmother would surely find it easier to accept if someone else were to blame. Barring such an outside influence, Peller needed a compelling reason to reject the inside man hypothesis, and he didn't have one.

He flopped backwards on the bed and closed his eyes. This entire line of thinking was warped, and he knew it. Whatever had happened had happened, Wanda Fletcher's dogged belief in Jayvon notwithstanding. But he couldn't squelch his concern for her. Why couldn't Jayvon have been goodness personified? Some explanation other than base greed had to be hiding among the faded evidence.

Maybe, Peller mused, thinking about Joan Churchill would be better after all.

Do you want to think about her?

"Don't do this," he muttered to the voice in his head.

What do you think about her?

"What do you think about her?"

That's not the question.

He draped his arm over his face and squeezed his eyes shut. "I miss you," he whispered. "You have no idea how much I miss you."

Silence.

Then...

Of course I do.

8

Thursday morning, and the reporter was back. Groggy following a largely sleepless night, Dumas welcomed Collins with as much civility as he could muster and motioned him to the chair beside his desk. Collins dropped into it with somewhat less than his usual enthusiasm. "Anything turn up?" he asked.

"Nope. I whittled down the list of names a tad, which counts as progress." Dumas pulled up the roster of Tamai's acquaintances on his computer. He found it hard to focus on it, but he knew what it said. "Tamai kept a long list of contacts. They could be anybody. Family, old school buddies, girlfriends. Some are likely accomplices. Based on what Denise Newville told us, which was corroborated by our interviews to date, probably most of those are also his victims. Quite an accretion. Unfortunately, we don't know who is which yet."

"There you go with the word-a-day thing again," Montufar said behind him.

Both men looked up, startled by her arrival. She smiled down at them, but their blank stares chased her smile away. "You know. 'Accretion.' Word-a-day. Get it?"

"Uh, sure," Dumas said, unable to muster any enthusiasm for her ribbing, good natured though it was.

She surveyed them critically. "Okay, who wants to go first? What's wrong?"

Collins shifted uncomfortably. "Just tired," he muttered.

"Likewise," Dumas agreed. "Someone kept me up too late."

Collins looked up with a sly grin.

Dumas wished he could stuff the words back into his mouth. Then he wondered why he cared what the reporter thought. *Probably because he could be my brother-in-law someday. I'm not sure how I feel about that.* To deflect everyone's thoughts—including his own—he turned back to his computer and tapped the monitor. "And this is my to-do list today. I'm not looking forward to doing."

Montufar leaned in to look. With Collins now watching their every move, Dumas found her uncomfortably close.

Montufar never took her eyes off the list but asked, "You're Jack Collins, aren't you?"

"Yes, ma'am," Collins replied.

"You and Ella should join us for dinner at Eduardo's house this weekend. I'll make sure Eduardo knows he's hosting." She slipped Collins a knowing smile, then asked Dumas, "Why's this name got an asterisk by it?"

"It was like that in Tamai's book. That and a few others. It could mean anything. Unless something better turns up, I'm going to interview one or two of them first. I might get lucky."

"Could I see the book?"

"Be my guest." He got her a pair of gloves and retrieved the evidence bag from a drawer.

She pulled on the gloves and carefully extracted the book from the bag. "How smart was Tamai?" she asked while leafing through the pages.

"Not very when he was drunk. According to his lady friend, he got beat up at least once after getting sufficiently lubricated to let slip that he'd cheated a partner. Aside from that, who knows? It's probably a good bet he never made the dean's list, though."

"Beat up once, killed once," Montufar suggested.

"That's the theory."

Collins had been watching the back and forth with interest. "Oh hell," he said and fished his tape recorder out of his coat pocket. He snapped it on and set in on the desk.

From the look Montufar gave the machine it was clear she disapproved, but she continued. "The marked names might not be the important ones. If he was smart, he wouldn't have been that obvious. He might have used a code."

"Like the third name down from the marked ones, or something?"

"Maybe."

"Why do you always complicate things for me?" Any other day he would have smiled when he said it. Today he couldn't muster the energy.

Montufar straightened. "Your gratitude is overwhelming." She slipped away as quickly and silently as she'd arrived.

The men watched her go. "Is she mad?" the reporter asked.

"Nah. That's just her *modus operandi*."

"I've noticed there's a, um—" Collins cleared his throat. "Kind of tension between you."

"Oh yeah." Dumas turned back to his computer.

"I really like her sister, but the women in that family are hard to figure. Ella and I...well, let's just say last night was strange."

Dumas exhaled and leaned back in his chair. He hoped this wasn't going to morph into true confessions time. He wanted—needed—to get out of the office and make some house calls. It wasn't just the investigation beckoning. He needed to lose himself in constructive action. "I hear all women are strange. Of course, they think the same way about men."

"She's afraid her father is dying."

Dumas wasn't sure if Collins meant Ella or Corina. "Understandable."

"Ella tries so hard to put on a brave face for me. I told her it's okay to let it out, but she won't until she can't take it anymore, then she's in hysterics. And then she apologizes like—I don't know, like she's killed somebody."

Dumas closed his eyes and locked his hands behind his head. *Please, Jack, don't walk us too far down this road.*

"And then she wants to make it up to me and goes overboard the other direction."

"It must be rough on her." He sat forward, put on a pair of gloves, and began inspecting Tamai's address book. There was no telling how long

Collins would ramble on, so he might as well try to get some kind of work done.

"I wonder if she's bipolar. But I really care about her, you know? I feel responsible for her, too. Like somebody has to save her from herself, and..." He made a vague motion with his hand.

"And it might as well be you."

"More than that. Like it's my destiny."

"That sounds like a dangerous basis for a relationship." Dumas suddenly noticed something he hadn't before: subtle marks on the page before him. He studied them, puzzled, until their meaning struck him.

"I know," Collins chattered on. "But she's really something when she's not going to pieces. I guess I have to take the bad with the good. I just hope—"

Dumas flipped a few pages forward. "Hold that thought. I just realized something. Corina, you're a genius!"

He set the book on the desk and beckoned Collins closer. "Look at this." He tapped several names in sequence. "Tamai counted down from this name, tapping the paper on every line and leaving little pen marks. Six times, then he put the asterisk here. And it's not the only one." He flipped backward to the page where he'd first seen it. "Same thing here. Six dots, then an asterisk. That can't be a coincidence." He took a few minutes to examine every page in the book that contained a starred name. There were no other dots in evidence.

Collins gazed at the page but didn't seem to get it.

Still working out the mystery of Ella? Time to snap you out of it. Dumas jumped to his feet. Grabbing his coat and snatching up the book, he crowed, "Come on, Jack! Let's see what we can find. Work is the best therapy in the world!"

*

Unlike Dumas, Montufar didn't feel any need to rush out. She suspected more than exhaustion gnawed at him but shrugged off his curt responses. He'd bounce back before long. He always did. Meanwhile, she had work to do.

After reviewing her notes on the arson case, she placed a call to the Dibbles' temporary home. Vincent would be at work today, but Candace had taken time off from her job at the college so she could focus on insurance claims and start the process of rebuilding. More important, unlike Vincent she hadn't seemed evasive. Montufar was sure the husband knew something he didn't want out, and odds were his wife didn't realize it. If so, she might unwittingly reveal some small detail that would point Montufar in the right direction.

"Hello, Sergeant," Candace said upon answering. "Any news yet?"

"Not yet. I just had a question."

"Ask away."

"I understand Vincent changed jobs about a year ago."

"Yes, he did. He felt stuck in his former position. He'd been a middle manager for nearly ten years and thought it was time to make the move to a senior leadership role."

"I guess he timed it right."

"Absolutely! He loves working at Filson."

"And they seem to love him. I talked with the CEO there. She was quite certain the fire couldn't have had anything to do with his job situation."

Candace considered that for a moment. "He already said it didn't."

"I know. I just wanted to be sure. Suppose he'd taken disciplinary action against someone, even over a small matter that he didn't remember anymore. The fire might have been motivated by revenge over something like that."

"Oh. Yes, I guess so. And you're wondering if it might have been someone from his former company?"

"It's one possibility."

"He could answer that better than I, but if you need to talk to someone sooner, I can get you a contact. The company name is Fastrak Engineering." She spelled it for Montufar.

"I'd appreciate that." Montufar waited while Candace found the information and relayed it to her. "I know it was a while back," she continued, "but do you recall anything troubling from that time, like problems with neighbors or coworkers?"

Candace didn't answer immediately, and Montufar wondered what that meant. "I don't think so," she finally replied. "There was a brief time last year when Vincent seemed a bit on edge, but I'm sure it was just normal work-related stress. It was about the time he started looking for a new position, anyway. I can't see how it could have anything to do with the fire."

"I'm sure you're right," Montufar said in her most soothing tone, although she wasn't. "With so little to go on, I need to cover every base. Thank you so much, Ms. Dibble."

After the goodbyes, Montufar made some notes and pondered what she'd heard. Vague suggestions lurked beneath the talk of all being well. She had nothing concrete, but a picture was beginning to emerge with Vincent Dibble a key figure.

*

Aside from the Jayvon Fletcher case, Peller's professional life was fairly boring at the moment. He had Dumas on the Michio Tamai murder and Montufar working the Dibble arson. Lower-ranking detectives dealt with the usual smattering of assaults and burglaries. The extreme cold—extreme for Maryland, that was, although Peller remembered much colder winters during his childhood in upstate New York—seemed to keep most of the criminal element indoors. Everyone had time to catch up on paperwork, complete training courses, and generally take a breath before the next crime wave heated things up again.

But Peller found he couldn't relax. The details of Fletcher's disappearance—the broken window, the bloodstained steps, the deep silence of unknowing—haunted him. They looped over and over in his mind like an unending trailer for a horror film. Unable to focus on anything else, he got up and paced out a circuitous course through the office, past the desks of colleagues and underlings, wanting but not daring to ask if he could help with something, with anything. He passed by Dumas' desk, but Dumas wasn't there. He slipped quietly by Montufar, who was on the phone. His course ended at Captain Morris' open door, where he forced himself to stop.

"What's up?" Her eyes shifted from her computer monitor to his face.

He sat in one of the chairs before her desk. "Frustration. What's up with you?"

"Reports and more reports and ongoing budget squabbles. I'm afraid that Lamborghini is still on the chopping block, but at least I've persuaded the powers that be to forgo any staff cuts for now."

"Score one for the Captain." Peller made an imaginary mark in the air with his index finger.

"Don't cheer just yet. They still might take our chairs away. It's all I can do to avoid foaming at the mouse." Morris shook the computer mouse rather more than necessary to make her point. Then she picked up the pen she perpetually kept on her desk and clicked it a few times. Peller had always found that pen habit annoying, but he knew it usually signaled either deep thought or stress. It wasn't hard to guess which held sway now. "By frustration you mean Fletcher's disappearance remains an enigma?"

"Impenetrably," Peller admitted. "Turns out he was involved with a religious group of which his mother doesn't approve. She hadn't brought that up in previous interviews. I'm in the process of contacting them, but so far they seem harmless enough. They don't sound like terrorists or nutcases, anyway."

"Religion can make people nuts."

"So can politics. Or race, or nationality, or sports, or who looked the wrong way at whom at the fast food counter."

"Granted. We're a touchy lot, aren't we? People?"

Peller looked out the window. Puffy clouds dotted the sky. It looked from this vantage point like a nice day, but he knew the temperature still hovered around twenty and more snow was forecast. Snow could drive people nuts, too, in this part of the world. At least this winter's snowfalls had been small, typically no more than an inch at a time. They hadn't caused a quarter of the havoc raised by those two-footers laden with Gulf of Mexico moisture that blew in every few years.

"What did you think of Joan?" Morris asked without any reason Peller could discern. He was desperate for distraction, but not of that kind.

"She seems nice."

"I thought so, too, although after being called away I'm afraid I didn't catch up with her again."

That hadn't escaped him. He'd wondered at the time if Morris was in on the plot but decided probably not. She never turned her gift for political maneuvering against her own people. He rose and nodded. "I should let you get back to your work. I'm sure you're eager to wrangle that budget."

She looked up as though to say something but didn't. Her eyes shifted back to her computer screen. "Thanks a lot."

He gave her a knowing smile then made his way back to Montufar's desk. She was off the phone now, leaning on her desk, fists balled as though about to punch an unseen foe. Peller knew she was troubled but could only hazard a guess as to why. "Corina? It's not your father, is it?"

She started to say something, then shook her head.

"If you need to go—"

"No, it's not that—not now, anyway." She took a deep breath. "Of course, well—"

"It's always at the back of your mind," Peller said quietly. *Like Sandra.*

She looked up at him. "Yeah." Her fists unclenched and she seemed to relax. "How busy are you?"

"Not half enough. Why?"

"Could you interview someone for me?"

Could he ever. "Sure, what's the story?"

Montufar told him about her visit to the Dibble home and her talk with Candace. "The man is hiding something. He has to be. But I don't think I can pry it loose."

"You're the smartest cop in the room, Corina. If anyone can weasel it out of him out, you can."

She gave Peller a twisted smile, half embarrassment, half rebuke. "You sound like my brother. But even if I am, there's one thing you are that I'm definitely not."

"What's that?"

"A man."

With a grin, Peller started, "I'm sure..." But it wasn't to be broadcast, apparently. He made sure nobody was near and dropped his voice. "...that Eric appreciates that."

A series of emotions from embarrassment to relief chased across Montufar's face, but she said nothing.

"Come on, I've known for months. I won't tell the world if you don't want me to. But it's nothing to be ashamed of. You're lucky to have each other."

She didn't reply to that, either.

"Okay, back to business. You think Dibble would tell me things he won't tell you?"

She relaxed, apparently glad to leave relationship talk behind. "Maybe, if you can get him away from his wife. Whatever it is, she doesn't know about it. He might be afraid that anything he told me would get back to her."

"Do you get the feeling there's something wrong between them?"

"Something's not quite right. They won't show it in front of me, but I get the feeling that she's head over heels in love with him, and he's trying hard not to broadcast anything. I'm sure he knows something."

Peller considered that. He supposed she had a point. Dibble might not trust a woman detective to keep a confidence. Stereotypes lived on. "Okay, I'll see what I can do. Do you have a phone number for him?"

"I'll email it to you." Her fingers danced on her keyboard. "And, Rick..." But she didn't finish the thought.

"Yes?"

"There may be another woman involved."

"Why do you think that?"

"The way he talked and acted. I could be wrong, but..." She threw herself backwards and ran both hands through her hair. "Why do I have to be the one to uncover it? I like Candace and her niece, and...damn it, it's not fair."

"I'll tread carefully," Peller promised. "But if he is cheating on her, it's going to come out eventually. That's not our fault."

She nodded absently. "Yeah."

On the other hand, Peller, told himself, he was as guilty as Montufar of allowing emotional entanglements to interfere with work of late. She didn't want to tell Candace Dibble that her man was adulterous; Peller didn't want to tell Wanda Fletcher that her grandson had been a crook. He couldn't in good conscience lecture her on the matter. Not right now, anyway. "I'll let you know what I find out," he said. "Maybe it's something innocuous. The man's house did go up in flames, after all."

"That's what Candace thought," Montufar agreed. "I hope the two of you are right." The look on her face, though, said she knew otherwise.

9

Under a pale blue sky tufted with hints of cirrus far above, Dumas shoved his gloved hands down into his coat pockets and waited for a response. Leaning on a shovel with his back to the detective, Charlie Sheffield stared into a hole at the side of the road, working overtime to ignore the fact that he'd attracted police attention. Not more than five foot eight, he looked overweight, but that could have been an illusion conjured by his thick black coat. The tattered garment could do with a cleaning, Dumas thought. An orange vest added a couple more imagined pounds.

"It's a miracle," Sheffield said.

That wasn't the answer to Dumas' question. "What's that?"

Sheffield pointed. "That line is crumbling. It's a miracle it lasted this long."

"I didn't come to discuss water mains."

Sheffield still didn't turn. "Yeah, I knew Michio. Mike, we all called him. Sorry to hear he's gone."

"You mind looking over here while we talk?"

Resigned to his fate, Sheffield turned. He had a wide, round face and a complexion that suggested a racially mixed heritage. He licked his lips, then wiped away the moisture on his sleeve before it could freeze.

"When did you last see him?" Dumas asked. At his side, Jack Collins shuffled and stamped his feet. His tape recorder hung from a lanyard around his neck; his hands were tucked warmly into his coat pockets. *Smart move*, Dumas thought, although he'd never seen a tape recorder on a string before.

"A month ago?"

Dumas looked down the road, where the rest of the repair crew milled about and chattered amongst themselves. He had intended to take

Sheffield aside, but the foreman said it was time for their break anyway. He wondered if that was true or if the crew was taking advantage of the intrusion. Behind them cars zipped by, their drivers uninterested in the goings-on.

"If you're asking me," Dumas said, "I wouldn't know."

Sheffield shrugged mightily.

"How did you meet him?"

"Friend of a friend. Mike was a kind of businessman?" Sheffield's eyes flickered to the side while he said this, or asked it. "Sometimes he needed help."

"What kind of business was he in?"

"Oh." He stamped his feet. "Just small stuff."

"Petty theft, maybe?"

"Hey, now," Sheffield protested.

"Hey now yourself. I already know what he got up to. And that he cheated nearly every partner he ever had. And that somebody, probably one of his good buddies, popped him because of it."

Sheffield put up his hands as if to ward Dumas off. "Look, I didn't know him that well."

"Not well enough to kill him, you mean? How well did you know him, then?"

"I just..." Sheffield looked over at his coworkers. They watched while trying not to look it, but they were too far away to hear. He lowered his voice anyway. "If I help you, you won't arrest me, right? I need this job. If the boss knew what I'd done before..." He nearly choked on the thought.

"I'm not after you. Unless you killed Michio."

"It wasn't me."

Dumas found his tone of voice suggestive. "Do you know who it was?"

"No, but I think I know why it happened." When Dumas didn't react, he licked his lips again and stole another look at the idle crew. "I talked to him two weeks ago. He needed a go-between to handle a big payoff. Said he couldn't meet the guy personally, you know? He promised me a cut if I handled it." Sheffield shuffled his feet again. Dumas wished he would stop.

"Did you bite?"

He shook his head. "Like you said, he was a cheat. And it wasn't right. Something was going down."

"Like what?"

"Don't know, but he was on edge. Not scared, exactly, but I could tell he didn't want to be in the same room as the guy who owed him. So I figured I didn't want to meet him, either." He shuffled his feet again. "Anyway, I landed this job and didn't need Michio anymore."

"Funny," Dumas said. "Everyone who knew Tamai seems to have suddenly gone straight."

Sheffield shook his head. "Liars."

"And you?"

He put up his hands again. "Honest. I swear."

Dumas smiled at him. "Did Tamai give you any details? Name, address, anything?"

"No. I turned down the job, so he didn't tell me anything." He frowned at the pavement for a moment. "But I think it was blackmail."

Now that was interesting. Dumas glanced at Collins. The reporter had perked up, too. "Why?"

"He threatened me. He said if I didn't take the job, he'd tell my girlfriend about my other women."

"That didn't bother you?"

Sheffield shed his misery and flashed an evil smile. "Wasn't much of a threat. She'd already found out and left me the day before." That out, he slipped back into pathetic mode.

Dumas figured it was the only victory he'd had over Tamai. "Let's try it another way. Who did Michio know who had money?

"Nobody. Not unless somebody scored big recently. He collected a hopeless bunch of lowlifes. And when we had cash, we blew it in on stupid stuff." His face scrunched up in thought. "You got my name from his book?"

Dumas nodded.

"Whoever it was, they're in there."

"Then maybe you could give me a guided tour of the names."

"Hey..." He looked at his idle coworkers again.

"Not here," Dumas assured him. "We can arrange a time. Here's my number." He handed Sheffield his card. "Call at your convenience. If you don't, I can always call at mine."

Sheffield took the card and frowned at it. "Yeah," he mumbled.

Dumas motioned Collins toward the car. As they left, he waved an all clear to the foreman, who straightened, surveyed his crew, and said something. They returned to work but looked none too enthusiastic about it.

*

"Mr. Dibble? This is Detective Lieutenant Rick Peller, Howard County police. I was wondering if we could meet sometime today." Peller jammed the phone between his ear and shoulder and called up a map on his computer. While he waited for Dibble to reply, he located Filson Control Industries.

"I thought Sergeant Montufar was handling the case," Dibble said, disgruntled.

"She asked me to lend a hand today. I hope you don't mind."

Dibble could hardly object, but he could make excuses. "I have a lot on my plate today, Lieutenant."

"Over lunch? My treat."

"Well..."

"I'm sure you want this resolved as quickly as possible. We need your help."

The dead air told Peller Dibble had little interest in helping, but apparently he couldn't think of a way to worm out of it. In a subdued, almost weary voice, he relented. "No more than an hour, Lieutenant. Meet me in the parking lot of the Elkridge library. I'll be there at twelve-fifteen." Peller heard the clicking of typing on a keyboard. "Bring me a hamburger."

Taking the demand in stride, Peller located the library on the map. "I'll be there."

He arrived five minutes early with fast food for two. The parking lot, large enough for about sixty vehicles, handicapped spaces included, was no more than a quarter full. Peller parked on the west side of the lot, where a stand of woods afforded an aura of privacy. He thought Dibble might feel less exposed there, facing the trees, his back to passersby.

Within a few minutes, a pristine white BMW crossed Peller's rearview mirror. He could have sworn he caught a whiff of new car. *Must be Dibble.* He got out and waved the driver over. The car slunk across the lot and pulled in next to him. Dibble looked none too pleased as he clambered out of the Beemer, nor did he speak.

"Mr. Dibble?" Peller asked.

"Yeah." Without invitation, Dibble opened Peller's passenger door and got in.

Peller resumed his position behind the wheel. He started the engine to keep them warm then divided up their lunch.

Without bothering to thank Peller, Dibble ate half of his sandwich before asking, "What do you want?"

"Same as you. To know why your house was torched."

"Seems obvious to me. Sergeant Montufar said arsonists get their kicks from setting fires."

"Sometimes. Not always."

Dibble maintained focus on his food. Peller took a long pull on his soda and waited patiently for him to answer, but no answer was forthcoming, so he decided to shake things up a little. "You don't think it was random, Mr. Dibble."

Dibble looked up sharply.

"Tell me I'm wrong."

"I...I don't know."

Peller settled his drink in the cup holder and gazed at the trees, stark in their winter slumber. "Sergeant Montufar told me a story. Last year, an arsonist torched three houses. We caught him and sent him to prison. A set of fingerprints lifted from a mailbox near the street gave him away. The investigator might not have thought to check for prints there, except one of the victims remembered receiving a juvenile sort of warning in her mailbox. At the time, she took it for a stupid teenage prank. Fortunately she remembered it and told the investigator about it."

Dibble, his mouth drawn into a tight line, looked out the windshield as though studying the woods, but Peller knew he was seeing a ghost from his past. "What's your point, Lieutenant?"

"Anything, even something that seems unconnected, even something that seems stupid, could be important. And to be perfectly frank, I think you know what it is. Why don't you tell me about it?"

Anger crossed Dibble's face. He refused to look at Peller.

"I'm not accusing you of anything. We know you wouldn't set fire to your own house." Actually, they knew no such thing, but Peller didn't think it likely. Dibble wasn't hurting for money, so unless he'd blundered into outrageous debt, he wouldn't have his heart set on an insurance payout. "Then again, you may be afraid of something. Someone may have threatened you, say, over something you don't want your family to find out. But weigh that against the fact that the next arson might kill somebody."

Peller took another drink and let Dibble mull that over. And he did take his time, ignoring the remains of his meal. When he spoke, he looked out the side window, away from Peller. "I didn't do anything wrong,"

"I'm sure you didn't," Peller replied quietly.

"There are photos." He shook his head and folded his hands in his lap. His gaze returned to the trees as though watching dangerous shadows moving among them. "I thought I'd gotten away from them when I changed jobs and moved. We would have moved anyway. Joining Filson boosted my income significantly. We could afford a nicer place. I changed jobs, we moved, and I thought I'd gotten away from them."

"Away from who?"

"Like you said, Lieutenant, it's something stupid. You sometimes go out for drinks with colleagues after work, right? Well, that's all it was. We always went to the same place, a respectable restaurant with a nice bar, good staff, decent prices. One night I met a pretty young blonde. Yeah, so I'd seen her there a few times before, and sure, I looked, but I wasn't trying to get her attention. She was just part of the scenery. But on this particular evening, we ended up next to each other at the bar. I didn't realize it until she said hello. I didn't think she recognized me. It seemed like a coincidence, like she was just being friendly."

Peller already realized it was no coincidence but said nothing.

"We got to talking. Small talk. Nothing important. That was all. I just talked to her. Just once, for maybe fifteen minutes, about absolutely nothing." He drew a long breath.

Peller knew what was coming.

"Two or three days later, a mailer came to me at work. Photos. Incriminating photos. Whoever took them knew what they were doing. It was like a documentary. The angles, the timing, all perfect. They made it look like we were a lot more intimate than we had been." He shook his head. "You'd swear from looking at them that we were touching, that she was whispering in my ear."

I bet they were, Peller thought. "What else was in the package?" Presumably a demand for hush money.

"Nothing." Dibble finally looked at Peller. His expression pained, he shrugged. "Just the photos. For a whole week I wondered who had done this, what they wanted, what they were doing with those photos, whether they'd sent them to Candace. Eventually I started hoping it was just a stupid gag. Maybe one of my coworkers thought it would be funny to embarrass me that way. Could you get photos like that with a cell phone? I thought maybe so. I told myself that had to be it." He shrugged again.

"No such luck," Peller suggested. "Just when you'd convinced yourself you were in the clear, the demands arrived."

Dibble pointed at Peller in acknowledgement.

"What did they want?"

"Nothing much. A mere three hundred dollars." Very little surprised Peller after nearly thirty years on the force, but that did, and Dibble could read it on his face. "A week," he added. "Three hundred dollars every damn week. The week I stopped paying would be the week Candace got the photos. In the event of our divorce or Candace's death, our sons would become the recipients. Can you imagine that, Lieutenant? It's evil. Absolutely evil." He pressed his head back into the headrest and closed his eyes.

Peller pondered that. Assuming Dibble had told the truth, he'd been set up for blackmail by somebody who knew where he worked, where he socialized with colleagues, his family situation, and probably his financial means. A great deal of planning and carefully coordinated execution had gone into the crime. "Did you pay?"

"Of course. It wasn't easy hiding it from Candace. I had to cut back my discretionary spending without being too obvious. I don't think she noticed. But I also decided I was going to get the bastards off my back. I'd already put out feelers for a new position. From then on, I moved quietly. As soon as I'd secured the position with Filson, I shopped around for a new place. I didn't even tell Candace. I sprang it on her as a birthday surprise. 'Honey, I've bought you a brand-new house. Here's a picture of it. We move next week.'" Dibble smiled crookedly. "You should have heard her squeal. She loved it."

If Peller had pulled that kind of stunt with Sandra, his new home would have been a doghouse. "You can't move a family quietly, though. People will know. Friends, family, coworkers, church members. What if the blackmailers were close to you?"

"You think that didn't occur to me? But I had to try, and it seemed to work. I made three more payments after we moved, then stopped. Nothing happened. Months passed. Life returned to normal. I'd escaped."

"And then the fire," Peller finished for him.

"And then the fire. That's the only message I've received. I didn't even connect it until Sergeant Montufar called it arson." His demeanor suddenly cracked. "They know where I am, Lieutenant. What if they torch Peter's house, too? What if someone is killed? How do I stop these monsters?"

Peller set a hand on Dibble's shoulder. "You don't. We do. And we will; that's our job. But you might tell your wife, sir. Sergeant Montufar tells me she's a good woman. She loves you and deserves your honesty."

Dibble shook his head, not in denial but in disbelief. "She might not understand. She might think…"

He didn't have to finish. Peller understood. But he also knew that people constantly misjudged each other, perhaps especially the people they knew best. "You said you did nothing wrong. Is that the truth?"

"I swear."

"Then trust her to know it."

"But what if she doesn't? Either way, I don't want to put her through that. She has enough to deal with as it is."

"Then try it this way," Peller suggested. "At your wedding, didn't you say, 'for better or for worse'?"

Dibble nodded.

"Well, this is the 'for worse' part. You'll get through it if you face it together. The blackmailers are counting on you not telling Candace and your sons. If you do, the sword is no longer dangling over your head. Those photos will be worthless."

Dibble drew a long, deep breath and slowly released it. "I'll give you that. But fire isn't so easily disarmed."

*

Dumas and Collins caught up with their next person of interest, Angelina Peralta, at a modest gym in Maple Lawn off State Route 216.

They'd been directed here by her older sister Maria with whom she shared an apartment in Columbia.

Dumas suspected the gym employee who greeted them was a personal trainer. A fit black woman wearing brilliant white spandex, she looked almost disgusted at the arrival of the police, but took them to see Peralta anyway. The main floor of the gym was the size of a modest grocery store, dotted with the usual collection of workout equipment—weight machines, rowing machines, treadmills—that appeared well-used but not tired out. A few customers were energetically shedding pounds and building up strength.

Peralta lie face up on a bench near the back, the muscles in her solid arms bulging as she pumped weights. Her brown skin glistened with sweat; her lungs worked overtime. After a few more reps she stopped, closed her eyes, and rested. Once her breathing slowed, she sat up. "You guys scouts or voyeurs?" She reached for a towel lying in a heap on the floor.

Dumas ignored her little joke. "Detective Sergeant Eric Dumas, Howard County Police. I have a few questions for you."

She gave Dumas a crooked smile, then settled her gaze on Collins and his tape recorder. "He takes your notes?"

"Something like that."

Collins shifted his weight uneasily.

"You know Michio Tamai," Dumas said rather than asked.

"Who?" She rubbed her face in the towel then threw it back on the floor.

"You're in his little black book."

"I'm in lots of little black books. Doesn't mean I remember names."

"He sure remembered you. In his long list of contacts, you're one of just a handful marked for special attention."

"Guess it was good for him."

"He was murdered early Monday morning."

Peralta looked up sharply, her denials stripped away in a moment of surprise. She realized it, too, because she immediately dropped all trace of pretense. "Damn. I didn't know that."

Dumas gave her a bland look. "Didn't you."

"Nope. Last time we talked—three or four weeks ago, I think—he was still breathing."

"What did you talk about?"

"I told him we were finished."

"In what sense?"

"All senses. Business and pleasure."

Dumas looked around for a chair but there weren't any nearby. He resigned himself to looking down at Peralta. "Let's focus on business for a moment. What did that entail?"

"Sometimes he needed to give somebody a talking-to. I was his go-to girl for that."

"Obviously," Dumas said.

She seemed to like that; her back stiffened with pride. "I also helped him with odd jobs sometimes."

"Like what?"

"You know. Sometimes things fell off a truck and he needed them picked up."

Dumas couldn't help show his surprise at the admission of thievery. "You say things like that to all the cops in your life?"

Peralta grinned then turned serious so fast it almost gave Dumas whiplash. "Only when they talk murder. Anyway, I've gone straight since then. I'm a good girl now."

"Oh yeah?" Dumas wondered why association with Michio Tamai had turned so many bad apples good so suddenly. If it actually had. Charlie Sheffield said otherwise, except where he himself was concerned. Of course.

"I'm into boxing now. I'm hoping to make a name for myself in the ring." She faked a few punches in his direction.

"Nice. Just don't incur brain damage along the way. What exactly made you break it off with Tamai?"

Peralta studied her hands before answering but apparently decided to keep on playing it straight. "He wanted to get back some of the money he'd paid me. He said he'd tell my mom about my activities if I didn't cough it up."

"Did you pay?"

"Sure, with a swift kick in the groin. Then I told him if he ever threatened me again, I'd break every other part of his body." She grinned. "He decided that was payment enough."

"You admit you threatened to kill him." He couldn't help but wish that all witnesses were as forthcoming as Peralta, but he also knew it might be an act. Maybe she'd decided to cooperate just enough to convince him not to look too deep.

"Sure, why not? I didn't actually do it."

Dumas gazed at her for a few minutes, but she wouldn't be intimidated. "How do I know that?"

"How did he die?"

"How do you think?"

"I wouldn't know. But if he was shot, stabbed, poisoned, electrocuted, or dropped off a building, it wasn't me. Now if you found a sack of jelly where a guy used to be, then it might have been me." She cocked her head and grinned that crooked grin again.

Dumas ignored the implied question and switched subjects. "Who else was he blackmailing?"

"God knows. Probably everyone. Loyalty wasn't his middle name."

Dumas considered that. He'd heard it from nearly everyone who knew Tamai. Nor was this the first suggestion of blackmail. "From what I hear, though, he wasn't very good at it."

She nodded agreement. "Might have been new territory for him. I don't know that he'd tried it with anyone else. That's just a guess."

Dumas moved on. "I heard he needed help collecting on a debt just before he died. What do you know about that?"

"News to me. He might have asked me to do stuff like that before our little talk, but not after, you know?"

"So who would he have asked?"

Peralta frowned in concentration. "Harold and Hannah." To Dumas' surprise, she shuddered as she said this. "They'd have been good at that kind of thing."

He knew the names; Harold and Hannah Bellamy were among the asterisked entries in Tamai's book. "What's the story on them?"

"I only met them once. They're one creepy couple."

When she didn't elaborate, he prompted, "Why?"

She scraped at her pulled-back hair. "Hard to explain. They don't act like normal people. It's the way they look at you. I felt like a piece of meat in a grocery store, one they thought didn't look too fresh, you know?"

Dumas found that interesting, but he also wondered if Peralta had read them right. It might have been a feedback loop: Peralta unnerving the Bellamys and they unnerving her. Still, they'd be his next stop.

"I appreciate your candor," he told her, still not sure how far to trust her. "Here's my card. Call me if you think of anything else that might be of interest."

She took the card, gave it a cursory glance, and dropped it on the towel. "Will do." Lying down on the bench again, she resumed her workout as though the conversation had never happened.

Outside, Collins paused before getting into the car. He looked up at the swirls of high cloud overhead and drew in a breath of chill air. "You think she's telling the truth?"

"I'll reserve judgement," Dumas said. "But offhand, I'd say probably so."

"Why?"

"I can definitely see her drawing and quartering Tamai. It's a bit harder to see her dispatching him with two clean shots. If she did use a gun, it would be a big, nasty piece that would paint the walls with her victim."

Collins winced.

"Sorry." Dumas pushed the button on his remote and the car locks thunked open. "Do this for a while and you get a sense of how different people would rid themselves of someone." As they got in, he gave Collins a probing glance and added, "You'd contract it out."

Scandalized, Collins blurted, "Why do you say that?"

"You wouldn't want to be there when it happened."

The writer turned off his tape recorder and stared at it as though it had caught his own confession.

*

Peller had just parked at Northern District Headquarters and turned off his car when his cell phone jangled. He didn't recognize the number and nearly ignored it, but something niggled at him, suggesting he knew the caller. He answered.

"Hello, Lieutentant Peller? This is Vicki Manshadi. I have a contact for you."

"Oh," Peller said. "You're with the Bahá'ís."

"That's right. Jayvon Fletcher contacted us through our website. I wasn't living here at the time. I just moved to the area about a year ago. But I found out that he attended a few of our firesides. Some of our members visited him in his home, too, several times."

"Fireside? Is that anything like what FDR used to do on the radio?" He got out of the car and closed the door quietly. The sky was clear, the air cool with the temperature gradually descending toward an overnight low in the teens. He almost felt like he was back home in Lockport. Almost.

"FDR?"

That surprised Peller. Didn't everybody learn about Roosevelt's fireside chats in high school history? Given her last name, maybe she was an immigrant? But no, she didn't have an accent. Likely she was second-generation American, which put him back where he started, which didn't boost his confidence in the education system. "Never mind," he said "What's a fireside?"

She recovered gracefully. "It's a sort of informational meeting about the Bahá'í Faith, often in somebody's home. There's usually a talk and time for questions and answers."

"I see. You can give me a contact, you said." He walked toward the building while she responded.

"Yes. The best person to answer your questions would be Winston Marley. Winston was the first person in our community to meet Jayvon. He remained his primary contact."

She gave him a phone number, and Peller scribbled it on the back of the fast-food receipt. "Thank you, Vicki, I very much appreciate it."

"You're quite welcome. I hope Winston can help."

Going through the door, Peller pocketed his phone and went up to the CID offices on the second floor where he found Montufar on a call of her own. She looked up hopefully at his approach but held up a finger, so he lowered himself into the chair beside her desk to wait. She jotted notes on a yellow legal pad, then told the other party, "Thank you. I'll be in touch if we need anything else." She settled the receiver in its cradle and turned. "That was Fastrak Engineering, Vincent Dibble's former employer. Guess what I found out."

Peller noted the dull look in her eyes. "Absolutely nothing."

"Right the first time. He was a good employee, they hated to lose him, of course nothing bad or disturbing or even moderately odd had happened while he was there."

"Oh, for the awesomeness of our company," Peller remarked drily.

"Pretty much. How'd it go with Dibble?"

"Paydirt."

She brightened considerably. "I owe you. What's the story?"

"Dibble was being blackmailed. Someone surreptitiously snapped photos of him talking to a sweet young thing at a company happy hour. He swears it wasn't what it looked like, but the photos are damning and he was afraid to tell Candace. He paid the hush money until he could change jobs and move, then he stopped. Nothing happened for a while, so he thought he'd gotten away from the blackmailers, but now he thinks the fire was their handiwork."

Montufar didn't look happy about that. "I had a feeling," she muttered. She doodled on her notepad, making little spirals and nested boxes.

"Gut instinct from you?" He said it lightly, but at her acid glance he dropped it. "I told Dibble he should talk to his wife. If he does, so much the better, but if not, well, it can't be helped. She'll find out one way or another." He tapped on Montufar's desk to get her to look him in the eye. "Right?"

"Yeah, yeah. It still stinks."

"Now if you don't need my humble assistance any further, I have a call of my own to make."

"Something new on Fletcher?"

"Maybe. He apparently got involved with one of those, what do they call them? New religious movements? I put in a call to them and they found me someone who'd had contact with him."

"What's the name of the group?"

Peller smiled, thinking she'd probably be able to tell him all about these people. "They call themselves Bahá'ís."

Her brow furrowed while she searched her internal files. "I've heard of them, I think."

"Of course you have."

"Oh, I know. You remember Seals and Crofts?"

"The musicians?"

"The musicians. They were Bahá'ís."

"Hold on. You're not old enough to know about them."

Montufar laughed. "Thank you, I think. They did an anti-abortion song that some of my Catholic high school acquaintances had picked up on. The song came out in 1974, so it was old by the time I heard of it. You know me. Naturally, I had to research them."

Peller nodded. "Yeah, that'd be you. Which means that can't possibly be the extent of your knowledge of the religion."

She gave him one of her dark looks, but then the corners of her mouth turned upward. "There actually are a few subjects I still have to study."

"I wouldn't have thought it. But never mind. When I find out more, I'll let you know."

*

Once a mill town situated at the confluence of the Middle Patuxent and Little Patuxent rivers, Savage now collected historic buildings. A community of older homes on well-wooded lots bounded by State Route 32 to the northeast and U.S. route 1 to the southeast had given way to mid-century bungalows and later apartment complexes, and although the town was never quite as tranquil as might be expected, still it had a comfortable feel.

Tailed by Jack Collins, Dumas navigated to the southern edge of town where one of those apartment complexes hugged River Island Drive. Behind the row of buildings on the south side of the street, the Little Patuxent flowed by, hidden by a stand of woods. In one of these nondescript buildings lived Harold and Hannah Bellamy, the couple who had given Michio Tamai's "go to girl" Angelina Peralta the shivers.

By all rights, the side of the building facing the parking lot should have been its rear. Getting out of the car and looking around the area, Dumas noted that the other buildings were identical on both sides. Maybe the architect hadn't been able to make up his mind where the front belonged, so he just left it off?

Dumas and Collins mounted the open-air stairwell to the second floor, protected from the elements only by a roof and a chest-high wall. Dumas banged on the door and waited, silently regarding the diminutive reporter and wondering if it had been a good idea to let him tag along on this particular expedition. Probably the Bellamys were harmless, but Peralta's discomfort had been real. He briefly wished he'd roped Kevin Graham into backing him up again. Unfortunately, Peralta's comments had left him too eager to get here, and he hadn't stopped to think.

Collins looked around impatiently as Dumas knocked a second time. "Maybe they aren't home," he said. "What then?"

"I have phone numbers, but I'd rather see them face-to-face, without advance warning if possible. It's best not to give people time to prepare a story."

Collins nodded sagely. Dumas wondered if he felt like an expert already. "I don't like this place," the reporter commented quietly.

Dumas didn't care for it, either. The concrete stairs were dished by the passage of many feet. The meager light struggling to penetrate the space barely illuminated the dingy brown apartment doors and floors stained with decades' worth of unnamed substances. He wondered what a Luminol spray would show. "It's the darkness. It might be brighter in the summer."

"Feels like a cannibal's cave," Collins remarked.

It was too close to what Dumas imagined. He knocked a third time. "Mr. and Mrs. Bellamy!" he called. "Anybody home?"

The opposite door flew open. "For God's sake! What the hell do you want?" demanded a thin, nasal voice.

Collins and Dumas both jumped, then turned to confront a shrewish gnome in a ragged blue robe and slippers. Dumas immediately thought of Rumplestiltskin.

"Howard County police," Dumas said, flashing his badge. "I'm looking for Mr. and Mrs. Bellamy."

The gnome scowled at them. "I don't care if you're the president of the United States! Some of us are trying to sleep!"

"My apologies, sir. Do you know if the Bellamys are at work?"

"How the hell should I know? All I know is, they're quieter than you!" He slammed the door shut.

Dumas and Collins looked at each other.

"Nope," Collins said. "I really don't like this place."

10

That evening, without being asked, Dumas gave Montufar a ride to the hospital. When they arrived, they found the siblings gathered around. Eduardo and Sylvia sat close together in a pair of uncomfortable plastic chairs probably scrounged from somewhere by a nurse. Ella stood at her father's bedside with Jack Collins, who kept a protective arm tight about her shoulders. Felipe Montufar slept, but not quietly. Occasional coughs disturbed his slumber. A nursing tech making her rounds offered Montufar and Dumas a quiet greeting as she pushed her cart out on the way to her next stop.

Montufar couldn't find voice to say hello. She scrutinized her father as though he might die any second and leaned into Dumas as though about to collapse. He held her steady and asked, "What's the word?"

"Hard to say," Eduardo told him in an unusually subdued voice. If anyone could stay upbeat in a crisis, it was Eduardo. But then, Dumas thought, this was his father. "I talked to one of the nurses earlier. He hasn't responded to the antibiotics yet. She said that's not unusual for a man his age."

Eyes fixed on Felipe, Corina moved to his side and took his hand in hers. "How long until they know?" Her father's eyes fluttered as though he recognized her. Dumas followed to the bedside, afraid that if he released her she would collapse. He told himself that was ridiculous. She wasn't that fragile. Yet he couldn't shake the feeling that only his strength kept her on her feet. He noticed that Collins, arm still tight around Ella, guarded her just as closely. Maybe they both had the same fear. Male protective instincts? Possibly, and possibly foolish, but Dumas didn't care.

Eduardo made a helpless gesture. "Nobody can say. I talked to Father Owen this afternoon. He came to see papá a couple of hours ago. I don't know if they were able to talk. I hope so. He said he'd call me tomorrow morning." Eduardo took a deep breath. "Or I'll call him."

For support, Dumas wondered, or to prepare for death? Would the priest perform last rites—or whatever they called it—before the end had unquestionably come? Would he petition Providence for healing? Would he counsel the family, try to help them find peace, share in their grief? He didn't know. He didn't know anything. He'd known no priests, no ministers, no preachers, except in the most cursory way. A handshake after a Christmas service and little more. His ignorance of the Montufar family's religion filled him with inadequacy. It wasn't his religion, but how could he support his bride-to-be through this and into the future unless he knew these things? He desperately wanted to ask but couldn't. Not now. There would be a better time, a more appropriate time. His questions—if he could even formulate them—could wait until Felipe recovered.

Assuming he did. If not, the answers would be given without his asking. He would, if nothing else, share the experience with Corina.

Ella fought down a sob. "There must be light. Somewhere in this, there must be. Show me where." She might have been addressing her father, but Eduardo's mouth twisted in frustration. The request had been for him, and he'd come up as empty as his sisters. Ella turned desperate eyes on him. "Please?"

Taxed beyond his strength, Eduardo said nothing.

Dumas found himself thinking of Peller and Sandra, of her tragic death, the pain the whole department had felt at her loss, and the years that tormented Peller before, in his words, he had made peace with her absence. The same act played out here with different costumes, different actors, a different script even, but the same theme. *How did Rick move on? How did I move on without family? How does anyone move on?*

Something intruded into his thoughts, pushed all those questions aside, spoke words of comfort. They were words Sandra might once have spoken. He felt as well as heard, as though she had come among them and reached out to embrace the whole family, her words flowing as soft as a forest stream. She might have been standing in their midst, but only Dumas knew. The others could not hear her. He had to speak for her.

"Ella," he said quietly. "Your father is with you. He always will be. You can't ever lose him."

At first nobody reacted. Maybe they couldn't hear him any more than they could hear Sandra. But no, they had heard. A small smile stole over Ella's face as a tear slipped down her cheek. Eduardo drew a deep breath and nodded. "Thank you, Eric."

Montufar squeezed her father's hand and leaned all the more heavily against Dumas, her other hand settled on his shoulder. He felt her breath stir the air. She was speaking what might have been a prayer, but so quiet that even he couldn't hear. Then she grew still.

"Strange," she told him.

"What's that?"

"My grandmother told me the same thing the other day."

Eduardo and Ella looked at her, surprised. "Corina," Eduardo said. "She's gone."

"Yes. But she's not."

Eduardo scanned the air as though their grandmother might indeed be there somewhere.

Dumas had never believed the dead could communicate with the living. But if not, then what had spoken to him with Sandra's voice? Memory? Hallucination? Wishful thinking? He wondered what Peller would say.

Felipe's breathing steadied. For some time, he seemed at peace.

*

It was approaching ten o'clock before they left the hospital. Neither had had dinner, so Dumas detoured to a fast food drive-through, where they ate in his car in the parking lot. Montufar had been quiet since leaving the hospital, and he didn't know what to say to her. He only knew her father's weakness had shaken her, and that his words, however much they might help, could never banish her worry.

Talk to her, Peller had advised. But what could he say? He couldn't say Felipe would recover, for in truth the man looked weaker every time Dumas saw him. He couldn't distract her by changing the subject or pulling coins out of her ear. He could only stay close, offer her his shoulder to cry on, and say absolutely nothing. But silence might be worse than saying the wrong thing.

He felt utterly inadequate.

Montufar took a half-hearted sip of her drink and set it in the cup holder. "You're very quiet."

"So are you."

"I don't need to say much, do I?"

Dumas took her hand. "No. Do I?"

She picked a french fry from the bag, gave it a dull look, and dropped it back in. "It *was* my grandmother."

He could neither agree nor disagree, but curiosity got the better of him. "It's funny. I was thinking Sandra had told me. Or a memory of her, maybe. I don't know." He picked up his soda but didn't quite manage a drink of it.

"Intercessory prayer is a powerful thing. We're all together, living and dead, no matter what anyone says." She took a sip and put down her cup. "Maybe somehow, sometimes, we can sense others praying for us."

Had anyone else said it, Dumas would have thought them nuts. Coming from Montufar, he had to give it credence. *Because I trust her. She wouldn't lie to me.*

She drew a ragged breath. "But papá..." She picked up a napkin and dabbed at her eyes. "I'm not ready for this. I should be stronger. Why am I finding it so hard?"

"Because he's your father. Because you're human." He reached out and stroked her hair. "And you need sleep. You're exhausted."

She nodded without seeming to mean it.

He watched her in silence, wishing he could do something, anything, to lift her burden. Only one thing came to mind: hold her close, ensure she wasn't alone. "Do you want to stay at my place tonight?"

She hesitated. He had never asked her that before, and maybe he shouldn't have asked it now.

"No, I'm okay."

"You can if you want."

She shook her head. "It wouldn't be proper."

In his mind, he saw her wake in the middle of the night, alone and frightened, with nobody to hold back the winter dark. "Nobody will know."

"That's not the point."

Crumpling his sandwich wrapper, Dumas dropped it into the bag. He reached into his pocket where the little box with the ring awaited his resolve. He needed to do this. Now. For her if not for himself. "Corina—"

"It wouldn't be right."

His fingers froze on the ring box. He felt like he'd blundered off a cliff. How could he have given her such a wrong impression? He frowned at her, feeling stupid, but before he could find his voice she snapped, "Why does everyone think self-control is a dirty word?"

"Corina, I didn't mean—"

"I don't just live my life right because I think other people are watching. You should know that."

Now he was angry at himself for his verbal clumsiness as well as with her for mistaking his intent. "Damn it, Corina, you don't have to go to bed with me! I just don't think you should be alone under the circumstances. I didn't mean anything more than that."

Montufar knotted up her napkin and slam-dunked it into the bag. "I know. I'm just..." She ran a hand through her hair and pressed her head back against the headrest. "I'm sorry. Just take me home. I'll be all right."

Without another word Dumas drove her to her apartment. Neither of them said goodbye. Exhausted, he passed Ozzie's door without bothering to tiptoe, then struggled with the lock on his own door until it reluctantly surrendered. Once in, he slammed the door and threw himself at the living room couch.

He wasn't even sure what to think. He'd never as much as nudged Montufar towards more intimacy than she wanted. He'd denied his own desires—rather heroically, he thought—so she wouldn't feel pressured. He thought of nothing but her needs.

Don't lie to yourself, Eric. You're just running scared.

Yeah, and with good reason.

Dumas had been with just one woman, long ago. Full of life and song, she had a laugh that could blow every care out to sea. Two years after meeting her, he proposed to her and she said yes. He had never been so happy. She would become the family he had all but lost—she and their children and grandchildren as far into the future as he could imagine. But three months before the wedding, she threw him over for a fellow police officer who he'd counted as a friend. She might as well have dug out his heart with a soup ladle. Less than a month later, his Uncle Ethan had thrown him out for good.

The double betrayal plunged him into a deep isolation. Years passed while he dragged himself out of the emotional grave and struggled back toward the light. Even now he held most people at a distance, afraid to get too close. He couldn't survive another loss. It was better not to get involved.

Except that he had.

A gentle knock at the door interrupted his one-man pity party. Could Montufar have changed her mind? He doubted that but rushed the door, hoping against hope.

It wasn't her. Cameron Terrell smiled brightly at him, beautiful in a tight red sweater and tighter jeans. She waggled her fingers. "Hi there. I heard you come in."

Dumas couldn't reconcile her with his expectations. He stared dumbly at her, then looked behind her. No Montufar. Nor, for that matter, his neighbor. "Where's Ozzie?"

"Asleep. He had a long day." She smiled at the floor as though embarrassed, but Dumas had a feeling she wasn't a bit of it. "I'm afraid I finished wearing him out."

That wasn't anything he cared to hear. "What can I do for you?"

"Talk to me. I'm feeling lonely. Homesick. You know?"

Did he ever, and although he suspected it was a bad idea, he held the door open and motioned her in. "Just for a bit. I have to get some sleep, myself."

She slipped past him with a demure smile and looked around as she made her way into the living room. "Where's Corina?"

"Home."

"I thought she lived with you."

"Not yet." He thrust his hands into his pockets and touched the ring box. "Maybe someday." The door closed behind him as he followed her to the living room.

Cameron sat on the couch and patted it, inviting Dumas to sit beside her. He opted for one of the chairs instead, which didn't seem to faze her. "I like your place. It's so simple, so peaceful. It's like just full of spiritual energy."

"You're from California, aren't you?" he asked without thinking, then rather wished he hadn't. The stereotype might be insulting.

"Why yes! I was born in Pasadena and lived most of my life in that area. How did you know?"

Dumas leaned back and studied her face. She was easygoing if nothing else. And even at this late hour she glowed, maybe because her makeup was perfect. She must spend a lot of time in front of the mirror. "You just have that California air about you."

"Were you ever there?"

"Once, briefly."

"Where?"

He didn't want to talk about it. Except for Montufar, he'd never told a soul. "A short vacation in the Sierra Nevada." He hoped that would put an end to it.

"I love the mountains. I could spend my whole life there." She sighed, pushed herself into the cushion, and arched her back.

The juxtaposition of words and action might have been unintentional, might have been suggestion. Dumas suspected the latter. "So what are you doing here in Maryland?"

"Trying to make a living, same as you. You're doing better than me, though. Ozzie showed me your newspaper story."

Dumas wished he'd never agreed to Collins' project. "Don't believe everything you read."

"Oh, but it's fascinating! I'll bet you'll have the case solved in no time!"

"I don't know about that."

Cameron leaned forward, elbows resting on her knees, chin cupped in her hands. Her eyes sparkled. Dumas couldn't help but look. And hate himself for looking. "The article said you were closing in on a suspect."

How could he cut short her seduction scene and get her out of his apartment? He didn't want to offend Ozzie by giving her too severe a boot—no doubt word of her innocent visit and Dumas' overreaction would get back to White—but he might have no choice. "No, it didn't. It said I was interviewing a number of persons of interest."

"Oh." She looked disappointed for a moment, then brightened. "But that's progress, right?"

"A little." He decided to go official on her. Maybe that would put her off and she'd go home. "I can't comment on an ongoing investigation."

No such luck. "I understand. We can talk about other things." Her eyes suggested she had other things on her mind anyway.

"Look, I may be reading you wrong, but…" He shifted uncomfortably.

She licked her lips and smiled. "How are you reading me?"

"Ozzie is my friend, Cameron. And anyway, Corina and I..."

She waited, but when he didn't finish she looked down, embarrassed. "I'm sorry. You probably think I'm horrible."

"It's just..." He motioned helplessly.

"No, I really do understand. Some people like committed relationships. Some of us, well you know." She tilted her head as if looking for him to understand in turn. "Don't worry about Ozzie. I've been up front with him. He knows I find you attractive. He's cool with it."

Dumas couldn't reconcile that with the Ozzie he knew. It was easier to assume Cameron was lying. But then, one never knew about people.

Changing subjects, Cameron asked, "You got anything to drink around here?" Before he could answer, she was halfway to the kitchen.

He followed, hoping to keep her from rummaging through everything. "Not alcohol, if that's what you mean."

She stopped and turned so quickly he almost collided with her. "Well come on, let's go get something! I'll buy."

"I mean I don't drink."

Her eyebrows nearly hit the ceiling. "Why not?"

"Alcohol killed a few of my friends."

She stared at him as though unable to comprehend a life without booze. "Well hell, what do you do for fun?"

He'd had enough. "Interview persons of interest," he snapped.

Her eyes popped wide and her mouth worked silently. Then she laughed a high, squeaky laugh. "So I have to commit a crime to get you interested in me?" She winked. "I'll get to work on that."

"No chance. I'm booked solid for the next few days. I'll probably have to search the whole state for that couple I couldn't find earlier today." His irritation had come completely out of hiding, and he didn't care.

Cameron didn't take offense. Instead, her eyes filled with pity. "You're exhausted. I'm sorry, Eric. I'll go." She leaned forward and pecked him on the cheek. "That's for friendship, nothing more. Honest."

Dumas stood as still as stone while she sashayed to the door, waved her little wave, and faded into the darkness of the hall. He touched the spot on his cheek where she'd kissed him. Without a doubt, he'd just blundered through his strangest night in a very long time. Now that she was gone and quiet enveloped him, he wasn't quite sure how he felt about her, but he was very sure of one thing: he'd better not tell Montufar about any of this. He didn't want her convicted of murder before he could propose.

*

Alone in her apartment, Montufar changed into a long flannel nightgown, took her rosary in hand, and sat cross-legged in bed. She wished she hadn't snapped at Dumas. He'd only been concerned for her well-being. She knew he'd never ask for something she couldn't give. She'd never met anyone so considerate, so much in control of himself, and yet she'd accused him of being practically an animal.

She also knew about his troubled past: how his father and then his mother left; how his cousin had become ensnared in selling illegal drugs and how Dumas had turned him in; how in anger over that his Uncle Ethan had exiled him. Rejection had made him distant. She could tell that he wanted her as much as she wanted him, but he couldn't bring himself to make the commitment she needed. *It wouldn't take much*, she said to herself, as though he were beside her. *Just ask me to marry you. You know I'll say yes.*

Or maybe she should do the asking. The traditional little girl in her said that wasn't how it was supposed to work, but maybe the time had come to throw tradition out the window. She'd only be helping him do what he wanted.

She looked at the clock: almost midnight. Propping the pillows behind her, she settled back against them, cleared her mind and began to pray the Rosary. She prayed it for her father, for her departed mother, for the man she loved.

In the midst of prayer she fell asleep against the pillows, and slept deeply.

*

For Peller, evening passed in blissful quiet until the phone call came.

He stopped at the grocery store on the way home and picked up a roasted chicken and some microwavable mixed vegetables for dinner. After zapping the veggies, he ate at his small kitchen table, cleaned up, and settled in his recliner in the family room with a Zane Grey western. By the time he'd read a couple of chapters, his eyelids had grown heavy, but he didn't feel like trudging upstairs to bed. He could sleep just as well here, and he might have had his cell phone not gone off. In his semi-somnambulistic state he didn't check the number before answering.

"Lieutenant Peller?" a baritone voice said cheerfully. "This is Winston Marley, no relation to Jacob or Bob." The man laughed at his own joke. "I hope this isn't a bad time?"

That woke him. He'd been waiting to hear from the Bahá'í. He sat forward and blinked the sleep from his eyes. "It's fine, Mr. Marley. Thank you for calling."

"Please, call me Winston. I don't stand on formality." The man's resonant voice conjured up the image of an old-fashioned black southern minister, genteel and authoritative all at once.

Peller set his book on the end table next to him and raised the recliner to upright. "I understand you knew Jayvon Fletcher."

"I did. Jayvon's a bright young man. I'm sorry to hear he's missing."

"You didn't know?"

"No. When he stopped coming to our events, I called a few times, both his cell phone and his home phone, but he never got back to me. It did strike me as odd. He'd been so interested in the Faith before, but sometimes people change their minds. If so, it wasn't my place to bug him."

Peller thought that was a refreshing point of view. "How did you meet Jayvon?" He already knew some of the backstory but was interested in how Marley would tell it.

"He called our information number and asked about our activities. We invited him to a fireside—an informal discussion, that is—at my home. That's where I met him."

"What did you talk about? Did he ask a lot of questions?"

"I can't say I recall the exact subject that evening, but yes, he had a million questions. He'd read about the Bahá'í Faith online and wanted to know everything about everything." Marley laughed at the memory. "I'll have to say, he did ask some strange questions."

"Like what?"

"Evil interested him." Before Peller could react, Marley corrected, "That came out wrong. I mean, evil seemed to puzzle him."

Given the pictures everyone drew about Fletcher, Peller had trouble imagining he'd even heard of the concept. "Can you be more specific?"

"Let's see." Marley thought for a moment. "I remember he wanted to know if we believe in demon possession. That had something to do with a young lady he knew. I think a friend told him to stay away from her because she was possessed. Jayvon must've taken it seriously."

If Peller wasn't already fully awake, that did the trick. Shifting to the edge of his seat, he asked, "What did you tell him?"

Marley chuckled. "It threw me for a loop. I think I just said no and babbled a bit about how evil comes from being ruled by our passions, whereas good comes from turning to God and letting Him guide us."

"No demons, then?"

"Nope. If you want to see Satan, just look in the mirror."

"How did he take that?"

"It didn't divert him. He kept harping on it. I think we all got a bit irritated, and finally one of us gave him some stuff to read on the subject."

"Did you ever convince him?"

"I don't know, Lieutenant. He didn't bring it up again."

"What about this girlfriend's name?" Peller asked. "Did he ever mention it?"

"Not that I remember."

Weird as it sounded, Peller had a feeling it was important. He made a note to ask Mrs. Fletcher about the woman. But for now, he moved on. "I spoke with Jayvon's mother recently. She didn't seem to approve of his association with your group."

"No," Marley admitted without hesitation. "She was never too happy to see us."

"Why not?"

He paused, and Peller wondered if he'd struck a nerve. People could be touchy and downright defensive about their versions of the truth. But the answer came calm and reasoned. "Some people fear the unknown. And she's a devout Christian. She probably thought we were leading Jayvon astray."

"That's what she told me," Peller said. "That you were leading Jayvon away from Jesus."

"No, we wouldn't do that. We believe in Jesus. But we don't believe that revelation stopped with him. The Bahá'í view of Jesus differs from the Christian view, that's all."

Peller wondered how different it was but didn't think it important right now. "Let's get back to Jayvon for a minute. When was the last time you talked to him?"

"I knew you were going to ask that," Marley said with a forced laugh. "I've been wracking my brains trying to remember. It's a bit hazy, but I think it was about two years ago, maybe a week or two before Christmas. He was interested in studying the *Kitáb-i-Iqán*. That's Bahá'u'lláh's primary theological work. Since he was interested I asked him to host the study, which he did. We met at his place about every other week for two or three months. He drank it up by the gallon, but then for no apparent reason he dropped off the face of the Earth. I was surprised and not a little frustrated. He didn't return my calls or emails. If his mother got any of the messages, she didn't return them, either. But I don't guess she would. Eventually we decided courtesy required us to let him go."

"You didn't drop by his place?"

"Once, but nobody was home. Or nobody answered the door, anyway."

"One last question," Peller said. "At that last gathering, did anything about Jayvon strike you as amiss?"

Marley didn't answer at once, and again Peller wished he could see the man's face. "Not that I recall. It was just another session. He seemed as happy and as interested as ever. Frankly, Lieutenant, I'm baffled. I can't think of any reason why he'd cut off contact with us, or run away from home, or anything like that. It occurred to me he might have been in an accident. I suppose you know more than you're telling, but if you can tell me, I'd like to know. I like Jayvon. He's a good guy. Wherever he is, I hope he's all right."

Peller scooted back in the chair. "I appreciate your time, Winston. I may have more questions later or need to meet with you. Can you be available?"

"Anything I can do to help," Marley promised, and he sounded sincere.

Afterward, Peller leaned the recliner back and ruminated for a time. The Bahá'í angle wouldn't pan out. He was sure of that. Their websites talked about unity and peace and justice and equality. The two adherents he'd talked to seemed decent enough people, interested in helping him ferret out Jayvon's fate. Moreover, they seemed to paint the same picture of Jayvon that his grandmother had, in spite of their religious differences. Even if their group self-portrait proved too good to be true, he doubted anything more sinister than solid PR lurked behind it.

But a demon-possessed girlfriend? Now that inspired some scenarios.

He fell asleep in his chair while pondering the implications.

He woke with a start from a dream in which a masked, shadowy figure held a flint knife over a struggling man bound to a table that ran black with blood. He shook away the dream and nodded off again, only to have it return. Opening his bleary eyes, he tried to focus on the familiar, but instead of his family room he saw a glow of light, and immersed in the light the hint of a face he knew and loved. She smiled, and though her lips remained still he heard her voice, calm and soothing: *That's enough of that. Go back to sleep.*

11

"Oh. My. God."

Friday morning, January twentieth, the fifth day of Dumas' investigation into the murder of Michio Tamai, and he felt like a truck had run him over. He sat at his desk, head cradled in both hands, and stared at his computer monitor. A few minutes earlier, the demonic contraption had locked up. He had turned it off and back on, and now it was refusing to boot, giving him instead some bizarre message about checking the disk. That's all he needed on top of his massive headache and even more massive lack of sleep. What time had it been, anyway, before he'd managed to doze off? Well after three A.M., he was sure of that much. Maybe four. His encounter with Cameron Terrell had rattled him more than he'd realized at the time.

Peller happened by just as he moaned his complaint to the divine. The lieutenant paused, peered down at him, and observed, "You look like hell."

Dumas raised his bleary eyes. "No, really?" And then he noticed that Peller, standing less straight than usual, circles under his eyes, could have been his mirror image. "So do you. What happened?"

"Bad dreams. I'd blame it on talking to a Bahá'í, but he was just the messenger."

Dumas leaned back and ran a somewhat shaky hand through his hair. "That makes about as much sense as what happened to me. What's a Bahá'í? A bohemian on drugs?"

"A follower of a religion called the Bahá'í Faith."

Dumas had glommed onto bits and pieces of several religions during his long quest, so the mention of a new one piqued his interest. Before he could ask questions, though, Peller realized what was coming and shook his head. "Never mind," Dumas told him. "I'll look it up myself. What did this guy tell you that gave you nightmares?"

"Seems Jayvon Fletcher had his eye on a demon-possessed girl."

That sure got Dumas' attention. He could feel his eyes bulging, cartoon-like. He straightened. "What, like in *The Exorcist*?"

"Probably not. One of Jayvon's friends used the word to describe her and he apparently took it seriously. I got to thinking about it, pondering implications and possibilities. And so..." Peller shrugged. "Bad dreams."

Dumas couldn't decide if that was scary or funny or a bit of both. "You could have thought about something pleasant, like fishing or hiking in the Rockies with your grandkids." But now that the subject had been broached, he couldn't help thinking about it himself, at least long enough to wonder if demon possession might explain Cameron's visit. *Don't be absurd*, he scolded himself.

Peller sighed wearily and sank into the chair by the desk. "I guess I'm a bit obsessed with Jayvon's fate. I'm afraid he was one of the bad guys, and I don't want him to be."

That, at least, Dumas could understand. Nobody wanted to tell a woman like Wanda Fletcher that her grandson had gone bad. "But demon possession? Do you even believe in that?"

Peller's eyelids drooped further. "No. But it's a lead."

"You're not really going to pursue it, are you?"

"Why're you being so literal, Eric? You've heard as much hyperbole as the rest of us. One of Jayvon's friends thought he was attracted to a bad news woman. That's all."

"Some people might mean it literally." Dumas wondered if Montufar was one of them. Catholics dealt in demons and exorcism, didn't they?

Peller, eyes closed now, shook his head. "Anyway, I might ask his grandmother, see if I can at least get the woman's name so I can locate her and have a little chat about her missing boyfriend."

The computer still wasn't cooperating. To encourage it, Dumas slapped the monitor. "Stupid thing." He powered off the machine again. "Instead of chasing ghosts, how would you like to do some actual work?"

"Like what?"

"Help me interview a scary couple."

Peller opened his eyes and watched while Dumas punched the computer's power button. "You think two exhausted cops are better than one?"

The computer beeped. This time, it seemed to be reluctantly cooperating. Dumas patted it gently and crooned.

When his colleague didn't answer, Peller added, "So what happened to you, then? Someone spike your mineral water?"

Dumas didn't want to talk about it or think about it or even remember it. He still didn't see how Ozzie could live with Cameron's antics, although he'd about convinced himself that desperation might drag his neighbor down some weird paths. "Don't ask."

"You and Corina didn't—"

"I don't want to talk about it."

Peller looked away. "So what makes this couple so scary?"

The computer was now applying operating system updates and cheerfully told Dumas to wait just a few moments. "Harold and Hannah Bellamy, associates of Michio Tamai. I spoke yesterday with a nice young lady who used to beat people up for Tamai. Being a good girl, she's gone straight and taken up boxing."

"Of course," Peller murmured sarcastically. "What else?"

"She said Tamai might call upon the Bellamy couple for debt collection services. They creeped her out the one time she met them."

"Why?"

"Nothing specific, just the way they looked at her. I don't know what that means. Maybe nothing. They might have found her as weird as she found them."

"Great. I dream about satanic rituals and you want me to meet creepy people."

"You can say no." Dumas hoped he wouldn't—Peller had a knack for noticing what escaped others—but given his miserable condition this morning, it was only fair to offer him an out.

"Nah. Sounds interesting. When are you going?"

"Right away." He whacked at the computer again, which persisted in cheerfully asking him to wait a few moments. "They weren't home yesterday afternoon. Maybe they will be this morning."

"You driving?"

The prospect of facing down Maryland drivers in his condition horrified Dumas. "Are you nuts?"

Peller rose and fished his keys out of his pocket. "If we die, it's your fault."

"I can live with that."

As they reached the door, Montufar rushed in from the cold. Seeing them, she slammed on the brakes. "Oh, Eric." She glanced at Peller, then looked away. "Um."

Alarmed, Dumas took hold of her shoulders, momentarily forgetting that others might be watching. "Your dad?"

"No." She glanced at Peller again who, taking the cue, walked outside to give them privacy.

"If it's about last night," Dumas said, then couldn't finish. He felt utterly stupid about the way he'd talked to her. It pained him that Montufar didn't seem to be able to meet his eyes. He must have hurt her more than he realized, but they couldn't talk about it here. They'd need privacy, and anyway he had to corner the Bellamys. "Look, Rick and I have to go. We can talk over lunch, okay?"

She started to object, then backed up a step, freeing herself from his grip, and nodded.

"See you shortly." He hurried after Peller. Only as they pulled out of the parking lot did it occur to him that he'd probably done something stupid yet again.

*

After the brush-off, Montufar felt worse than ever about how she'd treated Dumas the previous night. He had every right to be angry with her, but she could neither apologize nor make amends until he returned. Moreover, she had no time to brood. The prior year's arsons beckoned. The revelation that Vincent Dibble had been blackmailed opened new paths for exploration. From Trengove she'd learned that Karla York had received a threatening note prior to the fire. She got to wondering: could that fire have been fallout from a blackmail plot, too? She looked up York's cell number in the files and placed the call. York answered on the third ring, her voice crackling over a poor connection.

"Ms. York, this is Detective Sergeant Corina Monutfar with the Howard County police."

"Oh lord." She nearly squeaked the words. "He's not out already, is he?"

"No, not at all. I just need some information. There's been another arson that looks very similar. We're concerned there might be a connection. Could I stop by either your workplace or your home today?"

The signal faded in and out, and all Montufar could hear was "store" and something that sounded like "baboon." She pushed the phone tighter against her ear, as though that might help. "I'm sorry, you broke up there."

"I said I'm on the way to the store, but should be back about noon. Do you have my address?"

Montufar did—a home north of Fulton off Pindel School Road—and read it off to make sure it was right.

"That's the one."

"Thank you, I really appreciate it." As she hung up, she felt someone hovering behind her. Swiveling her chair around, she found Trengove's stony gaze boring into her. "What's up?" she asked.

"What can she tell you after all this time?" He didn't sound annoyed, or at least no more than usual.

"I don't know, but there's blackmail behind the current case."

His eyebrows arched upward. "No kidding."

"Nope."

Trengove looked as though he'd bitten into a green persimmon. "Mind if I tag along?"

She picked up her purse and stood. "Why not?"

"But, ah, I'm driving." His eyes challenged her to object.

She shrugged herself into her coat. "You don't like my little red car?"

His mouth maintained its grumpy demeanor, but a sparkle lit up his eyes. "I don't like your driving."

Montufar gave as good as she got. "So long as we get there before midnight."

"The point is, we'll get there alive." Shoving his hands into his pockets, Trengove led Montufar to his desk so he could don his own cold weather gear, a heavy black coat with a warm hood. As he zipped up, he studied her face, which she kept intentionally bland for him, until he cracked a rare lopsided smile. "Too bad I'm married. I could fall for a lady like you."

This time Montufar was afraid to even attempt a comeback. She'd probably blurt out something that would get the whole department talking, which would further bloat Dumas' anger. Trengove frowned at her uncharacteristic lack of retort but didn't question it.

Outside, an arctic blast streamed the flags full-length and violently shook the bare branches. The sky was filled with ragged, racing fragments of cloud. "Oh!" Montufar shrieked. "I hate this weather!" She turned her head sideways, but it didn't help. The wind slapped her cheek so hard she was sure it would leave a mark.

Trengove gallantly stepped to windward and put an arm about her shoulders, pulling her against his side. "Look down at your shoes," he instructed. "We'll be in the car in a moment."

She did as he said, and to her surprise the maneuver helped.

Once he'd packed her into the passenger seat, he trotted around and got in behind the wheel. The car, a 1997 Accura Integra of a color Trengove liked to call "stealth gray," coughed before coming to life. "It heats up pretty quick," he said as Montufar rubbed her hands together to warm them. "You just have to learn how to get around in the wind, that's all."

"This is the worst winter on Earth."

"Nah, only in the mid-Atlantic. If you want to see rough winters, you have to go at least to Minnesota. And I'll bet Canadians sneer at that." He backed out of the parking space.

"I don't know how they stand it."

Trengove didn't explain but said with some bitterness, "Turns out my son had the right idea after all."

Montufar wondered what that meant. She recalled Trengove's son was in college, but little more.

"He took off for Australia with some friends. They decided it would be cool to explore the outback instead of going to college this winter. Against my wishes. But I sure wouldn't mind being with them right now. It's summer down under, you know."

"You could have gone," Montufar told him. "You've got enough vacation accrued, don't you?"

"You've been looking at my pay stubs, maybe?"

"I don't have to. You're a workaholic. You never take time off."

Trengove turned west on U.S. 40 and passed by an expanse of car dealerships on the right. "That's the trouble with working alongside a bunch of hotshot detectives," he grumbled. "But you might have noticed that I took off December twenty-fifth." Before she could respond to the wisecrack, he added, "And November eighteenth. That was our twenty-fifth anniversary. I took Catherine all the way up to Lancaster County. She loves all things Amish."

Montufar found it touching that such a gruff man would do something so caring for his wife. It wasn't a big thing, but it must have meant a great deal to her. "Twenty-five years," she mused aloud. "What's it like being married that long?"

He pondered the question before answering, "I have no idea." Trengove veered onto the ramp to U.S. 29 southbound.

Montufar couldn't help but laugh.

He glanced at her in rebuke. "I'm serious. I can't imagine not being married to her by now. It's just business as usual."

She found that disturbing somehow, but couldn't quite put her finger on the reason. She didn't think Trengove took Catherine for granted, but to call marriage business as usual stripped it of its sanctity and magic.

Trengove's eyes fixated on the road ahead. "I'm surprised you don't at least have a boyfriend."

"Why?" She blurted it without thinking, then wished she hadn't.

"For God's sake, Corina, you're beautiful, smart, caring, funny, and I don't know how many other fine things. There must be a million men out there who'd be happy to—" He stopped short, maybe even blushed, although in the winter light it was hard to tell.

She couldn't help but grin at him. "Happy to what?"

"I'm sorry, I shouldn't talk like that."

"It's okay, Bill. I'm not offended."

"There, see? That's exactly the kind of thing I mean. Most guys you'd skewer for saying that, but you take pity on old Bill. You're not half as cold as you pretend."

Now she was embarrassed, too.

He turned a corner and grumbled, "Why the hell hasn't Eric asked you out? He's eligible and probably knows you better than anyone in the department other than Rick, who's hopelessly lost in the past, not to mention too old for you. Like me."

Montufar gave a sort of horrified giggle. The sound was ghastly, and she put a hand over her mouth to stifle it.

Trengove glanced at her in alarm. "Are you all right?"

She nodded but kept her mouth covered.

He squinted at her before turning his eyes back to the road. "Oh, good Lord. I should learn to keep my mouth shut."

Trengove had figured it out; Montufar wondered how many others had as well. Their secret was exposed at last. More fuel for Dumas' anger, probably. But now that Trengove knew, she wondered why either of them should care. They couldn't keep it hidden forever, nor should they. Before it had been a form of protection while they fumbled into their relationship, but those days were over. Why not let the whole world know?

She found she could only echo Trengove's own words: "That's the trouble with working alongside a bunch of hotshot detectives."

Trengove allowed himself another twisted smile, his second in one day. "That Dumas. He always was lucky."

*

For three miles Pindell School Road undulated gently up and down heavily treed hills. It had the appearance of land cleared for farming during Maryland's colonial era but long since repossessed by the forest. Now much of it had been cleared again, sectioned into housing developments by companies seeking a comfortable profit from farmettes sold to urban elites who had never seen a cow or a silo.

It was clear they had arrived at the place they sought when they spied a great stone sign bearing the name Pindell Chase. An assortment of petite evergreens and leafless shrubs surrounding it shivered pitifully in the wind.

Trengove eyed the real estate. "Welcome to Green Acres. Must be rough."

"Did the Yorks live here at the time of the fire?" Montufar asked.

"No, but they had a place about like this not too far from here. They moved here, rebuilt the old homestead with the insurance money, and then sold it. The financial juggling makes my head spin."

"And the other victims?"

"They all live in this general area and pretend to be lords. Whether or not filthy lucre made them happy is another story."

"The Dibble fire fits the pattern."

Trengove made a face. "I fairly hate where you're going with this."

The remark puzzled Montufar. It seemed clear enough to her; the connections were too strong, too neat. "Why?"

"Quite aside from the shattering blow to my fragile male ego, if you're right the real bad guys are still out there."

She smiled at him, although he wasn't looking. When she first met Trengove, she'd been a bit afraid of him, but over time she'd learned to like him and even become endeared to his mannerisms. "The bad guys are always out there, Bill."

"Yeah, I know. London, Munich, Moscow, 'Nam. Here. Maybe we should thank them for keeping us cops off the unemployment line, but do they have to burn down decent people's houses? You know what Howard County needs?"

"What?"

"More white-collar crime. If we could convince the thieves and thugs to turn over a new leaf and skim money from the First Global Bank of Satan, we'd still have jobs but nobody would get hurt."

Montufar laughed. "You want to run that by the captain? There's the house." She pointed to a beautiful stone-fronted home on the left set well back from the road amidst a scattering of trees. The long, curving driveway, perfectly cleared of snow, was lined with low hedges jutting up from the white blanket. An uncollected newspaper lay rolled up ten feet from the road.

Trengove pulled in and drove up to the five-car garage. "Last time I suggested something like that, she told me to take the afternoon off and get some rest." He stopped the car and they got out. Montufar found herself once more in a life-and-death struggle with the icy wind. At the massive oak front door, Trengove rang the bell.

Mercifully, Karla York wasn't long in opening it. "You picked a great day to visit," she quipped as she waved them in out of the cold.

Montufar looked over her host. She was a sleek woman, an inch taller than Trengove, with blonde hair falling over her shoulders in ringlets. Montufar thought she might be in her mid-forties. She looked elegant in a deep green 1940s-style dress that flowed gracefully to white heels. If she hadn't known they were coming, Montufar would have expected her to say she was just on her way to the opera.

After introductions, she led them to the living room, a wide space furnished with three separate seating groups whose eclectic styles complemented each other. "Let's sit here by the window," she said. "I like looking out on cold days. From the warmth of the house." She smiled mischievously.

Montufar sat on the end of the loveseat, Trengove in a chair to her left, and York on the sofa across from her. "I'm very interested in the note you received prior to the fire," Montufar said. "Lieutenant Trengove filled me in, but I'd like to hear how you remember it."

"Oh, that. At the time I thought nothing of it. I threw it away."

"Do you remember what it said?"

"Not exactly. Something like, 'Nice house. It might catch fire. Pay your insurance and it won't.'"

"You didn't take that seriously?"

York wrung her hands. "I wish I had, but no. It seemed so childish. Some of the neighborhood kids were pranksters, so I thought it was their doing."

"You hadn't received any other threats, even childish ones, prior to this?"

"No, and to be honest it's puzzled me ever since. It sounds like a demand for money, but it was totally out of the blue. No specific amount, no instructions, no nothing."

Out of the blue? Montufar doubted that, and glancing at Trengove she could see he was thinking the same thing now. But with Carl

Bradley incarcerated, that little detail must have seemed unimportant—until the Dibble arson and Peller's discovery of the associated blackmail. "You're married and have three children, is that correct?"

"That's right," York replied. "Two sons and a daughter. Our oldest son is away at college."

"Good boy," Trengove said irritably, and York's eyebrows shot up in surprise.

"Don't mind him," Montufar said with a grin. "He's got a college-age son, too. What about the other two?"

"They're both in high school, senior and sophomore years. Why do you ask?"

"There's no easy way to put this. Another arson has occurred. It looks very much the same as what happened to your family, but with a twist: the husband was being blackmailed. We think the fire was retaliation after he stopped paying."

York's hands flew to her mouth. "Oh my God. And you think—"

"We don't know yet. It's a possibility. If you don't know anything about it, maybe your husband was the target, or maybe one of the children, if they have access to enough money."

"Not without Stan or myself knowing. But that's too awful to even think about!"

Trengove leaned forward. "It doesn't necessarily mean any of your family did anything wrong."

"That's right," Montufar added. "It could have been a setup. That's what happened to the other family."

York looked lost, as though the revelation had upended everything she thought stable in her life. Montufar began to wish they'd never come here. She hated planting the seeds of doubt in the minds of people who appeared to have sound, happy marriages. She wondered if she and Dumas could ever be tormented by such doubts.

"I can talk to your husband about it," Trengove offered. "You don't have to."

Somehow, York found her bearings again, composed herself, and quietly refused his help. "Thank you, but no. This is something I have to do."

"You're sure?"

She nodded. "It'll be okay. I trust Stan. Whatever happened, I'm sure he's not to blame. What..." She straightened her skirt and bravely met Montufar's eyes. "What did the blackmailer have over the other family?"

Montufar didn't want to answer but wasn't about to lie to York, either. "Photographs of the husband talking with a young woman in a bar."

"That's all?"

"That's all, but they were timed to look incriminating."

"I see." York's fear had evaporated, leaving behind severe determination. Montufar understood the look. She wasn't going to let anything threaten her family. "I'll talk to Stan. I'll find out what if anything happened and let you know right away. And if anything did happen, I hope you catch whoever's responsible. I'll be there to cheer at the sentencing."

*

The dim stairwell outside of Harold and Hannah Bellamy's apartment, Dumas mused, felt even gloomier this morning than it had the previous afternoon. The wind penetrated the shaft, stirring a few stray scraps of paper someone had dropped on the steps. Dumas rapped on the door while Peller studied their surroundings, then asked, "What do you see?"

"A dark stairwell," Peller replied. "What do you see?"

"All joy freezing out of the air."

Peller looked up at the ceiling as though considering the concept. "Interesting image."

A clattering arose inside as a chain was undone and the deadbolt unlocked. The door slowly opened to reveal a tall, muscular young man. His wavy dark hair and square jaw somehow said movie star, while his expression was so blank Dumas thought he must have just woke from a sound sleep. He was dressed, though, in black jeans and a black turtleneck. He directed that blank gaze at Dumas for a moment, then at Peller, then said, "Hi."

"Harold Bellamy?" Dumas asked, and the other nodded slowly. Displaying his shield, he continued, "Howard County police. I'm Detective Sergeant Eric Dumas, this is Detective Lieutenant Rick Peller. We need to have a talk with you and, if possible, Mrs. Bellamy."

He stared as though not comprehending, then stepped back. "Come in, then." Leading them into the living room, he pointed to a beige sofa. "Hannah will be awake." He vanished into the recesses of the apartment.

"Late sleepers," Dumas commented quietly as he and Peller studied the apartment. It was simple and clean, with worn furnishings. Aside from the couch, there were two matching chairs, equally old, equally used. The chairs faced the sofa, but there were no tables, no place to set a cup of coffee or snacks. The dining area held only an empty dinette table and two chairs. A modest flat-screen television hung on the white wall, but nothing else. No photos, no artwork. It made Dumas' apartment feel luxurious.

Harold Bellamy returned with his wife, a beautiful woman much shorter than he, on his arm. She seemed to glide rather than walk. Soundlessly, she and her husband took chairs across from the detectives. Dumas began to understand Angelina Peralta's discomfort in their presence. Their eyes held no interest, no curiosity, no fear. Nothing whatsoever. He almost felt they were looking through the whole world.

"Good morning," Mrs. Bellamy finally said. Her cultured voice was colored with a faint accent Dumas couldn't place. Boston? England? "What can we do for you?"

"A friend of yours, Michio Tamai, has been murdered," Dumas told them. The pair didn't react. The silence felt eerie, as though he'd been walking through the forest when suddenly wind and birds and every creeping thing had fallen still. "That doesn't seem to surprise you."

"Not in the least," Hannah said. "Mike had enemies."

At least she wasn't denying their connection with Tamai. "Why is that?"

"He took advantage of people."

"Did he take advantage of you?"

Hannah shook her head. Strangely her eyes didn't seem to move along. They maintained a laser focus aimed towards but not on Dumas' face.

"Why not?"

She shrugged, and Harold shrugged in synchrony.

This wasn't natural. Were they drugged? More to the point, were they even human? Dumas felt a primal urge to run. "What was the nature of your relationship with Tamai?"

"We performed various tasks for him," Hannah replied in her cool voice.

"Tasks. Illegal jobs?"

Harold held up a defensive hand. "We will not answer questions like that until we have a lawyer."

"We already know the nature of Tamai's activities," Dumas snapped. "Your names are in a book he kept. You're marked as special, along with a few others, all of whom were involved in his schemes. You were his partners in crime."

Hannah pushed Harold's hand down. "Officers," she said, her voice faintly scornful. "You certainly understand that we cannot answer these questions unless a lawyer is present."

Dumas met her empty eyes with a hard glare, but to no avail. He wondered what she saw. It certainly wasn't him.

Peller leaned forward into the silence, focused on Hannah. She must have noticed but didn't bother acknowledging his attention. Then he nodded to Harold and asked, "How did you two meet?"

The change of subject didn't throw Harold off balance. It seemed to Dumas the man had no need of balance. No force in the universe could move him except perhaps one, and she was seated next to him.

"At college."

"Did you have a class together?"

"I saw her in a play."

"What play?"

Hannah interrupted. "Is this relevant, Lieutenant?"

"You interest me," Peller replied. "I've never met a couple quite like you."

"You never met a couple deeply in love?"

Dumas glanced at Peller. Hannah couldn't have known about Sandra, but her words might sting.

Peller gave no hint of that. "Sure."

"Not like us. He is all that exists for me. I am all that exists for him. You are not here. This conversation is not happening. You cannot understand that, can you?" She slowly turned her head to look at Peller but once more didn't seem to notice what was right before her eyes.

"I think I can," Peller told her.

A hairline crack opened in Hannah's control, just for a moment. For that one moment, surprise overtook her. But she forced it away, and the breach sealed.

Dumas wondered whether Peller was telling the truth or just trying to rattle her. Whatever the case, he took advantage, or tried. "You killed Michio Tamai, didn't you?"

Hannah's head moved in negation.

Dumas looked to Harold. "Then you did."

He likewise denied it without a word.

"If either of you did, we will find out. It would be much easier if you confessed right now."

The couple spoke not a word nor even gave any sign that they'd heard.

Dumas knew they'd get nothing more. He stood and flung his card into Hannah's lap. "If you have anything to tell me, call." He heard Peller rise, too, and as he turned to leave noticed his boss scrutinizing Hannah closely. The woman was oblivious to his attention.

Back in the warmth of the car, Dumas let out a long breath. "God, that was weird. What do you think?"

"You said Tamai was killed with two clean shots," Peller mused. "Any word on the weapon?"

"Yeah, a nine-millimeter that belonged to him. It had been stashed under the sofa where he was killed, thoroughly cleaned. No prints, no nothing."

Peller eyeballed the apartment building. "I'm thinking we need to watch them. Be on our guard. It was a cold killing. They're cold people."

"If they're even people." Dumas shook himself. "There's no emotion at all there. She said they love each other. I wonder if they actually do."

"Not like Sandra and I, not like you and Corina, but oh yes. They're addicted to each other. They care about nothing else. If Tamai had crossed one of them, the other would have had taken him down with neither thought nor remorse."

"That woman could kill without any weapon at all." Dumas gazed up at the building, too. "Too bad we don't have probable cause for a search warrant."

"You wouldn't find anything. That apartment feels like a ghost town. I'd check on their college background. Hannah didn't care for that subject."

Dumas nodded. "You think she's the brains of the outfit?"

"Could be. She did most of the talking. Whether or not she's book smart, she strikes me as deep."

Dumas put the car in reverse and pulled out of the parking space. "An actress. That whole thing might have been staged."

Peller looked out the side window for a time as Dumas drove. "Maybe," he finally said, "but I don't think so. Even if she was acting, I don't think Harold was. I think they really are that weird."

12

Two steps into the CID office, Dumas pulled off his coat and slung it over his arm. He'd committed himself, nerves notwithstanding, to talking to Montufar before anything else. But now he saw that she wasn't alone. Across the room, she and Trengove stood near the windows, close together, deep in conversation. Dumas felt his every muscle tense. Why would she let Trengove stand that close to her? Hot anger coursed through him. He had to turn away until it subsided.

What was happening to him? This bordered on lunacy. Montufar and Trengove were colleagues talking business, nothing more, certainly not replaying that ancient scene in which Dumas had lost the woman he loved. He had killed and interred that pain years ago in the Sierra wilderness. How had it clawed its way out of the earth and hunted him down? What motive had it for returning to torment him? Why couldn't the past simply die?

He probably should have joined them, but he couldn't. Instead, he returned to his desk and threw himself into his work. He looked up the smattering of area colleges and in short order compiled a list of their registrars' phone numbers. He'd just set hand to phone, ready to place the first call, when it rang. Startled, he jerked his hand back, stared at the possessed device while it rang twice more, then snatched up the receiver. "Dumas," he snapped.

"Sergeant?" the caller, a man, said tentatively.

"Yes."

"Charlie Sheffield. You told me to call you."

He had indeed. "Right. When can you come by?"

"I get off work at three today. I can be at the station about four?"

Sheffield sounded so cowed that Dumas nearly felt pity for him. "I'll be here. You need directions?"

"No. I've been there before."

Obviously, Dumas thought. "All right, Mr. Sheffield, I'll see you then." Neither bothered with a goodbye. Dumas pressed the switch and released it. The tone buzzed in his ear, but before he could dial the first college number, Montufar appeared at his side and slipped into her usual position on his desk.

"Hey there," she said quietly.

He swallowed and looked up, forcing himself to smile. "Hey there."

"We still on for lunch?"

He'd completely forgotten. Once more, he felt like an idiot. "Sure. What takes your fancy?"

"How about our Chinese place?"

She couldn't have chosen better under the circumstances. Dumas pushed himself to his feet. "You got it." he said, then offered, "I'll drive." It wasn't much of an offer, but he owed her something.

Montufar pretended to pout. "Even *you* don't like my driving."

"I was just trying to…" It came out more snappish than he'd intended. The corners of her mouth drooped, this time genuinely. Shoulders slumped, Dumas mumbled, "Sorry. I had a bizarre morning. I didn't mean…"

Montufar carefully slipped her arm through his and gave him a gentle tug. "Come on. You need a break."

He looked down at their entwined arms, wondering why she'd thrown caution to the wind. People would see and talk.

She understood. "Let's not hide anymore."

Right now he felt like hiding from the whole world, maybe even from her, but he nodded and they walked out together arm in arm, paying no heed to who saw or what they thought.

They drove to "their" Chinese place, a little family-owned storefront restaurant hidden away at the end of an unobtrusive strip mall. It had become their place to celebrate or commiserate or rejuvenate or just escape for a short time. Dumas ordered his usual General Tso's chicken and watched as Montufar skillfully wielded her chopsticks. The shrimp with lobster sauce never had a chance, and the ten-thumbed Dumas envied her talent. A few other diners, some in business suits some dressed casual, busied themselves with their meals. The place hummed with a low chatter.

They didn't talk aside from ordering until halfway through the meal when Montufar said without looking at him, "I'm sorry."

Surprised, he set down his fork. "You are?" He had no idea why she would be apologizing. Everything of late had been his fault.

"Shouldn't I be?" She looked up, as astonished as he.

He patted his mouth with his napkin to hide his confusion.

"About last night," she explained as though Dumas might have forgotten. "I know what you meant. I shouldn't have flipped out on you. I was just…" She made a vague motion.

"Scared and tired," he finished for her. "I know."

Montufar nodded and looked down again. "So I'm sorry."

"It wasn't your fault. I haven't done one thing right since we left the hospital last night. So I'm sorry, too."

She smiled at her meal. "We're pathetic, aren't we?"

"Irredeemably."

"There you go with the ten dollar words again." She picked up her napkin and nearly tied it in a knot.

The apologies should have resolved the tension, but something still hung between them, the source of all this fumbling, and Dumas knew what it was. He merely had to ask the question. No elaborate setup, no magic tricks, no gimmicks. Even the place was perfect. But still the words wouldn't come.

When he couldn't break the silence, she did. "I was wondering…" she began, but the sentence died a death as pathetic as his own attempts at speech.

Dumas gave up. He'd never get through it. Feeling more miserable than when they'd come in, he asked, "Wondering what?"

"Would you..." She looked up, studied his face, lowered her gaze.

Astonished, Dumas realized she was having her own crisis of inaction. What, he wondered, could she find so hard to ask?

"Would you come to mass with me on Sunday?" She winced as she said it, as though that hadn't been what she'd meant to ask, but continued in a breathless rush. "I mean, if you don't have anything going on. It starts at ten. You don't have to, but, well, it would be nice."

He certainly hadn't expected that request and had to wonder what really was on her mind. Yet maybe that was it, after all. It at least made sense. Her father was probably dying. She needed Dumas' strength and support to shore up the tottering structure of her life. After everything he'd done wrong over the past fourteen hours, he wasn't about to take another false step. It was too important. "Of course I'll come." He reached out and took her hands in his. Her fingers trembled in his. "Although, I might need some coaching. I've never set foot in a Catholic church."

Her only reply was to gently squeeze his hands, which Dumas took for a thank you. He squeezed back and wished for even a hint of a smile, but instead he got a puzzled frown. "Wait a minute. Your last name is French."

What did that have to do with anything? "My great-great-..." He released her long enough to count on his fingers. "...great-great-great-great-grandfather? I've lost track. However many greats he was, he came from Marseilles and settled in New France. His descendants lived in New Orleans for ages. I still have a few distant cousins there, I think. Most of the family scattered on the winds over time."

He could see her working out the implications. He knew that focused expression well. "So why aren't you Catholic?"

"Oh. The story is, my great-grandfather Charles Dumas had an altercation with his parish priest which ended with the irate father telling dear old granddad that he'd earned a one-way ticket to hell. Charles left the church, probably out of spite. They say he could be mule-headed. He took his whole family with him. I've always wondered how that sat with his wife.

Nobody ever mentioned her role in it. Since that time, most of my branch of the family has been Christmas-and-Easter Protestants, if that. I've heard that one of my cousins went the fire-and-brimstone route, but that may be an exaggeration. You'd be surprised what some of my relatives consider fundamentalist."

Montufar laughed. "They might not even think of them as Christian!" She squeezed his hand. "Now you've done it, you've made me laugh."

Dumas smiled and said in an atrocious French accent, "It is my job to amuse mademoiselle."

Montufar's expression returned to its pensive state. She picked up a chopstick and twirled it absently in her food. "So what are you today? I know you believe in something."

Dumas could almost feel Peller prodding an answer out of him: *Talk to her.* "I believe there's something out there, something bigger than any of us. Whatever it is, it's pure good, pure love, and I'm okay with calling it God. Most people mean pretty much the same thing by that word, from what I can tell. I also believe none of us have a very good handle on God. If we did, the world would be a lot different."

Montufar pushed back her half-full plate. "That's all?"

"In a nutshell. You don't want me to deliver a sermon on reality according to Eric Dumas. Or do you?"

Smiling, she shook her head. "I just mean I don't see how a do-it-yourself religion could give anybody much structure."

"It doesn't," he admitted. "But what about you? How long has it been?"

"How long since when?"

"Since you had structure. Since you went to church."

"Oh." She laid down the chopstick and sipped at her tea. Dumas gave her time. He felt as though he could give her all the time in the world just to prolong this moment. "The last mass I went to—that I actually *went to*, not just going through the motions because it was my cousin's wedding or something—was my mother's funeral Mass."

"When was that?"

"About eight years ago." She looked into his eyes but didn't seem to see him. "I was fourteen when we came to the U.S. Papá had a job with an engineering company in northern Virgina. We lived in Gaithersburg then. I went to a Catholic high school and attended Mass every Sunday and said grace at every meal and my prayers every night. All that slipped away when I was at the academy. I missed it at first, but I kept telling myself I didn't have time for it, and eventually it just evaporated. Not the belief, but the practice. That wasn't a very good excuse, though, was it?" She gave a half-hearted laugh. "I was so focused on proving I could be a good cop, I didn't think of much else. But it was in me all along, and now that it's all bubbling back to the surface, well..." She studied their entwined hands. "I guess I'm afraid of the lightning bolts." She looked up and gave him a weak smile.

"You're joking, right?"

"Yes. And no."

Dumas wasn't sure he understood, but he patted her hands. "I don't think you have to worry about that. But if any do flash your way, I'll take the hit for you."

Montufar's eyes looked a bit dewy, and he knew she understood: although he'd spoken lightly, he'd meant every word. "Likewise," she promised.

*

When Peller arrived for his second visit with Wanda Fletcher, she was waddling out into the cold, bundled in a bright orange coat. "Good afternoon, Lieutenant," she said brightly, pulling up the hood and tying it securely beneath her chin. "Any news?"

"A little, but mostly more questions. I guess I've come at a bad time."

"No, I was just going for a walk. You can join me."

Peller looked up at the sky, where clabbered clouds scudded and rushed. It looked to him like snow was on the way: the temperature had risen to twenty-eight, but the wind bit through his coat as though it were tissue paper. "Do you usually go out in weather like this?"

"My doctor wants me to walk regularly." She gave him that motherly look and added, "My husband was stationed in Alaska right after we got married. This ain't cold, so don't you whine about it."

Peller laughed. "I'm used to it myself," he said. "I'm from upstate New York." They crossed the parking lot, then took to a sidewalk that looped around the perimeter of the complex. "I talked to one of Jayvon's Bahá'í contacts, a Winston Marley. Do you remember him?"

"Nothin' to me." Mrs. Fletcher shrugged as though she wouldn't care if he'd been Prince Charles.

"Marley said he was surprised when they lost contact with Jayvon, but they figured he wasn't interested anymore."

"They were wrong about that." Bitterness tinged her voice.

"Unfortunately. He did mention something odd, though. He said Jayvon was worried about a young lady he knew."

"He sure should have been. That girl was trouble."

Peller wondered whether that might be run-of-the-mill grandmotherly disapproval, but one look at her disgusted expression disabused him of that notion. Her face looked as though she'd caught a whiff of decaying mouse from behind the refrigerator. "How so?"

Mrs. Fletcher set her lips firmly and shook her head.

"Please, Mrs. Fletcher. I have almost nothing to go on. Anything might help explain what happened to Jayvon."

Mrs. Fletcher shook her head again. "All right, but only because you're a good man trying to do something about it. She was a stripper in some club somewhere. Bad news from the start. I don't know how Jayvon met her, and I don't care to think about it."

"Ah."

Mrs. Fletcher stopped and stared up at the clouds as if seeking guidance. "Although he did say he wanted to save her. Ain't that just like a man?

I told him to let the Lord save her, and not go looking for trouble himself. But he wouldn't listen. I guess it was a case of bad woman, good reason, to Jayvon anyway. But he wasn't Jesus. He couldn't cast out devils."

There were those demonic suggestions again. Peller could at least understand them now. "I guess it makes sense, though. Jayvon being who he was, he must have seen some good in her. No one is all bad, after all."

She harrumphed at that.

Peller avoided showing any amusement. "Regardless, I can't see a connection between her line of work and a break-in at a veterinary clinic."

"Well, that's your job, Lieutenant. I'm just an old lady."

They came to a patch of ice, and Mrs. Fletcher shuffled into the grass to avoid it. Peller followed suit. "What was her name?"

"Shania North."

Peller was surprised she remembered it so readily after the lapse of two years. He didn't suppose she wanted to remember the least detail about the woman. "Was there anything else about her that struck you as wrong? You mentioned devils, and one of Jayvon's friends told him the lady was possessed."

Mrs. Fletcher snorted. "Lady? Not her. Dancing on tables in her birthday suit. Some lady. Now, possessed? Only the Lord knows that. I can tell you one thing, though— there are lots of devils in the world. She might have been on drugs. A lot of girls like that are on drugs, aren't they?"

"Some," Peller acknowledged.

"Possessed. Huh." Mrs. Fletcher pondered that for a moment, then shook her head. "All I can say for sure is she was a stripper. God knows what else she got up to."

"But you don't?"

There was that look again.

"Okay, we'll drop that subject, then."

"About time."

The ice behind them, they regained the sidewalk. Peller was starting to feel the chill and shoved his hands farther into his pockets, but Mrs. Fletcher didn't seem in the least cold. Peller had run out of questions, except the pointed ones Dumas suggested he'd have to ask. He wondered if he could blunt them for Mrs. Fletcher's sake.

Presciently, she said, "You got somethin' ugly on your mind."

"Yeah."

"Well, spit it out and get it over with."

He didn't know whether to laugh or cry. "You're one remarkable lady, ma'am," he said, and meant it. She looked embarrassed but didn't challenge the assertion. "Was Jayvon at all..." He had to search for the right word. "Impressionable?"

"Some. He wouldn't fall for just anything, but when did fall, he fell hard. That..." Her nose wrinkled again. "...woman. That's one case. Those Bahá'ís were another."

"Suppose somebody approached him with a money-making scheme, one they made sound safe and easy but that turned out to be illegal. Could he be sucked in by it?"

"Nope. He wouldn't break the Commandments. Not my Jayvon."

"How can you be sure?"

"Because that wasn't him, Lieutenant. Once he ordered a camera online. Nothin' too pricey. He got two of them, three days apart. Most people would keep them both, but Jayvon sent the second one back. Didn't even hesitate. So you tell me. Can I be sure?"

Peller didn't know, but he had no grounds to argue.

"If I wasn't sure, what would you be suggesting?"

"It's not a suggestion," he said, a bit defensively. "Just a speculation."

She glanced at him, expression unreadable. "Go on."

"Given what we know, the incident at the clinic looks like a robbery involving two or three people. If it was two, Jayvon must have surprised them."

Mrs. Fletcher nodded grimly and spoke in a whisper, "And he'd be dead."

"I'm afraid that's most likely. The other possibility is that somehow the thieves recruited him as their inside man."

"You said that before." Whether she was considering the possibility or refusing to do so wasn't apparent, but after a moment she asked, "Where would he be then?"

"Given what we found at the scene, most likely dead."

"Then I'll keep on believing in his goodness. If it's all the same to you." She stopped and set a hand on Peller's forearm. "Most likely is no good. I got to know."

"I know you do," Peller replied gently. "I want to know, too. I can't promise anything, though, only that I'll keep at it as long as I can."

Patting his arm, she released him and began to walk again. "You're a good man, Lieutenant. I wish you could have known Jayvon. You're a lot like him."

He nearly quipped that he'd never dated a stripper but thought better of it. Curiously, Mrs. Fletcher tossed him a wry smile, as though without hearing she'd gotten the joke. "I better get you home," he told her. "Before I freeze to death."

"Sissy," she replied.

*

About one thirty, Peller arrived at Northern District Headquarters. Snow was beginning to fall, as he'd predicted. A thin dust of tiny white crystals settled on the grass and on the windows and hoods of parked cars. He doubted it would amount to much; it looked too dry to accumulate.

Dumas saw him come in and sauntered over to his desk, trailing Jack Collins. "When did you get here?" Peller asked the reporter.

"Apparently five minutes after you all left this morning," he said. "But that's okay. I had a few other things to do anyway. I stopped by again twenty minutes ago. Eric filled me in on the day's activities so far."

Peller motioned Collins to a seat while Dumas asked, "So how'd it go?"

"Better than I expected. Mrs. Fletcher is one tough lady."

"That's something, at least." Dumas absently took a half-dollar from his pocket rolled it between his fingers. Peller and Collins watched, fascinated.

"The possessed woman, it turns out, was a stripper," Peller told them. "Mrs. Fletcher didn't know any more about her than that."

"That's a bit of a letdown. You had nightmares for nothing."

Peller gave Dumas a crooked smile. "What would nightmares be good for? But I'll check up on her, just in case. Our stripper is one Shania North." He jotted the name down on a sticky note and plastered it to the bottom of his monitor.

Dumas folded his fingers around the half-dollar and peered as though trying to see the coin through them. "I know that name."

Surprised, Peller said without thinking, "Why would you know a stripper?"

Dumas sighed. "I know the name, not the woman. Just a minute." He rose and disappeared in the maze of cubicles.

"The book—" Collins began hesitantly, but Dumas returned with Micho Tamai's address book before he could continue. Thumbing through it, the detective parked himself against the wall of Peller's cubicle and placed the open book on the desk.

"Shania North." He tapped the page. "Here she is. But why would any of Jayvon Fletcher's acquaintances be in here?"

A hundred possibilities flitted through Peller's mind, none of which he could wish true.

Counting through the entries, Dumas added, "She's not one of the marked names."

"What are the marked names?"

"I'm still working on that. Shania lives in Laurel, or did when this entry was made." He looked up. "Shall we pay her a visit?"

Peller rose. "After you."

Collins joined them without invitation, and the three headed out into the snow to Peller's car.

Twenty minutes later, they arrived at a rundown ranch home that looked like it had crash-landed dead center in a tangle of weeds. A junkyard overflowing with decaying automobiles sprawled behind it, imprisoned by a huddle of scrawny trees. The house, isolated from its neighbors by wide stands of woods, felt beyond forlorn.

"Are you sure anybody lives here?" Collins asked from the back seat.

"I wouldn't." Peller could scarcely believe anybody would. Certainly the place must be abandoned? But no. They parked in the gravel driveway behind a surprisingly new slate Ford Focus and crunched up to the front door. When Peller pressed the doorbell, they heard no sound from within. He tried again and got the same result.

Dumas banged on the door, then shuffled his feet in a futile effort to generate some heat. "What is with this winter?" he griped.

Collins turned up his coat collar and readied his tape recorder.

The door finally opened with a wheeze. A tall man, thin to the point of emaciation, stood behind it. He could have been anywhere from twenty-five to sixty-five years of age. Dark skin stretched over his frame as though it had been dried to fit. "Eh?" he mumbled, his eyes unfocused and blank.

Dumas flashed his shield. "Howard County police," he said. "Does Shania North live here?"

"Eh," the man repeated, only the inflection differing. Leaving the door open, he faded into the house, feet scraping across the floor.

"I guess that means yes," Dumas remarked.

Peller peered into the dim interior. The dingy carpet and stained walls mirrored the same neglect as the exterior of the house. There were a few beanbag chairs on the floor, but he couldn't tell their color, nor could he see any other sign of furnishings or decorations. A vague cloud of smoke hung in the atmosphere. It may have been the most depressing home he'd ever seen.

Shania North's arrival did nothing to lighten the mood. Her feet shuffled across the floor exactly as the man's had. Although not as skeletal as he, she didn't have much meat on her. She leaned against the left door jamb, her dark eyes vacant, and ran her right hand slowly down her body from left shoulder to right thigh. "Tweny five," she spewed rather than said.

Peller and Dumas exchanged a glance. "I'm sorry?" Peller said.

"Tweny five dollahs?"

Collins looked at his shoes in embarrassment.

"We're not customers. We're detectives with the Howard County police. We'd like to ask you a few questions."

Her brow slowly furrowed as she tried to work that out. "Fifteen?"

"We just want to talk," Dumas tried. "We're detectives. Police."

"Um." She stood a bit straighter now and slowly waggled her head as though not comprehending. "Kay, how 'bout ten for jus' talk?"

"Ma'am," Peller said, his voice flat, "we're police. We want to ask you about Michio Tamai and Jayvon Fletcher."

At least one of the names sparked something in her. Her face grew taut and after a delay she turned her head and spat on the floor. She hadn't bothered to aim for the outdoors. "Mike can go to hell."

"He already has. Somebody shot him dead earlier this week."

A sudden light flickered in the sunken depths of her eyes. "Good." Finally registering the chill soaking into her bones, she shivered. "In," she said and backed away from the door.

Peller thought he'd rather risk frostbite, but he and Dumas and Collins stepped through the door and she closed it behind them. The warmer air within smelled of mold and weed. She didn't invite them to sit on the beanbag chairs, an omission that suited Peller. "Why do you want to send Mike to hell?" he asked her.

"He ruined me." Yet her voice held zero emotion.

"How so?"

She motioned at herself head to toe, then sank to her knees and started to sob.

Before Peller could think what to say, Dumas had worked it out. "He supplied you with drugs? Forced you to do something in exchange for them?"

North wiped her eyes with her hand and flung the moisture away as though it were a disease. "Yeh."

"What are you on?"

"Stuff. Ox..." she looked around, then whispered, "Oxatin. An' stuff."

"OxyContin?"

North tried to think about the name but quickly gave up.

Peller would have shot Tamai himself had he been there. He struggled to keep his voice gentle. "What did he want?"

She looked up at him. Her pupils were pinpricks. "Names."

Dumas cocked his head in inquiry.

"Guys with money," she explained.

"Customers?" Dumas asked.

"Yeh."

With a nod, he said to Peller, "It fits. The marked names seem to be associates Tamai tried to blackmail. He had trouble with that crowd. Maybe he tried to hit the big time with Shania's customers."

Peller felt his gut knot up at the word, but before he could say anything, North whimpered, "Had to. Din't wanna. Most guys were good to me."

"How did you meet Jayvon?" Peller asked, changing the subject before she lost control.

She smiled through her tears. "From a guy, used to pay me good. He worked with Jay." She frowned in concentration. "Worked with animals. Hired me for a party. Jay was there."

Saint Jayvon at a party featuring a stripper? After so long not believing the man could have been that good, Peller found himself unable to swallow this revelation.

"I din't look like this then," North told the carpet. "I was hot. Real hot. But Jay wouldn't watch. Told me I was better'n that. Said he'd help me get out." A small chuckle forced its way up from her throat but sounded like retching. "White knight, yeh?"

God knows you need one, Peller thought. "Did you let him help you?"

She chewed on her lip for a moment before answering. "A little. Not really. Mike woulda killed him. But I wanted him, so I played along for a bit."

"Was Mike jealous?"

She shook her head slowly. "He was okay with me gettin' 'round. Just business. I was money to him."

Peller gingerly took a seat on the filthy floor and looked into her eyes. "Did Mike know about Jayvon?" He could see Tamai killing Fletcher over money, if not the woman.

North shook her head lethargically.

"Where is Jayvon now?"

Her mouth drew into a pout and her brow furrowed. "Gone," she said at last. "Gone. I think. Gone."

"He just stopped coming around?"

Following another great shrug, North said, "Gave up on me." She looked hurt. "Everyone does."

Peller wished he could give her some good news, but as he couldn't, he offered the next best thing. "We won't. We'll get you into a recovery program. Get you away from this nightmare."

Her eyes flitted over the wall without seeing it. Whatever they did register, she kept it to herself. Peller's only answer was her shallow breathing and befuddled stare.

"The guy Jayvon worked with. What was his name?"

Peller didn't think she was going to answer. Her expression had slipped towards oblivion and what little light had been in her eyes had dimmed. He clambered to his feet, feeling age seeping into every muscle and bone. Collins was staring at the woman, his eyes so sad Peller thought he might start bawling, too.

"Bob," she finally said.

"Bob what?"

"Jus' Bob."

They got no more from her. Peller couldn't force her to go with him without a court order, but he vowed he was going to help her. He could imagine how he would feel if a child of his had ended up this way. Unfortunately, that would have to wait until later.

So Shania North's eyes haunted him for the rest of the day.

*

Charlie Sheffield slung his black coat over the back of the guest chair by Dumas' desk and sat, trying to look anywhere but at the detective. He shed a few pounds along with the coat but might still have benefited from some time at the gym.

Dumas turned his monitor so Sheffield could see it. "This is a transcript of Mike's address book," he said. "Let's scroll through it, and you tell me about anyone you happen to know." Dumas had a recorder of his own today to capture everything Sheffield said. He amused himself momentarily with the thought of his and Collins' recorders dueling.

Sheffield swallowed apprehensively but nodded, and the work began.

Forty-five minutes later, Dumas snapped off the recorder, thanked Sheffield, and, mouth knotted in annoyance, watched him leave. Aside from the names Dumas already knew, Sheffield had only been able to identify a couple of Tamai's ex-girlfriends, one high school friend who had lived in Arizona for the past eight years, and three guys currently serving time for armed robberies. As far as Dumas could tell, he hadn't avoided any names He sounded more subdued than usual when pointing out the Bellamys, but he hadn't denied knowing them.

At best, Dumas could cross one more useless item off his list.

*

"I have to go." Hannah threw back the sheets, rolled over, and swung her sleek legs over the edge of the bed. Air currents swirling through the leaky bedroom window played on her skin. She shivered luxuriantly at their chill caress.

Harold reached out and stroked her bare back but said nothing.

She rose and dressed, aware of his eyes drinking her in, enjoying his attention.

"Do they suspect?" he asked.

"Of course not," she assured him. "People are idiots. Even detectives."

She inspected herself in the mirror, turning this way and that, pleased that she still looked as beautiful as she had in college. Her beauty was her gift to Harold, and she meant to always be able to give it to him.

"Do you like it?" he asked, voice tentative.

Hannah glanced at him. He'd agreed to this, so she didn't understand why he would doubt. Other men would, but not Harold. "It's an act," she said. "It's not real. There's nothing to either like or dislike."

He settled back on the pillow, hands behind his head, eyes fixed on the ceiling.

"I wouldn't lie to you. I never, ever lie to you."

"It's just weird, you know?"

She crawled onto the bed, pressed herself against his muscular chest, kissed him delicately. "The whole world is weird. Except us."

She started to rise, but he took her shoulders and pulled her down. She couldn't have gotten away if she wanted to, but she didn't want to. He kissed her again, passionately, for a long time.

When finally he ceased, Hannah tweaked his nose with her forefinger. "If you don't stop that, I won't get to work."

"You'll get to work, all right," he said with a grin. But he relented and helped her to her feet. "Go do your stuff."

She did. They didn't see each other until the following day.

13

Karla York called Montufar just after four o'clock that afternoon. "I asked Stan about the note," she said, an edge in her voice.

Montufar had been shuffling through the arson file once more but set it aside. "Something did happen."

"Yes. And he wasn't entirely innocent, but that doesn't matter. It was a group effort. He just let himself get roped into it."

Montufar didn't want to hear anything of the sort, but York seemed to be taking it in stride. "Let's have it from the beginning, then,"

York launched headlong into the story. "It started as a bunch of guys at the office going out to lunch on Fridays. They took turns picking the place and driving. One day about a month before the fire, one of them said he had a surprise for the group. He drove them to a strip club somewhere near route 40. Stan said he wasn't comfortable with it, but he didn't want the guys making fun of him, so he didn't object. While they were there, one of the dancers got friendly with him. He told her more than he should have. His name, where he worked, how many kids he had, stuff like that. A week and a half later, the first threat arrived. It said they had photos of him with a naked woman and demanded monthly payments of five hundred dollars. There were instructions for how the money was to be delivered."

Had Stan York been all that hesitant to join his buddies in their indiscretion? Maybe not, but he'd likely been truthful about the key details. If he was going to make something up, it wouldn't have been this. "Did he pay?" Montufar asked.

"No. He demanded to see the photos."

"Brave. Or foolish. What happened next?"

"More threats. He never saw any photos and suspected they didn't exist, so he didn't pay."

"And then they torched your house."

"Stan's sure that's what happened, but he's satisfied that you caught the guy."

"So's Lieutenant Trengove," Montufar said, "and I imagine they're right. Yet something very similar has happened again."

"You don't think the arsonist is the blackmailer?"

"Maybe not. The arsonist could have been hired help."

York pondered that for a moment. "Let me know what I can do. Anything at all."

"I appreciate that. I think I have what I need for now. How about you? Are you okay?"

"Of course." Montufar could almost see the woman dressed to the nines, a smug smile on her face as she twirled her pearl necklace. "Stan's a good man. He wouldn't cheat on me. Still, he's as much a man as any other. Maybe he wasn't as reluctant as he claims, but I do believe he was a bit uncomfortable. Why else would they have targeted him? I bet that dancer could tell he didn't want people to know he'd been there. Either way, I don't care. My family has been attacked. I want whoever did it to be very sorry."

"I'll do what I can," Montufar promised, although after she hung up she wondered if the matter wasn't getting too personal. She was sworn to serve and protect, to enforce the law, not to exact revenge. It was far too easy to identify with the wife in a case like this. She could imagine what she'd feel if Dumas fell into a blackmailer's trap, and unlike Carla York or Candace Dibble, she'd have a gun in her hand.

Dumas slipped into the chair by her desk. "Whoever it is," he said presciently, "please don't shoot them. We have enough paperwork as it is."

Instantly her burden lightened. She laughed and reached out to take his hand, but froze when she realized that Peller and Collins had come up behind Dumas.

"Go ahead," Peller said with a mischievous smile. "We'll close our eyes." And he did, too, just for a moment.

Montufar could feel herself blushing, but she took Dumas' hand anyway. *I thought I was ready to be open about this,* she scolded herself.

"Yeah, so," Dumas muttered, equally embarrassed. "What's the face of fury for?"

Montufar filled them in on Karla York's report.

Collins remained in the background, his tape recorder whispering, while Peller moved to the side and leaned against the desk. "There's a lot of blackmail in the air. What did you say about Tamai, Eric?"

"He definitely tried his hand at blackmail, although he seems to have bungled it with some frequency. Based on the interviews I've conducted so far, it looks like the marks in his book designate some of his targets. So far only the Bellamys haven't admitted it. But they wouldn't admit to anything, not even the fact that they're really aliens from Alpha Centauri."

Usually Montufar knew what Dumas was talking about, but that threw her way off. "Aliens?"

"Those two are strange," Peller supplied.

"Strange is hardly the word," Dumas added. "But yeah, taken together, all this is beyond suggestive. Tamai had a stripper on his payroll who he used to find blackmail victims. Stan York was blackmailed after visiting a strip club, and Vincent Dibble was blackmailed after meeting a pretty young thing. What are the odds?"

Montufar turned the new information over in her mind. "So the blackmailer may be Tamai, and he's dead. Who's the stripper?"

"A pitiful woman named Shania North," Peller supplied. "Tamai used drugs to control her—OxyContin, she said. She looks like death itself. Talking to her is like talking to a mummy. I'd be surprised if she lives out the year."

Montufar's heart turned over. She hadn't seen Shania North, but she instinctively knew how she would look—eaten from within by the contagion of drug and evil, her husk to be tossed aside after all life had been drawn from her. *How do we fall so far?* "Do we know where Shania worked? Do we have a photo, preferably a 'before' picture?"

She turned to her computer and searched on North's name. It was just possible she'd show up in connection with one or more clubs. Nothing came up, at least not immediately.

"Didn't think to ask," Dumas told her. "I was focused on her connection with Tamai, and Rick wanted to know about her relationship with Jayvon Fletcher."

Montufar whipped around and nearly knocked the keyboard onto the floor. "What's that?"

Peller shrugged. "Apparently Jayvon met her at a party and tried to save her from herself."

"The kid who makes Superman look like a pervert met a stripper at a party?"

"About the same way Stan York met his nemesis," Peller replied thoughtfully. "A coworker named Bob invited him. He only found out what was going on after he got there."

Pushing to her feet, Montufar paced in the space between the cubicles. The men watched her furious movement with amusement. "Tamai uses North to find blackmail victims. When they refuse to pay, he hires Bradley to torch their houses. Bradley gets caught and goes directly to jail. North is destroyed by the drugs Tamai gave her and is no use to him anymore. So he hires someone else to set up Vincent Dibble and just for fun starts blackmailing his own people. But then Dibble stops paying, so Tamai hires a new arsonist. Finally, someone's had enough of Tamai and terminates him."

"Don't forget the early days," Peller added, "Before all that, Fletcher meets North, tries to rescue her, and vanishes from the face of the Earth."

Montufar paused in her pacing. "But you think that was a robbery during which he surprised the thief."

"Thieves. Eric thinks the evidence suggests two people with different temperaments. Maybe three. Jayvon could have been in collusion."

She made a face at the latter suggestion and resumed pacing.

Dumas pulled a half-dollar from his pocket and studied it thoughtfully before performing a vanish. "Regardless, we're left with a murderer, an arsonist, an accessory to blackmail, and a thief turned killer all on the loose. One step forward, two steps back." He pulled the coin out of his own left ear.

Montufar smiled, impressed with his dexterity.

Collins nearly applauded. "You'll have to teach me how to do that sometime."

Montufar reseated herself and squared her keyboard. "I need North's photo and work history. Maybe Stan York can identify her." She began typing, still hoping she could find what she needed somewhere in cyberland.

"And my next job," Dumas said, "is to find out about the Bellamys' college background. Rick likes them for the murder."

Peller slid off the desk and sighed heavily. Montufar stopped typing and turned, wondering what was weighing on him. "Did we miss something?"

"No," he told her. "It's just that I have the really tough job. I have to find some guy named Bob."

*

Seriously, Peller knew that finding Bob wouldn't prove difficult. Being Fletcher's coworker, Bob had worked at the South Howard Veterinary Clinic. Even if he'd moved on, the clinic would have a record of him. Peller called and asked. A no-nonsense woman answered his inquiry in predictable fashion: "I'm sorry; I can't give out personnel information."

"I'm sure Dr. Meadows would allow it in this case," Peller told her. "We're trying to locate a missing former employee."

"There are rules about confidentiality. Don't you have to have a warrant or something?"

He couldn't fault her caution. "Is Dr. Meadows available?"

"She'll be here this evening, after six. But she's booked full."

"How late are you open?"

"Our last appointments are at nine. We're usually here until ten."

It was now nearly four o'clock. "Do me a favor. When she gets there, tell her I'll stop by about seven-thirty. If she's okay with it, she can leave the information for me at the front desk. If not, I'll speak with her when she has time."

If the receptionist was miffed, she didn't show it. She merely double-checked his name and promised, "I'll give her the message."

Before Peller could decide what to do next, his cell phone rang. He let it go to voice mail, then a minute later noted that the caller had left a message. Probably a salesman or a scam, he figured, but just in case it was his Bahá'í contact Winston Marley, he checked.

"Hi there, Sherlock!" Joan Churchill chirped. Astonished, Peller wondered how she'd gotten his number. He hadn't given it to her. "It's Friday and I'm all alone with nothing to do, so I wondered if you'd like to get together for dinner or drinks or, or, or something. I mean, it's not a date. Just, you know, getting together and, um…" There was a pause, then she added, embarrassed, "I rehearsed this for an hour and it still won't come out right. I hate talking to answering machines. You can never tell what they're thinking." She laughed nervously, then ended sadly, "Well, give me a call if… if you want."

Peller wasn't sure whether to laugh, grumble, or feel sorry for Churchill. He managed all three simultaneously but didn't have the heart to leave her hanging. He tapped the call button.

She answered a bit too quickly. "Hi, Rick!"

"Hi, Joan. Got your message." Lightly, he added, "Or whatever it was."

"I hate telephones," she laughed.

"Unfortunately, I have to make an official house call this evening."

"Oh." Disappointment weighed down the lone syllable. "Maybe another time, then?"

Peller replied without thinking. "If you don't mind fast food, I guess you could tag along." As soon as the words were out, he felt like kicking himself. Hard.

Churchill didn't answer immediately. For a moment he hoped she'd beg off. Maybe she wouldn't want to interrupt his work? But no.

"Are you sure you don't mind?" She sounded delighted and not at all hesitant.

It's your own fault, he told himself, but still he couldn't say no. "I'm sure. It shouldn't take long. I might just be picking up a piece of paper."

"Then I'd love to," she told him, definitely delighted now.

"I'll pick you up. Say, five-thirty?"

"Five forty-five," she countered. "I have to get home from work and slip into something more comfortable. These heels are killing me. I never should have bought them."

Peller got her address at the Orchard Meadows apartments in Ellicott City then promised, "Five forty-five. See you then."

"See you then, Sherlock."

It looked like he was stuck with the nickname. He hoped she wouldn't advertise it too widely.

*

Darkness had blanketed the eastern seaboard by the time Peller pulled into the Orchard Meadows parking lot. Majestic in a crystalline sky, the first quarter moon cast its cold light upon the Earth. The temperature had already fallen below twenty and was forecast to descend into the single digits overnight.

Peller turned up his coat collar against the cold and made his way inside the building. Although he could see little of it in the dark, it seemed an ordinary apartment building: four floors, some small trees that might blossom come spring, a comfortable air that spoke of an attentive landlord. Somewhere in the dark, traffic rushed by on route 29. Inside, Peller mounted the stairs and walked halfway down the third-floor corridor to Churchill's door. He rapped on it and waited, wondering what he was doing here. He didn't dislike the woman, but he wasn't interested in being pulled or pushed or tricked or stumbling into a new relationship. Could nobody understand that he still had Sandra and always would? That was enough for him.

Are you sure?

"Why wouldn't I be?" he quietly answered the voice only he could hear.

You always were stubborn.

He didn't have time to react. The door opened and Churchill stepped out. She wore dark jeans, but from neck to waist was lost in a plush wooly sweater. Dark threads rambled up and down the length of the oversize garment, and to Peller's eyes she looked like a deliriously happy sheepdog. A dark red coat was draped over her left arm. "That's some outfit," he remarked.

She looked down at herself, pleased. "You like it?"

"Sure," he said, although he wasn't. "It'll be hard to misplace you." She laughed while he motioned down the hall. "Shall we?"

"Let's." She unfurled the coat and pulled it on, buttoning it up as they walked.

Once they were in the car and on the way, Churchill decided it was time for conversation. "What made you decide to become a detective?"

Although it seemed trite to him, Peller played along. He'd been asked the question so often over the years that the answer had become reflexive. "Columbo."

She grinned before noticing he was serious. "Really?"

"Really. In my childhood, I thought he was the cleverest guy on the planet. I liked the trench coat, too, and the fact that he didn't carry a gun. He did everything with his mind."

"You don't wear a trench coat, do you?"

Peller couldn't help but crack a smile. "No. Should I?"

"You'd look good in one. What about the gun? Do you carry one?"

"Of course."

"You have it on you now?"

"I do."

She looked him over as though searching for it. "Ever use it?"

"When necessary. Fortunately it usually isn't."

Talk of guns stole some of her cheer away. Peller thought she looked pensive.

"Ever kill anyone?" Churchill kept her eyes on the traffic.

Ah, he thought, *that would do it*. "Once."

She started to ask but decided against it.

It was a rough memory: a bad incident on a day connected to Sandra's fate. He didn't care to talk about it, but he felt he owed her some explanation. "A gang of thugs ambushed my team. They only had knives, but they got the jump on us and cut up a few cops pretty bad before we took them down. I killed one of them. Shot him in the heart point-blank. I can still remember the look on his face."

Timidly, she touched his shoulder, just for a moment, then drew her hand back. "Pain? Fear?"

Peller shook his head. "Surprise. I think he'd just learned he wasn't invincible."

Churchill considered that. "How did you feel afterward?"

"Horrible. About a number of things. But Sandra was there to…" He cut himself off, realizing it might be awkward for Churchill to hear that part.

She stared at the taillights before them as though hypnotized. "She was your anchor, wasn't she?"

Peller nodded.

"What's your anchor now?"

Sandra. Of course, Sandra. She always will be. That's what he told himself, and in some measure it was true. Yet often, he couldn't deny, he merely drifted from one day to the next without charts or rudder or anchor. He got up, went to work, did his duty, returned home, went to sleep. He had no purpose outside of his work, no higher calling, not even a hobby.

His only goal in recent years had been to survive to retirement and move to Denver to be near his son and daughter-in-law and grandchildren.

When he didn't answer, Churchill graciously changed the subject. "Bacon cheeseburger with large fries and a large iced tea. You can pick the brand."

"Yes, ma'am," Peller said. Be it only fast food, it was a welcome distraction.

*

The top of his bed raised at a forty-five degree angle, Felipe Montufar's heavy eyelids blinked slowly at his daughters. Ella's hands enfolded his, rubbing gently to remove the chill. The room felt unnaturally cold to her this evening. She hadn't bothered to remove her coat.

"Where," Felipe began, then paused for a wheezing breath. "Where are your husbands?"

Ella glanced at Corina. Her big sister would have an answer. She could always find the right thing to say. But no, that wouldn't do any more. She couldn't cower behind others any longer. Looking at her father, Ella saw the future. Someday it would be Eduardo or Corina knocking on death's door, no longer able to protect her, no longer able to hold her up. She had to find and nurture her own strength, not only for herself but for them, too, and also for Jack.

Jack. Just the thought of him filled her with warmth. Ella so wanted to be with him now, and she was sure he wanted to be with her. Another reason to stand up on her own. Most men she had dated had fallen for her weakness like superheroes swooping down from the sky to rescue a damsel in distress, but that never lasted. Although she knew Jack felt a similar impulse, she also knew he recognized the danger. Instead of taking on the world on her behalf, he led her into the fray, at her side but not shielding her from every blow. Ella feared she might lose him if she couldn't prove herself.

To Ella's surprise, Corina said nothing. Fortunately, she found words: "They wanted to come, papá, but they had work to do."

Felipe slowly pulled one hand out from hers and settled it on her fingers. "Está bien," he said, then reverting to English added, "They work hard for their families."

Corina frowned at the sheets.

"They do," Ella told him. "Very hard."

"I am going," he said simply. "But you will be well with them."

"You'll pull through. The nurses all say you're strong."

Felipe wheezed again, closed his eyes, and slowly settled into the sheets. "Tell mamá I shall be home soon."

Fighting back tears, Ella wrapped her hands around his again. "I'll tell her," she promised. Corina place an arm around her shoulders and drew her close, and they stood together quietly weeping over their dying father.

*

Jack Collins' thoughts were on his story that evening. Dumas had contacted the few colleges on his list and found what he needed: Harold Bellamy and Hannah Childress had attended Howard Community College, where he had been a key player on the baseball team and she had studied theater and performed on stage. Although the registrar's office couldn't or wouldn't tell him much beyond that, they had put him in touch with one of the theater program's professors, Lenora Mendez. By then it was late in the afternoon and Mendez was about to walk out the door, but she invited Dumas to speak with her in her Columbia home at six-thirty. He agreed and Collins asked permission to tag along.

A short drive deposited them before a moderately large house set amidst a cluster of heavily wooded lots on the side of a hill. Collins wasn't sure what he expected in a theater professor, but Lenora Mendez wasn't it. The woman who opened the door stood not quite five feet tall, her head topped by a mop of frizzy graying hair cropped short. She wore a severe expression and an uninspired outfit—faded jeans and a dull orange turtleneck. A simple gold wedding band encircled her ring finger. She greeted them in a small voice that wouldn't carry to the back of a classroom, much less through a crowded theater.

"Come in, gentlemen."

She led them into a neat but similarly uninspired living room done in tans and blues with heavy wooden end tables. The walls were occupied by a strangely pedestrian arrangement of landscapes and still-lifes. A man Collins assumed was her husband rose from one of the chairs as they entered.

"This is Trent Jordan," she said, "our baseball coach. I invited him along. He knew Harold better than me. My husband Frank is around here somewhere, probably hiding." She looked around as though he might be behind the sofa or under a table. "Please, have a seat."

Dumas and Collins settled on the sofa. Collins quietly took out his tape recorder and activated it, then smiled at Jordan. The coach actually looked his part: probably in his late fifties, about six feet tall, barrel-chested, dressed in neatly pressed blue slacks and a burgundy, gold, and blue sweater emblazoned with the college logo. Even at his age, he probably could knock a few balls out of the park.

"What's that for?" Jordan asked, nodding at the recorder.

"Mr. Collins is a reporter," Dumas told them, "but he's reporting on me, not you."

Mendez brightened "Oh! I saw your article. It was very good. You're doing a series, right?"

Collins wasn't sure whether to blush or swell with pride. "Thank you, ma'am. Yes, it's a series."

Getting down to business, Dumas told them, "Then you know I'm investigating a murder."

That made the professors' eyes widen. Mendez replied, "Oh, that's right. But what would that have to do with…"

When she didn't finish, Dumas explained. "Harold and Hannah are connected to the victim. I can't say more than that right now."

Jordan shook his head definitively. "You think one of them killed somebody? Ridiculous. Harold was a fine student. A bit on the quiet side, not a leader in the usual sense, but serious. Dedicated. The other students looked up to him."

"And Hannah was just plain timid," Mendez added. "Except when on stage. Then she could be anything. She was one of the best actresses I've taught."

Walters wondered how good that made her. It was, after all, only a community college.

"I understand they met at school," Dumas said.

"Correct," Jordan answered. "I don't recall when they started dating, but it was rare to see one without the other. Hannah came to all the games and hung around at practices. She was one pretty lady. The guys liked having her around, but they all knew she was Harold's girl." He smiled at the paintings on the wall behind Dumas, or perhaps at a memory. "She left a trail of broken hearts, I'm sure."

"Harold came to her performances," Mendez said. "Somebody told me he never missed a single one. I recall him hanging around backstage a couple of times. I never spoke to him, but I knew who he was from talk among the other students."

"What did they say?" Dumas asked.

"Just that he was Hannah's boyfriend and that he was protective of her. I imagine Trent is right. A lot of the guys would have given their right arms to go out with her. And he was a good-looking guy, too, so I'm sure more than a few young ladies had their eyes on him. But in vain."

"Were they ever in any trouble?"

Both professors shook their heads, and Jordan said, "Harold was steady, the kind of guy you could count on. He'd go out of his way to keep things on the level. I remember once during a game an opposing pitcher hit two batters in a row. Harold was the second victim. He took a pretty hard shot on the upper arm, and it sure looked intentional. The rest of the team was ready to mob that pitcher, but Harold stopped them with just a shake of his head. And his next at-bat was a homer. If he wanted revenge, that's how he'd get it: by the rules. As for Hannah, I don't know." He looked at Mendez for the answer.

"Like I said, she was timid. I don't think she could have caused trouble if she wanted to."

"But on stage," Dumas reminded her, "she was different."

"Oh yes. That's true of most good actors. We all have a surprising array of characters hidden within us. Actors learn to unlock them."

"What if she turned the whole world into her stage?" Dumas asked.

Mendez looked at him as though he was a student who'd given an egregiously wrong answer. "You don't know what you're suggesting. It would take enormous concentration. Only the best actors can manage that for any length of time. I said Hannah was good, not that she was Katharine Hepburn."

"I talked to them the other day," Dumas said, and Collins sat forward, curious how the detective would play it. He knew Dumas has been creeped out by the Bellamys. From what he'd said, today they were far removed from the couple the professors recalled.

"They're strange people now," Dumas continued. "Intensely devoted to each other and nothing else. They didn't seem to care that a man was dead. Hannah went so far as to say that nothing was real to them except each other. Of greater interest, she didn't want me to know that they had met at your school."

Jordan thought about that for a moment. "How did you find out?"

"Harold let it slip. Hannah shut him up, unobtrusively but efficiently."

The professors exchanged a puzzled glance. "That sounds exactly backwards," Jordan decided, and Mendez nodded agreement.

Dumas waited for more, but nothing was forthcoming. Collins felt the urge to interject a thought. Probably he shouldn't have, but he said it anyway: "Maybe something's changed them since you knew them."

Mendez folded her hands in her lap and studied them as though working out a difficult problem. "If so, it must have been traumatic. What could transform Hannah from a mouse to a, well, not a lion exactly, but you know?"

Dumas glanced at Collins thoughtfully. "Maybe. Something must have happened at school, too, something public enough that Hannah would fear its discovery."

"Not a thing as far as we know," Jordan told him. "Harold played baseball. Hannah played roles on the stage. They were a couple people noticed, but they didn't take advantage of it. Maybe even then they weren't fully aware the rest of the world."

Dumas leaned back and studied the ceiling for a few moments then rose. "Thank you for your time. Let me leave you a card. If you think of anything or find out anything that might be of interest, please give me a call."

Collins rose with him and turned off the tape recorder. He had a funny feeling that in all that talk about apparently nothing, something significant had been said, but not being the detective in the room, he had no idea what it might have been.

*

Behind the counter, Dr. Barbara Meadows was scribbling on a clipboard when Peller and Churchill came in. She glanced up and smiled. "Be right with you," she told Peller, then finished her notes. The waiting room was empty and quiet, although frantic barking issued from one exam room and human chatter from another.

Setting the clipboard down, the doctor rounded the end of the counter. "Nice to see you again, Lieutenant." She smiled at Churchill and added, "And you must be Mrs. Peller?"

Smiling demurely, Churchill said, "No, just a friend."

Meadows seemed to have a hard time keeping her eyebrows level or from checking Peller's left hand to make sure that was indeed a wedding ring, but she didn't remark further. "Here's the information you asked for."

She pulled a legal envelope from one of the deep pockets in her coat and passed it to Peller. "The guy you're interested in is an ex-employee, Bob Jankowski. He left us about a year ago to work for an emergency clinic. I hated to lose him. He was a good worker." She nodded at the envelope. "Just out of curiosity, why do you want to talk to him?"

"It's probably nothing," Peller told her. "We found out Jayvon had been trying to help a woman who was in a bit of trouble. He met her at a party at Bob's place. The woman may in turn be connected to another crime."

Dr. Meadows took a surreptitious look around, then nodded toward the front door. "Sounds complicated. Like I said, all the info is in there." She escorted them to the door and followed them outside. In a confidential tone, she said, "I've heard about Bob's parties. I didn't approve, but so long as he did his job I figured it wasn't my business. He never came to work stoned, at any rate. If he had, I'd have kicked him out the front door. It's hard to imagine Jayvon being at one of those parties."

"He may not have known what kind of party it was until he got there," Peller said. "The woman said he didn't like the goings-on."

"Well that's a relief. I suppose she was part of the entertainment?"

"That's one way of putting it."

Dr. Meadows wrapped her arms around herself in a vain attempt to ward off the chill. "I can see Jayvon as a knight in shining armor. You think that's what got him in trouble?"

"Hard to say. I'm hoping Bob can shed some light on that question."

"I hope so, too. I'm going back in before I freeze solid." She nodded at Churchill and added, "Nice meeting you," then hurried into the warmth of the clinic.

"Nor does she approve of you running around with me," Churchill said with a twisted grin.

Peller shrugged. "Lots of people don't approve of my activities."

Surprised, Churchill gaped at him.

"But most of those people," he added wryly, "are criminals."

*

Peller returned Churchill to her apartment and, in spite of himself, allowed himself to be invited in for coffee. She had just placed the steaming cup in front of him when his cell phone went off. *Slaves to our technology*, he told himself for the second time that week. But he felt a wave of elation when he saw his son Jason's name on the screen. He said hello while Churchill put a sugar cube into her coffee and stirred.

"Grandpa!" a bright young voice chirped.

"Susie!" he replied, and his granddaughter giggled. "What are you doing up so late?"

"Daddy said we could stay up late because it's Friday."

"So it is. What have you been up to?" Peller swiveled the base of the phone away from his face and quietly told Churchill, "My grandkids."

Churchill smiled and waved him on.

Susie filled him in on school, the teacher she really liked, the teacher she really hated, the dumb boys who kept causing trouble on the playground, and anything else that came into her head. She reminded grandpa that her birthday was coming up soon, in about three months, and Peller promised to send her something really nice. A minor skirmish ensued in which her younger brother Andrew wrested the phone from her and said, "Hi Grandpa!" and proceeded to relate his own tales of adventure in the public education system. Peller listened with a grin affixed to his face, and when the boy ran out of steam, asked, "Is your dad there?"

The phone changed hands again, and Jason came on the line. "Hi dad. How's it going?"

"Not bad. A few crazies on the loose, but there always are. Nothing we can't handle."

"Work is all you think about, isn't it?"

Peller laughed. "And I suppose you don't."

"Since I'm talking to a cop, I'll plead the fifth amendment. But there must be something going on in your life besides crooks. "

Peller glanced at Churchill, and she raised her eyebrows as though she'd heard the question. "Well, Uncle David sent me a letter. He's planning on visiting this summer."

"Wonderful! I haven't seen Uncle Dave and Aunt Theresa since mom's funeral. Maybe we can get out there, too."

"I'm sure they'd like that. I'll see you either way. If you can't get here, I'll go there."

"Family reunion?" Churchill asked.

"Looks like it."

"Who was that?" Jason asked, a playful undertone in his voice.

Peller felt himself flush. "I'm having coffee with a friend."

"Hi," Churchill said toward the phone. "I'm Joan."

Jason greeted her in return. "Aside from the breaking news the kids relayed, I wanted to let you know that Belinda's finally landed a job. She's going to head up marketing for a local media company. She won't be making quite as much as before, but it looks like a solid position and she says the company is growing."

"That sounds promising," Peller agreed. "Tell her congratulations."

"I'll do that. I'm afraid I have to go now. I have a few things I have to get done before bedtime. But I'll try to call next week when I have more time."

"All right. Have a good night. Tell Belinda I said hi, and give the kids hugs for me."

"I will. Good night dad. And Joan."

Peller gently set the phone on the table. "My son Jason. He says to tell you hello and good night."

Churchill smiled, took a sip of coffee, and warmed her hands on the cup. "Shouldn't I have interrupted?"

"It's okay."

"But?"

Peller shook his head. "Really, it's okay."

She didn't look convinced, but she didn't press him further. "A family reunion sounds like fun. I've never been to one."

"No?"

"Nope. I come from a small family, and we've always lived in Maryland. We were never really apart. Which could sometimes be good and sometimes be bad."

Peller drank his coffee.

"If they all do visit, I'll be happy to help out. I know how to cook, anyway." She grinned over her cup. "You can do the dishes."

"I'll keep that offer in mind," Peller said. He suddenly realized how tired he was. "I suppose I should get going soon. This might keep me awake long enough to get home, but not much more than that." He raised the coffee cup and nodded at it.

"Okay, Sherlock. Get some sleep." She reached across the table and patted his hand. "Thank you for dinner."

Peller couldn't help but smile at her persistence. "Such as it was. You're welcome."

14

Saturday, January twenty-first. Felipe Montufar, though slowly weakening, still lived.

Dumas' telephone beeped at him just as grey light crept over the horizon. Corina's voice crossed the line, trembling as though she'd been shocked awake. "Eric. Eduardo just called me. You'd better come now."

He glanced at the clock. "I'll be there in fifteen minutes."

He dressed hurriedly, dragged a comb through his hair, and didn't bother with breakfast. When he screeched to a halt outside Montufar's apartment building, she ran out and dove into his car. He didn't say anything, just drove like fury.

The entire family was at the hospital. The first thing Dumas heard was Eduardo's son Jimmie reading in a clear young voice, "For I am convinced that neither death, nor life, nor angels, nor prin-ci-*pal*-ities..."

Sylvia's face was a study in contrasts as she smiled through tears at her son. "Very good," she murmured.

Corina came to her father's side. He lay so still Dumas could barely see him breathe. "Has there been any change?"

Eduardo shook his head. "I don't think he's going to make it." He drew a ragged breath. "But he's ready to go. Father Owen was here late last night. Papá was awake then. The nurses say he drifted off shortly after we left, and there's been no change since. Right after we got here, I called to ask Father Owen to come back. He said he'd be here as soon as he could."

Silence fell again. The old man slept. To Dumas' eyes it was clear that the family patriarch had little strength left for the fight. He found himself staring helplessly at the floor, unable to change events and ignorant of how to lighten the family's burden. He could feel Corina stiff at his side as if she, too, couldn't fathom her feelings or find a way to express them.

"Now that you're here, maybe we should say the Litany of the Saints," Eduardo suggested, although it seemed more command than suggestion.

Corina opened her mouth as though to protest, then apparently changed her mind. "All right. But it's so awfully long—"

Eduardo handed his sister a prayer book. "I marked it for you."

Corina took one wild, helpless look around the room, then opened the book to the ribboned page.

Dumas, to whom most things Catholic so far remained a mystery, wondered what a litany was, and how long "awfully long" was. He peered over Corina's shoulder at the words on the page.

Eduardo led the group in the Sign of the Cross and began, "Lord, have mercy."

"Lord, have mercy," the others responded. Dumas joined in, his voice but a whisper. He'd plunged head first into unfamiliar religious territory before. He'd taken communion with Methodists, meditated with Zen Buddhists, even sat in on a Wiccan ritual. Where others lived in the certainty of their truths, he had found no more than elusive glimmers of it. Still, he searched wherever he could. So now he immersed himself, paying careful attention to the changes in the response. Beside him Corina prayed; the chorus of the others, united in prayer, seemed to fill the room much more than was possible.

"Saint Joseph," said Eduardo; the family answered, "Pray for us." Dumas could hear every voice: Eduardo's, firm; Sylvia's, confident; the children's, trusting; Ella's, full of tears; Jack's, uncertain but game; Corina's— her voice was a heartbroken petitioner's. He knew her father had meant a lot to her—probably more than he suspected. He tried to stop the flood of insight and concentrate on the prayer.

His eyes again fixed on the page, Dumas quickly learned why Corina had seemed intimidated by the length. The prayer continued in what seemed to him a call-and-response, naming saint after saint without ceasing. *Saint Peter and Saint Paul, Saint Andrew.* Soon the litany passed into names Dumas didn't recognize. He hoped he didn't stumble too badly over any of them. Occasionally a familiar name surfaced—Augustine; Francis—and was gone. The wealth of names roared silently around him, and in a sudden flash his mind's eye glimpsed a great and noble family, both dead and improbably alive, gathered to join the prayer, transforming the crowded hospital room into a great cathedral filled with chorusing voices.

Then Corina said, "Amen", and the hospital room returned.

Was that real? Dumas wondered. *A vision? Or am I imagining things?*

There was a gentle tap at the door and Father Owen entered. His spare figure seemed thinner and grayer than usual as he moved to the bedside and silently regarded Felipe.

"Thank you for coming so quickly, Father," said Eduardo. "The nurse told me he's been like this since eight-thirty last night."

"No change at all?" Father Owen asked.

"No. I think…" Eduardo shifted his weight and looked around. "I think he's leaving us. I know he's had a good life, and he's seventy-three, so we have to expect it. Still…"

Father Own reached into an inner pocket of his coat. "Yes. It's always difficult." He pulled out what looked to Dumas like a tiny makeup case and gestured toward the family. "Come a bit closer."

There was an awkward moment as chairs were pulled into position and people rearranged. Corina found his hand and squeezed tight. Dumas looked at her, startled by the pressure, but her attention was completely on her father and the priest.

With something from his kit Father Owen drew a cross on the unconscious man's forehead. A fragrance that seemed to be paradoxically composed of both mighty trees and trackless deserts stole into the room. Dumas remembered the cheap incense that had been so popular in his youth. This scent was purer than the cherry concoction his long-ago girlfriend had favored, clean and heartening.

Corina snuffled and dug in her purse for a tissue. Dumas put an arm about her shoulders. As priest and family prayed, he found himself thinking about Uncle Ethan. The man who had thrown him out had since then lost his entire family: his son had been killed, his daughters had left and never returned, and his wife had sunk into the abyss of depression. Dumas had no true reference for family except these people gathered before him to bid farewell to one of their own. What must it be like, he wondered, both the joys and the sorrows of family? He had no idea, but possibly, it occurred to him, the Montufar clan might teach him.

The priest stayed with them for a further half hour but then received another call and had to go. Children growing restive, Eduardo and Sylvia departed shortly before noon to seek out food. On and off, Dumas held Montufar and Collins held Ella. Dumas found no words to speak, but if he could he would have assured Montufar that he would always be beside her. Somehow he knew Collins wanted to tell Ella the same. Something in his eyes, in the way he looked at her. Inevitably, that thought led Dumas back to his long delayed marriage proposal.

Now's not the time, he scolded himself.

So when is the time?

Soon. I hope.

At the rate he was going, he feared never was more likely. He needed a push, or maybe a taskmaster with a whip. The more he thought about it, the more he liked that idea, and he knew the perfect man for the job.

At one o'clock, Ella leaned into Collins and asked, "Would you mind if Corina and I stepped out for an hour or two?"

"If you want," he told her.

Montufar gazed at her blankly, then gave Dumas a questioning look.

"Go ahead," he told her. "I need to talk to Rick about something anyway."

"You're off duty," she reminded him.

He didn't try to undeceive her. "It shouldn't take long. Call me when you want me back."

Montufar pulled him close and kissed him. "I always want you back."

After the women left, Dumas and Collins watched Felipe until Collins said, "Don't take this the wrong way, but I hope this ends soon."

Dumas understood and nodded.

"You're not talking business with Lieutenant Peller, are you?"

"Not police business. You can put away your tape recorder for the day."

"Gladly. I have other things to get done."

After Collins left, Dumas remained for a few minutes longer. He drew close to Felipe, set his hand on the old man's shoulder, and made a promise: "I'll take good care of Corina. I'm sure Jack will do the same for Ella. He seems a decent fellow. You can go now and get some well-deserved rest."

He shuffled out of the hospital and through the parking lot. High, thin clouds brushed across the face of the sun. It was supposed to warm up today, all the way to thirty-one, balmy by this winter's standards but still frigid in the eyes of most Marylanders. His mind on other matters, Dumas couldn't have said whether it was warm or cold. He slipped into his car, took out his cell phone, and pulled up Peller's entry in the address book. He stared at it, hand trembling, for a full minute before tapping the screen to place the call.

"Hi Eric," Peller answered. "What's up?"

"Do you have some free time? I'd like to stop by."

"Of course. I'm just vacuuming, which I don't want to do anyway."

Twenty-five minutes later, Dumas slipped into a chair at one end of Peller's dining room table, Peller slid a mug in front of him, then seated himself at the head of the table with one of his own. The fragrance of mint and honey filled the room. Peller looked inquiringly at Dumas. "What's on your mind?"

Dumas hardly knew how to start, which was his whole problem. Why couldn't he ever find the right words? There was no reason to fear his friend. This wasn't his former life. He wasn't in danger of rejection. The people around him now—particularly Corina and Rick—wouldn't pitch him into the cold to fend for himself. He put a teaspoon of sugar into his tea and stirred, listening to the spoon clink against the mug.

"It's not about work," Peller said.

Dumas shook his head and took a careful sip. The tea was still nearly hot enough to scald.

"Ergo, it must be about you and Corina."

Maybe he didn't need to speak. No doubt Peller could figure out the whole business from his grimaces and winces.

"Eric?"

"Okay," he said, but once more he found himself tongue-tied.

Peller suddenly straightened, alarmed. "Is her father gone?"

"What? No. He's on his way out the door, but it's not that."

"I'll be happy to come to the hospital if—"

"It's not that, Rick." Dumas felt utterly stupid now.

Peller leaned back and gave Dumas a careful scrutiny. "Okay, we've established that much. Come on, then. Let's get this resolved before the sun sets and rises again."

And there he was, the taskmaster with the whip. Somehow, it made a difference. "I need your help with...something."

"Well, that's a start." Peller took a sip of his tea. "What something?"

Dumas almost felt he was choking and realized it was indeed the old fear grasping for his throat. Suddenly angry at himself, he spat out, "I'm going to propose."

Peller looked amused. "Not in that tone, I hope."

Dumas relapsed into misery. "I'll be lucky to get through it at all. That's why I need your help."

Peller leaned back, stretched his legs under the table, and regarded his colleague as though studying a new species of animal. "Why is this a problem?"

Dumas sipped at his still-steaming beverage. "It's me. I suffer from a long history of rejection."

"Corina's not going to reject you," Peller reassured him. "She loves you. You know that. She knows that. Heck, the whole second floor probably knows it by now."

Dumas wasn't sure he could make Peller understand without reciting his whole miserable history, something he didn't care to do. Only Montufar knew any of it. He kept his past locked safely away so it couldn't interfere with his present, so that others wouldn't probe too deeply, so that it wouldn't rise up to overwhelm him at every turn. Except that lately it had.

"I can't help if you don't say anything," Peller told him.

"I just have problems with this, okay?" Dumas snapped.

"Why?"

He shoved himself back from the table. Cups jostled and drops of liquid splattered onto the table. "Because! Because my father left, my mother left, my uncle threw me out, and my friend stole my woman! Everyone I've ever been close to walked out on me, Rick. Everyone!"

Peller's eyebrows raised while Dumas exploded. When he'd finished, Dumas knew he now had no choice but to explain. Peller would ask a million questions, and they'd be here hours turning it every which way as though it were an investigation, as though somewhere behind it all lurked someone responsible, as though their identification would resolve the whole matter. But it wasn't anybody at all. It was everyone. Including Dumas himself. There could be no resolution.

Peller, though, surprised him. "Okay, Eric. I won't press you. But have you told Corina?"

Dumas crossed his arms over his chest and started at his shoes. "Most of it. Not about the girlfriend."

Peller lifted his mug to his lips but set it down again without drinking. "Corina isn't like her."

"I know."

"Nor has everyone has walked out on you. Some of us would stick by you to the death."

It wasn't a rebuke, but Dumas felt embarrassed anyway. "I didn't mean you."

Peller rose, refreshed his cooling cup, and offered the last of the tea to Dumas. Dumas shook his head. Peller poured the remaining liquid into his own cup and rinsed and washed the teapot. He returned to the table, sat, and crossed his arms on the tabletop. "I'm no good at psychotherapy, but it seems to me you need to get this done before you turn your whole life inside out."

Dumas started to object that it wasn't that critical, but Peller shook his head to stop him.

"I'm serious. It's eating you up, and for nothing. It's not that hard to ask. It's just four words. Start with 'will you' and end with 'marry me.' That's all it takes."

"I've tried, Rick. Believe me, I've tried. Five or six times. I haven't gotten the first word out, much less all four."

"So what do you want me to do? I can't say them for you."

Finally, Dumas thought, *we can get to the point*. "I want you to be there."

Peller shook his head, but not in refusal. "I don't see how an audience will help."

"You're not an audience."

"Then what am I?"

How could he say that Peller served as overseer, that without him the proposal would never materialize? It sounded stupid even to Dumas. "You're my friend, is all. And you went through this yourself. I suppose it was easy for you, though."

"I suffered a minor case of nerves," Peller said. "But I had my dad to coach me, too."

Dumas sure wished he'd had a father to coach him in these matters, instead of an absentee dad and an uncle who couldn't handle the truth. "What did he tell you?"

"He told me to ask Sandra. Without delay."

"Without delay." Solid advice, Dumas knew, but delay seemed to be all he could muster.

"Exactly. So tell me, when do you want to stage this coup?"

If he thought it over, he'd come up with a million excuses, so he didn't think at all. He said the first thing that leaped into his mind: "How about my apartment, tomorrow evening over dinner?" But excuses followed hard on the question's heels anyway. "I hope," he mumbled.

Peller smiled encouragement. "If you ask her to dinner, she'll come. That's been business as usual with you two for months."

Dumas wasn't quite sure how Peller knew that. The problems, though, weren't only in his mind. "Her father might die anytime now." He rubbed at the headache threatening his brow. "This is so complicated."

Peller took another drink. "It's the simplest thing in the world. Just ask her. It doesn't matter who's there or who's watching, whether you're alone or in a crowd. There's no bad time to ask. In fact, this may be the best time. Eduardo has Sylvia and their family, Ella has Jack, but who does Corina have? Yeah, she's a tough woman, but everyone's strength fails sometimes. She needs you by her side. Nothing can be bad about promising her you will be. It will give her something else to think about, too, and a future to look forward to."

As always, Peller made sense, but Dumas couldn't shake off his doubts.

"Anyway, you've got it easy. You just want to propose to your girlfriend. You don't have my problem." Peller grimaced.

Dumas couldn't imagine how Peller could possibly have any greater problem than he. "What's that?"

"A woman who wants to call me Sherlock."

At first Dumas thought he was trying to be funny, but Peller's dead serious expression made it impossible not to laugh. "You're joking."

"No joke."

"Who is she?"

"Her name is Joan Churchill."

In spite of himself, Dumas laughed again. "Well, that's appropriate. As English as Holmes. How did you meet her?"

Peller cracked a smile, too. "She's a friend of Andy's wife, a double divorcee about my age. They conspired to introduce us at the shindig at Victoria's Wednesday evening, and I foolishly agreed to have something approaching dinner with her last night."

"And she calls you Sherlock."

"Scout's honor." Peller raised his hand in the Boy Scout sign.

Funny or not, Dumas knew Peller must be suffering. "Do you like her?"

Peller examined the depths of his tea.

"You do," Dumas decided.

"That's half the problem."

"Maybe you'd better take back what you said."

Peller raised his eyebrows.

Dumas grinned. "You sound entirely as woeful as me."

Peller laughed. "Well. Let's wait and see how your proposal goes before we draw that conclusion."

*

Had it been springtime, Ella would have driven her sister the five miles north to Cedar Lane Park and walked with her in the warm sunshine among the new grass and unfurling leaves. With that option out the window and the window securely closed to keep out the January chill, she did the next best thing: she took Corina to the mall.

Three dresses and a pair of shoes later, they stopped for lunch at a little Mexican counter in the food court. Juggling their purchases and food-laden trays, they located a two-person table on the edge of the dining area. A constant stream of Saturday shoppers washed by them: teenagers in jeans, mothers pushing strollers, white-haired grandmothers. Corina, eyes turned on the tabletop, barely seemed to be there.

"Hey," Ella prompted. "Aren't you going to eat? This place makes pretty good tacos."

Her sister looked up, blank.

"Come on, Corina. Let's try to have a day together, like we used to."

"Nothing's like it used to be."

"I know," Ella said gently. "It's horrible, and it hurts. But we can't cave in."

Tears suddenly stood in Corina's eyes. "I'm so tired, Ella. So scared, and tired. I can't work, I can't think, I—I—" She wiped fiercely at her eyes. "I wish it was over. I wish he was just gone. And then I want him to live forever. I know he can't. But why does he have to go now?" She covered her face with her hands.

Ella sat quietly. She'd been waiting for this moment, when Corina would finally crack, and they would have to face the inevitable together. She nibbled at her taco and waited.

Finally Corina took a deep breath and wiped at her eyes one last time. "I'm sorry."

"You don't have to tell me."

"But I don't usually go to pieces."

Ella didn't have to be told that, either, but maybe she knew something her sister had never realized. "Unless it really hurts. Remember that weekend after your first month at the academy?"

Pain of a different sort flickered across Corina's face, just for a moment before she pushed it aside. "Yeah. I remember."

"You couldn't say two words without bawling."

Corina nodded, picked up a taco, took a tentative bite while she reflected. "I guess I've toughed up since then. But what about you? You're the one with the reputation for falling apart in an emergency. How is it you're not?"

Ella had wondered when the question would arise. Unlike Corina, she'd never been forced to grow a thick skin, so she hadn't. Until now, when she no longer had a choice. "For Jack."

Corina smiled weakly. "Thought so."

"I want to marry him."

"Really?"

"Yeah."

The conversation dropped into a pensive lull, and they both turned their attention on the food. Ella wasn't sure why Corina needed to mull it over. After all, she and Eric Dumas were traveling the same road. Weren't they?

"Have you talked to him about it?" Corina finally asked.

"No."

"Oh."

Ella propped her chin on her folded hands and waited.

"Eric and I haven't talked about it, either."

"Why not?"

Corina shook her head and drank her soda.

Ella sighed and picked up her cup, too. "Same here."

Corina scowled at her food, then her mouth curled into a suddenly sly grin. "I didn't think you'd ever marry. You always seemed to enjoy trailing men wherever you went."

Ella laughed and blushed simultaneously. "I did! But we're not that young anymore, are we? Time is speeding up, or we're slowing down. I feel like I'm missing out on something important. You know?"

"Don't tell me your biological clock is running down."

"It's more like, I don't know, like I've only half lived. When I'm with Jack, I feel complete." She winced at her own words. "Okay, that's corny."

Corina set her elbows on the table, then quickly pulled back and inspected the surface for cleanliness before resettling them. "Believe me, I get it."

"Why didn't you ever go out with anyone?"

"All the guys I knew were jerks."

Ella laughed, but she wasn't sure whether Corina was joking or being serious.

"All the available ones, anyway," Corina affirmed. "Besides, I was too busy proving myself to the world. I didn't have time for frivolity. Thinking back on it, I probably fell in love with Eric the day I met him. I just didn't know it at the time."

That didn't surprise Ella. Corina hadn't exactly gushed about Dumas over the years, but she sure had mentioned him a lot. "What attracted you to him?"

Now it was Corina's turn to blush, a rarity with her. "It's stupid."

"Come on, *hermana*. You know I'll badger you until you tell me."

"Little brat," Corina joked. She drew a long breath and told the story without once looking Ella in the face. "I hadn't been on the force very long. Maybe four months. This happened the day Eric came on board. He'd been introduced around, but I hadn't talked to him yet. I picked up a big stack of files from my desk, and they started slipping every which way. I tried to corral them but dropped every last one. Papers flew everywhere. So I got down on the floor to pick them up, and one of the men passed by. He made some imbecilic lewd joke about me on the floor. I was so angry I don't remember what he said, but the next thing I knew Eric came around the corner full tilt and *accidentally* smacked him in the face with a three-ring binder! After apologizing in a totally unapologetic tone, he helped me pick up the papers. That guy never said a word to me again."

Ella laughed and reached across the table for Corina's hands. "That's not stupid; it's great! But you didn't fall into each other's arms until now?"

"Not until last year, anyway. Before then, we kept our relationship professional and friendly, nothing more."

"There was something there, though."

Corina nodded thoughtfully. "I guess so. But we both had issues to work through. Maybe that's what took so long."

For the first time in her life, Ella found herself feeling sorry for Corina. It felt strange—she was used to being the recipient of her sister's pity—but somehow liberating, too. Maybe she'd finally grown up enough to face the world after all. "You know what I think?"

"What's that?"

"I think we should give the guys one week to propose, and if they don't then we should serve the engagement rings on them."

Squeezing Ella's hands, Corina put on her most serious cop face. "That's a deal, ma'am."

Passersby couldn't help but look in the direction of their laughter.

*

Shortly before four o'clock, Dumas received a text message from Montufar letting him know the family was returning to the hospital.

"I don't know her father," Peller said, watching as Dumas shoved himself into his coat, "but if you want I can come along."

Dumas considered the offer. He wouldn't mind the company, and he doubted either Montufar or the rest of her family would, either. "Why not," he decided.

They arrived in the hospital lobby at the same time as the family. Jack Collins rushed in from the cold two minutes later. Reunited, the gathering trooped up to the third floor. They were passing the nurse's station as a young doctor with wiry red hair emerged from Felipe's room. He immediately spotted them and approached with downcast mouth.

"I'm Dr. Byrne," he told them quietly. "I'm very sorry. Felipe passed away about twenty minutes ago."

Corina gripped Dumas' arm and choked back a sob. Ella, unable to contain her grief, nearly collapsed against Collins, tears flooding her eyes.

Eduardo let out a long breath and gave his sisters a distressed glance. "Thank you, Doctor. May we go in?"

"Of course." But before letting them go, he drew Eduardo aside and spoke quietly, so that Dumas couldn't hear. The brief conversation ended, Eduardo motioned the family into the room. They surrounded the bed where Felipe's body lay covered. Byrne followed them in and gently turned down the sheet so they could see his face, peaceful, silent, empty, then the doctor slipped out.

Eduardo waited until he was gone to speak "Adios, papá. Da besos a mamá de todos nosotros." He translated for the northerners: "Goodbye, father. Give mother kisses from us."

Eyes moist, Sylvia gathered her children to her and held them as they cried into her skirt.

Peller had hung back, but now he stepped close and put one tentative hand on Corina's shoulder and another on Ella's. Simultaneously, the women each set their hands on top of his and squeezed.

"I didn't think this would come so soon," Corina said. "But maybe it's for the best. He was so seldom himself anymore."

"It is God's mercy," Eduardo agreed. "I'll call the funeral home and Father Owen. I suppose the funeral will be Monday or Tuesday." In turn, he looked pensively at his wife and children, at his sisters, at Dumas, Collins, and Peller. "We should all attend Mass together tomorrow. Please join us?"

At first Dumas thought he was specifically asking the men, but the women nodded first, and he realized that like Corina, Ella must not have given much attention to religion for a long time. "Corina and I were already planning on it," he told Eduardo.

Collins looked uncertain, but after a glance at Ella, still leaning into him and crying, he said, "Of course."

That only left Peller, who without hesitation answered, "I'd be honored."

"Thank you," Eduardo said. "Let's say a prayer, and then we should go so I can make the arrangements."

This time, instead of reaching for a prayer book, Eduardo simply began, "Hail Mary, full of grace..."

As Corina slid seamlessly into the prayer, Dumas listened. Tomorrow, he thought, was going to be one strange, stressful day. Nothing short of Cameron Terrell popping in for another late night visit could ratchet up his tension. Just thinking about her nearly gave him hives. He hoped she'd keep her hands off of Peller.

As the family chorused, "Amen", Peller leaned over and whispered, "You okay?"

Dumas wondered if he looked as ill as he felt. With all these thoughts chasing each other around his brain, he probably did. "Yeah."

Silently, the family filed out and down to the lobby, where Sylvia offered, "Would you like to come to our place for dinner?"

"Thank you, but I don't want to intrude," Peller told her.

"It's no intrusion."

"Just the same, I'd rather give you folks your space."

The others accepted, though, and Eduardo bundled up the children and led his crew out into the cold, with Ella and Collins close behind. Montufar gave Dumas a gentle tug, but he held up a finger. "I need one word with Rick."

She looked miffed but let go of him and went to wait by the door.

"You're not all right," Peller concluded.

"I'll live. I just want to give you fair warning about something, or rather someone. You remember me telling you about my neighbor Ozzie?"

"Sure, the guy on a mission to get you hitched."

"That's the one. He's got a girl of his own now, or rather again, and she's a wild one. She came on to me the night before last. She says Ozzie knows about her escapades and is okay with them. I'm not sure I believe it."

Peller fought down a laugh.

"What?" Dumas asked.

"I can just imagine you desperately trying to fend her off."

"Ha ha. I'm not telling you this to amuse you."

"So the point is?"

"Forewarned is forearmed. If she gets half a chance, you'll be next on her list."

Peller rolled his eyes, a bit too theatrically Dumas thought. "So I have two women after me now? Thanks a lot."

"At least you like Joan. I don't think you'll like Cameron."

"Speaking of not liking things," Peller said, and nodded at Montufar, who was staring at them with growing impatience.

Dumas waved her an acknowledgement. "See you tomorrow," he told Peller, and hurried to her side. They walked out into the frigid evening arm in arm.

"What was that about?" Montufar asked without looking at him.

"Nothing. Just a bit about tomorrow."

"He probably knows more about what goes on in a church than you do," she said, and nudged him gently.

He let it go, not wanting to speak a lie or tip his hand, and she didn't press, thank God. Maybe his Catholic ancestors were praying for him, after all.

15

Peller took his time going home. The deep blue of evening was fading to gray as he pulled into his driveway. Next door, Jerry Souter lumbered down his front steps in a heavy white coat. Peller thought first of polar bears and then of winter camouflage. Either image seemed to fit. Souter waved to him, so Peller got out of his car and walked over. "You're not going out in this cold, are you?"

"Gotta eat," Souter told him. "Care to join me? I'm going down to the corner deli."

"May as well."

They walked in silence, an unlikely pair of friends: Souter old enough to be Peller's grandfather, striding along slowly, ramrod straight; Peller with hands shoved in his pockets, eyes seemingly directed at the sidewalk but taking in everything they passed—houses with glowing windows; streetlights scattering glare about the neighborhood; cars swishing by, bearing people home from the mall or out to nightlife.

The deli overlooked an intersection a few blocks from Peller and Souter's homes. The mingled aromas of soups and breads escaped its door and wandered along the streets. Souter pulled the door open, motioned Peller inside, and followed, trailed by a swirl of freezing air. Even with the heat cranked up, the storefront felt cool. They approached the long glass-fronted counter where meats, cheeses, and salads were temptingly arranged.

Souter ordered a bowl of chili, and Peller a reuben sandwich and onion rings. They stood at the counter until the food arrived, then carried it to one of the red tables lining the front window. The only people in the place, they chose the table farthest from the door to avoid the draft. After sampling his chili, Souter asked, "Not to meddle, but did you find anything yet?"

"Not a lot," Peller told him. "It's an odd case, though."

"Odd how?"

"For one thing, Jayvon was mixed up with a woman who had a connection to a crook who got himself popped last week. It could be a coincidence, I guess." He bit into his sandwich and chewed thoughtfully.

"You don't think so," Souter guessed.

"No. I'm reasonably certain the incident at the vet clinic was a botched robbery attempt. Tamai—that's the crook—used the girl as bait to collar blackmail victims. There's an unpopular theory about Jayvon being the inside man in that robbery. I doubt he would have done such a thing voluntarily, but if he was being blackmailed?"

Souter nodded and gazed out the window. "His poor grandmother."

"She's strong, Jerry. Amazingly strong."

"I guess."

"Anyway," Peller continued, "the connection between Jayvon and the girl is a guy he worked with, a fellow named Bob. I'll be paying him a visit on Monday." He looked at his watch. It wasn't even six yet. "Or maybe I'll call him this evening. I don't have anything else to do."

Souter regarded him evenly. "Don't you ever take a day off?"

"Occasionally," Peller said with a grin, but he found he couldn't maintain it for long.

Souter noticed his lack of good cheer. "What's wrong, son?"

"Corina's father passed away today." *Winter has penetrated everything. Absolutely everything.*

"Old men do that." With a twinkle in his eye, Souter added, "Good thing we're still young."

"You are, I'm sure."

"You're not?"

Peller shrugged. "Eat your chili, young fellow."

Souter ate but raised an eyebrow when Peller didn't follow suit.

Peller wasn't sure he wanted to talk about it, but somehow he couldn't hold it in. "People seem to think I'm still young," he said. "A colleague even tried to fix me up with a friend of his wife."

"And you didn't want him to," Souter remarked between spoonfuls.

"Not particularly."

"So don't get involved with her." He looked up, eyebrows arched. "Unless you do want the lady."

"You never remarried," Peller told him. "Why should I?"

"I had an excuse."

"Oh?"

"I was a terrible husband."

Peller found that so ridiculous that he had to laugh.

"I'm serious," Souter objected. "I don't mean I beat Amanda. I just was no good at all those little things women like their men to say and do. So when she died, I figured no sense in disappointing another woman. Best if I toughed it out on my own."

"A disappointment?" Peller asked, surprised. "That's how you see yourself?"

"Uh-huh."

"She might have seen it differently."

"She did," Souter admitted. "She was crazy about me. Little fool."

Peller had never known Amanda, had never given her much thought even. She had died shortly before he and Sandra moved to Maryland. But now he found himself wishing he could have met her. She must have been as fascinating as her husband.

"So what's your excuse?" Souter asked.

Peller wanted to say it wasn't an excuse, merely the truth, but Souter might have an opinion on that and he didn't want to get into an argument. "I can't give Sandra's place to someone else."

"You won't," Souter assured him. "But if you'd a mind to, you could add on a room in that big ol' heart of yours."

Peller didn't want to pursue that course, so he changed the subject. He pulled out his cell phone and said, "No time like the present. Let's see what Bob can tell us." The envelope Dr. Meadows had given him was still in his pocket. He extracted it and looked at its contents, a printout with a phone number, an email address, and a residential address in Jessup. Calling the number, he leaned back and looked out the window at the darkness.

"Hello?" The tenor voice sounded thin and suffused with the fuzz of a bad connection.

"Bob Jankowski?" Peller asked.

"Speaking."

"This is Detective Lieutenant Rick Peller with the Howard County Police Department. I'm doing some follow-up work on the disappearance of Jayvon Fletcher. Dr. Meadows tells me you worked with him."

"Yeah," Jankowski replied without hesitation. "He was a good friend and a good coworker. Have you guys found anything yet?"

Peller ignored the question. "I hear you introduced him to a woman named Shania North."

Jankowski didn't respond immediately. Peller wondered what that meant. It could have been anything from embarrassment to fear. "I did," he finally said. "Big mistake."

"The introduction or the party in general?"

"Both I guess. I didn't realize Jayvon was such a holy roller."

"Meaning?"

"He got real upset at the goings-on. I guess he found it sinful or something."

Peller found Jankowski's tone dismissive. Apparently Jayvon hadn't made a convert of him. "What in particular did he find objectionable?"

Again the pause, then, "I probably shouldn't say too much."

"I don't care what you do at your parties, Mr. Jankowski. I'm trying to find out what became of Jayvon. Presumably you want me to find out."

"Yeah, okay, sorry. We were drinking and smoking stuff. I guess you already know Shania put on a show for us."

"I'd gathered that, yes. So Jayvon didn't like it. How did he react?"

"Before the lady did her stuff, he pulled me aside and lectured me about the drugs and said he was leaving. I told him to wait for the main attraction. I figured he'd like Shania. Everybody did. She knew how to move."

"This wasn't the first time you'd hired her, then."

"Nope. I'd hired her a few times before."

"Were you wrong about Jayvon's reaction to her?" Peller already knew the answer.

Jankowski gave it without hesitation. "So wrong I couldn't believe it. When she started to take it off, he stormed out."

"Did he speak with her before he left?"

"Not then. Two days later."

Surprised, Peller waited for an explanation. He could almost hear Jankowski squirming.

"We were at work. He took me aside and told me he was sorry about blowing a gasket. He said he wanted to apologize to Shania. So I arranged for them to get together."

"Where did that take place?"

"My place. I thought maybe he'd changed his mind, so I told Shania I'd pay for anything Jayvon wanted." He laughed. "What an idiot. He could have had her all the way, but he really did just want to apologize."

Peller wondered why Fletcher hadn't cut off contact with Jankowski, even if it meant finding a new job. There were plenty of veterinary hospitals around. With his stellar reputation, he wouldn't have had any trouble finding work. "What happened?"

"He was such a perfect gentleman that she fell for him. I could see it in her eyes. And after that, they started hanging out together. He even introduced her to his grandmother. Can you imagine that? 'Hi granny, this is my new friend. She's a stripper.' That went over like a lead balloon."

"I can imagine," Peller said, although he didn't have to. He'd seen it in Mrs. Fletcher's eyes and heard it in her voice. "But how do you know that?"

"He told me. He didn't understand. I had to explain it to him. Nice guy, but pretty clueless, huh?"

No more than you, Peller groused to himself. "If Jayvon objected to her profession so seriously, why did he take up with her?"

Jankowski laughed again, but this time it was bitter. "White knight syndrome. He thought he could save her from herself. Dumb, dumb, dumb. Anyway, she didn't need saving. She was fine the way she was."

"How do you know that?"

"Come on, Lieutenant. You know what she did. She made good money, and you could tell she enjoyed everything about it. She loved it."

Peller's tone turned dangerous. "That was an act. Her enthusiasm cranks up yours until you're throwing money at her. Secretly, she might have hated it."

"Nah. She liked working my parties. She told me so. Told me I was her best customer."

The man's gullibility didn't surprise Peller. He should have stopped there, but he couldn't help bating the fool. "Have you hired her lately?"

"No. I tried a few times but couldn't reach her. I guess business is good."

"Business is dead, Mr. Jankowski, and Shania isn't far behind. She's been used up and spit out by men like you. Now she's hooked on opioids and dying a miserable death." Without a further word, he cut the connection. He found his hands shaking as he pocketed the phone. He felt like smashing the window with it. When he looked up, Souter was eyeing him, expressionless. "What?" he snapped.

"Good man," Souter told him. "We could've used you in the war."

*

The family reassembled on Sunday morning in the parking lot of St. John the Evangelist Catholic Church in the Oakland Mills Interfaith Center. Montufar had been here just once before, the previous year when she asked Father Owen to convince her stubborn brother to talk to his doctor about his speech problems following a concussion received in an automobile accident. She still couldn't reconcile this blocky, corporate building with a church. Growing up, her parish church had been San Juan Bautista in Amatitlán, a beautiful structure lifting itself up to heaven. This place just looked like every other building in Columbia.

They arrived in miniature convoy, with Eduardo driving his family and Jack Collins ferrying Ella, Corina, and Dumas. Peller hadn't arrived yet, but with the temperature again stuck at about twenty degrees, it wasn't a day to wait outside. The sunshine lied. As they crossed the parking lot, Montufar asked Eduardo, "Do you like attending Mass here?"

"Oh yes. The people are wonderful."

"But it looks like a warehouse."

Eduardo regarded the building for a moment. As he held the door open for his sister, he said, "Maybe it's like the lepers Jesus healed, or St. Francis embraced."

Surprised, she looked up at him, expecting to see his teasing smile. But no. He was serious. "What do you mean by *that*?"

"Ugly on the outside, beautiful on the inside. Where it counts."

He had a point, she supposed, but she still preferred churches that reflected the glory of God.

They waited in the vestibule for a few minutes until Peller arrived, dressed in a sharply tailored navy suit. Montufar thought he looked particularly handsome. She could imagine him walking into a formal gathering with an elegantly gowned Sandra on his arm. They would have turned heads for sure. After exchanging greetings, he fell into line with the family

Montufar hesitated. It had been so long since she had attended Mass—years, while she studied and worked and forgot who she had once been. As she reached for the font she had a sudden wild mental image of her fingers flaming in the holy water, like a vampire's in a B-flick. But the water was cool as she blessed herself.

Dumas looked quizzically at her. "Something wrong?"

"No. It's okay."

She followed Eduardo, Sylvia, and the children into what she expected its architects might have termed a sanctuary. The room was large and well-lit, but there all resemblance to a church ended. The seating suggested a lecture hall. Set into wood-paneled walls, the windows carried colorful abstract designs that didn't recall to her anything spiritual. There was a table that Montufar assumed to be the altar, for a crucifix hung behind it. After a careful search, she found what she thought must be the tabernacle.

She wished she could hide herself somewhere in the back, but apparently the family seats were near the front of the church, and she couldn't leave her siblings. When they arrived at the chosen spot, Peller stepped aside to let her take a place beside Susannah. Susannah smiled at her, delighted to have her aunt beside her. Maybe it helped chase off the sadness of the day.

Montufar genuflected in the vague direction of the altar and sat down beside Susannah.

Dumas settled beside her and murmured in her ear. "Are you sure you're okay?"

"Yes. I don't know. Nothing's right."

She could see the questions in his eyes, but he didn't press.

Or was she just predisposed to see this ultramodern building, designed as a sort of religious lowest common denominator, as an irreverent pile of sheetrock and wood? Maybe Eduardo was right. Maybe the building didn't matter that much. Mass was Mass, whether it was celebrated in a cathedral or a village church or on the hood of an Army jeep. What mattered was that she was there, for the first time in longer than she cared to consider.

Montufar closed her eyes. *I'm home. When I open my eyes I will be in a stone-walled sanctuary with the Virgin Mary and the saints and windows full of light. It will be Easter Sunday and there will be flowers and incense and candles glowing in ranks and the choir in joy and old women praying the Rosary and I will be with my grandparents and my parents and my big brother and little sister and I will be eight years old.*

Home.

She felt a warm trickle down her cheek. Dumas's finger wiped away the moisture.

He'll think I'm just crying for papá.

*

Following the mass, the family returned to Eduardo and Sylvia's home for lunch, accompanied by Dumas, Collins, and Peller. This time Peller didn't resist, possibly sensing that Sylvia wouldn't have let him say no.

While Sylvia bustled between the kitchen and dining room, carrying trays of sandwiches and tubs of premade salads, Eduardo touched Montufar's shoulder, whispered her name, and drew her aside.

She looked up into her brother's eyes. "What's on your mind?" she asked, a bit flippantly, for his expression was sober.

"Corina," he repeated. "You look exhausted."

"Are you surprised?"

He shook his head. "I watch the news. I know what goes on out there in the world. But I don't see what you see. What I see is cleansed for public consumption. You look evil straight in the eye day after day. I don't know how you stand it."

She wanted to object that it wasn't nearly so bad as that most days, but he put a finger to her lips to silence her.

"And now papá is dead. You're a tough lady, as tough as mamá was, but even tough ladies shouldn't have to carry such burdens alone."

Corina looked back to the others. Dumas had squatted down and was saying something to Jimmie and Susannah, his fist balled up, no doubt with a coin about to either vanish or appear within.

Eduardo followed her gaze. "Eric is a wonderful guy. He'll stay by your side, I'm sure. He's right for you. But you need something more."

Suddenly irritated, she snapped, "You're not talking about therapy, are you?"

He shook his head and smiled patiently. "I'm talking about Father Owen."

"Oh. I don't think I could—"

"Corina. You talked to him for me once. He's not that scary."

She had, but neither she nor the priest had ever mentioned it to him. How had he known?

Eduardo's smile broadened, telling her he understood the unasked question. "Like you said once, I'm smarter than I look. Just talk to him. For your own sake this time. He can help you find yourself again."

Big brothers can be so annoying, she told herself, but she knew that was just deflection. "What makes you think I'm lost?"

"Don't you think you are?"

"I don't know. Maybe."

Eduardo smiled. "You were a deadly serious little girl, too, but you were serious about different things. Life in this country has changed you, changed what you see and what you don't see. You've grown hard and cold on the outside, maybe for a good reason. But how far down does that shell reach? Is the real Corina still in there? She must be. You must find her again. Find your way home again." He drew a breath and released it. "Talk to Father Owen. He can guide you. He can help you come home."

Sylvia called them to the table, but Corina, simultaneously unsettled and comforted by her brother's words, didn't move. Maybe he understood her struggle better than Eric did. He'd known her all her life. "Okay." Her eyes burned with sudden unshed tears. "Okay."

"Good girl." He hugged her. "Now let's go eat."

*

While they ate, the Montufar siblings traded stories about their father. Peller listened to their memories with interest.

"He never said an angry word to me," Eduardo recalled, then with a chuckle added, "Although I did a few things that made him mad."

"I can't imagine that," Corina said with a sly wink at Ella.

"Mamá gave me the thrashings. Papá would just look at me and shake his head, and I'd know I messed up."

"I got some of that, too," Corina acknowledged.

"Not me," Ella told them. "I was his little angel."

Eduardo grinned at Collins. "Our little sister could get away with anything. Be on your toes."

Collins smiled, embarrassed, but he reached for Ella's hand and squeezed it. "I think I can handle her," he said quietly.

The mischief vacated Eduardo's face. "He gave up a lot for us. I didn't realize how much until Susannah was born." Susannah was dissecting a turkey sandwich and didn't seem interested in the mention of her name. "When he held her the first time, he said to me, 'This is why I brought the family to this country.' I asked him what he meant. He said it was for his children and grandchildren and all the generations to follow. He loved Guatemala. He had family and many friends there. But the politics. The violence." Eduardo shook his head. "He couldn't trust anyone anymore. So when the opportunity arose, he brought us here."

Everyone reflected in silence, then Ella said, "Thank you, papá. From all of us."

Peller hung around for a time after the meal. The family talked sports and news and the mundane affairs of life. Ella pressed Dumas into performing a few magic tricks with coins and cards, which everyone applauded. Once the talk moved beyond prestidigitation, Dumas pulled Montufar and Peller aside. "My place for dinner?"

"That would be great," Montufar told him.

Already knowing the plan, Peller pretended to hesitate. "You sure you want me along?"

Dumas didn't have to insist. Montufar did so for him. "We'd love to have you join us." She turned a hopeful smile on Dumas. "Wouldn't we?"

"Like the lady says."

"In that case I'd be happy to," Peller told them, satisfied that Montufar had no idea of the surprise in store.

*

It was full dark by the time they arrived at Dumas' apartment complex. As they mounted the stairs, he set a finger to his lips. Montufar smiled demurely, but Peller had no idea why silence was necessary. He gave Montufar a quizzical look.

"Don't want to alert Ozzie," she whispered.

That seemed odd to Peller, but following his companions' lead, he crept silently down the hall to the far end, where Dumas carefully unlocked the door. The process seemed to take two lifetimes. Once inside, their host motioned them to the sofa in his spare living room. "I'll fix us something to eat," he said.

Inexplicably on pins and needles, Peller didn't think he could eat a bite. His case of nerves irritated him; this was Dumas' big moment, not his.

"Thank you for coming with us today," Montufar said, and it took Peller a moment to realize she was talking about earlier in the day, not the forthcoming proposal.

"You're welcome. How are you holding up?"

She shrugged. "I'll be fine until the funeral, I think. I don't know how I'll be then."

"You'll get through it."

"I guess." She leaned back and closed her eyes. In the kitchen, Dumas clanked things around. "I have to. But I feel like I'm on a roller coaster. Arsons. Eric. Blackmail. My faith. My father. My brother, bless his soul. Down and up and down again until I don't know what I'm feeling anymore."

"It's called life," Peller said, but not without sympathy. "We all go through it in our own way."

She opened her eyes and stared at the ceiling. "Sorry."

"For what?"

"Being so self-indulgent. What have I got to complain about? You've lost more than I can imagine."

"I don't know about that. I'm not sure there are any degrees in the loss of a loved one. But if I have, then rest assured you'll come out the other side. Because I did."

She looked at him, eyes moist, and smiled. "But you're…"

When she didn't finish, Peller said it for her. "A man? You think that makes a difference?"

"I don't know. I don't like to think so, but maybe."

"We might process it differently, but pain is pain."

Dumas slipped from kitchen to table to set out plates and utensils and food. "All set. Come on over."

To Peller's surprise, Dumas had merely heated up some canned spaghetti and supplemented it with a loaf of Italian bread and bagged salad. "I didn't have enough energy to make a seven-course meal," he explained.

"This is fine," Montufar told him, settling in. Making the Sign of the Cross, she silently said grace while Dumas and Peller waited. Peller said his own prayer. He'd long since grown accustomed to this procedure. Sandra had always said a silent prayer before meals without ever insisting upon anyone else's participation. They had given their guests and even their son Jason time to pray—or not—as they wished. Jason readily picked up the habit and carried it forward as tradition in his family.

Once the meal began, they ate in silence, Peller waiting for Dumas to do something, Dumas probably waiting for the propitious moment, and Montufar just looking drained. At length the plates sat empty. Dumas set aside his fork, pushed himself back and fidgeted with his napkin. Peller didn't have to guess what was running through his brain—his eyes were feverish, and his jaw quivered as he licked his lips.

Peller gave him an encouraging smile and a nod just as Montufar patted her mouth with her napkin and looked up. She frowned first at Peller, then at Dumas. "Was it something I didn't say?"

"I have dessert," Dumas said. Laughter bordering on the maniacal bubbled in his voice, but Peller thought he was holding up well under the circumstances. Now if he could just make it to the finish line.

"Oh, I couldn't—" Montufar began.

Dumas fished in his trouser pocket. When he extended his clenched fist, she frowned at it, then gave him a questioning look.

What is it? Peller thought on her behalf. *A fortune cookie?*

She had a different thought. "You want me to chew on your hand?"

Dumas' hand trembled, but he slowly uncurled his fingers. Lying in his upturned palm, an unpretentious diamond, glowing with an inner light, sparkled in a slender gold ring.

Just your style, Eric, Peller thought. *Simple and beautiful.*

"Is that for real?" Montufar said, as though she couldn't expect anyone to give her such a thing. The look on Dumas' face convinced her. "It is for real. Oh. Oh."

"Will you…" Dumas's voice faltered. He looked to Peller, desperate.

Like a stage prompter, Peller silently mouthed the second half.

Dumas swallowed and focused on Montufar again, and somehow he got through it. "…marry me?"

To Peller's astonishment and delight, Montufar broke into tears, then began to laugh hysterically. Alarmed, Dumas tried to rise, but Peller pushed him back down into his seat.

"Marry you," Montufar said when she got her breath. "Marry you! Yes, Eric, *obviously* I'll marry you. Even Eduardo says you're the right man for me. I can hardly disagree with him." The giggles threatened again, and she muttered, "Now I will have to go home."

Neither of the men understood what she meant by that, but her consent was clear. Dumas sat, dumbfounded, until Peller motioned toward the ring still in his hand. Recalled, he reached across the table for Montufar's hand, and slowly, as though afraid of breaking her, slipped the ring onto her finger.

"You don't know how—" he began.

"Oh, shut up, Cyrano."

Peller smiled at the allusion—Cyrano de Bergerac indeed!—and turned to give them some privacy. While he waited for some sign that they had remembered he was there, he relived the moment he had proposed to Sandra so long ago. He'd been a quivering mess, too, but only because he'd bravely—or foolishly—popped the question in a crowded restaurant. Even now, he could still feel Sandra's arms around him, her body pressed tight against him, her lips fusing with his as though they had become a single person.

"Well," Corina finally said, turning to Peller. "Roxane would like to know how long Cyrano had to coach Christian. I'm sure you had something to do with it."

Peller tipped an invisible hat. "Just applied a little grease, ma'am."

Montufar gave him a hug and a peck on the cheek. Peller shook Dumas' hand heartily.

"Congratulations to you both," he said. "It's about time. And it'll be nice to have some good news at the station."

"Now Jack needs to propose to Ella," said Montufar. "Then we could have a double wedding!"

Dumas began, "Now, for the culinary dessert—", but a sudden wild hammering at the door interrupted. Peller jumped at the noise. Dumas just shook his head and half grinned, half grimaced. Montufar laughed.

"Shall I tell whoever it is to go away?" Peller asked.

"I'll get it," Dumas said. "That's Ozzie's knock. He must've heard me slip the ring on Corina's finger." He went to admit the interloper

"How's that?" Peller asked Montufar.

"Ozzie's senses are uncanny. No matter how quiet we are, he always knows when Eric or I come down the hall."

That explains the tiptoeing, Peller thought.

Ozzie hadn't come alone. He and his lady friend followed Dumas into the living room, all smiles and energy. Dumas introduced them. "This is Rick Peller. Rick's our boss. Rick, this is Ozzie White and Cameron Terrell."

"Nice to meet you both," Peller said. Ozzie replied in kind and Cameron smiled a cute, embarrassed little smile and waved minutely. Remembering Dumas' warning about her, Peller merely nodded politely. But he found it hard to take his eyes off of her, not because of her considerable beauty but because something about her seemed familiar. He had the strange feeling she might be sister to someone he'd known long ago.

Dumas, braced against the inevitable squeals of delight, made the necessary announcement: "So, I've just asked Corina to marry me."

He got what he'd expected. Ozzie clapped him on the back and pumped his hand while Cameron squealed and jumped up and down on the balls of her feet. She couldn't have been happier if she had received the proposal.

Beaming in the midst of the ruckus, Montufar glanced at Peller. Peller figured she was gauging his reaction to Cameron's antics, but he was already looking beyond that. What was it about this woman? Something in the turn of her mouth, the angle of her cheek bones, the shape of her nose.

The explanation slowly dawned. At the realization, his gut knotted up.

Shocked, needing to be sure, Peller scrutinized her, feigning attraction so she wouldn't suspect that he suspected. Out of the corner of his eye, he saw the smile slip from Montufar's face. She didn't like the look he was giving Cameron, but he couldn't drop the pretense now without giving himself away.

Cameron smiled knowingly, inviting his pursuit. She turned a bit this way, curved a bit that way, adjusted her golden glasses just so, not so much that Ozzie would notice but enough to entice the man she really wanted. Peller didn't doubt she'd find a way to get him alone if he gave her half a chance.

Except it didn't last. Something in his face must have signaled trouble. Her smile faded and, as though not really interested after all, she straightened and attached herself to Ozzie. Irritated at himself for messing up, Peller wondered what he'd done wrong, how she knew that he knew. She hooked her arm through Ozzie's and drew him close. "We should go, baby. The lovebirds need some privacy."

Ozzie didn't look like he wanted to leave, but Cameron gave him a coy smile to suggest they had better things to do anyway, and he fell for it. "Okay. But I'll want to hear all about it tomorrow, Eric."

Montufar laughed as Dumas rolled his eyes and said, "You got it."

Cameron waggled her fingers goodbye and nearly pulled Ozzie from the apartment. After they left, Peller stared at the closed door, wondering what to do next.

Montufar had stepped close to him. "You're creeping me out, Rick. I've never seen you look at a woman like that. Not even Sandra."

Dumas looked at them, surprised. "What?"

Peller couldn't keep the ice from his voice. "You know her, Eric."

"Slightly. She's been around for about a week and come over…" He glanced at Montufar. "Once or twice."

"That's not what I mean. That woman is not Cameron Terrell."

"What are you talking about?" Dumas' eyes shifted in confusion between Peller and the door. Alarmed, Montufar took his hand and squeezed it.

"Think, Eric! Her face. Her height. Her weight. Her figure. Wash that brunette dye from her blonde hair, and who have you got?"

Dumas shook his head, still not getting it.

"That's Hannah Bellamy."

"*What?*"

Stunned, Montufar asked, "Are you sure?"

She shouldn't have to ask, Peller thought. *She knows I am.*

"What's she doing with…" Dumas began, but the answer was obvious. He collapsed onto the sofa. "Oh my God."

Montufar sank down next to Dumas and took his hand." She must have read Jack's article about you."

"She did. Damn it! She even *told* me she did."

"Did you talk to her about the investigation?" Peller asked.

Dumas looked up sharply. "I'm not that stupid."

"She's that smart. She could have weaseled something out of any of us. Even an offhand comment might tell her how close you're getting to Harold."

Dumas seemed to be chewing on something bitter. "Tamai had a lot of enemies," he objected.

"It was Harold." Peller had no doubt of it. "Why else would Hannah risk spying on you? She doesn't care about anyone else. Nobody but Harold exists for her."

"But this makes no sense," Montufar said. "If she's that devoted to Harold…" She looked like she was choking on the thought. "Rick, she's in Ozzie's bed!"

Peller almost wished he'd terminated Hannah on Ozzie's behalf. "She's an actress. It's not real. It's a role she's playing." Another piece of the puzzle fell into place. "That must be why she shut Harold up the day we questioned them. She didn't want us to know she's an actress."

Tears welled up in Montufar's eyes again, but no longer tears of joy. "Poor Ozzie. He'll be devastated."

"Moron!" Dumas snapped at himself. "I should have recognized her."

Things had become too personal. Peller took a few breaths to clear his mind and forced everything away except what had to be done. "It's not your fault. That woman has definite talent."

"So how did you see through her?"

"Mostly the shape of her face. I don't forget faces. Once I blocked out the glasses and hair and makeup and the cutsie smiles and seductive glances, I could see her."

Dumas leaned back and exhaled. "Damn it. So what do we do now?"

Good question. Hannah suspected Peller knew about her. She would be on high alert. They had to get her to drop her guard, make her think she'd dodged a bullet. They needed time. They didn't have enough evidence to arrest the Bellamys yet, even if they now knew where to focus their attention. "Is there any indication she's defrauding Ozzie?" he asked, fishing for something, anything, to use against them.

Dumas shook his head. "I'm not even sure she's moved in with him yet. I just know she's usually there when he's there."

Peller considered his companions. A death, an engagement, and now this. Dumas looked like he'd been hit by a truck. Montufar leaned against him in no better shape. "Poor Ozzie," she muttered.

"It can wait until morning," Peller decided. "Let's get together then and come up with a plan." When they didn't respond, he added gently, "Do you want me to stay for a while, or do you need time alone?"

Absently, Dumas stroked Montufar's hair. "After this, we won't be very good company, but you're welcome to stay if you want."

Mentally, Peller was already flipping through files, organizing, connecting dots. Something occurred to him, a small hole in the picture, a detail he should fill in. The hour notwithstanding, he decided to deal with it at once. "In that case I'll let you be. Get some rest. Don't beat yourselves up. This could be a gift. Hannah's made a huge mistake right in front of us."

Dumas looked up but didn't reply.

"I guess," Montufar said quietly. "But my God, Rick. Poor Ozzie."

16

Another cold night descended upon the mid-Atlantic under a crystalline sky and a brilliant waxing moon. Peller thought he might have been on that moon as he trudged up the walk to Shania North's shambles of a home, surrounded by the desolation of its yard. Reaching the door, he heard a faint moaning within. He knocked and listened. The sound continued unabated; nobody answered his summons. Alarmed, he pounded on the door and called, "Shania! It's Lieutenant Peller. Are you okay?"

The sound dissipated for a moment, then returned louder, followed by fumbling at the doorknob. The door flew open as though it had been ripped off, and North threw her emaciated body at Peller, wailing piteously, hanging onto him as though drowning.

He caught her and kept her from crashing onto the frigid concrete. "What's wrong? Are you hurt?"

"He won't wake up! Whas wrong wit him? He won't wake up!"

Still holding her, Peller hurried inside. North's companion sprawled in the middle of the floor, empty eyes wide, staring heavenward. A terrible stench suffused the room, something Peller couldn't place. Tendrils of smoke curled through the air. He lowered North onto one of the beanbag chairs and kneeled by the man. "Are you okay?" When there was no response, he snapped his fingers beside the man's ear. Not even a blink. He checked for a pulse but felt nothing. Peller pulled out his cell phone and called for an ambulance, knowing he was too late. He took a quick look around. Nothing had changed since his last visit. No signs of a struggle, no indication that the man had been injured. This was likely a drug overdose, nothing more.

Sobbing uncontrollably, North stared at her lifeless companion. "Why won't he wake up?"

"I've called an ambulance," Peller told her, unable to break the news. "Shania, I want you to come with me. Let me get you some help. Will you do that?"

She couldn't even wipe the tears from her face, much less answer.

"Listen to me. You need help. You need to get off this stuff or you'll end up..." He looked back at the body and couldn't finish.

"I wanna die," she moaned.

Sirens wailed in the distance. "No," Peller told her. He scooted to her on his knees, took her by the shoulders, looked her in the eyes. At first she didn't react, but as the sirens screamed up road and into the driveway, she met his gaze, blank, devoid of comprehension. A newborn infant understood more than she. "Don't give up. Let me help you."

She sniffed and wiped her eyes. A tiny glimmer of light returned. "He's not sleeping?"

Peller shook his head. The paramedics appeared in the open door. Peller flashed his shield at them and nodded at the deceased. "Over there." He watched North as she blinked through her tears at the newcomers. Once they had her companion covered head to toe on a gurney, she looked away and closed her eyes and choked down a wail.

I never even asked his name, Peller realized. *I should have asked his name.* He couldn't ask now.

One of the paramedics returned and asked quietly, "Is she okay?"

Peller shook his head.

"I'll go," North whispered. "I got nothin' else."

A wave of relief washed over Peller. "Thank you, Shania." He motioned the paramedic over and lowered his voice. "OxyContin. God knows what else."

The other paramedic returned. They checked North over before half leading and half carrying her to the ambulance, where they put her in the front so she wouldn't have to sit by her late companion. Peller followed and stood by the open door. She reached out a trembling hand to him, and he took it. "You'll pull through," he promised her. "I'll keep in touch and make sure you get whatever help you need."

She nodded absently.

"I know this is a bad time, but I need to ask you something. Is that okay?"

Again, she nodded.

"Do you know Harold or Hannah Bellamy?"

Her mouth opened and she shivered before replying. "Yeh."

"They worked for Mike, right?"

"Harold an' Mike were friends."

That surprised Peller. He couldn't see Harold calling anyone but Hannah friend. "Good friends?"

"Yeh. From school maybe? Mike gave 'em tips on jobs they could do. One time…" She shuddered.

What's causing that? Peller wondered. *The drugs, the death, or the Bellamys?* "What is it?"

"They came over late one night an' woke us up an' were sayin' things."

"What kind of things?"

North leaned back and closed her eyes. "Don't remember. Awful things. I stayed in bed and hid under the pillows. Din't want to know." Her eyes slowly opened, and she rolled her head towards Peller. "Denise knows."

"Denise?"

"Mike's girlfriend."

Peller wondered if she were confused. "Why were you sleeping there? You were never Mike's girlfriend, were you?"

With a little shrug, she closed her eyes. "Guess not."

One of the paramedics climbed behind the wheel and gave Peller a look. He nodded and stepped back. "All right. Thank you, Shania. I'll check up on you tomorrow. I promise." As he closed the door, she almost managed a smile. She looked like a little child. Where were her parents?

How could they have let this happen to her? He wasn't her father, but he felt as responsible for her as if he had been.

The flashing red lights moved out of the driveway and down the street until they were swallowed up by the darkness. Peller considered calling Dumas to let him know that Denise Newville hadn't told him everything, but it could wait until morning. Besides, he thought he knew what he needed to know. Michio Tamai had involved the Bellamys in something so foul it frightened Shania North.

Then he blackmailed them over it.

And that had been his fatal mistake.

*

Monday, January twenty-third dawned clear, cold, and still. The overnight temperature had dipped into the single digits, not a record but well below normal. Forecasters predicted no relief from the chill for at least eight more days.

Peller arrived first that morning, reserved the conference room, and checked email while waiting for his colleagues. They arrived as haggard as he'd left them the previous night. Only Montufar's ring glowed. The rest of her looked as though she'd been squeezed through the wringer on an old fashioned washing machine. "Get some coffee," Peller told them. "I'll meet you in the conference room."

On the way there, he picked up a tail: Captain Morris followed. She nodded in the general direction of the break room. "The lack of exuberance is stunning even for a Monday. Something up?"

"Several somethings. We think we have Tamai's killer."

"And that's cause for despair?" She slipped into a chair opposite him and crossed her arms on the table, ready for action. She liked to keep tabs on key cases. Peller figured she also needed a break from budget negotiations. She'd been a top-notch detective before ascending to her present rank and may sometimes have missed being hip deep in crime.

"Not in itself, but it's complicated. Also, Corina's father passed away Saturday. The funeral is tomorrow at ten."

"How's she holding up?"

"As well as can be expected."

"Poor woman." Morris shook her head. "What about Tamai's killer?"

Peller gave Morris an edited version of the previous evening's events, excluding any mention of Dumas and Montufar's engagement. That news should be theirs to share.

After listening, Morris said, "That's disturbing but maybe a blessing in disguise."

"That's what I told Eric and Corina."

As if on cue, they came into the room, coffee and napkins in hand, and took seats to the captain's left. Morris glanced at them, then did a double-take. She pointed to Montufar's ring. "Is that what I think it is?"

Montufar tried her best to smile. "Eric asked me last night. I said yes." She held out her hand so Morris could get a good look.

"This is beautiful. Not so many rocks as you usually see these days, but beautiful."

"Maybe the extra rocks went in the budget cuts," Peller quipped.

"I like it just the way it is." Montufar smiled at Dumas. Her look seemed to warm him more effectively than the coffee.

"Congratulations," Morris said. "I'll refrain from making a public service announcement, but don't keep everyone guessing. People will notice that ring." She patted Montufar's hand. "And I'm sorry about your father. Rick told me."

Montufar nodded her thanks.

"Okay," Morris said, turning to Peller. "Batter up."

He launched into it. "I paid Shania North a visit last night. Good thing I did. Her boyfriend had died, likely from an overdose." He exhaled heavily, seeing the sprawled form in his mind, hearing the woman's wails, looking into her lightless eyes. "She consented to treatment, thank God."

"Why did you go back?" Dumas asked.

"I wanted to find out if she'd ever met the Bellamys. That wasn't a question we knew to ask during our first visit."

Dumas nodded. "Right. And had she?"

"Yes. She wasn't entirely lucid, but apparently Mike and Harold were good friends, if you can believe that. Tamai gave Harold work from time to time. She remembers a night when the couple dropped by and had a disturbing conversation with Tamai. She doesn't remember what it was about, just that it was so awful she didn't want to hear it. She says she hid in bed until it was over."

Dumas frowned. "Was this before Denise was with Mike?"

"No, she was there."

"Tamai was sleeping with Shania while Denise was in the house?"

"Apparently. We already knew he wasn't humanity's finest."

"Yeah, but that's low even for him. She may have been a fool, but Denise loved him."

Montufar broke in with the logical question: "Was Denise party to this awful conversation?"

Peller nodded and watched Dumas' face, wondering if the revelation would surprise him.

Apparently it didn't. "I'll pay her a visit today, find out what happened." He looked up at Peller. "Unless you already know?"

"Nope. I only know that whatever it was, it scared Shania."

Montufar leaned forward with a frown. Peller could see the wheels turning in her head. "Harold and Hannah worked for Tamai. So did Shania. And Jayvon Fletcher knew Shania. It's a fair bet she learned where he worked. If that got back to Tamai, it might have given him the idea for the robbery. Shania could have tried to recruit Jayvon to help."

Peller started to object, but simultaneously she shook her head and went on, "No, he wouldn't have gone for it. If he wouldn't watch her perform, he certainly wouldn't follow her into a crime. But Eric, you said before you thought there were at least two people involved, two people with different temperaments. Harold and Hannah?"

"I don't know," Dumas said. "They strike me as very similar. Hannah does seem more controlled, maybe even bolder. At least today. According to their professors, that wasn't always the case."

"Life is her stage now," Peller said. "Nothing is real to her except Harold. However that happened, it could well have changed their dynamic."

Montufar still wore her look of calculation. "So much blackmail. Could Jayvon have been a victim, too?"

Peller shook his head. "I thought of that, but he was completely open about Shania. He even introduced her to his grandmother."

Dumas had just taken a sip of coffee and nearly spit it out. He picked up his napkin and dabbed at his mouth. "Say it isn't so."

"He wanted to save Shania," Peller explained. "He might have thought his grandmother, being so strongly Christian, would be a good influence. Unfortunately, Wanda Fletcher has her own flaws and couldn't overlook Shania's profession. But as your near-explosion so eloquently demonstrates..." He paused to grin at Dumas, who was still dabbing at the table with the napkin. "...most of us wouldn't expect a dotting grandmother to reach that height of nobility."

"I guess not," Dumas acknowledged.

"Anyway," Peller concluded, "as far as Shania is aware, Tamai didn't know about Jayvon. Even if she's wrong, Jayvon couldn't be blackmailed. He was open about their relationship and had nothing to hide. Another thing. Shania liked Jayvon. His disappearance devastated her. She thought he'd given up on her."

"So she didn't know about the incident at the clinic," Montufar said. "And Tamai probably didn't know about Jayvon."

Dumas studied Montufar's face for a moment. "You don't like it."

"It's too much of a coincidence. There has to be a connection."

"Then I'll lay you odds Denise Newville will provide it."

"Why?"

"Just a hunch."

She gave Dumas one of her long-suffering looks, but with a faint hint of a smile.

*

This, Dumas thought, was where it had all started: the North Laurel townhouse, the leftmost in its row, that had once been shared by Michio Tamai and Denise Newville. He arrived just after ten o'clock. The air felt as cold as the first time he'd been here, but somehow the place looked different without police tape and the prying eyes of neighbors: serene, ordinary, safe. Life in the neighborhood could indeed have returned to normal, although who knew what whispered gossip yet passed from ear to ear behind the closed doors.

He'd called ahead to make sure Newville was still in residence. She was, although packing up preparatory to moving to her cousin's place in Virginia. When he arrived, she led him through the tiny foyer, its green tiles dulled with age, and into the living room with its muddy brown carpet, its threadbare tan sofa, its oversized TV on the wall, and the stacks of old boxes along the back wall, folded shut and gathering dust. Little had changed since he first saw Tamai dead on that sofa. Newville might have done some cursory cleaning. A shabby blue blanket now lay across the seat cushions, perhaps to hide the blood stains. But she hadn't wasted much energy on a place she would shortly abandon.

As if reading his thoughts, Newville said, "I'm not fussing over how it looks. My name isn't on the lease. They can keep the security deposit. Michio sure won't be needing it."

Dumas sat in the same chair from which he'd previously interviewed her and waited while she settled opposite him. "You're looking better," he told her, and she was. Hair neatly braided and lips carefully painted with dark red lipstick, she wore a bright green sweater and snug jeans and wasn't smoking a pack a minute.

"I'm feeling better. It occurred to me two days ago that this could be the best thing that's happened to me in ten years. That probably sounds horrible. I don't care."

"You didn't have a good life with Michio," Dumas acknowledged.

"No."

"Not to spoil your good mood, but I need to ask you about something."

She leaned forward and set her elbows on her thighs, hands clasped between parted knees. The way she looked at him, Dumas almost expected her to start with the suggestive comments again. "What's that?"

"We talked to Shania North. You knew her, I believe."

Newville's expression darkened. She shook her head once, sharply, before deciding it wasn't worth denying it. She looked down and muttered, "Yeah, Michio kept that slut around for a few months. Why?"

Her hostility didn't surprise Dumas. He wondered whether it would work for him or against him. "She said the Bellamys came by late one night."

"They did that from time to time," Newville replied, feigning boredom.

"Frequently?"

"No. They were unpredictable."

"This particular visit was special. The talk gave Shania a serious fright. She didn't recall details, but she said you were in on it."

Newville swallowed and sat up straight. "You can't believe anything she says."

"Why not?"

Newville studied her fingernails. "She tried to take Michio away from me. I didn't let her. So now she hates me." She glanced up at Dumas just long enough to gauge his response.

He figured from that glance that the woman was deliberately poisoning the well. "How well did you know the Bellamys?"

She squirmed as though to get more comfortable. "Well enough to stay away from them."

"They had that effect on people, it seems. Why?"

Newville absently patted her left hip pocket as though searching for her smokes. "The way they look at you, you feel like an insect. One they might squash."

"What was their relationship with Michio?"

"I think Harold knew Michio from before. I didn't pry into that. But when it came to business, Michio only had one script. He hired people to do illegal things then bilked them out of their share."

"Can you be specific?"

She nervously clasped her hands and entwined her fingers. "I didn't get involved in the dirty work. I just know he cheated everyone else, so why not them?"

"Because," Dumas said, his voice suddenly sharp, "he was just one more insect to them. They would have killed him without thought."

Newville looked up, eyes wide with fear.

"That's what happened, isn't it?"

She soundlessly mouthed something, but no response formed.

Dumas added, just as sharp, "If you know anything about Michio's death, I suggest you tell me."

Newville shook her head. "I—I can't tell you anything."

"Can't, or won't?"

She squeezed her eyes shut as though that might make Dumas disappear.

He wished he'd brought Kevin Graham with him. This sort of thing was easier when he didn't have to play both roles. But since he had no choice, he now softened his tone. "I don't think you're a bad person, Denise. You didn't have your head on straight when you got involved with Michio, but you're not like him. You're not a criminal. Don't make yourself an accessory to murder. You don't owe him anything. Especially not that."

Newville slumped and covered her face with her hands. Her chest heaved as though she was sobbing, but Dumas heard nothing. After a moment she dropped her hands to reveal tears tracking down her cheeks. "I already am."

Dumas hadn't expected that. He stared at Newville, who took his silence as a prompt. "Michio and some of his accomplices went out for drinks on occasion. I didn't know it at the time, but usually their outings ended at a strip club up by route 40. That's how he met Shania. He fell in lust with her the first time he saw her dance. He threw money at her, she got friendly with him, he threw more money. That's how they work, I'm told."

Dumas knew nothing about the subject, but he nodded to keep her talking.

"I don't know how many times he went to see her. All I know is, one night he convinced her to come home with him. I don't remember much, just that he introduced her to me, told me he was taking her to bed, and laughed while I had a meltdown. Finally he shoved a pile of cash in my hands, told me to go have some fun of my own, and literally pushed me out the front door."

Dumas felt a deep anger welling up on Newville's behalf. He barely kept his voice level. "Didn't Shania object?"

"She was too stupid to realize what was going on. She looked confused. She wasn't confused in the morning, though. I staggered in plastered at about five thirty. I have no idea how I found my way home. And she was there, smiling and making breakfast for the three of us. She moved in that weekend. I should have left, but like I said before, I had no place to go. So stupid me, I tried to compete with her for the next few months. Michio loved it, I'm sure, two women practically killing themselves to make him happy."

"He used her as a criminal accomplice, too, didn't he?"

"Oh hell yeah. He told me she'd be a goldmine. While watching her do her thing, he realized there were a few regulars with money to burn who were just as smitten as he was. One night he told us those men had families and would pay a lot to keep their little secret. Shania didn't like the idea, but Michio had already started feeding her drug habit, so in the end she couldn't do without him any more than I could."

"Opioids?"

"Not at first. Pot and some less dangerous pills, I think. That was enough for a time. Once it wasn't, he upped her all the way to OxyContin."

"Where did he get the stuff?"

"I don't know. I didn't want to know."

"Did he make money off of her?"

"Some, but he had trouble getting clear photos. He had to fake it sometimes. When his victims figured it out and refused to pay, he went ballistic."

"And hired someone to torch their houses," Dumas finished.

Surprised, Newville gaped at him. "How much of this do you already know?"

"Let's find out. Did Michio know Shania was seeing another man?"

Newville's voice emptied of all emotion. "Was she."

"You know she was."

"Yeah. I'm a woman. I could tell. Michio didn't know, but after a while he suspected. She started spending more time away, seemed a bit happier, stuff like that. He didn't care who she was doing. He only cared that it might interfere with his blackmail scheme. He confronted her one day and she denied it. He told her if she was lying, he'd cut off her drug supply. She told him she could get some from a friend who worked at an animal hospital." Newville shook her head. "You should have seen the light bulb go on over Michio's head. It lit up the whole neighborhood."

And that, Dumas thought, tied everything into a neat package. Jayvon Fletcher's disappearance, the arsons, Tamai's death. Montufar had been right: no coincidences here. "He organized a robbery to get the drugs."

"Bingo. An easy job, Mike said. He got them white outfits, so they'd be less visible in the security lights. He lifted that idea from another job, one Kennedy set up a long time back. Ken always had smart ideas like that.

Shania even got the alarm code from her friend. Probably watched him enter it. Nothing could go wrong."

Dumas nodded. "Until something did."

"You do know everything," Newville whispered.

"Not everything. I need you to fill in some details."

"Please don't ask me for that." She sounded like a frightened child. "I can't do this. I wouldn't survive two days in jail."

"Did you kill anyone?"

"No! I just helped..." She closed her eyes and leaned her head way back. "Please don't make me."

"Denise, listen to me." Dumas stood and went to her side. He took her hands in his and held them firmly. They trembled with fear. "If you cooperate, we can cut a deal. Unless you did something really horrible, which I don't for a minute believe you did, we likely won't charge you at all. But I need the whole story."

Fear and tension held Newville in their grip. Tears dribbling down her face, she sobbed for some minutes, then pulled her hands free and wiped her face on her sleeve. "Okay. I'll tell you. But promise me something."

"If I can," Dumas said.

"Please don't hate me. I was so afraid."

"I'm sure you were." Dumas released her hands and resumed his seat.

Newville composed herself as best she could, then she told him the story of one terrible Christmas morning two years before.

17

"Come to bed with me." Tamai, standing behind Newville, wrapped his arms around her. The stench of alcohol liberally mixed with a sickening current of burnt marijuana overwhelmed her. She tried to detach herself from him, but his hands were everywhere, groping wildly.

"You're in no condition," she snapped. "Besides, you don't need me. You have *her*."

Tamai released her and staggered backward a step. "Denise baby, she's just a toy. She's not important. Not like you. Just a toy. Come on up. We'll play with her together."

The words slurred so badly she was surprised he could get them out of his mouth. "You're a pig." He'd likely hit her, but she didn't care. She'd taken his abuse for so long that she'd learned to absent herself from her body while it happened.

He laughed, pushed up the end of his nose with his forefinger, and snorted loudly, over and over. When she didn't signal amusement, he shrugged. "It's Christmas. Time to party, yeah?"

"Great. Celebrate the birth of Jesus with debauchery. No thanks."

"You're no saint, either, babe." He leered at her.

"No." She sat heavily on the sofa, arms crossed over her chest, face directed as far from Tamai as possible.

She could feel him glaring and wondered when the blows would start, but to her surprise nothing happened. After a moment he said, "You don't know what you're missing. I guess I'll just do her extra hard."

When she finally turned, he'd vanished upstairs.

She didn't cry, didn't get angry, didn't even care. She'd wasted too many tears on him already, and anyway, when all was said and done he always came back to her. She pulled her deep red and gold afghan about herself and curled into a ball beneath it. *Be rational. You need Michio for food and shelter. Love? No. Faithfulness? No. All you need is his money.*

Thankfully, Newville heard nothing from upstairs. Tamai might already have passed out. Outside, a cold wind whispered through the trees. She listened to it for a time, straining to hear whatever words it might be murmuring. There were none, but the sound emptied her, drained her of care and thought until finally, well after midnight, she drifted into a restless sleep.

Shortly after three A.M. the doorbell startled her awake. Heart pounding, eyes wide with alarm, she pulled herself up and backed into the corner of the sofa. Nothing good would call on Tamai at this hour. The bell rang again, several times, harried, frightened, like someone desperately trying to escape encroaching evil. Frozen with fear, she didn't dare investigate.

From upstairs Newville heard Tamai unleash a string of curses, and a moment later his feet pounded down the stairs. Not wearing a stich of clothing, he yanked the door open to confront the cold and whatever it had borne to his door. "What the hell!" he barked

"Mike! Thank God!"

She recognized Harold Bellamy's voice, but unlike every other time she'd heard him, he was terrified. He pushed past Tamai and circled the living room over and over, seeing nothing, saying nothing but, "Oh my God," over and over.

On his heels, his wife Hannah lunged into the room, pale and shaking, and followed him around in circles like a lost dog. Michio slammed the door behind her, pressed his hand to his forehead, and grimaced in pain. Only after the fourth pass did Hannah stop and stare and her host's nakedness. "Hell, Mike," she sputtered.

Gathering her wits, Newville rose and hurried to Tamai with the afghan. She draped it around him and pushed him toward the stairs. "Get dressed. I'll find out what's going on." As he ascended the steps, she turned and motioned toward the sofa. "Sit down." Alone with the Bellamys, she felt a sudden upwelling of fear. This couple transmitted danger signals by their mere presence. Being alone with them felt like standing before a firing squad without a blindfold.

But something was very wrong. No longer the cold, unfeeling couple she knew, they were scared to death. Hannah took Harold in her arms and pulled him to the sofa, where together they huddled, shaking. "The vet clinic," Harold muttered.

So Tamai had hired this pair for that job. Newville wondered why. She didn't know their particular skills, but she didn't see them as burglars. Hired killers, yes. Not cat burglars. She put a hand to her mouth to stifle a nervous chuckle at the unintentional pun.

"Somebody was there," Hannah told her when Harold couldn't continue. "He caught us just after we got in. He must've heard us break the window."

Harold put his protective arms around Hannah and pulled her close. Newville waited for the rest of the story, but she could already guess how it ended. Cold washed over her as though the front door stood wide open. She had to look to make sure it didn't.

"You could've taken him," Hannah whimpered. "I should've let you." She choked back a sob.

"He's dead," Harold said. "I got into a scuffle with him. Hannah hit him on the head with…" He looked at her and stroked her hair. "I don't even know what it was."

Hannah shrugged.

"And then I…" He squeezed his eyes shut. "All I could think was I had to be sure. I crushed his throat with my…"

Harold couldn't finish and Newville neither wanted nor needed him to. She'd been right about them. A pair of killers sitting on her sofa, probably trailing cops, leading them right to Tamai and his harem. "Why did you come here?" she squeaked. She'd be furious if only she weren't so frightened by the implications.

Hannah, the timid one, looked up, and Newville saw something in her eyes, a glimmer of calculation, of determination. Realization dawned. Harold, crippled by the shock, no longer directed their affairs. Somehow Hannah had found the strength to assume command. Newville never suspected Hannah of that much backbone, and the revelation only added to her fear. What would this woman not to do protect her man?

"We need help," she said simply.

"Help?"

"The body is in the trunk."

Denise put her hands to her mouth and muttered, "Oh my God," just as Michio thumped down the stairs in ratty jeans and an old blue sweater.

"What?" he demanded.

Newville rose on shaking legs and staggered to him. She grabbed his shoulders and held on as though drowning. "I should get dressed," she said, although she didn't know why. Tamai nodded and helped her to the stairs. After the first unsteady step, she gripped the railing and ran for her life, ran to the top and into the bedroom and slammed the door behind her, oblivious to the strained voices in the living room. She switched on the light and pulled some jeans and a sweater out of the dresser and began stuffing herself into them.

In bed, Shania North sat up from her drug-induced haze. As the sheet slid off her body she fumbled to pull it back up, then realized it was only Newville, gave up, and let it drop. Newville didn't want to look at her competition. She focused on getting dressed.

"Wha's goin' on?" North mumbled.

"Stay in bed," Newville told her, bitterly aware of the irony. "Don't come downstairs, don't look out the window, don't do anything. Put the damn pillow over your damn head and don't hear or see any damn thing."

She hurried back downstairs, where a volcanic Tamai was erupting in obscenities and randomly hurling any object he could lay hands on. Harold held a trembling Hannah close, although Newville couldn't tell whether Hannah trembled in fear or in anger.

Halfway down the stairs she stopped. She didn't dare approach Tamai. What should she do? She didn't know, but throwing things and making noise had to be just about the worst possible course. If the cops weren't already on their way, somebody would call them. Only one thing made sense to her. "Let's take care of the body."

Tamai turned and lunged violently at her. But before he could reach the stairs, Harold sprang from the sofa. In a huge leap, he overtook Tamai, pinioning him in crushing arms. "Don't you dare. One stiff is enough. What are we going to *do*?"

As Harold maintained the pressure, Tamai's eyes bulged with fear. "Okay!" he sputtered. "Okay! I wouldn't hurt her!" He held up his hands to show his pure intentions.

"You damn well won't," Harold said. "We need help!" He eased his grip. Tamai twisted away and backed up, keeping a close eye on the other man.

Grateful for the intervention, Newville cautiously descended the remaining steps. She expected police sirens to scream down the street at any moment, but they hadn't yet. She only had one thought: when they did come, the body couldn't be here. It was her only hope. "We have to bury him," she said.

Everyone stared as though she'd lost her mind.

"I didn't say to give him a funeral! Just *bury* him."

Harold and Tamai, still squaring off, couldn't wrap their heads around it, but Hannah nodded. "Where?"

"Out back where the power lines run. Nobody goes back there. Nobody would think to look there."

A small sound behind her caught Newville's attention. North stood naked at the stop of the stairs, holding onto the wall to keep from falling, chin hanging down, eyes vacant. "Get back to bed!" Newville snapped, and North vanished into the darkness. *My God, I'm living in an asylum!*

"How do we get him back there?" Hannah asked. "We can't carry a corpse through the neighborhood."

Newville hoped Tamai would have an idea, but the men continued to watch each other, neither willing to drop his guard. It was up to the women. Ironically, she found herself drawing strength from Hannah's look of concentration. "Okay," she said. "The power lines cross Leishear Road about half a mile from here. I think we can get the car down there." She closed her eyes and tried to envision the place. "I think there's a strip of pavement down there. If we can get far enough back from the road, maybe we can get him out without being seen."

Hannah mulled that over. "Does that work, Harold?"

Harold finally took his eyes from Tamai. "I guess. We'll need shovels."

"I have a couple in the shed out back," Tamai said, perhaps hoping the offer would make everything right again.

They gathered the equipment and as quietly as possible loaded it and themselves into Harold's car. Newville directed Harold to the spot on Leishear Road where the power lines crossed over. A track used by utility vehicles came up a rise to meet the road there. Harold pulled onto the track, stopped, and turned off his headlights. The road stood empty in the dark, nothing moving on it but a whisper of chill wind. He carefully maneuvered his vehicle onto the track and bumped downhill to the strip of pavement Newville had remembered. They followed this beyond the first pair of towers which loomed over them like giant aliens. When the pavement ended, he continued around a slight bend until they were out of sight of the road.

Harold brought the car to a halt. Newville thought they must be very close to their home, perhaps even right behind it. Everyone stepped into the cold and together they prepared to remove the body from the trunk. Harold and Hannah had stashed it there as quickly as possible, and Newville could only be thankful for the darkness so she didn't have to look into the vacant eyes, the crushed throat, the blood that must certainly have coated the man's hair. The men hefted the body from the trunk, Harold lifting the shoulders and Tamai the feet. Once it was clear of the vehicle the women took positions to support it at either side, and together they waddled down the clearing for what seemed an eternity.

Finally they stopped near the tree line and dropped the body on the ground. The thud sickened Newville. Tamai went back for the shovels. When he returned, digging commenced. Cold seeped into their joints and dark obscured their vision as they dug. It was horrible, miserable work. Newville had no idea how long it took, but she had a sense of being covered head to toe in half frozen earth, as though she was the one being buried.

Eventually the job was done. They picked up the body once more and heaved it into the depths, then shoveled the soil back in. They did their best to hide their handiwork with leaves and sticks but couldn't see well enough to know how it looked. They could only hope that nobody would come by here before Mother Nature awoke in the spring and covered the bare ground with new growth.

Filthy, exhausted, and freezing, they trudged back to the car. Harold dropped Tamai and Newville off at the townhouse, then the Bellamys escaped into the early dawn.

Tamai shuffled into the foyer with Newville following. No sooner had she closed the door than a small voice from above asked, "Where'd ya go?" Still undraped, North gazed down at them, eyes not quite so vacant, a shiver in her voice.

Tamai looked at her as though not sure where she'd come from. "Nowhere. Go back to bed."

She didn't move. "I wanna know. You're all dirty."

Newville mounted the stairs, set her filthy hands on North's perfect shoulders and forced her to turn around. "Do as Mike says." She pushed the other woman toward the bedroom. North tried to turn and object. "If you don't go to bed right now, Mike will come up here and slit your throat."

North craned her neck and gaped at Newville.

Newville had a sudden vision of her fingers wrapping around North's scrawny neck, squeezing, choking the life out of her, snapping bones, pulling her head right off. Maybe Michio wouldn't find her so damned attractive then. It was a vison both tempting and terrifying.

"Damn it, girl!" she snapped. "Do as you're told or I'll kill you myself!"

Terrified, North scampered into the bedroom and slammed the door.

Newville dragged herself downstairs, feeling a thousand years old. She wanted nothing more than to lie down and die. She found Tamai standing at the French doors, holding the curtains slightly open, staring into the early morning glow now illuminating the tops of the high-tension towers. She came up behind him but didn't touch him. So much had tainted him that she wasn't sure she ever wanted to touch him again.

"She can't ever know," she told him. "She'd talk. You have to send her away."

He nodded absently.

"Will we be safe, do you think?"

Tamai shrugged. "Nothing ever goes right," he muttered.

That does seem to be the case with you, she thought.

"If they left a mess..." He shuddered. "We're in big trouble."

She couldn't dispute that, either. Then again, she had to wonder. Hannah, scared as she was, had shown considerable presence of mind in absconding with the body. Maybe she wasn't as dumb as she seemed.

*

Dumas watched Newville break down once more. He could do nothing but let her cry, yet he wasn't done with her. One last question remained.

Ten minutes passed before she'd vented her pent-up emotions. She excused herself and vanished upstairs for a few minutes, then returned composed if red-eyed and took her seat again. She looked tense, as though knowing what he was about to ask.

"Can you show me the spot?"

"I don't know. It was two years ago and pitch black."

"Will you try?"

She studied her fingernails.

"Denise?"

"You must think I'm a monster."

"You might have told me this before. But no. I don't."

She tried to smile her relief, but her face could only grimace. "Okay," she said quietly. "I'll try."

18

When Cameron Terrell's eyes blinked open earlier on that Monday morning, she found herself lying in a double bed. Morning light streamed through a gap in the pale blue curtains, and the aroma of cinnamon filled the air. At first she didn't know where she was and felt as though she had been stolen from her home and deposited somewhere fantastical—perhaps Oz, perhaps Wonderland, or Narnia, or simply another universe altogether. Only when Ozzie White appeared in the open doorway with a plate in his hand did she remember that she was in his apartment.

She watched the steam rise from a stack of pancakes neatly arranged in the center of the plate, fascinated by the way it curled about White's round, boyish face.

"Good morning, beautiful," he said with an easy smile.

Terrell kicked the sheets off and stretched long and slow, giving White time to drink in every curve of her body. She wore a pale yellow nightgown that showed more than it covered. She shifted to enhance the effect, reveling in his attention. "What's that?"

"Cinnamon pancakes." The tone of his voice assured her that his mind wasn't on the food. "My specialty."

Terrell sat up and motioned him over. He sat next to her on the bed and offered her the plate. The pancakes were smothered in real maple syrup. Two slices of bacon lay neatly beside them. "I'll get your coffee," he said but didn't move. So beautiful was she that he couldn't take his eyes from her.

She knew how smitten he was. She'd heard it in his breath, felt it in the beating of his heart when he held her close. Taking the plate from him, she cut a small wedge from the stack and sampled it. "This is divine!"

He just about melted. "You shouldn't spoil me like this. A week from now I won't want to do anything but lie in bed all day and let you take care of me."

"I wouldn't mind that," he said, and she giggled until he couldn't help but laugh along with her.

"But you have to go to work sometime." She cut off another bite.

"Not today. I called in sick."

"Oh, poor baby, you shouldn't be pampering me if you're not well." She set a hand on his forehead to check his temperature.

White took her hand in his and kissed her fingers one at a time. "I'm fine. I just wanted to spend the day with you."

"That's so amazingly sweet of you."

For a few minutes they didn't speak. White watched her eat, and once she mischievously dripped a bit of syrup down her nightgown and giggled while he cleaned it up. She never did get her coffee, but that was okay. It might have been the best breakfast she'd ever had. She finished and handed the plate back to him.

"I'm really sorry, Ozzie," she said, her voice bathed in sorrow, "but I have to go out for a bit." He looked crestfallen. She did so hate to disappoint him, but it couldn't be helped. "I have a job interview at ten thirty. But I promise I'll be back just as soon as I can, and you can spoil me all day long after that. Okay?" She stroked his cheek and kissed him gently on the lips.

"I guess an interview is important. But the rest of the day belongs to us, right?"

"Absolutely, I promise."

"With one small intrusion. I want to invite Eric and Corina over for dinner. Is that okay?"

"That would be wonderful! I really like those two. I wouldn't miss it for anything."

White set the plate on the floor, gathered Terrell into his arms, and didn't let go for a very long time.

Terrell melted in his embrace. She loved Ozzie White to death. He was the most amazing thing that had ever happened to her, and she hoped and prayed she could stay with him and make him happy forever and ever throughout all eternity.

She had only lied to him because Hannah Bellamy needed to get away from him for a few hours.

*

While waiting for Dumas to report back, Peller stopped in at Howard County General to visit Shania North. He found her sleeping beneath a rumpled sheet, fluids coursing into her left forearm through a clear tube, the head of her bed slightly raised. Her mouth hung open and her left hand hung off the side of the bed, a sensor clipped to her index finger. The machine at the other end of a tangle of cords beeped regularly, marking out her heartbeat and breath. The device displayed numbers higher than what Peller understood to be normal, but North appeared to sleep peacefully.

Pulling over a large, well-padded green chair, Peller sat by the woman and watched her for a time. He didn't entirely know why he'd come. The world overflowed with sad stories like hers. He probably couldn't save her. He knew the odds of successful long-term recovery, knew that even with the best of intentions and the best help, Shania North would likely end up back where she started, probably sooner than later, and from there progress to the grave. Few slave drivers tortured their victims worse than opioids. He only knew he had to try.

He sat with her a full hour before leaving. When he rose to go, his footfalls woke her. She made a small noise, and Peller stopped to look back.

"Oh," North said. "Hi."

Peller returned to her bedside. "Hi." He couldn't think of a thing to say; asking how she felt seemed ludicrous if not cruel.

"You're here," she told him needlessly.

"For the past hour."

She tugged weakly at the sheet but couldn't make it move. He pulled it up a couple of inches for her and tucked it around her bony shoulders. She closed her eyes and tried to smile. "Thanks."

"You need anything?"

She shook her head. "You going?"

"Yeah. I'm afraid I have work to do."

"Come back later?"

"Of course."

Again the little smile, and her eyelids closed and sleep took her once more. A nurse was just coming in as he was leaving, a tall, dark-skinned woman with a no-nonsense face. She looked too young, Peller thought, to be that severe. "What's the word?" he asked.

The nurse raised her eyebrows.

Peller produced his shield in explanation. "I sent her here last night."

"She's not dead yet."

"I know. I talked to her. Briefly."

Craning her neck to see the patient, the nurse frowned. "That's something. I expect she'll be out of here in a couple of days, but after that?" She shook her head.

What could he say? He thanked her and moved on, feeling powerless to change anything for the better.

*

When the photo finally surfaced, it wasn't one Montufar cared to look at herself much less show to Stan York. She found a blog run by someone hiding behind the screen name "Secret Shopper" portraying in lurid detail his "investigations" of strip clubs and porn shops around the Baltimore area. Obviously intoxicated by if not addicted to the stuff, he must have spent two thirds of his life making the rounds of area sex establishments, writing reviews of their wares, and taking surreptitious photographs with his cell phone camera. The amateurish photos were often blurred and dark and thankfully lacking in detail. Even so, Montufar angled her monitor so passers-by wouldn't catch a glimpse of what she was looking at.

In a post from three years earlier, the blogger had given rave reviews to a dancer named Shania at Olga's Dollhouse, a route 40 club. The accompanying photo of the dark-skinned dancer in the altogether was so poor that Montufar doubted anyone could identify her. Yet this had to be Shania North. Further research revealed that Olga's was presently the only strip club in Howard County. Baltimore harbored a sizeable red light district near its main police station, and others dotted eastern and western Baltimore County, also along route 40, but other Maryland counties had done their best to oust them in the early 1990's by prohibiting nudity in establishments that held a liquor license. Although not one hundred percent successful, the ploy had significantly damped the sin business.

History lesson absorbed, Montufar created a free webmail account and sent from it an email to the blog owner. She posed as an interested male visitor and begged for more photos of Shania. Within half an hour, she had her reply. The blogger did have one other photo of the lady—his term, not Montufar's—taken at a private party where she'd performed. In it, the dancer appeared to be writhing on a couch, back arched almost to the breaking point, nothing left to the imagination except her face, the only part Montufar cared about. Shadow half buried that.

Ignoring the accompanying text, which was at least as lurid as the blogger's posts, she closed the email and squeezed her eyes shut as though that might exorcise the image from her brain. Then, feeling horrid about it, she picked up the phone and called Karla York.

"More questions?" York asked when Montufar announced herself.

"Not exactly. I have a photo of the woman we think was involved in blackmailing your husband. I was wondering..." The question lodged in her throat. She couldn't make herself spit it out.

"You want to know if he can identify her?"

"Yes. But..."

The silence between them was so deep they might have been cut off. Finally York said, "Oh. It's that kind of photo."

"If you'd rather not..." *Come on, Corina, just do your job!*

"Could you cut off her head and send me that?" After a pause, York laughed bitterly. "That would be poetic justice."

Montufar couldn't suppress a snicker. "Unfortunately not. Her features aren't that clear. The ones on her face, anyway."

York mulled that over, then gave up. "What the hell. He's already seen what she's got. I don't suppose one more glance will hurt."

Still churning inside, Montufar said, "It's an electronic copy. Can I email it to you?"

"Sure." York gave her email address.

After a glance over her shoulder to make sure the coast was clear, Montufar saved the photo from the original email, attached it to a new message, and sent it on. "On its way."

"I've got my laptop here. Let me check."

Montufar could scarcely breathe. Within ten seconds, she heard a faint chime from York's computer.

"Here it is. So…"

That should have been followed by something—a yelp, a curse, nervous laughter, something. But Montufar only heard the faint hiss of static. "You okay?"

Again that silence. York might have passed out or died. When she spoke, she sounded distant. "That's one athletic woman."

"Apparently," Montufar told her. "You okay with showing that to Stan?"

"No, but you need him to identify her, so I'll deal with it."

"Thank you. I owe you dinner or something."

"At least," York said, sounding more herself. "I'll let you know what he says. About whether or not it's her, that is."

Off the phone, Montufar told herself without enthusiasm that she'd need to add the photo to the files, which meant printing it on the shared network printer. She'd have to do that when the place was quiet. She sure didn't want to be caught carting smut around. She'd never hear the end of it.

To her surprise, York called back within fifteen minutes. "That's the girl," she said.

"Stan's positive?"

"Yeah. Subdued. Almost morbid. But positive."

"I thought he'd be at work."

Playfully, York said, "Oh, he was. I emailed it to him there."

Montufar nearly choked on her surprise. "Couldn't that get him in trouble?"

"I called ahead to warn him. Anyway, you needed a quick answer. And I didn't want to be there when he looked at it."

Montufar supposed that made sense, although she could see it the other way, too. Maybe it would have been best to keep an eye on him. "Thank you. For whatever it's worth, that ties a lot of things together."

"You know who the blackmailer was, then?"

"Yes."

York waited, but when Montufar didn't say more, she prompted, "And?"

"He died last week."

"Serves him right. One of his victims plugged him, maybe?"

"I can't comment on that."

"Okay. But if so, I hope you don't catch them. They did the world a service."

Montufar understood York's bitterness, but given what she knew about the Bellamys, she doubted they served anyone but themselves.

*

The trio reconvened in the conference room at Northern District Headquarters just after eleven o'clock. Dumas filled them in on Denise Newville's story, and Montufar relayed Stan York's confirmation that Shania North had been the dancer involved in blackmailing him.

"Will Newville testify?" Peller asked Dumas.

"Yes. She's afraid of the Bellamys, but she's moving out of state, and I told her we'd do everything possible to keep her safe."

"Then we have them for the death of Jayvon Fletcher. That gives us breaking and entering, voluntary manslaughter, and concealing a homicide. They sound like prime targets for another of Tamai's blackmail schemes, which could mean a murder charge waiting in the wings."

Dumas' cell phone dinged. He pulled it out to check the message. "I vote we arrest them on what we have and work out the remainder later."

"Too dangerous," Peller objected. "They'll be watching for us. I'd rather given them a little time to let their guard down."

Dumas swiped at his phone's screen. "I don't like...oh great." He looked at Montufar. "Ozzie invited us to dinner. He and Cameron want to hear about last night."

Montufar smiled weakly. "And to plan our wedding, I suppose."

"And to find out if Rick really did see Hannah lurking behind all that makeup and ditz."

Peller didn't doubt it. White's interest in his neighbor had played right into Hannah Bellamy's hands. "You should go. Act casual. Don't let on that we know. That might put her off her guard."

Montufar grimaced at the table. "She'll want to know why you were so interested in her. She'll probably ask roundabout questions."

Peller felt Montufar's discomfort at the prospect. "So tell her the truth."

She looked up sharply. "How's that"?

"Tell her my wife died a few years ago. Let her work out the implications."

Dumas nudged Montufar. "Yeah, tell him Rick's gotten interested in women again."

She stared at him, probably thinking he was making one of his strange jokes. Peller hadn't mentioned Joan Churchill to her, and apparently Dumas hadn't, either.

"I'll give you that story later," Peller said, rolling his eyes so she'd know it wasn't as it sounded. "But that's not a bad idea. Just don't overplay it."

"She's the actress," Montufar said, "not us."

"Precisely the problem." He pondered it for a moment. "If this doesn't work, things could go south pretty fast. You'd better have backup standing by. Arrange for a couple of officers to wait in Eric's apartment. Agree on an emergency signal, like a preset text message."

"We'll do that," Montufar agreed.

"And hope it isn't necessary. If we tip our hand, people will get hurt." Overtaken by misgivings, Peller almost told them to forget the whole idea, but he couldn't see how his companions could excuse themselves from the party without raising Hannah's suspicions. They had few choices: spook the couple into fleeing, go in guns blazing, or try to quell suspicions.

"Meanwhile," Dumas said, getting back to the subject, "we need to connect the Bellamys to the murder. The room was clean. The gun was clean. No witnesses to the event. Assuming they did the deed, they probably took care not to be seen coming and going."

"The address book connects him with his accomplices," Montufar said. "We have statements from some of his blackmail victims. The marks in the book correlate with those victims. I wonder if he kept any other records?"

"None that we found," Dumas told her. "The place was utilitarian, just the usual furnishings. He didn't even have a computer."

There ought to have been something, Peller thought. "He couldn't have run his whole operation out of his head."

Dumas shrugged "It wasn't complicated. Seems whenever he got an idea, he recruited one or two people and executed it." But as he thought about it, a look of surprise stole over his face.

"Another crazy idea?" Montufar prompted.

"Something I overlooked. Tamai had a bunch of boxes stacked in the living room. Denise Newville said they were books. I checked one, and she was right. She said he got them from dumpsters at the mall and sold them when he could."

"Okay, boxes of books. And?"

"I checked *one*," he repeated. "I didn't check them all. Newville was so guileless I didn't question it further."

Montufar nodded. "You think she was lying?"

"No. She avoided involvement in Tamai's business as much as possible. If he told her the boxes contained books, she wouldn't have dug any deeper than I did. But there are books and there are books, you know?"

"What became of them?"

"With luck they're still there. Newville wasn't planning on cleaning out the place. The landlord will dump everything, but not until she turns in the keys. I'll get on it when we're done here."

"I think we are," Peller said. "I'm going to visit Wanda Fletcher while you do that."

"Before we have everything worked out?" Montufar objected.

"She's waited long enough to hear why her grandson never came home. We'll have to locate Jayvon's remains so she can give him a proper burial, but at least she'll know what happened."

Montufar seemed to accept that, but still she looked pensive. Dumas took her hand and squeezed it gently. "It's frightening how much misery one man can cause," she said. "And he wasn't that clever or charismatic or anything, just selfish and without scruples. Thinking about it leaves me cold."

Peller looked out the window at the sky where gray clouds gathered, perhaps presaging more snow. "It does. But colder people than Tamai are out there."

He didn't have to elaborate. From their expressions, he knew Montufar and Dumas knew precisely who he meant.

*

Immediately after the meeting, Dumas called Denise Newville who answered on the first ring. "I was about to leave," she told him. "Everything's packed. I never want to see this place again."

"I'm sure. Before you go, I need to check on one more thing. Those boxes in the living room. Are they still there?"

"Yeah, I haven't touched them."

"Great. I'd like to go through them in detail."

She didn't reply immediately. Dumas figured it must seem a strange request. But in the end, she didn't object. "You can have them, but I'm not waiting around. I'll leave the front door unlocked for you. You can lock up when you go."

"That'll be fine. Have a safe trip. I'll be in touch."

He pulled on his coat. After negotiating the moderate traffic, he arrived one more time at Tamai's place. The neighborhood remained quiet. A few dry flakes of snow fluttered down from above as he strode up the walk, and as promised he found the front door unlocked. Inside, the boxes stood where he had first seen them, a thin film of dust coating their tops. The mess in the kitchen likewise sat undisturbed. Wondering if Newville had taken all her meals elsewhere since the murder, he hefted one of the kitchen chairs, set it next to the boxes, and went to work.

Although Newville wanted nothing and the landlord would toss the lot in the trash, Dumas couldn't bring himself to throw books around. He stacked them carefully on the floor, riffling through them as he went. When finished with each box, he repacked it and set it aside. Seventeen boxes in all awaited his attention, stacked three and four high. He cleared fourteen before finding what he wanted: a collection of binders hidden under two layers of thin, coverless books.

"About time," he mumbled. Rather than unpacking the binders, he closed up the box and set it aside. He then checked the remaining cartons but only found more books. The carton of interest he took to his car and placed in the back seat. Returning to the front door, he turned the lock and closed it, then checked to make sure it was secure.

And that, he assured himself, would be the last time he set foot in that place.

*

Wanda Fletcher peered through the cracked door. Satisfied that her visitor was indeed Lieutenant Peller, she undid the chain and let him in. She led him into her living room, where a steaming cup rested on a saucer on the coffee table. "Care for some coffee?" she asked, but he declined with a shake of his head. They settled on opposite sides of the table. "What'll it be today, then? More questions? Or answers?"

"Answers, at long last," he told her, but didn't immediately go on. He wasn't sure how she'd take the news after all this time. He guessed she knew Jayvon would never come home, but sometimes people hoped against hope far beyond the point of rationality.

Bravely, she met his eyes. "He's dead, isn't he?"

"I'm afraid so, ma'am. But we know the general location where he was buried. We should be able to recover his remains for you."

Mrs. Fletcher swallowed, hard, but said nothing.

"Two years ago," Peller explained, "a man and a woman broke into the South Howard Veterinary Clinic on Christmas Eve. They were after drugs. They didn't know anyone was there. They also didn't know the drugs were locked up, inaccessible to them. Jayvon surprised them. There was a struggle, and he was killed. They panicked and took his body to the guy who had hired them for the job. He helped them bury Jayvon nearby, beneath some high tension power lines."

She squeezed her eyes shut during his recitation. Her head bowed and her lips moved silently as though she were praying.

"I'm very sorry," he told her.

Her eyes remained closed. "He was no inside man."

"No. Jayvon was a good man who had the misfortune to be in the wrong place at the wrong time."

She was silent for a long time then finally opened her eyes. "And the thieves?"

"We know who they are. We have a witness."

Mrs. Fletcher looked up, eyes narrowed. "A witness?"

"Yes, ma'am." When she shook her head, Peller realized she was wondering how they could have overlooked a witness for two years. "Not to the robbery. To the burial."

She thought about that for a moment. "Have you arrested the killers?"

"Not yet."

"Why not?"

"It's complicated. We're still working out a few details. But rest assured it won't be long."

"You'll let me know." It wasn't a question.

"Of course."

Mrs. Fletcher patted herself on her knees a few times then rose and took Peller's hand in hers. "Thank you, Lieutenant. You don't know how much this means to me." Before he could contradict her, she added, "Or maybe you do. I guess you must." She drew a ragged breath and for a moment looked like she might break down, but then her resolve strengthened and she motioned to the door. "Not to rush you, but I need some time alone."

Peller nodded and rose. She led him to the door where he again promised to be in touch when he had more information. After she closed the door behind him, he stood in the hall for a moment, eyes fixed on his shoes, wondering if she could find some measure of peace now. He hoped so. But he knew well that such a loss could not be forgotten, nor did such wounds ever completely heal.

19

Harold pulled Hannah's body against his and kissed her deeply. "I missed you last night. Tell me this will be over soon."

"It will," she promised. She pushed on him and obediently he released her. But then she leered, threw her arms around his waist, and yanked him back into a tight embrace. "I missed you, too."

He pulled her down and didn't stop kissing her until they were side by side on the floor, limbs haphazardly entwined. When he finally let her breathe, she said, "We either dodged a bullet last night or we have a problem."

"How so?"

His hands were all over her. She reciprocated while explaining. "Sergeant Dumas had a little department get-together at his place. He proposed to his detective girlfriend. Their detective boss was with them. Ozzie and I crashed the party. The boss man, that Peller guy, looked real interested in me."

"He's not the only one."

She slapped at him playfully but her voice was heavy. "He may have recognized me."

Harold's lightheartedness sublimated. He stopped groping and frowned. "Are you sure?"

"No. Maybe he really was turned on. But I got a funny feeling, like he was searching me for my soul." She shuddered, remembering how strange it had felt.

"We'd better find out." Harold pulled her close again, this time protectively.

"Ozzie invited Dumas and his woman to dinner tonight. I'll see what I can get from them."

"Be careful," Harold told her. "They aren't as smart as you, but they aren't idiots."

"I will be," she promised. "We should have a plan. Just in case." She wished Harold could come with her. They stood a better chance together than alone. Yes, she'd grown bolder over the past couple of years, but he was still her strength. Unfortunately Harold was no actor, and she doubted even with different hair and a different face he could fool Dumas. Besides, how would she explain his presence to Ozzie?

Thankfully, Harold formulated a plan for her. "I'll follow you and wait in the parking lot. I'll text you a few times to see how it's going. Pretend you're getting some silly messages from a girlfriend. Get all giggly and stuff." He tickled her waist. She squirmed and did her giggly routine. "Send a reply now and again. If things turn serious, let me know. Nobody will suspect."

She liked it. It was simple and fit her established act. "What would I do without you?" She rested her head against his chest.

Harold stroked her hair thoughtfully. "I guess you would cease to exist."

Hannah looked up, filled with a sense of wonder. He was absolutely right, and she could tell by the intensity of his eyes that he felt the same way about her. Wishing they could merge into one being, she pulled him as close as close could be. The room, the furniture, the window, the ceiling, even the floor upon which they rested faded away, leaving them alone together in an endless void. Deeply content, she lost herself in a universe where nothing but their embrace was real.

*

Dumas dropped the box onto Montufar's desk.

"What is that?" She eyed the container and her fiancé with equal suspicion. "You're not trying to move into my desk already, are you?"

Dumas laughed. "Not yet. These are Tamai's books."

"Oh. That's different." She stood and opened the box, and together they unpacked, cataloged, and inspected the eleven three-ring binders inside. Four were white, three dark blue, two green, and two red. Most contained pocket folders and sheaves of college-ruled paper. Four held nothing but blank paper and empty pockets. Records of sorts had been squirreled away in the others, hastily scrawled, disorganized, sometimes illegible. Stuffed into the pocket folders they found news clippings about crimes—mostly thefts and break-ins—receipts, notes on slips of paper, an occasional five- or ten- dollar bill, and one petrified fragment of pizza crust.

"Anybody hungry?" Dumas quipped.

"No, thanks." Montufar tossed the object into the wastebasket, fished a napkin out of one of her desk drawers, and scrubbed her fingers.

"It's like the frat house from hell," Dumas said. "What's next?"

Montufar pulled another batch from a white binder and leafed through it. "Either Tamai had no organizational skills or he was trying to be clever. He split up information about operations. Some here." She set aside the white binders and pulled one of the green ones close. "Some here. Probably some elsewhere."

Dumas picked up her discards and examined them. "It's not consistent, though. It looks like he recorded payments here, but also over there. I guess a green binder doesn't mean money."

"Look at this. 'Dog food, three hundred dollars. Discount, fifty.' What's that mean, do you suppose?"

"Beats me." Dumas' eyes widened. "Wait. Dog. Wolf. Wolf Spensely. He said Tamai didn't cheat him. Looks like he was wrong."

Montufar turned a few pages. "Here's another one. 'Seeds, five hundred dollars. One hundred saved.'"

"Maybe Kennedy Farmer. He was Tamai's ideas man. I wonder what scheme he seeded?"

"There's more in that entry," Montufar told him. "He really stretched the metaphor. Plowing fields, harvesting. Lining up the north star. Weird." She looked up. "Shania North? You think Farmer planned the blackmail scheme?"

Dumas looked pleased. "Kevin and I should pay him another visit."

They worked through the books for an hour, struggling to make a coherent story from their contents. Sometimes cryptic references and scattered fragments formed a pattern matching the reports from Tamai's associates, but often the entries appeared completely random. No doubt, Montufar thought, they told tales of criminal ventures so far unmentioned, escapades that might remain forever buried. Overall, the material only confirmed what they already knew. It filled in only a few unimportant details, and the speculation required to turn it into something meaningful would be useless in court.

Until, as the scrawling blurred before her eyes, she tripped over something astonishing. "Whoa," she whispered.

Dumas looked up from the book he was examining. "What?"

"Water bill, twenty thousand dollars. Collect monthly, term one year." She looked up at Dumas. The number made no sense. "That's ten times anything else he recorded."

He moved closer to her to look. "Water bill. I wonder what that was?"

"Maybe it's code for another of his buddies?" This wasn't her area of expertise. Without coherent data and a connecting logic, she couldn't see her way through. Intuition and sudden leaps of inspiration were Dumas' forte, not hers.

True to form, he delivered. "You're right. Water. H_2O. Harold and Hannah."

"Brilliant. But where would the Bellamys get twenty thousand dollars?"

"You got me," Dumas replied. "But if you killed somebody and the guy who helped you bury the body came back for his wages, how much would you pay to shut him up?"

"A hell of a lot," she admitted.

"Or if you're the Bellamys, nothing. Rick called it right. One of them killed Tamai."

"But we still can't prove it." Montufar glanced at the clock on her computer monitor. "We should finish up so we aren't late for Ozzie's shindig." From the look he gave her, she knew Dumas didn't relish the prospect any more than she did. Regardless, they couldn't refuse Ozzie, and somehow they had to convince Hannah, in her role as Cameron, that she hadn't been discovered. They repacked the binders and returned the box to storage, logged off of their computers, and headed out into the twilight.

*

"Eric, you sit there. Corina, you sit next to him." Ozzie, frothy with enthusiasm, positioned his guests along the side of the table next to the wall. His chrome and glass décor shone nearly as brightly as he did. Plush upholstery patterned in burgundy and white covered every seat in the place, including the dining chairs. Montufar could only imagine the consequences of a dropped forkful of spaghetti.

Ozzie pulled out the chair opposite Dumas and held it for his lady. "You sit here, Cameron." The adoration in his eyes pained Montufar. What would he do when he learned the truth about the woman?

Cameron, fiddling with her cell phone, smiled and took her place, setting the phone face-down beside her plate. Ozzie settled next to her, across from Montufar. The places were set with china and silver. A massive serving dish filled with pot roast and vegetables sat proudly in the center of the table, a basket of cloverleaf rolls nearby. A fluted glass of something pinkish and fizzy rested at each place. Cameron peered into the liquid, puzzled. "What is this?"

"Sparkling cider," Ozzie told her.

"Not wine?"

He patted her on the shoulder. "Our guests don't drink."

"Oh." She blinked befuddlement at Montufar. "Okay."

"Help yourselves," Ozzie directed, and the meal commenced.

Food dished up, Montufar sampled the roast. It melted in her mouth. "This is delicious, Ozzie!" she said, and he fairly melted, too. His cooking prowess never failed to surprise her. On the surface, he didn't seem the sort who would be much accomplished at anything, but he threw himself into everything he tried and, apparently, never settled for second best.

"Now let's hear all about it," Ozzie said, grinning at Dumas.

Dumas put down his fork and patted his mouth with his napkin. "It was pretty simple. We had dinner, and I gave her the ring for dessert."

Cameron laughed. "You make it sound like doing the laundry."

"I don't mean that." He looked helplessly to Montufar.

"He embarrasses easily," she supplied. "No, really, it was like a balcony scene, except we were all sitting at the table. Until the ring made its appearance, anyway."

Ozzie smiled rather dreamily. Clearly he was every inch the hopeless romantic. Cameron clapped her hands and, voice sparkling, cheered, "Perfect!"

"Was it in something?" Ozzie asked.

Dumas looked at him, confused. "In something?"

"The ring. Did you put it in a cupcake, or…" He motioned vaguely.

"Oh. No, I just gave it to her. She doesn't like wearing cupcakes."

Cameron found that hysterical. Laughing, she leaned against Ozzie and gazed into his eyes. "And then we came in."

"Pretty much," Dumas replied. "Like I said, it was simple."

"Simple can be good." Ozzie said it, but he looked dubious. "I guess."

Cameron nodded. "I'm glad we could be there. It's such a special moment, and to share it is so, so, I don't know, special."

I'll bet, Montufar thought. She could guess where Cameron would go next: how special it was that Peller had been there, and what a special guy he was, and what was with that special look he gave me, anyway?

Cameron's phone chimed. She checked it and laughed. "Oh, you!" She tapped at the screen, then put the device down. "Sorry. One of my friends in California. I was telling her about Rick. He looks a lot like her husband. She said, well, maybe I shouldn't say what she said. You can guess, though." She winked at Montufar. "He's one cute guy, yeah?"

Fortunately Montufar hadn't been drinking or she'd have spit cider all over her host. "Cute" was hardly the word she would use to describe Peller! But she forced herself to smile. "You said it."

Ozzie grinned and waggled his finger back and forth between the women. "We'd better watch it, Eric, or Rick will steal these two!"

Dumas forced a smile. "I think we're safe."

Cameron's eyes widened. "What, he's not interested in a couple of hot ladies like us?"

Lips pinched into a grimace, Dumas picked up his fork and toyed with his dinner.

"I bet he'd like to try." Cameron winked at Montufar just as her phone chirped again. She picked it up and read the message, head cocked. Then she began to enter an answer.

As Montufar watched her with the phone, she wondered whether Cameron was actually typing anything. Her fingers seemed to flutter over the screen rather than move in a directed manner. It reminded Montufar of pretend telephone conversations between five-year-olds. Was the other woman really answering a message, or was the phone just an electronic prop to her airhead act?

Cameron finished with her phone and set it down again. "He sure was checking me out last night, anyway. And him a married man." She giggled.

Ozzie's smile slipped. "Huh?"

"Not jealous, are you?" She kissed her forefinger and brushed it over his cheek.

"No, of course not."

He was sliding that direction, though, so Montufar came to his rescue. "So he looked. Men do that. Rick knows the boundaries."

Cameron giggled again. "I don't get many looks like that, honey. If his wife had been there, he'd be sleeping on the couch for a month."

In a terse conversation-stopper, Dumas stated, "His wife's dead. Let's stop talking about this."

Montufar wondered whether Dumas' forbidding expression was just as much an act as Cameron's contrived girlishness. Either way, he'd slipped Cameron the information Peller had suggested, and her act swung to embarrassment with a side of pity.

"Oh, no. Hey, I'm sorry. I didn't know." She picked at her food. "What happened to her?"

She was good at what she did, Montufar admitted to herself, but she knew the wheels were turning in Hannah Bellamy's head. "Car crash," she told her. *Like Rick said. Let her work it out.*

"Recently?"

"Four and a half years ago."

Now Cameron exhibited an exaggerated concern for Peller's well-being. "Can't he move past her?"

"Move past her?" Dumas exploded. "She was his wife, not a pet parakeet!"

Although she hadn't taken a bite recently, Cameron patted her mouth with her napkin. Her hands trembled, again a bit too much. *You're not Sarah Bernhardt*, Montufar thought.

"God, I can't say anything right," she said with a false laugh, but even the attempt at stage levity fell flat. "I just mean, you know, life goes on. Right?"

Dumas eased up on her. "Yeah, I guess."

Ozzie, who had been watching with horror as his carefully-planned party disintegrated, gave a feeble smile and raised his glass of pink non-alcoholic bubbly. "Come on, guys, we're celebrating. Here's to your future happiness!"

Four glasses were clinked, faux champagne was sipped, and everyone tried to look happy. Ozzie placed his glass carefully on the table. "So Eric, when's the next super-detective article coming out?"

Dumas waved him off. "Oh, stop that."

"Don't be so modest." Ozzie turned to Cameron. "He doesn't know his own worth."

Dumas gave up. "Wednesday, I guess. It's a weekly thing."

Cameron leaned forward. "I can't wait. I've never known anyone who was in the papers before."

Is it my imagination, Montufar wondered, *or did she actually bat her eyes at him?* She could feel Dumas's irritation surface again. No doubt about it: this time it was real. Why was he letting her get to him? She put a hand on his arm to quell him, but too late.

"Damn it, Cameron, it's not entertainment. A man was murdered."

"Eric—" Ozzie began, but got no further.

"I'm trying to compliment you," Cameron objected, an edge in her voice now. "Why does everything I say tick you off?"

"Because it's all a game to you! Don't you care about anything? Or anyone?"

Without warning Ozzie pushed his chair back from the table and stood. "Back off, Eric. Leave her alone."

Who would have thought Ozzie had that in him? Montufar wondered. *It's certainly not the Ozzie I know!*

Dumas' mouth opened, then shut again. He scowled at his plate, picked up his glass, swirled the liquid, and set it down. "Sorry, Ozzie. Long day."

Cameron fidgeted with her napkin and studied his face until her phone dinged again. Setting the napkin aside, she picked up the phone and read the screen. "Things aren't going as well as the papers say, huh?"

Montufar took Dumas' hand in hers before he could answer. "Eric's a smart guy. He'll work it out."

"Is he." Cameron set the phone carefully on the table, but when she looked up at them, it wasn't Cameron. Hannah Bellamy's dead eyes stared a hole through them.

Damn, Montufar thought. *She's figured us out.*

Ozzie, seeing the sudden change in his lady friend's face, frowned at her. "Look, let's just—"

"Shut up." While Ozzie mouthed a silent objection, Hannah looked through Dumas. "Clearly you suspect us. Why?" She picked up her phone and turned it over and over in her hand. The obsessive motion drew Montufar's eye. Cameron—Hannah—began to tap at the phone again, and Montufar realized suddenly that she had been communicating with Harold all the while they had been talking. But where was Harold? At home? Or somewhere nearby, as ready to come to Hannah's aid as the pair of officers waiting in Dumas' apartment were ready to come to theirs? *A disaster waiting to happen*, she thought.

Dumas watched her toy with the device. Montufar eased back in her chair, slipped her hand into her skirt pocket, wrapped her fingers around her own phone. "I can't comment on an ongoing investigation," Dumas finally said.

"Your favorite line." Hannah turned to Montufar and pierced her with those empty eyes. "What else are you unable to comment on?"

Montufar didn't understand.

Hannah's dark smile suggested she might enjoy cutting out Montufar's heart. With her words, she tried. "So you didn't tell Corina about you and I and Friday night."

In her pocket, Montufar's fingers tightened on her phone. *I don't hear your lies. Nothing you say is true.*

Hannah fixed Dumas in her sights again. "Keeping secrets already," she said sweetly. "What a poor start. Mistrust kills relationships."

"Hey." Ozzie reached out to touch her, but she slapped him away as though he were a mosquito. He looked helplessly from Montufar to the woman he knew as Cameron, unable not only to find words but to even find the right thought. Montufar could imagine the turmoil in his mind.

Hannah ignored him, her face hoarfrosted steel. "You have no basis on which to arrest us." She stretched her arms toward Dumas, fingers balled into fists. "But if you do, then do so."

While she locked eyes with Dumas, Montufar sent the prearranged phone signal to the officers. Simultaneously, Dumas pushed back from the table and stretched as though ready for a nap following an excellent meal. "I thought we were celebrating," he said easily.

The misdirection worked. Hannah never as much as glanced at Montufar. "You are one damn lousy actor," she said. She pulled her hands back. "Still. Since you cannot make an arrest, let us indeed celebrate. Let us finish dinner." She stabbed a chunk of potato with her fork and shoved it into her mouth.

Ozzie had had enough. He slapped the table so hard it must have stung. "What's going on?"

Come on, Montufar pleaded with their backup.

Hannah didn't hear Ozzie. He had no further utility, so he'd slipped back into the void of nonexistence. Cameron, too, had left the universe, probably never to return.

"Cameron!" Ozzie demanded just as a heavy fist pounded on the door.

Hannah skewered a piece of meat. There was no Cameron. No Ozzie. No pounding. No cops demanding entrance.

Answer the door. Montufar tried to beam the words into Ozzie's brain, but he just sat there. *For God's sake! Go!*

The pounding repeated, louder. Ozzie turned. A muffled call rose over the third round of hammering: "Howard County police. Open the door."

Hannah continued to eat, oblivious to her surroundings. Ozzie finally got up, dazed, and found his way to the door. The moment he turned the knob, the cops shouldered their way in, hands on holstered weapons.

Ozzie shrank against the wall in fear. "Eric!"

Dumas motioned him to silence while keeping Hannah in his sights. Nor had Hannah taken her eyes off of Dumas. Montufar wondered if she registered anything but him: police or guns or fear or danger. Probably not. Her roles had swallowed her completely—certainly nothing with power over her existed. All about her was shadow and illusion.

But she knew the shape of the shadows. "Now I understand. The dogs carry the cuffs."

Dumas gave her a thin smile. "You were wrong. I'm going to arrest you after all."

"You have no grounds."

"Actually, I do."

"On what charge?"

"Breaking and entering, voluntary manslaughter, and concealing a homicide. We'll discuss murder later."

No reaction. Montufar had never seen eyes so empty of emotion. Hannah ought to at least have hated Dumas. But no. Why not? "We need to get this wrapped up," she told him. "She's been texting Harold. He might be nearby."

Dumas stood and motioned to the officers. "Check the hall. Her accomplice is a big guy, athletic, with wavy dark hair."

One of the officers nodded, drew his weapon, and edged into the hall.

The chill that raced up and down Montufar's spine while she waited for Dumas to recite the Miranda warning didn't fade when the officer returned from the hall and announced, "It's clear."

"Keep watch," she told him. "He's out there somewhere."

Hannah rose with the grace of a monarch. "I will not speak until my lawyer is present."

"You have one?" Dumas asked. Hannah gave no sign that she'd heard, so he motioned for the handcuffs.

At long last, Ozzie separated himself from the wall and stepped forward, eyes pleading. "I don't understand."

Reptile-like, Hannah turned her head slowly to eye him. "Oh, God, Ozzie. How does a worm like you survive even one hour?"

"Who are you?"

She turned her unfeeling eyes on Dumas. "I could destroy all three of you at once. It would not take much. I need only kiss you again."

Montufar's gut knotted up. *What do you mean, again?* She felt Charity Dibble and Carla York crowd her from behind, watching, holding their breaths, all three of them praying that the answer wouldn't be as it sounded.

In the same instant, Hannah puckered her lips and leaned toward Dumas. He pulled back, but before he got out of range she slapped his face so hard Montufar thought she heard the smack echo off the walls. Dumas grabbed Hannah's wrist and twisted her arm around behind her. She grimaced but made no sound.

Hot with anger, Montufar ripped her gun from its concealed holster, but before she could take aim, the officers waded in, grabbed Hannah, and wrested her from Dumas. With one on each side of her, she went limp, knees buckled and arms flaccid. They dropped her on the floor. One of them reached for the cuffs at his belt.

An explosion sounded.

The officer with the cuffs grunted as a spray of red erupted from his chest. Montufar's rage melted into horror as the man crumpled to his knees. Before he hit the ground, a second explosion sounded and the other officer went down. Now Dumas had his weapon out, but Hannah had already lunged for the door. As the detectives found her and took aim, a hand grabbed at Hannah from the dark of the corridor and pulled her away.

Montufar fired. Wood splinters exploded from the doorjamb. A yelp echoed from the hall. Dumas charged the door. "Call for backup and an ambulance!"

"Eric!" Montufar cried, but she knew he wouldn't stop. Dropping to her knees by the wounded officers, she fumbled with her cell phone and called in. Simultaneously, she checked their injuries, her mind on automatic. One of the men had no breath left in him. The other was gasping his last.

Phone pinned between her shoulder and ear, she leaned all her weight on the still-living officer's wound, hoping beyond hope to stanch the bleeding with her bare hands, but the warm river of red poured undiminished over her fingers to soak into her skirt and the carpet. A battalion of sirens wailed, closing rapidly on the building.

She looked around desperately for something, anything, to plug the wound. She heard a soft sound that might have been a whimper and for a moment thought the man still lived, but no. He had lost too much blood. What she had heard must have been the outrushing of his breath as his heart and lungs fell silent.

Yet the whimper remained, behind her. She turned and found Ozzie curled into a ball on the floor. "Oh God, Ozzie, are you hurt?" She took her blood-encrusted hands from the dead man's wound and crawled to Ozzie's side, wiping her fingers on the pristine carpet as she went, leaving a long, scarlet trail in her wake. "I'm here, Ozzie. It's okay. I'm here."

She took him by the shoulders and helped him sit, back to the wall. Tears streaked his ashen face, but he hadn't been shot. The only blood staining his clothes had come from her hands. Montufar gathered him into her arms as a mother would her child, smearing blood all over his shirt. "It's okay, Ozzie," she whispered. "I've got you. You're safe."

She didn't know how much time passed. She cradled him and whispered to him while he moaned and sobbed. Police and paramedics flooded the room, but still she didn't release him. She couldn't. She had to keep him safe from this horror.

They had to pry him out of her arms to get him to the ambulance.

*

Dumas lunged into the hall, half expecting to be met by a storm of bullets. But the Bellamys were running and wouldn't stop, not with so much carnage in their wake. And they didn't: in the dim he saw them, hand in hand, vanishing down the stairwell. The pounding of feet rose to meet him when he reached the stairs. Descending two steps at a time, he tried to cut their lead, but they had too great a start. The front door banged shut below him. By the time he reached ground level, Harold and Hannah had disappeared into the darkness.

Dumas lunged from the fourth step and hit the floor hard. He felt the shock all the way up to his shoulders. Throwing himself against the wall, he shoved the entrance door open, still anticipating a barrage of gunfire. Nothing. He stepped into the night, blinded by the blaze of floodlights above the parking lot. Somewhere among the ironic fusion of glare and darkness, the Bellamys hid.

Tiny snowflakes floating out of the night accumulated on the grass and sidewalk. Dumas had no idea which way this quarry had gone, but Harold's car had to be nearby. The detective ran for the parking lot and skidded to a halt between two cars. An SUV lumbered onto the lot to his left. He heard car doors slam and teenagers laugh, heard an engine rumble to life, but of the Bellamys he saw no sign.

Eyes darting every which way, he hustled to his own car. He had just yanked the door open when an old Ford Escort roared by as though on the interstate. Dumas caught a glimpse of two occupants. It had to be Harold and Hannah. Not even Marylanders drove like *that* in a parking lot.

He slipped behind the wheel and backed out, nearly ramming the car on the opposite side of the lane. As the Escort squealed off the lot and into the street, Dumas noted the shape and brightness of the taillights. Once on the road himself, he called for backup. The Bellamys had a considerable lead on him already. He kept his eyes on their taillights and followed as they careened through the residential area, through stop signs and red lights, leaving a trail of screaming horns and squealing tires and at least one driver run off the road.

It looked to Dumas like they were making for route 100. He radioed that information, floored the accelerator and tried to close the gap, but to no avail. Sirens cried in the darkness. In moments, a stream of flashing red lights followed him up the eastbound ramp. Dumas didn't have time to wonder where the Bellamys were going. The snow was falling more heavily now, and the increasingly slippery road required his full concentration. Fortunately the traffic was light, and the tumbling snowflakes had intimidated most drivers into slowing down.

But not the Bellamys. The Escort wove from lane to lane, onto the shoulder and back, playing dodge with the other vehicles while brake lights flared all around, cars skidded, and horns blared. Dumas stayed on their tail with the other cops following. Frightened and irate Marylanders took evasive action, knocked into each other, and slid off the road.

What a nightmare! Dumas hoped nobody had been hurt.

As they sped east, traffic further diminished. With that pulsing red glare threatening to overtake them, drivers pulled off and gaped as the chase passed by. Dark hulks of trees flew by, littered with flashes of light from homes and businesses. The Bellamys gave no quarter, taking slippery curves at nearly one hundred miles an hour. *How do their tires hold to the pavement at this speed?* Dumas wondered, but he managed it, too, noting that whenever he had to ease up to stay on the road, they did likewise. Though desperate, they weren't completely off their rockers.

The police radio crackled with instructions and curses. Dumas heard Anne Arundel County police and Maryland state police join the pursuit, so he knew he had either left Howard County or soon would. That meant the Bellamys were running out of road. Ahead the expressway ended, and they'd be forced onto main streets and back roads. What then? If the combined forces of Maryland's finest managed to cut them off, what would Harold and Hannah do?

He had a pretty good idea.

Snatching up the speaker, he added his two cents to the chatter: "This is Howard County Detective Sergeant Dumas. Do not blockade them. Repeat: do not blockade them!"

"Why the hell not?" somebody responded.

"Because they'll ram the blockade."

"Are they suicidal?"

"They'd rather die than be captured. And they'd love to take a dozen cops with them."

That seemed to quell the chatter for all of half a minute.

White-knuckled, Dumas fought the increasingly slippery road, and still the Bellamys didn't slow. As the expressway ended, they flew onto the Mountain Road ramp, barely keeping to the asphalt. Dumas gained on them as they slowed, but not by much. The other units still trailed, giving the Bellamys the choice of route. Somehow, Dumas thought, the good guys needed to force them to stop without killing anyone, but for the moment all he could do was stay on their tail.

The snow grew heavier still. Dumas negotiated the winding road as fast as he dared, passing through dark, leafless woods until someone on the police band said, "Approaching Gibson Island." He didn't know where that was. "Five units moving up from the south."

"Don't blockade them!" Dumas insisted.

"We'll take out their tires," the reply came. "We're getting a sniper in position."

Will that work? Somehow he didn't think a couple of flats would stop the Bellamys.

The surrounding darkness opened wide as though a great, unseen mouth gaped to swallow Dumas and his car whole. The trees receded behind him. Water lay to either side. He was on a causeway with the ice-covered Chesapeake to his left, glinting in the light of a rising moon that hadn't yet been overtaken by the clouds. Flashing red lights erupted in the distance ahead, newly-arrived units lying in wait with their sniper.

Harold and Hannah saw the lights, too. Without warning their brake lights flared and their vehicle went into a skid. Dumas took his foot off the accelerator but had no time to brake. The Escort spun out of control, its headlights blinding him momentarily as they flashed across his bow. By the time he recovered his vision, he was almost on top of them. They'd spun full circle and then some. His car slammed into their driver's side trunk, knocking them across the road and pushing him onto the right shoulder. Squad cars flooded the area, tires and sirens screaming while vehicles scrabbled for space, barely avoiding a massive pileup.

Head whirling, Dumas threw open the door and jumped out, hanging onto the frame for support. "Where are they?" he yelled. Other officers piled out of their cars, guns at the ready. Police lights stabbed through the darkness, blinding him. *No gunshots. Why aren't they blasting the hell out of us?*

He wove between patrol cars and across the slippery asphalt toward the other side of the causeway. Only when he left behind the mass of vehicles did he realize where the Bellamys must be. He hurried to the edge of the road and across the adjacent parking area to the rocks that fell away to the surface of the water. Out in the darkness he sensed motion, ice bobbing up and down, slowly closing the puncture inflicted by the Bellamy's car. The headlights, glowing eerily in the depths, illuminated the crazed ice from below, and a weird singing seemed to rise from the waters. "Damn it," he muttered as officers converged and gazed with him into the bay. A state trooper stood to his left. Dumas felt the cold seeping into his joints. "We need a rescue team."

"We're calling in now," the trooper acknowledged. "But that water." He shook his head. "They aren't coming out of there alive."

20

Montufar had never understood the English expression "on pins and needles." Now she did. She had followed Ozzie White on his forced march through Howard County General, all the while desperate for news from Dumas. While doctors and nurses treated Ozzie for shock, worst-case scenarios played through her mind, refusing to be silenced. Dumas might be trapped in a pile of twisted metal on some darkened road. He might be lost in the cold night, succumbing to exposure. He might have been shot dead.

She sat by Ozzie's bedside in the emergency room, watching his restless sleep, wishing for news, any news; wishing she could sleep, too; wishing that she could simply close her eyes and wake hours later wrapped in Dumas' arms, the nightmare over.

Hours passed. Shortly after ten o'clock, her cell phone vibrated and she fumbled the device as Dumas' name flashed across it.

"Hey, babe," he said. He sounded as exhausted as she felt.

"Hey. You okay?"

"I'm fine. My car got a little banged up, but it's fixable."

"Thank God."

"Yeah, at first I was worried it might not live."

She couldn't help but laugh at his teasing. "I meant you."

"I know."

For a full minute neither said anything. Montufar leaned back and closed her eyes, letting her fears drain away.

"The Bellamys are dead," Dumas told her. "Their car dove into the bay."

That surprised her. "The bay?"

"Yeah. We brought in a recovery crew and a medevac helicopter, but it took too long to locate them and pull them out."

"Where are you?"

"Someplace called Redhouse Cove. In the summer it's probably nice, but right now it reminds me of Dante's lake of ice at the bottom of Hell."

Montufar shuddered.

Dumas drew a long breath. "Did the officers make it?"

She couldn't get the word out.

"It's my fault." His voice dripped misery.

"Eric, no."

"You warned me. I should have –"

"Don't do this to yourself. Hannah played us all. Even Harold was just another prop."

Dumas didn't reply. She had a feeling he didn't fully agree, but at least he didn't argue. "What about Ozzie?" he finally asked.

She looked at the sleeping form of her fiancé's neighbor, his chest slowly rising and falling, his face ironically calm. Soon, she thought, he would be her neighbor, too, if he survived this. "I'm with him at the hospital. He wasn't injured. They're treating him for shock. He's asleep now. The doctor says he can probably go home in a few hours."

"Stay with him," Dumas requested.

"I will."

"I'll call again when we have this wrapped up. Wherever you are then, that's where I'll go."

"I love you," she told him.

"I love you, too."

After she tucked the phone away, Ozzie opened his eyes and rolled his head her direction. He blinked and squinted at the light. "Who's there?"

Montufar took his hand in hers. "Corina."

He smiled weakly. "Oh, Corina. Hi."

She returned the smile as generously as she could. "Hi."

"Where am I?"

"Where do you think?"

Only moving his head, he took in his surroundings: the bed, the IV stand, the TV mounted on the wall. "Hospital, I guess."

"That's right."

"Did I fall?"

"You don't remember?"

White frowned at the ceiling. "A little. There was a lot of noise. And..." Tears filled his eyes until he blinked them away.

Montufar waited while Ozzie worked through whatever nightmare images formed in his mind.

"Who was she, Corina?"

Montufar kept her voice soft in spite of the anger Hannah's memory sparked. "An actress. A thief. Maybe even a killer. She used you to find out what we knew about her. I'm sorry we didn't see through her sooner, Ozzie. I wish we had."

He mulled that over. "Who did?"

"Rick."

Closing his eyes again, Ozzie fell silent for a time, although his breathing told Montufar that he wasn't sleeping. "I'm such a fool. She was so perfect. I really thought this time..."

Still holding his hand, Montufar patted his fingers. "You're not a fool. She was a very good liar. Someday you'll meet the right lady, and when you do, you'd be a fool not to fall for her."

"Two kinds of fool, huh?" He put his other hand on hers. "I can still see her smile and hear her laugh." His voice cracked on the last word, and he began to quietly sob.

Montufar held his hand for a long time and cried with him.

*

Tuesday afternoon, Dumas called Denise Newville at her cousin's place in Virginia.

"Is it over?" she asked.

He could hear dishes clanking in the background as though someone were cleaning up after a meal. "Yes," he told her, knowing that his voice betrayed his weariness.

"Harold," she said simply.

"Or Hannah. We won't ever know for sure. We're pretty sure Micho tried to blackmail them."

"When's the trial?"

"There won't be one," Dumas said. "They fled when we tried to arrest them. Their car slid into the bay. They're dead. And you're safe."

Newville didn't reply.

"You okay?" he asked.

"Yeah. Just thinking. It's funny. Strange, I mean. Other than the Bellamys, everyone Mike tried to blackmail went straight after falling out with him."

Dumas had to choke back a laugh. "I'd heard something like that. I wasn't sure I believed it, though."

"It's true."

"Why do you think that was?"

Newville didn't need any time at all to answer that one. "He made people feel tainted. You touched him, you were polluted, and maybe you couldn't ever get clean again. They were just getting as far away from him as they could. You know?"

He thought he did. "What about you?"

"Who knows? I'll live, anyway. That's about all you can ask for."

Dumas wished her luck and they said their goodbyes. He hoped she might do more than just live, but he knew she had a lot to work through before that could happen. Feeling twice his age, he rose and shuffled to Peller's desk, where he found his boss finishing up a phone conversation of his own.

Dumas sat in the guest chair and waited. When Peller hung up he asked, "Who was that?"

"Winston Marley. My Bahá'í contact. I figured I owed him the explanation for Jayvon's disappearance."

"Must've been a shock for him."

"Yeah, but he took it in stride. He said Jayvon had had a good life even if it was short. And something else, too, that was a bit curious."

"What's that?"

"He said that when he dies, he wouldn't be surprised to find Jayvon among the 'supreme concourse'."

"The what?"

Peller shrugged. "I didn't want to get into it, so I didn't ask. But it rather puts me in mind of angels."

Dumas thought of angels singing praises on high, and then another sound intruded in his mind, the eerie ringing he had heard the previous night at the edge of the bay. He could almost believe it had been demons chanting curses deep below, except that was ridiculous.

Peller looked at him curiously. "Something wrong?"

"Huh?"

"You just shivered."

He hadn't noticed, but he could believe it. "I just remembered something. After the Bellamy's car went into the water, I was standing there looking at the hole in the ice and the headlights fading into the depths, and I heard the strangest sound. Like singing, or maybe bells chiming. It sounded like, I don't know, something supernatural." He shivered again and knew it this time. He could feel the cold and hear the sound. "I'm probably just going nuts. I told Corina the place felt like the bottom of Dante's *Inferno*."

Peller laughed. "Don't doubt your sanity. You just heard ice."

"Ice?"

"Sure. I've heard it myself once or twice, when I was much younger in the land of real winter. When a sheet of ice breaks up and the pieces rub together, they make that sound. It's eerie, all right."

"I guess I'll have to trust you on that. So what about these angels? What made you think of that?"

"Well. When good people die, others sometimes talk about them becoming angels and getting their wings. Like in that old movie *It's A Wonderful Life*. Becoming part of this 'supreme concourse' rather sounds like that, don't you think?"

Dumas cracked a smile. "Except that according to Corina, *It's A Wonderful Life* is all wrong. She tells me the angels were created separately, and a person can't become one, no matter how good they are."

Peller laughed. "I'm certainly not going to debate theology with her. All I know is, whatever this 'supreme concourse is', Marley is sure Jayvon will be right there with them. And part of me hopes he is. Or wherever Corina's preferred designation for such a thing might be."

Dumas didn't see how anybody's preferences could dictate the shape of the afterlife. *Something real surely waits for us*, he thought, *but it doesn't depend on our whims.* He leaned back and gazed up at the ceiling, remembering the gathering of saints he had felt at Felipe Montufar's bedside as the family prayed. A gathering. A concourse. Is that what Marley meant? Could Jayvon, who'd never been Catholic, who'd been a Protestant possibly edging toward Bahá'í, join with a gathering of Catholic saints? All questions about the nature of angels aside, what if all, dead and alive, were somehow joined in a single, great gathering of souls? What if the lines people drew to separate themselves from each other were mere illusion?

What if they are? someone asked playfully in the recesses of his mind, and whether because Peller was sitting before him or for some other reason he couldn't fathom, it sounded for all the world like Sandra.

He had no answer but decided to ask Montufar what she thought.

✱

On Wednesday morning, Dumas snagged Kevin Graham for one more visit to Kennedy Farmer. The notations in Tamai's books notwithstanding, Farmer denied any wrongdoing and refused to answer questions put to him, especially those regarding his role in Tamai's blackmail schemes. He pointedly ignored Graham's goading until Dumas, tired of the stonewalling, took a chisel to the masonry. "How much does your wife know about your criminal background, Mr. Farmer?"

Farmer gave him a sour look.

"Shall I find out?"

"Leave Rachael out of this."

"Does she know you're an accessory to arson?"

"I know nothing about any arson."

"I asked what your wife knows."

Farmer stood. "Get out of my house."

Graham gazed at him and said quietly, dangerously, "Get yourself a lawyer, mon. Advise your wife to get one, too. If she knows what you did, she'll be on the hook for it as well."

Dumas and Graham didn't wait for a reaction. They were almost out the door before Farmer called, "Wait."

Dumas turned.

Farmer looked ready to chew a hole in the wall. "Maybe we can make a deal."

"That's the D.A.'s job, not mine."

"Leave Rachael out of it. I'll get a lawyer and come to the station and talk."

Graham rolled his eyes. "Come to the station? You've been watching too much TV."

"Just leave Rachael out of it, okay?"

"Sure," Dumas agreed. "So long as you're straight with us."

Not that Farmer would be, he was sure. They'd no doubt have to threaten to prosecute Rachael a few more times. But it was a start. Once they reached the end, maybe a few wives could rest easier knowing exactly who had set up their husbands and burned down their homes, and knowing that they had all, finally, been brought to justice.

*

Late Wednesday morning a weary Corina Montufar pulled up outside the Interfaith Center for the third time since Sunday and found her way to Father Owen's office. When he opened the door, she smiled weakly and croaked, "Bless me, Father, for I am exhausted."

"Corina," he said warmly, and embraced her. "It's been a very difficult time for you. How are you doing?"

She shook her head. "It got worse on Monday."

"I saw the news. I imagine the full version would be enough to send me out into the desert with St. Antony. But come in, come in."

She took a chair and looked around. The room was as comfortably cluttered as the first time she'd seen it. A chasuble—white this time—hung in a clear plastic bag from the coatrack, and the stack of books on the table was missing only a sleeping cat curled atop it.

"What can I do for you?" Father Owen asked.

"Uh…" She found herself strangely at a loss for words. She glanced at the chasuble again. It seemed to draw her attention irresistibly. "Listen to me ramble, I guess."

"Rambling is fine."

She didn't know where to start, so she started with it all. "Nothing feels right anymore. I can't seem to make sense out of anything. Except maybe Eric, but even he can't fill this hole in my heart." She thought about that for a moment, wondering if she'd said it right. "He should be able to. Shouldn't he?"

Father Owen said nothing, but his silence was curiously comforting.

"Okay, maybe I should start at the beginning. Papá brought us to the U.S. He said we had no future in Guatemala. Eduardo knows more about it than I do, but I think people were disappearing, soldiers running all over the place fighting. I guess it got pretty bad."

"I remember that news, too," Father Owen said. "The country seemed to be tearing itself apart, like an animal in a trap desperate to get free."

"Losing papá has made us all think about ourselves and each other. Ella is changing. She's finding her inner strength now. Eduardo is getting more…" She struggled to find a word. "Not protective, exactly, but he worries about us, I think. Spiritually." She studied her fingers, not sure where to go from there.

"What about you?"

"Me?"

"How are you changing?"

"I guess that's the problem. Eduardo seems to think I've grown too cold."

"Didn't seem that way to me," Father Owen said with a little smile. "Then again, Eduardo is unusually sensitive, and he is your brother. Why do you think he thinks that?"

Montufar took a deep breath. The chasuble glinted at the corner of her vision. White and gold. Christmas and Easter. Redemption and Resurrection. "When I was eight or nine years old, I wanted to be a nun. A sister, at least. I think I wanted to live with God, the way a child might feel. If that makes sense."

Father Owen nodded. "Sure. Many of us have thought that." He winked at her.

"When I was in high school, I got interested in police work. Protecting people and serving justice seemed a good career choice. No more convent for me. I don't think Papá was heartbroken over my loss of vocation. He was more interested in making sure I could find my way around our new home and had prospects for a steady job."

"He took fatherhood seriously," Father Owen observed. "Rare these days, and refreshing. And I think your choice of career was admirable, especially given the integrity with which you pursue it. That's another thing that seems to be dying out."

"But that's what Eduardo was talking about, Father. I've had to work so hard at proving myself. I had to grow hard and cold to make it in the police world. Over the past year, though, some of the cases we've worked have been so terrible that I've started wondering what happened to that little girl who wanted to be a nun. Eduardo says I need to find her again. It's like I've burned away the center of my soul. Nothing's left. I barely have anything to spare for Eric, and that scares me."

"You know," Father Owen mused, "there was a young man once with your sort of problem. Name of Augustine. He had a very supportive mother. He finally found what he was looking for."

Montufar reflected on that for some minutes in silence. The hanger ticked against the rack again. "When I came to Mass last Sunday, for the first time in so long, I told myself I was home. But that wasn't enough. I want to come home, Father. I need to come home. Will you…"

Father Owen waited patiently for her to finish.

"Will you hear my confession?"

*

On Thursday, January twenty-sixth, Dumas asked Peller to do him a huge favor. He left work at noon and drove to Dumas' apartment building where he picked up Ozzie White. Together, they headed out into the cold.

Ozzie rode in silence, Peller drove in silence. He was unsure what he was supposed to say or do and equally unsure why Dumas had singled him out for this task. He wasn't even sure why Ozzie wanted to do what he planned to do. Peller barely knew the man and certainly was no psychiatrist. But he drove on, east along Maryland 100, out of Howard County, across Anne Arundel County, until the expressway ended. He merged onto Mountain Road and drove its meandering path until, passing down a wooded peninsula, it came upon the causeway to Gibson Island.

The Chesapeake froze on the rocks on their left. To the right, Redhouse Cove reposed beneath a blanket of white. Parking in the lot that overlooked the docks on the cove, he left the warmth of the car and waited beside it until, finally, Ozzie got out. Together they crossed the road and looked out over the bay.

"This is it?" Ozzie asked quietly.

Peller motioned. "They went off about here. I understand the recovery team had a hell of a time getting them out. It was dark, and the water is so cold. Dangerous work."

Ozzie stared into the ice, no comprehension illuminating his face.

Peller said nothing more for a long, long time. The wind nipped at them, threatening to suck all warmth from them.

"Eric says your wife died in a car crash."

Peller nodded.

"How do you get over something like that?"

The detective shuffled his feet to stay warm. "You don't."

The wind stole away a cloud of Ozzie's breath.

Peller recalled something Jerry Souter had said at the dinner party that had launched this chain of events. It was the only thing he could think to say, as little comfort as he knew it would give. "Death is a part of life. Sometimes we see it coming and sometimes we don't, but we all have to face it. Acquaintances die. Friends die. Relatives die. Eventually it's our turn."

Ozzie shivered.

"It may feel like the end, but it's not. It's like this winter." Peller motioned across the expanse of white groping at the horizon.

Ozzie looked. Peller watched him for a time and saw that, gradually, he understood.

There was ice on the bay. But in time it would melt, and the warmth of summer would return.

Further Reading

Thank you for reading! Please leave a short, honest review wherever you bought this book. I greatly appreciate it, and it will help others discover my books.

Rick Peller, Corina Montufar, and Eric Dumas return in more Howard County Mystery novels, available in print and ebook through your favorite bookseller:

The Fibonacci Murders (HCM #1)

"I start with zero. Nobody dies today." The strange note delivered to Rick Peller proves to be a warning shot. He, Corina Montufar, and Eric Dumas are soon pursuing a cunning killer basing murders on the Fibonacci series, a mathematical sequence in which each number is the sum of the preceding two. And the only thing Peller knows for sure is that the series never ends.

True Death (HCM #2)

Four years ago, Rick Peller's wife Sandra died on a country road. The driver who rammed her car vanished without a trace, leaving police stunned and baffled. Now, a bungled robbery raises new questions. As Corina Montufar and Eric Dumas investigate, Peller's memories awaken, triggering a series of insights that shine new light on Sandra's death.

A Day for Bones (HCM #4)

A catastrophic flood in Ellicott City unearths a human skeleton. Did a colonial settler wash out of his grave? Or is it murder? As Rick Peller and his team investigate, the descendants of James Ferring, a local business icon from a bygone era, become the focus, and Peller is sure they're hiding something.

About the Authors

Dale E. Lehman is an award-winning writer, veteran software developer, amateur astronomer, and bonsai artist in training. He principally writes mysteries, science fiction, and humor. In addition to his novels, his writing has appeared in *Sky & Telescope* and on Medium.com. He owns and operates the imprint Red Tales. At any given time, Dale is at work on several novels and short stories.

Prior to her passing in 2022, Kathleen Lehman defined herself as Grandma, but in a previous existence she worked at a library reference desk. She spent 45 years mentoring Dale in the art of writing and was frequently found with a crochet hook and yards and yards of yarn.

Together, Dale and Kathleen have five grown children, six grandchildren, and a pair of fiesty cats.

Visit https://www.DaleELehman.com to find out more about Dale's books.